All he coul[...]ps. They moved closer to his, whispering words he could not hear. Their noses touched, and Gavin could not find the strength to pull away. Finally, he could make out her words.

". . . think it's fate that two strangers could meet on a night destined for human contact? That the couple might find their destiny in a kiss shared even without the smallest knowledge of the other's name?"

Her voice rang like a song in his ears. He wanted to speak, wanted to tell her that he did, in fact, know her name, thereby making whatever fantasy she'd conjured in her sweet mind false. Instead, he found himself nodding.

A moment later, with her hands resting upon his shoulders and his on her hips, she pressed her lips to his and stole his breath away.

and see her grinning line. They

Destiny's Warrior

Heather Waters

BERKLEY SENSATION, NEW YORK

THE BERKLEY PUBLISHING GROUP
Published by the Penguin Group
Penguin Group (USA) Inc.
375 Hudson Street, New York, New York 10014, USA

Penguin Group (Canada), 90 Eglinton Avenue East, Suite 700, Toronto, Ontario M4P 2Y3, Canada
(a division of Pearson Penguin Canada Inc.)
Penguin Books Ltd., 80 Strand, London WC2R 0RL, England
Penguin Group Ireland, 25 St. Stephen's Green, Dublin 2, Ireland (a division of Penguin Books Ltd.)
Penguin Group (Australia), 250 Camberwell Road, Camberwell, Victoria 3124, Australia
(a division of Pearson Australia Group Pty. Ltd.)
Penguin Books India Pvt. Ltd., 11 Community Centre, Panchsheel Park, New Delhi—110 017, India
Penguin Group (NZ), 67 Apollo Drive, Rosedale, North Shore 0632, New Zealand
(a division of Pearson New Zealand Ltd.)
Penguin Books (South Africa) (Pty.) Ltd., 24 Sturdee Avenue, Rosebank, Johannesburg 2196,
South Africa

Penguin Books Ltd., Registered Offices: 80 Strand, London WC2R 0RL, England

This is a work of fiction. Names, characters, places, and incidents either are the product of the author's imagination or are used fictitiously, and any resemblance to actual persons, living or dead, business establishments, events, or locales is entirely coincidental. The publisher does not have any control over and does not assume any responsibility for author or third-party websites or their content.

DESTINY'S WARRIOR

A Berkley Sensation Book / published by arrangement with the author

PRINTING HISTORY
Berkley Sensation mass-market edition / December 2007

Copyright © 2007 by Heather Waters.
Interior text design by Laura K. Corless.

ISBN: 978-0-425-21962-1

BERKLEY® SENSATION
Berkley Sensation Books are published by The Berkley Publishing Group,
A division of Penguin Group (USA) Inc.,
375 Hudson Street, New York, New York 10014.
BERKLEY SENSATION and the "B" design are trademarks of Penguin Group (USA) Inc.

PRINTED IN THE UNITED STATES OF AMERICA

10 9 8 7 6 5 4 3 2 1

*To Tiffany Nakkole—for lending me
your name and your beauty.*

*And, as always, to my husband Kyle.
You know why.*

ACKNOWLEDGMENTS

Though writing is a solitary profession, it takes a team to make a book come to life. For me, those people are:

My family—all of you are a part of the person I am—I hope that's not an insult!

My critique group—The Plot Queens. Marge Smith, Vickie King, Dolores Wilson, Laura Barone, Kat McMahon, and, for this particular book, Jo Ann Ferguson, who is not my critique partner but who gave me permission to delve into the fantasy more deeply than I'd thought I would be allowed. I admire all of you for chasing your destinies.

My outstanding agent, Roberta Brown—the most generous soul I've met in years.

My editor, Kate Seaver. I hope I've grown at least a little since the last go-round. My thanks for your patience.

To all, may your destinies be found and cherished in each breath you breathe.

One

~

The Desolate Caves of the Otherworld

Queine Elphina pressed her spine against the sapphire cushions of her throne. Aventurine and turquoise stones bejeweled the scrolled arms where her fingers tapped with impatience. On her shoulder, her beloved pet raven, Rancor, lovingly bent its head toward hers. Whether good or bad, Rancor had always been able to sense Elphina's emotions, and for that alone, she had become Elphina's only true friend. The rest of the pathetic beings kneeling at her feet were nothing more than parasites, feeding off Elphina's power and hoping to be spared from her fury.

They were not wrong to worry.

"Whichever among you cost me the Orb of Truth will have his eyes fed to Rancor."

The dozens of creatures—peches, maras, succubi, a few redcaps and incubi—glanced up with fearful expressions. Their gazes darted about, eagerly seeking out one brave enough to save them all with a confession.

None would do so, and if numbers weren't so vitally important to her quest, she would have killed them all for their cowardice.

The air in Elphina's throne room shifted, if possible,

growing more tense. She glanced up to see her mother, Lucette, wafting through the doorway, her long, stringy, silver hair falling over her face, making her appear even more grotesque than she usually seemed to Elphina. That the blood running through Elphina's own veins was half succubus never failed to make her skin crawl. They were horrible creatures, with gnarled hands and skeletal faces. The greenish tint of Lucette's flesh had tainted Elphina, giving a faint blue aura to her body, her breath, her kingdom.

But thankfully, other than the blue aura and the twiglike shape of her fingers and toes, Elphina had not taken after her succubus mother. Instead, she looked like her father—the beautiful, powerful king of light magic, Arrane. One vigorous use of Lucette's glamour had seduced the king into bedding her, resulting in Elphina's birth. But he had never come for her, never acknowledged that she was his eldest child, destined to inherit his throne.

Even more than she hated her mother, Elphina hated *him*.

"None will tell you the truth," Lucette hissed as she floated toward Elphina. "The loss of the Orb is not the worst of it, daughter."

The closer she drifted, the stronger the swampy scent of her became. Elphina pressed herself even farther against her throne, struggling not to breathe in the putrid stink of her own mother. "You were lurking again, Lucette? Spying on those who do my bidding?"

"Someone needs to. Look at the lot of them." Lucette lowered herself into the jeweled chair beside Elphina's, her eerie pale stare bouncing over the shaking shoulders of the terrified congregation before them. "Who among you is brave enough to tell Her Majesty the identity of the Orb's thief?"

No one uttered a word, which brought a cackle from Lucette. "This is your mighty army, oh, *Elph Queine*?" She cackled a moment longer, making Elphina itch to rip out those horrid vocal cords.

"If you have truth to speak, Lucette, then speak it," she said through clenched teeth.

It took several seconds for Lucette to cease her laughter, then she sighed and puckered her wrinkled mouth. "Your father took the Orb from your little army, Elphina. *Your. Father.* Once again, he forbids you to have your heart's desire, while I sit here and bow to your every whim, a good mother, a tolerant mother. A mother whose lofty hopes for her daughter have flittered into—"

"Silence," Elphina warned, her long, pointed nails scratching at the aventurine stones. Her intestines quivered in rage. Her father. "He took the Orb, himself? Has he recovered, then, from his pathetic broken heart?"

Lucette's eyes narrowed briefly, and a flicker of compassion soothed Elphina's temper as she realized her mother had also been denied time and again by King Arrane. She'd craved his heart for so very long, and he'd given it to a filthy human, just as he was prepared to give Elphina's throne to a son whose birth order did not deserve such a gift.

"Even the almighty Arrane is not strong enough to overcome the loss of his soul match. He still withers away, pining for her, since she left him so long ago. But it was those he commands who stole the Orb of Truth, and, on his orders, they're after the other two Orbs, as well."

Elphina swallowed the tangy bile in her throat. A small droplet of water dripped onto her forehead, condensation from the dewy earth above them. Though her cavernous palace was in ill repair and her army was dwindling, her desire to right the wrongs done to her had never been stronger.

"Arrane means to stop me from awakening his brother," she whispered, her gaze flickering toward the wall opposite her. Ancient symbols marked the clay and stone, awaiting their invocation upon the placement of the Master Trinity. The Trinity of powerful Orbs that Arrane was attempting to keep from her. The Trinity that had the power to free the Dark King. "He won't succeed."

"If he brings his son into our world, he will. You cannot hope to be more powerful than Arrane's child born of his soul match."

Elphina shot her mother a scathing look. "He is a man, Lucette. He cannot kill me. My succubus lineage will protect me against him."

Lucette drew in a long, sickly breath and sneered at

Elphina. "Because he cannot kill you does not mean he cannot stop your efforts to bring back the Dark King."

"And just because he cannot kill me does not mean I cannot kill *him*. Should my *brother* dare enter our world, he will die. The king is weak. The time to strike is perfect. I'll not have his son ruining everything."

Too embittered to continue the deliberation any longer, Elphina stood and kicked a pech out of her path. The ugly, long-limbed creature moaned and scurried across the room like a filthy rat.

"You would leave before you hear the rest of what I've to tell you?" Lucette called out, her raspy voice ending in a parade of offending coughs.

Her games annoyed Elphina. She wished, not for the first time, that killing her own mother wouldn't bring the wrath of the other succubi upon her head. Their fear of the power of destruction she had inherited from Arrane had enabled her to crown herself their queine, but the succubi did not fear her enough to allow for murdering their own kind.

She gently prodded Rancor from her shoulder, tightened her dark blue, velvet cloak around her shoulders, and turned slowly to face her mother once again. "If you have more you wish to say, then say it."

Lucette grinned, her toothless mouth caving in on itself. "Your darlings weren't so useless today. I saw them looking into the Orb before it was taken. I maneuvered myself so I could have a glimpse, as well."

Elphina opened her mouth, ready to berate the occupants of the throne room for daring to peer into what rightfully belonged to her, but quickly changed her mind. If Lucette was daring to bring up such a deed, what was seen must have value.

"What did you see?"

Reaching out a long, thin arm swathed in filmy gray cloth, Lucette pointed toward a succubus near the door. "Tell your queine what was seen in the Orb."

The younger succubus pushed her long hair out of her face. Though not quite as horrifying in appearance as Lucette, this creature was no more pleasant to look upon. She inched forward on her knees, her deformed fingers clawing at the red, dusty earth as she moved. When she arrived at Elphina's feet, she pressed her cold lips upon them before lifting her head to meet her queine's gaze.

"I saw *him*, Your Majesty. Your brother."

From behind her, Lucette cackled once again. "You see, daughter? We've seen where your brother lives. You've no need to wait for Prince Gavin to come to our world to kill him. You can go after him now."

Elphina's gaze fell to the hairy red maras kneeling around her, their small, flaming eyes carefully avoiding her stare. Anticipation of a lifetime goal finally fulfilled made her ache a bit. Happiness, perhaps?

She felt the corners of her mouth curl up slightly and narrowed her eyes to glare at the leader of the mara. "Kill him," she commanded. "And bring me his soul."

The Forests of Normandy

If it is your desire to stare so intently at a man, might I suggest one who is worthy?"

Abunda's voice dripped around Nakkole's ears as easily as the wind brushed aside her coppery locks, but Nakkole knew without turning that she would find only Abunda's apparition in the small, muddy pool beneath the towering oak canopy.

Nakkole sighed and removed her gaze from the human male now traveling down the path on which she had directed him. "And who in your eyes would be worthy, Mother? For certain, not the humans you find so lacking. A merman such as Raventail, then? A princely dwarf, perhaps?"

She'd spent the last hour inspecting the trespasser who'd approached her spring, uncertain whether he meant the inhabitants here any harm. She had finally found him kind and gentle and had pointed him safely toward his village where a lovely wife was likely holding supper for him. Thanks to Nakkole, he would be safely home come twilight, no longer wandering about lost. If she had her way, she would have accompanied him in hopes of an offering of fresh cream or milk and an interesting human tale or two.

"You've done your duty," Abunda said. "You danced with him and found him good-natured. He returns home even as we speak. Cease wishing to follow him."

Staring in the water, Nakkole scowled at her mother's image.

As the leaves above swayed and gave way to a beam of sunlight, Abunda's likeness glimmered and winked at her. Even the watery portrait of the queine stunned Nakkole with its beauty. 'Twas not the first time Nakkole wondered how a mother and daughter could look so very different. As much as the hair upon Abunda's head was the color of night, Nakkole's was the color of early morning sunrise. As queine of the White Ladies, Abunda had mothered Nakkole and her sister-kind in both spirit and body, yet Abunda's life of ninety-six springs showed nary a mark on her youthful beauty.

The reflection pool rippled, and Abunda's face disappeared. A moment later, Nakkole felt a cool hand press her shoulder through her thin gown. Glancing back, she smiled at Abunda who now stood in full form behind her, her tart apple scent wafting around Nakkole on a blissful breeze.

An easy grin spread over Abunda's legendary face. Her cheekbones, high and delicately carved, rose with her show of affection, and her dark eyes sparkled with their usual faery mischief.

She clucked her tongue and eyed Nakkole with amusement. "I know you better than that, *ma fille*. You wish to follow him home as you did the handsome traveler last moon." Her smile dimmed, and her face turned serious. "Your curiosity for humankind will lead you to no good end."

Nakkole shrugged. She did not wish to have this discussion with Abunda yet again. She knew she was a frustration to Abunda and the other White Ladies. While they felt comfortable in the fae world and made easy friends with the faeries outside of the White Ladies, Nakkole's interest in the mortal world steadily grew. Simply protecting her forest spring was no longer enough to satisfy her curiosity of humans.

Alongside other duties, it was a White Lady's responsibility to make certain humans didn't stumble upon the mer-people inhabiting the waters they guarded.

Nakkole performed her duty here well enough. She also found lost travelers, danced with them until she determined whether they were worthy of her assistance. She sent the good ones home and the rotten ones farther into the maze of trees, just as all the other White Ladies did. She kept her waters pure and well tended. Froze them when they needed freezing and thawed them come spring. But she had never been satisfied with her station here, as though a piece of her had become as lost as these travelers, and that piece couldn't find its way back to her.

"Why aren't you resting as you should be?" Nakkole muttered.

Noon had long since come and gone, and this was the hour Abunda should be communicating with their ailing king through dreams. Her presence here meant either she had already communicated with the king or her need to monitor Nakkole had seemed more important. The latter did not warm Nakkole's mood in the least.

"There is news," Abunda said. "It seems our king has managed to prevent Elphina from collecting the Orb of Truth."

"We have it, then?"

Abunda nodded. "It is being taken to the Isle of Arran even as we speak."

Having one of the Master Trinity safely out of Elphina's reach was hope inspiring, but the other two Orbs were still out there somewhere and dangerous enough all on their own. Nearly a century ago, when the rivalry between the brothers of light and dark magic had reached its peak, Arrane had banished his brother Krion to a stony prison beneath the earth. The magic used had been so powerful the great Sphere of Life had split into three smaller spheres—the Orb of Truth, the Orb of Knowledge, and the Orb of Creation. The explosion scattered the orbs throughout the worlds, hidden until recently when the Orb of Truth had been discovered. There was no telling where the other two might be.

True, Elphina would not be able to raise the Dark King, as was her plan, unless she possessed the entire Trinity, but that did not mean that each Orb, alone, wasn't powerful in its own right. In Elphina's hands, even one of the Trinity could prove disastrous to light fae.

Abunda must have sensed Nakkole's thoughts, for she brushed a lock of hair from Nakkole's cheek and smiled grimly. "We will not stop seeking the other Orbs. With any luck, the Orb of Truth will aid us in our search, and we might finally be able to locate its brothers."

Her expression sobered, her flawless brow furrowing in a very un-Abunda-like manner.

"There's something else," Nakkole offered. "Something else that's happened?"

Abunda nodded slowly. "Before the Orb was taken, Elphina's minions peered within and saw what we've so desperately tried to keep hidden." Her eyes widened and filled with worry. "They have found him."

A shudder ascended Nakkole's body, the meaning of Abunda's words bringing a tingle of expectation to her belly. "Our prince?"

The circlet wrapped around Abunda's forehead glimmered, the gold star dangling between her brows catching the light and sparkling like the morning sun. Knowing she would soon become mesmerized by its shimmer, Nakkole looked away.

"He resides in a place called Grey Loch, though now he is no longer safe there. The time has come to bring him home."

Beside her, a vine wiggled at the base of the oak, and a leaf unfurled to reveal a wakening pixie beneath its cover. Noticing the cause for her rude rousing, the pixie put her tiny hands on her hips, then spread her butterfly wings and flittered away.

"Nakkole . . . Do pay attention." Abunda bent and carefully unrolled the other three leaves along the vine, and when they showed nothing within, she lowered herself to the ground. "We must be careful of curious ears."

A strong breeze ripped through Nakkole's hair, sweeping it over her shoulder and across her eyes. The small puddle near their feet rippled in the wind. Abunda turned slightly and beckoned to something in the forest. Nakkole's eldest sister, Timpani, stepped through the trees, looking as aristocratic and confidant as ever.

"Come, Timpani. You must hear this, also," Abunda said.

Timpani offered a look to Nakkole that suggested she knew naught of Abunda's purpose, either.

"Elphina's army grows by the number each day," Abunda said. "Her band of maras continue to collect more and more human souls, turning them into every sort of creature who is against Arrane. Elphina and her mother will stop at nothing to ensure Arrane's throne is claimed by the Dark King."

Her heart pounding, Nakkole swallowed. "Elphina still believes Krion will allow her to rule at his side?"

Abunda nodded. "If she manages to free him from the pit Arrane has trapped him in, he will have no choice. He will be bound to his liberator. No matter that, as Arrane's brother, he is Elphina's uncle. Together they will rule the Kingdom of Arrane through darkness."

"Should we manage to bring Prince Gavin safely home to his rightful kingdom, Elphina will not get so far as that," Nakkole said, disliking the uncertainty in her own voice. "She might be Arrane's oldest child, but she is certainly not more powerful than the prince."

Those born of soul matches were always more gifted than fixed unions and most certainly were more gifted than those conceived through dark glamour such as the spell Lucette had cast over Arrane so many years ago to conceive Elphina. Elphina might have inherited a power or two from Arrane, but Gavin would have inherited so much more.

"He cannot destroy her, Nakkole. She is half succubus, and Arrane's daughter as well. It will take a woman with blood ties to Arrane to finish Elphina off."

Nakkole would not allow her hope to be diminished so easily. "But Prince Gavin will be strong enough to subdue her."

Timpani snickered. "Perhaps he'll even place her in a pit beside her revered Dark King."

Releasing a sigh, Abunda slid a loving glance over her daughters' faces. "There is much about our prince that you don't know—that no one, save for a few, knows. Just now, that is a good thing, however, for it means Elphina likely knows little, as well.

"He doesn't understand the power he wields," Abunda continued. "Furthermore, he is not yet aware of the dangers facing him."

Nakkole's prepared retort stuck in her throat.

"What do you mean, he doesn't understand?" Timpani asked, a foreign glimmer of confusion in her eyes.

"Exactly that." Another gust of wind lifted Abunda's hair, hiding her face from view for a brief moment, but Nakkole thought she saw a momentary flicker of panic in her mother's eyes. "He knows nothing of his heritage, or of his powers. He's been raised without magic by his human mother."

Appalled, Nakkole dug her toes into the damp earth. "Sweet mercy, why? Why would she do such a thing to him?"

"To keep him safe, I suppose, though only Geraldine and Arrane know for certain." Abunda shrugged, paler than Nakkole could ever remember seeing her. "It's my belief that Geraldine hoped to prevent Gavin from using any magic, therefore making him more difficult to locate."

Scowling, Nakkole reached for a small twig on the ground and snapped it in two. No place in this world was safer than the Kingdom of Arrane. What sort of foolish woman was Lady Geraldine to pull her son away from the one being who could keep him alive and well?

She didn't dare voice the question aloud however, for no one spoke ill of Lady Geraldine without risking the wrath of Arrane himself.

"Elphina will attempt to kill him now that she knows where he is," Timpani stated, the confusion in her eyes seemingly replaced by an understanding Nakkole hadn't fully come to yet.

Abunda looked up, her black brows arching to meet the star dangling from the circlet on her head. "Not if we are there to prevent it. We'll have precious little time to allow him to become used to the idea of being a fae prince, but once he's accepted it, he'll be brought here."

Timpani scoffed. "Accepted it? We should force him

here. Let him grow accustomed to his heritage in Arrane's palace, where it is safe."

Narrowing her eyes in a menacing style, Abunda pursed her lips. "You would dare force your king's son to do *anything*? Think you Arrane would allow it? They are his orders that we follow, and he wants Gavin to have time to adjust before bringing him here. He is only to be taken by force if the danger becomes more than we can handle."

The worry in her mother's tone dried Nakkole's throat. Like Timpani's, Abunda's confidence had always been an admirable trait. To see it shaken now did nothing to soothe Nakkole's own worry.

Abunda stretched out her legs and lowered her chin toward her chest, studying the earth around them. "If we could just snatch someone from the human world and bring them here, we would have done so to Arrane's beloved Geraldine years ago. With her here, Arrane would never have lost his strength and none of this would have been happening at all. He wouldn't be suffering the loss of his soul match and slowly finding his way to death. But who would dare bring Geraldine here against Arrane's wishes? You? Me?" she scoffed. "Not if we wished to live."

"But—"

Abunda narrowed her eyes, refusing to let Nakkole speak. "He'd rather Geraldine be happy away from him than miserable close by. As for Prince Gavin . . . how would it be, with Arrane's ever-waning health and power, to have our only hope loathe the sight of us? What good would it do us to have him flee at his first opportunity?"

After a long, agonizing moment, she scooped a palmful of the murky rainwater into her fist and let it rain down upon the puddle.

"Our fair prince is not an old man as I had expected. I was shown him through the Orb of Truth in my dream-talk with Arrane. Time flows differently in their world. Prince Gavin is a lord far away from our sweet Normandy. A Scottish man by the name of McCain."

Nakkole raised her head and chewed her lip. "Who will Elphina send, do you think? Surely, she won't travel such a distance herself unless she must. Whoever is protecting the prince needs to be ready for whatever army she chooses."

Apparently thinking the matter over, Abunda continued to play with her puddle. Then, she nodded faintly. "There aren't many in her army who can cause great harm in the human world. Mostly mischief makers. I suppose she would either try to have him taken into our world where their mischief can be deadly, or else she'll send the maras as a first strike against him."

Nakkole's mouth grew dry. No matter that the maras stood only two feet high, or that their only powers lay in killing mortal men in their sleep. Their ability to create fae of all kinds from human souls was a terrifying prospect. Gavin was half human, and should they manage to steal his soul, they would have a deadly ally in him to battle against Arrane. Such a thing would be devastating to Arrane's aim to keep the world of dark magic out of his kingdom. Already the maras had stolen the souls of more than two hundred men and had turned them into such creatures as banshees, ogres, and succubi. Nakkole didn't even wish to ponder the demon a powerful faery like Gavin might turn into.

"This cannot happen," Nakkole whispered, her voice threaded with cold fear.

"The prince is to be protected at all cost," Timpani added.

"He must be shown his heritage, shown his powers. Arrane is not getting any stronger. Whether our prince chooses to reside in the human realm or with us, we need him to claim the crown when the time comes. To be ready to fight with us."

Nakkole's head swam, and she suddenly wished she was not privy to all the burdens of the world. "But Scotland is not so near to Normandy. How will we gather enough protection in such a short amount of time?"

"I've many friends all over this world who will be more than willing to protect their prince's future, as well as their own. I'll send for them straight away. We cannot all abandon our mountains and springs here to travel the distance, however. We must stand guard should Elphina's minions try to slither their way toward our king. I'm sending you to take command over Gavin's guidance."

Timpani smiled. "Of course, Mother. Just tell me what you wish me to do."

Abunda cupped Timpani's cheek lovingly. "You know I hold you in the highest esteem, Timpani. But this duty is meant for Nakkole."

Nakkole gasped. Had she not already been sitting, she would have had to do so. "Me?"

"For everything, there is a reason." Abunda smiled.

Timpani looked as disturbed by this turn of events as Nakkole felt. "Mother? Are you certain—"

Abunda held up a hand to silence Timpani's protest. "Nakkole has an affinity for the humans that is rare in our kind. Arrane believes, and I agree, that her . . . empathy . . . toward them will be the most useful tool we have to convince Prince Gavin he must return to us."

Her empathy? The very thing her White Lady sisters had teased her about since birth? How could that possibly be a virtue now?

"Find the mermen of our seas," Abunda continued. "They'll take you to the waters of Scotland to meet a large Scottish faery by the name of Ness. She is very knowledgeable about mankind and will carry you to Grey Loch."

"But my duties here—"

"Will be seen to by your sisters until you return. 'Tis of great importance that you keep our prince well guarded until he is ready. He's never been without at least one guardian at all times—even though he may not have been aware of it— but one guardian isn't nearly enough any longer."

Abunda's face softened. "Use your compassion, Nakkole. I admit, it's a gift of yours I never thought valuable—until now. You'll have the sensitivity your prince will need in order to understand all of this. You will consider his feelings as you do your lost travelers here in the forest, and therefore will know the right way to tell him all he needs to know."

Nakkole wrung her hands together and stood. As much as she would have relished being sent into the human world she had often fantasized about visiting, this was not a task she would have asked for, nor one that she savored. "How am I to convince a powerful faery of his might when he has no knowledge of his heritage?"

"Trust yourself. Guide him. Discover which of his father's powers he wields, then teach him how to use them if you can. Arrane has shown me this man knows naught of his heritage, but also that he holds no belief in our kind. His mother made certain he was raised to believe we are naught but the creation of foolish minds, so he'll need a gentle hand."

"Why would she—"

"I cannot begin to understand Geraldine's reasons for teaching her son we do not exist."

"Mother—" Timpani started.

"Timpani, have faith in your sister," Abunda commanded. Then, her voice softening, she said, "I do."

Nakkole felt the unfortable knot building in her throat but could not dislodge it. And Avalon save her, a swell of pride so large, it was nearly enough to assuage her fear. "You really mean to send *me*, Mother?"

Abunda slapped at Nakkole's knee. "Don't look so amazed. It's not as if I've never shown any faith in you, Nakkole. I know the strengths and weaknesses of all my daughters well. You will be successful."

Nakkole opened her mouth to balk again, but Abunda cut her off.

"Timpani will accompany you. I will send more details along the way. Go now, both of you. There's no time to waste." She leaned forward and placed a light, feathery kiss on Timpani's cheek, then did the same to Nakkole's. "Too often you've implied that I do not know what is best. Trust me when I say your part in securing Arrane's kingdom will be far more vital than any other's."

But Nakkole was barely listening any longer. Her entire body had gone numb. She was going to live among the humans for a while, had been given a duty so important, she could hardly believe her mother's faith in her.

"I can't believe she chose you," Timpani muttered, softening the insult with a playful shove and a small grin.

"I know." Nakkole tried to smile but found it impossible. "Neither can I."

Two

Scotland

By the time Nakkole and Timpani arrived at Grey Loch, the May Beltane festivities had already begun. Ness, the large faery of the Scottish lochs, had deposited them on the rocky shores little more than an hour before, and now, as a bewildered Nakkole stood among the forest trees, watching the village come alive with merriment beneath the pink sunset, her stomach twisted as though she'd consumed curdled milk.

Couples danced around a blazing fire, most locked in the familiar embraces the White Ladies used on their trespassers. Music, loud and slightly off rhythm, sang through the air, causing Nakkole's heart to beat off course along with it. There were so many of them! Far too many to count.

Nakkole closed her eyes and tried to focus on the task she'd been sent here to perform. By now, the people of Grey Loch would be expecting her as the clan's new healer, here to care for the laird's mother. Abunda would have seen to the preparations of creating the facade. At least, Nakkole hoped the deed had been done.

From what she understood, Geraldine McCain, a woman who'd spent the last thirty years bedridden with a broken heart, barely able to communicate with the world, was coming home to die. Under the guise of a healer, Nakkole was meant to make that death as comfortable as possible.

She had no knowledge of how to do so.

She stepped from the shelter of the trees, repeating in her mind all that Ness had relayed about their prince. Though Ness had been a wonderful source of such knowledge regarding the people of Grey Loch, Nakkole still felt ill prepared to meet her future king. All she knew of him was that he didn't believe in magic.

Although Abunda had said as much, only now was it sinking in what an obstacle that fact would prove to be. Convincing a man who did not believe in magic that he was a fae prince would be more difficult than convincing a blind man he could see.

She could not do this. As she treaded toward the crowd of dancing villeins, their raucous laughter overwhelmed her and her head spun. For a moment, she contemplated turning and fleeing, but doing so would shame her beyond repair, would never allow her to return to Eaux Blanches, the White Waters Forest in Normandy. She had no choice but to stay.

And in truth, a tiny piece of her wanted to do so. Here was her chance to not only prove she was as good a guardian as her sisters but also assuage her curiosities about the humans. She would be able to explore their world to her heart's content.

Nakkole smoothed her hands down her white, shimmering gown. The people here looked very much like the ones she'd seen in Normandy. But that notion didn't comfort her much, either, for she had never before seen so many of them all at once.

Timpani followed, wearing the same expression of dismay that built in Nakkole's heart.

"Are you frightened?" Nakkole whispered.

"Not as much as I am anxious to return home." Timpani presented Nakkole with a satchel. "We'll need to fit in, and without their wardrobe, we'll look suspicious."

"Where did you get that?"

Timpani grinned. "Ness. It was sent from some of the mermen along the way. Apparently, we've a few mischie-

vous friends on our side who don't mind borrowing a bit of
ladies' clothing."

Nakkole frowned. How was she to command the prince's
protection if she hadn't even thought of such necessary details? Of course, Abunda had sent her off without much
preparation. Nakkole wouldn't have even known of her facade as a healer if it had not been for her message through
the Norman mermen. Having such important information be
given by a source secondary to the queine did not sit well
with Nakkole. Ill-preparedness did not even begin to name
all of the fears coursing through her.

Silently, she cursed her mother for having brought this
upon her.

"Well," she said. "We should hurry. The laird is expecting
us."

Timpani did not move. She stood still, watching the
evening light frolic across the village dancers, a slow smile
creeping upon her face. "Are they like this all the time, you
think?"

"No more so than the Norman people. Beltane is their
time for celebration."

Nakkole stood beside Timpani, drinking in the sight of
her new world. Tiny houses lay in a neat pattern of rows a
fair distance from the stone walls of Grey Loch's castle.
Smoke curled from the chimneys, and the sound of musical
pipes began to play. Flowers abounded, placed around each
of the houses' exteriors. A maypole, much like those she'd
seen in Normandy's villages, stood near a large fire burning
in the center of the field, and tiny children danced around it,
wrapping their glorious ribbons round the large base.

This was why she'd loved following her trespassers
home. Humans seemed to do everything with purpose. No
moment of their day was wasted; everyone worked so very
hard. Even in these moments of celebration, they seemed to
know exactly what they should be doing . . . when and how
it should be done. Everything came so easily to creatures of
fae that life did not seem as cherished in her world as it did
in this one.

Nakkole sighed and turned her gaze away. In the distance, the large structure of the keep loomed in the darken-

ing shadows of twilight, flanked on either side by smaller, wooden structures of which Nakkole could not identify. The scent of earth and body mingled with the roasting meats, and even from their distance, she could smell her favorite scent of all—milk.

"Come, my lady," Timpani urged. "Before they see us."

"I am not your queine, Timpani. You do not have to address me so."

"If I am to act as your lady's maid, I must."

"I could take sore advantage of that . . . but I won't." Nakkole's gaze drifted over her sister's filmy white dress, the gold belt dangling on her hips, and the long, flaxen braid settling over Timpani's shoulder. "Let's find more suitable dresses in that satchel and don them quickly."

Timpani didn't question her. She obeyed, and several moments later, they stepped back onto the field, Timpani wearing an uncomfortable-looking garment of blue, and Nakkole an itchy one of yellow. On Timpani's feet were a pair of boots—another accessory Nakkole hadn't thought of.

"Is there another pair of those horrid-looking things in that bag?" she asked.

Her own feet were still bare; she'd never before worn a pair of shoes, and the very notion made her uncomfortable. How were they to fit in here? Bound feet. Bound bodices.

Timpani grinned, dug into the satchel, and withdrew another pair of black boots. Nakkole frowned and stooped to squeeze her feet inside.

"I suppose I'm ready," she said. "Try to look . . . human."

Timpani fell into step beside Nakkole. "Will they accept us, you think?"

Much of Nakkole's journey to this new world had been consumed by this worry, but it was odd to hear her sister sound so unsure of herself. In *their* world, Timpani was consistently the calm one, the confident one. She protected the largest river in the White Waters Mountains and required assistance from none.

Here among the humans, she did not seem herself. It was as though Nakkole had suddenly switched places with her older sister, and Nakkole wasn't certain how she felt about her new role of leadership.

"So long as they don't take a strong aversion to our presence, we can make certain they accept us well enough."

Timpani pulled on Nakkole's elbow, stopping her from walking farther. "*Glamour*, you mean?"

"If need be. Abunda never said we could not use our gifts to ensure our places here."

"But to enchant them? It could be dangerous should husbands fawn over us before their wives."

Nakkole stared deep into the blue depths of Timpani's eyes, trying to make her sister understand that enchantment might be the only way to seduce these people into accepting them as part of their world. Glamour came from within a faery's belly only to be used as a last resort on humans who needed a bit more convincing to leave soil claimed by magic. Because glamour gave its user the ability to bend the enchanted to her will, never was it to be used lightly. Timpani would simply have to understand that succeeding in their duties here may not be achieved if they did not ensure themselves a warm welcome.

"We use it all the time on human men, Timpani. If done carefully, it should work on the women as well. A tiny bit of charm to make certain we leave a good impression. No more. Not like the holds we use in our forest."

Timpani's delicate features relaxed. "Just enough to make them like us? To leave a good first impression."

"Yes," Nakkole agreed. "Just enough."

After spending the better part of the afternoon alone with naught but his thoughts for company at the loch, Laird Gavin McCain wearily pushed open the great door of the keep and stepped inside, eager to find a hot meal.

"The Lady of White Waters has arrived, Laird."

Gavin glanced up from the doorway to look at Rufous, the one member of the McCain clan, besides himself, who had chosen not to partake in the festivities outside. Gavin stopped untying his mantle. He'd known Rufous since he was a lad, and in many ways considered him the father Bruce McCain had never wanted to be. Rufous had been one

of the few people Gavin had been happy to see when he had
returned to Grey Loch a year before as the new laird of the
clan.

Smiling at his friend, Gavin nodded. "Where is she? I
want to meet with her before I take my supper."

Rufous yawned. The man spent far too much time pursu-
ing somber matters and took his position as Gavin's most
trusted councilman far too seriously. The McCain brooch
still gleamed on Rufous's plaid, pronouncing him laird in
Gavin's absence. Though Gavin's most recent journey to
King James's side had ended more than three days ago,
Gavin was not eager to have the McCain brooch returned.

Matters other than the clan claimed his mind these days.

His mother was due to arrive in the morn, too ill, according to Father Donnelly, for anything to slow her declining
health. She was coming home to die, and there was naught
Gavin could do but allow her to leave this world in the comfort of her home at Grey Loch. It was what Geraldine
wanted, according to the missive sent by Sister Margaret—
the only caregiver in recent years who'd been successful at
communicating with Geraldine at all. A pity she couldn't accompany his mother home, but the woman wouldn't be
bribed into leaving all those who needed her care for the
sake of one alone.

Instead, the healer Lady Nakkole of White Waters was
coming to help ease his mother's pain in these coming
moons.

Bending to tug off his boots, he gazed around the entranceway, trying to see it as his mother might. All of the
frivolous embellishments Bruce McCain had insisted upon
were now sold, the profits gone to Grey Loch's people
who'd needed it more after last year's harsh winter. Naught
but a large, lone mirror and a row of hooks to hold cloaks
stood in the entrance. If he allowed himself time to think on
it, he'd likely be a bit ashamed of allowing his mother to see
the barren keep. But Gavin rarely gave pause to think of her
in more than passing. He hadn't the time or the inclination
to become the melancholy, self-absorbed laird Bruce
McCain had been.

Gavin looked up to find Rufous smiling, his old face

wrinkling into a dozen grins. "Since your mother isn't due till morning, I sent the new healer out to enjoy the festivities."

Groaning, Gavin thought about the boots he had begun to remove.

"You look as if you'd prefer a bit of resting," Rufous said. "Want me to fetch the lass and bring her to you?"

"Nay." Gavin sighed. "I suppose I should put in an appearance for the merriment, anyway."

Lady Nakkole was not difficult to locate, as her name was being tossed about on the curious villeins' lips. Gavin found her dancing with the woodcutter's son, their arms linked together as she gracefully led the young man around the fire. The crowd watched the pair, whispering amongst themselves. They were obviously in awe, and Gavin could see why. Never had he seen a woman more fluid in movement, more fated for dance. Her yellow, form-fitting gown swirled around her booted feet. Red waves of untamed curls caressed her shoulders, her arms, her lower back. Gavin could do naught but stare.

"Bonnie lass, ain't she?" a man beside Gavin said.

Gavin nodded, his mouth suddenly too dry to speak. What was wrong with him? He had seen plenty of bonnie lasses in his day, some even more beautiful than this. Still, something about Lady Nakkole called to him, made his flesh tingle with excitement.

He moved closer to the dancers and gently removed the young man from Lady Nakkole's arm. She glanced up at him with questioning eyes.

"Do you mind?" he asked, though at the moment, he truly did not care whether she minded or not. He simply *had* to dance with her, *had* to touch a lock of her fiery hair. He was mesmerized. Enchanted.

Lady Nakkole said nothing, but slowly began her steps once more, her fingers sliding between his. With a mind of their own, Gavin's feet followed as if he had performed her odd dance a million times before, when in truth, he'd never

seen aught like it. It looked and felt more like floating than
dancing and brought their bodies together far closer than
proper dancing allowed. Her hips swayed provocatively
against his, a movement so seductive its normal place would
have been a bed.

They rounded the fire three times, her hips occasionally
pressing to his, her eyes closed in sweet concentration. On
their fourth jaunt around the flames, Gavin opened his
mouth to introduce himself, trying to remember the things
he wanted to discuss with her about his mother, but it was as
though he had lost his ability to form words. At the moment,
he could not even remember his own name.

Finally, the Norman beauty opened her eyes, and as her
gaze met his, a stunning smile graced her mouth. "You're a
quiet man," she whispered, a trace of rich accent in her
words.

He tried to reply and winced when he could not.

Apparently, his silence did not bother her. She continued
to smile up at him, kindness radiating through her gaze.
"'Tis Beltane, a day of celebrating the heart and body."

Gavin nodded, his feet slowing their movement to match
hers and the new choice in song. The world around them
seemed a foggy dream, and he could only compare the heaviness of his body to a night spent swigging too much ale. He
focused on her mouth, on the sweet, pointed peaks of her
upper lip. Should he kiss her, no one would pay mind.
Beltane was a day of love freely given. All around them,
couples embraced as though they had no care as to who
watched. Hell, he could just about ravish her in front of all,
and no one would think of it come morrow.

Oh, but *he* would. If he kissed her, he was likely to never
recover. Why? What was it he saw shining in her eyes? What
was the glow that radiated from her skin, from her whole
person? Even the long strands of her hair seemed to sparkle
in the moonlight.

He glanced around. Several other couples had rejoined
the dancing. The sound of laughter echoed in his ears.
Scents of sunshine and fresh, mountain air rippled off Lady
Nakkole's body to waft beneath Gavin's nose. What the
devil was wrong with him?

She smiled again, and the fog around them vanished. Time seemed to accelerate, making him dizzy beyond reason. All he could see were her grinning lips. They moved closer to his, whispering words he could not hear. Their noses touched, and Gavin could not find the strength to pull away.

Finally, he could make out her words.

". . . think it's fate that two strangers could meet on a night destined for human contact? That the couple might find their destiny in a kiss shared even without the smallest knowledge of the other's name?"

Her voice rang like a song on his ears. He wanted to speak, wanted to tell her that he did, in fact, know her name, thereby making whatever fantasy she'd conjured in her sweet mind false. Instead, he found himself nodding.

A moment later, with her hands resting upon his shoulders and his on her hips, she pressed her lips to his and stole his breath away.

Nakkole closed her eyes, drinking in the scent of the man she clung to. He opened his mouth, his tongue dampening her bottom lip until, finally, she parted her lips and allowed herself to taste him. She knew she should stop—knew her behavior wasn't proper—even for a White Lady. But she couldn't. Their bodies continued their graceful dance in a crowd of a dozen other bodies, but to Nakkole, no other being in the world existed at that moment other than herself and this lovely stranger who drew her like a butterfly to nectar.

She moaned and moved her hands to his nape, clutching his hair in her fist.

She shouldn't have directed her glamour so strongly toward this one man. But when he had taken her in his arms, and she had set her gaze upon him, she knew she had wanted nothing more than to indulge in this one act. The feel of his mouth on hers made the risk well worth it. He was so very . . . human. She could very well become drunk on the taste of him.

His tongue massaged hers. A strange, intimate thing, this kissing. She found herself liking it more and more each second. Men were no strangers to her. Some had even kissed her, or tried to before she had tossed them into the nearest ditch for their bad manners. But this one, this one was different in every way imaginable. This kiss *she* had initiated, had, in fact, coerced it with the use of her glamour. Upon seeing him, she had known she would stop at nothing until she had felt his touch. Still, it was no excuse. Glamour was *never* to be used lightly.

If Abunda could see her now, Nakkole would most definitely be in for a lecture. Her goal was to seek out and protect Prince Gavin, not to frolic with a glorious stranger like a wanton woman.

Oh, but this strong reaction to him terrified her. It was far more powerful than any magic she had ever performed in her lifetime.

"Lady Nakkole," the harsh, feminine whisper pulled Nakkole from her desire. Then, a hand to her arm yanked her from her dance partner and turned her around. Timpani stood, hands on hips, and a frown upon her face. "I see you've met Laird Gavin."

Nakkole stumbled backward. The glamour disappeared, and she cursed herself for ever casting it at all. If she had only learned his name before indulging herself . . .

"Lady Nakkole," he whispered, his voice husky, his eyes glazed. He appeared confused, dazed, and Nakkole felt the burden of guilt upon her shoulders. She had just enchanted the man she was bound to protect. "I tried to introduce myself, but . . . I can't explain why I didn't."

An emotion Nakkole had never encountered before consumed her—she burned straight down to the painful boots encasing her feet. Her cheeks hot, she shrugged, hoping to look as baffled as he.

"I can assure you, it is not in my nature to act so recklessly," she said, an uncomfortable giggle threatening to escape her lips.

"Nor is it in mine," he said.

Timpani pulled on Nakkole's arm. "Might I have a word, *my lady*?"

Grateful for the reprieve, Nakkole turned to Gavin. "Begging your pardon, Laird."

He nodded, then, as though trying to rid it of the lingering charm, shook his head. "I'd like to speak with you before you retire. You'll find me inside, supping."

Praying she did not appear as uncomfortable as she felt, she forced a smile. "A moment, then, and I will seek you out."

Sweet Avalon, but she felt guilty. At the moment, Gavin was probably doubting his own sanity. Appalled at herself, Nakkole swallowed. This man would have never kissed her had she not used her glamour on him. She hadn't intended to enchant him. It had just happened. She had to learn to control herself. She had barely started her assignment and already she was faltering.

"Imagine my surprise when I asked the young woodcutter who you were dancing with and was told he was the very man we are here to protect. What would possibly possess you to behave so foolishly?" Timpani started the moment they were out of hearing range.

Nakkole opened her mouth to defend herself, but Timpani held up a hand, obviously not ready to hear any excuses.

"'Tis bad enough that you would seek out and kiss a man on our first night as guests, but you had to choose the laird? May I remind you that he is our future king?"

Timpani's cheeks reddened in anger, and Nakkole looked away. She had done everything Timpani accused her of, but had she known who he was, she would have done no such thing.

Would she have?

Just because she now knew him as Laird Gavin did not change the fact that he was the most glorious man she had ever laid eyes upon. Black hair as dark as a raven's wing slightly curled around his neck. Full mouth. Strong, broad shoulders. He looked so much like King Arrane had years ago—so striking and beautiful—it had truly stolen her good sense. Had she known his identity at the time, would she have truly resisted the urge to taste him?

She wasn't certain.

Something about Gavin had spoken to her soul the moment she had seen him striding toward her. That very notion frightened her more than anything in her memory ever had.

He was her future king. Desiring him would lead to no good for her.

Swallowing hard, Nakkole turned back to Timpani. "Like it or nay, you're here under the pretense of being my servant. It'll not do to have others overhear you giving me such a set down." Nakkole breathed deeply, uncomfortable with the sight of her trembling hands. The prince's kiss had affected her in a way she had not expected. While she'd used her glamour on him to ensure the embrace, she felt as though it had been she who had been enchanted.

"Besides," she continued. "I don't think he minded all that much. 'Twas the same as we did on all the other good people here. They wouldn't have been taken by the glamour had they not already held some curiosity, some interest in us."

Timpani's eyes narrowed. Nakkole sighed and brought her hands to her side. "I know. 'Tis no excuse. I shouldn't have directed my charms solely on him. It will take a bit of getting used to these new ways here. Our normal days allowed us to bend others to our will with our glamour . . . to make them leave when they wanted to stay, make them stay when they wanted to leave. Will it be so easy for you, do you think? To remember not to use your gifts?"

This time it was Timpani who sighed, her taut face smoothing into a wistful stare. "Probably not. 'Tis only *who* you chose to charm that worries me."

"Had I known he was the McCain, I vow to you I would have done nothing more than introduce myself." At least she hoped she wouldn't have. She still couldn't explain the unescapable urge she had had to fall into his arms. Then, as a thought struck her, she smiled. "His powers. I *knew* I felt enchanted when he began to dance with me. Now that I know who he is, I understand why."

Timpani laughed. "Ah, he used glamour on you as well, you think?" She turned and led Nakkole through the crowd toward the keep. "Do you think his use of the power was intentional?"

"Abunda made it clear that he hasn't been raised to know of his sire, his powers, or his bloodline." Nakkole brought her hand up to press her fingers to her mouth, recalling the taste and feel of Gavin McCain on her lips. " 'Tis a mess I've gotten myself into, isn't it? How am I to face him as a healer to his mother, when he no doubt thinks I'm free with my body?"

Timpani giggled. "You are free with your body. As are we all."

Nakkole smiled. In the mountains, it was not an unusual sight to see the White Ladies traipsing about wearing naught but their precious spring waters. Modesty was not in their nature, but most had never indulged in the sort of dalliance Nakkole had just partaken in. "But we do not freely give it to anyone."

Timpani's giggle turned to hearty laughter.

"Are you laughing at me?"

Shaking her head, Timpani waved her free arm in the air. "No, no. Not at all. But . . . did you see his face when the glamour broke?"

Nakkole frowned. Gavin had appeared bewildered, as though secretly he thought he'd lost his mind. She found no humor in that at all. It was one thing to charm the trespassers in White Waters, and quite another to baffle a kind stranger—especially one destined to become her king.

As they approached the large stone walls of the keep, Nakkole made a silent vow to control her magic unless its use was necessary. She turned to give her pledge to Timpani when a slow, shadowed movement near the forest caught her eye. She pulled on Timpani's hand, turning her to face the trees.

Timpani gasped and clutched her chest.

Doubt and fear shook through Nakkole's body. There, on the outskirts of the Scottish pines, stalked a dog blacker than night. It possessed a head the size of a large boulder. Two horns protruded from behind its ears, and its eyes glowed first yellow, then red.

Barguest. The faery omen of bad things to come.

Death had danced among them this night.

Three

~

"I believe we underestimated Elphina's determination." As they stood on the steps of Grey Loch, Nakkole firmly pressed her hand against her bosom. "To see Barguest so soon after our arrival cannot bring good tidings."

Her gaze followed the languid movements of Barguest's pacing. His stare clung to her own, his red eyes blazing at her beneath the coiled horns atop his head. His presence meant doom, perhaps even death, was coming, or had just been delivered, to someone near. She glanced around to see if anyone else had seen the omen, but they carried on with the festivities, oblivious of the beast.

The keep's door opened swiftly behind Timpani and Nakkole. A young woman rushed from the keep into the evening air, tears coursing down her ashen cheeks.

"What is it?" Nakkole asked, stepping beside the girl when she stopped to breathe deeply.

The girl lifted a hand to point behind them, into the keep. "Rufous," she whispered. "Sweet Rufous."

A sense of dread filled Nakkole's gut. Something had befallen the kind man who had shown them their rooms and offered them their first friendly smile. Her gaze flicked back to the forest's border. The spot Barguest had paced so determinably moments before now stood empty save for a lone oak. He had stayed until his presence was no longer needed to warn them of death, and now he had gone.

Must it start so soon? She hadn't had time to prepare, hadn't even located the other guardians Abunda had sent to Grey Loch. And now, already something had happened.

"What's wrong with him?" Timpani asked, her voice a bit cold.

The girl looked up, blinking, and sobbed. "D-dead." Then she lifted her skirts and rushed toward the celebration, likely to spread the news.

Timpani placed a hand on Nakkole's shoulder. "Rest easy. It wasn't our prince."

Nay, but it was a clansman. She must discover how he had died, must know for certain whether Elphina was behind this tragedy.

❧

Gavin stood at the foot of the bed staring at his friend's lifeless body. Rufous lay in the center of Gavin's mattress, his chest no longer heaving with life. He would remain here, on Gavin's order, until it was time to prepare him for burial.

It had been little more than an hour since Gavin had left Rufous's company. Just enough time for the man to fall asleep in front of the great hall's fire and die alone. Had there been a symptom of whatever sickened him? Had Gavin been too preoccupied to notice? The man had appeared as fit as always. Aye, he was older. But not so old that age alone should have claimed his life.

Gavin whispered a quiet prayer. "Brotherhood till death and beyond, my true and worthy friend. I will miss you greatly."

The burning of tears stabbed Gavin behind his eyes, but he ignored them. He would not dishonor Rufous by whimpering like a fool.

"How did it happen?"

The voice brought Gavin around to face the doorway, his

fingers still resting lightly on the sheet. Lady Nakkole of White Waters stood there, as beautiful as she had been at the fire, but her glow had paled.

"I'm sorry to startle you, Laird. Your friend was kind to us when we first arrived. It seemed his nature to always be so."

Gavin gave a curt nod. While he had been dancing with and embracing Nakkole, his friend had been taking his last breath. Had Rufous cried out? If Gavin had remained in the keep, would he have heard?

"'Tis an irony that on the day our healer arrives, a well man finds his death," he muttered.

She said nothing, but stared intently at Rufous's form. The man's plaid had not been fully covered by the sheet, and her gaze had fastened on the brooch affixed to Rufous's shoulder.

"The McCain crest," Gavin said, more to fill the silence than to answer her curiosity. "He acted as laird in my absence."

And had been a far better fit for the title. Gavin loathed the thought of taking the charm back, loathed even more stepping back into his duties without Rufous's aid.

"How did he die?" she whispered again.

With sorrow heavy on his heart, he lifted the sheet and lay it carefully over Rufous's face.

He hated her for being there, did not want to share this moment, this last memory of his friend with anyone else— most especially this strange woman who made his body awaken while his heart mourned.

"In slumber," he stated simply.

Her eyes widened. She looked anxiously at Rufous's body. "We should wait till morn to speak. There will be time before I meet your mother. I will leave you to grieve in peace."

She turned and left him standing alone, and though moments before he'd wanted solitude, now he longed to call out, to bring her back, to make him think of anything other than Rufous's untimely fate.

"I am sorry, Rufous," he whispered, then turned and made his way to the anteroom outside of his chamber. But before he could settle himself down in the quiet of his solar, the sound of a throat being cleared invaded his privacy. He glanced up to find his closest friend, Alec, in the doorway, his face pale as he stared down at Gavin through glassy eyes.

"We will all miss him, Gavin," Alec stated simply, his voice a tad unsteady. And without another word, he left Gavin in solitude.

To Gavin, Alec was as much a brother to him as Rufous had been a father. The only true family he'd ever known resided in those two men, and now . . . now there was only Alec. Even his own mother—who he admittedly knew little about—was preparing for death.

How very tiny the world seemed just now.

He called for a bath to be brought up, and once it was delivered, he ordered linens to be carried into his solar so he might sleep on the floor. He stripped from his still-damp clothing and stepped into the warm water. The barrel tub allowed the water to warm him only to mid-chest, but he welcomed every inch of it.

He hadn't had a day go as horribly wrong as this in so very long. He only wanted it over. He wanted to close his eyes and pretend he would awaken to Rufous's concise report of the workings of the village. Pretend he hadn't fallen all over his new healer like a besotted fool.

He had never acted that way before, not even when Madeleine O'Connor pulled down her bodice to reveal a perfect pair of breasts when he was a lad of twelve. He hadn't had the presence of mind to speak to Nakkole about his mother's illness. He had not even had time to apologize for treating her like a common trollop.

He shut his eyes and scooted under the water as far as the tub would allow, his neck finally resting on the hard rim. The healer was the least of his problems. Rufous was dead.

Dead. Gone. Forever.

Gavin's chest tightened. He'd lost many a friend to death in times of war and rivalry, but never so abruptly and unexpectedly. Dampness burned his eyes, and he let his tears fall freely.

Nakkole's feet carried her swiftly down the stairs to the great hall where she hoped to find Timpani. Her heart raced. Her palms sweated. Neither were normal occurrences in her body. She hated both.

She found Timpani standing by the fire, gesturing wildly to a woman who stood only as tall as Timpani's waist. The woman replied in a thick Irish lilt that rang like music to Nakkole's ears. As Nakkole hurried over to them, she felt the slightest bit of relief at the sight of the woman, for the twinkle in her eyes revealed her as fae.

"Oh, Nakkole. Look who I've found. She's come to keep Grey Loch running smoothly while she helps keep an eye on Laird McCain."

A house faery. Nakkole's relief dissipated as quickly as it had come. The only magical help this woman could offer would be from filth. But another pair of wary eyes was always welcome.

Nakkole nodded a greeting. The woman mimicked the action. "Call me Beanie, me girl. I was told you might be needing me aid. I've a useful set of ears on me wee head."

"'Tis very nice to meet you, Beanie. I suppose Timpani told you of Barguest?"

Beanie gave a heavy sigh, her slight shoulders sagging with the motion. "That she did. As well as the dead man upstairs." She looked over her shoulder at a servant who entered the room, then cast another glance at Nakkole. "Remember, they're not able to see my kind. Keep silent when others are about, else they'll think you're odd in the mind, speaking to yourself. I've got me duties to see to now, but I'll make certain to keep me eyes and ears open."

Unable to reply with the servant girl within hearing distance, Nakkole nodded. The solid form of Beanie evaporated into a teeny sparkle, then drifted toward the hallway. Odd creatures, house faeries.

The servant retrieved a few scattered goblets, and when she left the room, Timpani grabbed Nakkole's arm and led her farther into the corner of the great hall.

"Was it Elphina?" Timpani whispered.

"I'm not certain, but it definitely sounds like the work of

her maras. Gavin says Rufous was in fine health, and yet he died in his sleep."

Timpani gasped. Nakkole understood her reaction. The very fact that Rufous had died in his sleep made the maras suspect. It was their power to sit their tiny red bodies on the chests of men and ride them through unimaginable nightmares, steering them toward their most dreaded fears and even to death. At the moment of death, the human soul escaped through the mouth, allowing the maras to catch it and in this case take it back to their queine where the human soul would be transformed into a dark creature to help fill Elphina's army.

Gavin's friend Rufous was likely no longer an ally, but an enemy instead.

"There is something else," Nakkole continued, wringing her hands as she thought about how very close they'd come to failing their duties this night. *Her* duty. The pride she'd felt when given this task was quickly becoming overrun by fear. "Rufous died wearing the McCain brooch."

"They thought Rufous was the laird."

Nakkole nodded. "I believe so. We were not given details of what our prince looked like. I can only assume the maras were as ignorant. They found a man wearing the brooch—"

"And thought him the laird. My word, Nakkole. What if it had been Prince Gavin?"

"We cannot think such thoughts!" Nakkole took a deep breath and tried to dismiss the tension in her body. "He is not to be left unwatched. The maras could try to strike again when he sleeps, and there are others who might strike out during the waking hours." She sighed and squeezed her eyes shut. "Abunda gave us far too little information to arm ourselves with."

"Well," Timpani answered, "our first duty is to teach him of his powers."

"Aye, but first we must keep him alive."

K*eep him alive.*
The words rang over and over in Nakkole's mind

that evening. Gavin would want his privacy and would not welcome a stranger's compassion on a night when such travesty had occurred. But she couldn't very well guarantee his safety from a distance.

Nay, she needed to remain close to hold guard against the maras.

Pacing the short length of floor in front of the open window in her chamber, she strained to peer through the night's darkness and into the forest trees. Barguest had come and gone, leaving his mark on this place in every tear now being shed for Rufous. She closed her eyes and allowed the cool night air to seep through the fabric of her gown and caress her skin beneath. Thoughts of her Norman springs carried nostalgia through her body, making her feel as though she had been away for years.

With a sigh of surrender, she stuck her head out of her window and tried to ignore the stifling confines of the chamber she'd been given. She suddenly found it difficult to breathe. In all her years of dreaming about coming to this world, she never guessed she would miss home so soon. Shaking her head, she pushed thoughts of Normandy from her mind.

A plan to remain near Gavin tonight was of the utmost importance.

Gavin the Immortal.

Around the Beltane fire, she had heard the villagers proudly refer to their chieftain by the name. *Immortal*. She knew not why he claimed such a title, but if she failed to guard his sleep, they could very soon discover how mortal their laird truly was.

Her only hope was to conceal herself. She stared at the dewy night grass and summoned the tiny iridescent drops into her outstretched palms. They coated her skin with a slick layer of damp armor.

With a slight wiggle of her fingers and deliberate command of her eyes, the drops spilled from her hand like a tiny stream and circled her ankles. A spiral of ascending rain crept from the floor below, cloaking her legs, her waist, her breasts, her head. She could still see well, but knew to any who encountered her, she would appear to be naught more than a faint fog let in from a drafty window.

She would stand guard in Gavin the Immortal's bedchamber and make certain his name remained truth on her watch. It was a duty she both dreaded and craved. For she longed to know more about the man who had set her blood aflame with a mere kiss.

❧

Gavin awoke to naught but eerie quiet, his chest heaving, his breath shallow. He sat upright in the makeshift bed on the floor of his solar. His gaze darted about the darkened room as he tried to recall what had awakened him.

What had he been dreaming? He could not remember, but the helpless feeling it left behind lingered within him. As did the heaviness upon his chest that felt as though something had been resting there.

Gavin squeezed his eyes shut and rubbed his hand over his face, trying to wipe the powerless feeling away. He thought of rousing himself fully, oddly afraid of falling asleep once again, but instead lay back against the blanketed floor, now damp from his sweat.

He turned onto his side, allowing the blanket to slide off of his hips and the cool night air to dry his perspiration. A thin wisp of fog drifted along the wall like a lone, wandering cloud. He watched its armlike tendrils spill around his floor bed, then disappear from sight.

Odd, he thought, as he gave in to his burning lids and closed his eyes for sleep. There had been no signs of fog when he had retired. An eerie chill crept up the back of his neck, and he forced open one eye, focusing on his window.

The shutters were closed. It couldn't possibly have been fog he had seen. He shifted his gaze to the floor, noting with a bit of relief that the fog had dissipated into nothingness. Perhaps he'd imagined it? Lord knew, he was weary enough to still be dreaming. Yet he could not shake the feeling that he was being watched.

Frustrated at his apprehension, he sat up once more and lit the candle on a nearby table. From his blankets, he guided the light into the corners of the room, and when he saw nothing, extinguished the flame and lay back down.

Rufous's death had made him uneasy, that was all. Closing his eyes, Gavin tried to reassure himself that his sanity was still intact.

❧

The next morning, Nakkole found herself sitting alone with Gavin in the Great Hall after the others in the keep had broken their fasts. The hall was nearly empty, the trestle tables all stacked against the walls leaving only one still topped with the morning meal. Nakkole picked at her food, hoping she at least appeared to be paying close attention to the words Gavin spoke rather the the array of food and drink around her. She wanted to sample everything, from the eggs to the bread, but dared not while he watched her so intently.

"My mother will be arriving within the hour," he was saying. "The chamber you've been given is next to hers. It should make it easier to tend her should she need you in the night."

Sipping the white, foamy milk, she savored its sweetness, then forced herself to put the cup down and focus on the matter at hand. She adjusted her body on the uncomfortable dining bench and tried harder to focus on their conversation.

"It would help to know exactly what ails your mother so I might better plan how to tend her needs. What sickness has befallen her?"

How much did he know of his mother's illness?

Gavin set his serving knife atop his trencher and leaned forward. "No one knows. She fell ill shortly after I was born and has never recovered. No one has been able to name her sickness."

Nakkole looked away, suddenly guilty that she knew more about his mother than Gavin. He may not know it yet, but it was heartache that steadily killed Geraldine. It was much the same sickness that had begun to lead King Arrane to his deathbed.

Now was certainly not the time to try and explain such to Gavin.

Struggling to think of something a true healer might ask, she grasped her cup and took a deep swallow of milk. When she replaced the cup on the table, Gavin stared at her with the beginnings of a grin on his face.

"What?" she asked, unsettled with his close scrutiny.

"You have a little . . . here . . ." He reached across the table, leaning close enough to her that Nakkole could see the tiny flecks of gold rimming the stone gray of his eyes. A sign of his fae heritage.

His thumb brushed her upper lip. It lingered there for a moment, but the tingling sensation of his touch forced her to pull back. Gavin cleared his throat and sat back in his chair.

"You had a bit of milk beneath your nose," he muttered.

Nakkole turned her stare away. She had kissed the man and had wanted him to all but consummate their meeting just the day before. Then she'd spent the previous night watching him through her fog cloak as the blanket he'd slept beneath crept lower and lower, nearly revealing every inch of him to her hungry, curious gaze.

Now his simple touch nearly undid her control.

" . . . the nuns haven't been able to tell."

Nakkole jerked and realized she had missed even more of his words.

"Pardon?" she asked.

He shook his head and pushed his chair away from the table. "I said, the nuns haven't been able to understand what plagues Mother. She just drifts in and out of slumber. Now she seems to be sinking into senility. Seeing things that don't exist."

Nakkole froze. "Things? What things?"

Gavin stood, chuckling. "Don't look so mortified. Silly things. Things that some who are considered sane actually believe in. Gentle folk and such."

"Gentle folk?" Nakkole swallowed. "You mean faeries? She sees faeries?"

A look of sadness crossed Gavin's face. "Aye. It's nonsense, but harmless enough."

It took a bit of will, but Nakkole managed to swallow the retort perched on the end of her tongue at being referred to as nonsensical.

She could not help but wonder if perhaps Geraldine truly did suffer some illness of her mind. Either she was imagining the creatures, or . . . was it possible that she could have retained the gift of Sight Arrane had given her when they had been married? Could she truly still see fae-kind? Without the gift of Sight, some faeries, like Beanie, weren't visible at all. Others, like Nakkole and Timpani, would appear as human as any other woman. But someone with the Sight would see beyond all that.

Could her soul kiss with Arrane have transferred a bit of that power into Geraldine? That was the purpose of such a kiss, after all—to give a bit of oneself to another when a child had been created between two soul matches.

She cleared her throat. "As you said, many people all over this world believe such things exist. I hardly think such would make your mother appear mad."

Running a hand through his hair, Gavin shook his head. His exasperation was clearly written all over his tense features. "Aye, for anyone other than my mother, it would be so. Those who know Lady Geraldine McCain, however, know how very ill she must be to claim to see such things." He paused, his gaze falling to rest upon her chest. "I'll have plaids brought to your chamber, as well as to your lady's maid's. You stand out far too much dressed as you are, and I wouldn't want you falling prey to anyone who might think you're worth English coin."

He said no more, instead turning and striding from the hall with no further instruction for Nakkole. Knowing he was eager to finish preparations for Rufous's burial to be held at sunset, she didn't try to keep him longer with her questions. She watched him go, her mind turning with the implications of his mother's "illness."

Did this mean Geraldine would see Nakkole and Timpani for what they truly were?

If so, Nakkole's task to fit in as a human had just increased in difficulty tenfold.

Four

～

That afternoon, several long strips of fabric nearly identical to the ones the clansmen wore were delivered to Nakkole's chamber. After a long bout of trying unsuccessfully to manipulate the cloth around her body, she sighed and wrapped the bulk of the plaid around her shoulders, then pushed open her shutters.

On the grounds below, two men engaged in a mock battle. Nakkole recognized Gavin instantly. He stood a good head above the others, his long, black hair clinging to his cheeks. She watched him raise his sword high, then bring a solid blow to his opponent's blade. The clanking sound of steel against steel echoed throughout the quiet morning air, seeming to bounce off the stone walls of Grey Loch. She imagined his skill in fighting had been the genesis of his nickname, the Immortal, for even the dread of seeing him without his guards in the bailey could not diminish her appreciation of his abilities.

In fact, she could do naught but appreciate the beauty of everything about him. Pressing a fingertip to her partially open mouth, she recalled his taste and the feel of lips far too soft for such a hard, solid man. Such gentleness in a man his size had been a treasure to discover. And oh, sweet Avalon, how she wanted to discover it again and again and again.

But she could not. She was here to prepare him, not seduce him, no matter how strong her urges.

Gavin pivoted and brought his sword down on yet another of his men, felling the opponent with the ease of a falcon targeting its prey. If only his foes were human, she would have no need to fret for his safety, for it was apparent he could well stand on his own.

But one could not fight an unknown enemy.

Nakkole sighed and fumbled through the belongings Timpani had given her, searching for something appropriate to don until she could be shown how to use the plaid. She yawned, already too fatigued to do much more than toss a few garments from the satchel. In the mountains, she spent her days in a more leisurely manner. That included napping at several intervals throughout the day, worshiping the warm grass as she awaited the next traveler to pass through.

Here, at Grey Loch, there had been, and would be, little chance for rest. Already her eyes burned with fatigue, and she had only just arrived the day before. She had spent the night watching over Gavin, her only comfort in the pillow of her shielding fog. Her days would be spent watching, worrying, hoping to catch a glimpse of whatever powers Gavin might unknowingly possess, dreading to catch a glimpse of Elphina's minions. And most important, getting to know the future king so she could figure out the best way to tell him the truth about his heritage, his destiny.

She hadn't even had a chance to explore the bed she'd been given, and she so wanted to spread out atop it and discover whether the blankets were as soft as they appeared. She bounced her bottom on the edge of the mattress and stifled a giggle. Then she sighed. The joy of coming to this human world and exploring all its wonders would have to wait.

"'Lo, Duncan! Open the gates!" she heard Gavin shout.

Half dressed, Nakkole hurried back to the window, her eyes focusing instantly on Gavin. He handed his sword to the man he had been targeting, then started toward the opening gates, his stride quick and purposeful. Struggling to fasten the bodice of her dress, she strained to see his destination. He was quickly joined by a man she'd been introduced to when she'd first arrived. Alec, she thought his name was.

Movement along the road leading from the gates to the village caught Nakkole's eye. Three horsemen and one large, covered cart headed toward the keep. Gavin and Alec strode from the field toward the arriving party.

Timpani stepped onto the bailey, and Nakkole breathed a sigh of relief. Timpani's eyes would serve in Nakkole's stead, at least until she could finish dressing. Without bothering with the horrible boots, she hurried from her room and outside. As she rushed to the gates, however, her wariness subsided. The cart's driver was dressed in a frock, and Nakkole knew instantly that this was the priest escorting Lady Geraldine McCain home.

The gates creaked open, and the cart and horsemen entered the bailey. The three riders dismounted, and a young man Nakkole guessed to be the stable master led their horses to the stables. The frocked man stepped forward and greeted Gavin with a polite nod. No one, save for Timpani, seemed to notice Nakkole's presence.

"G'day, Father Donnelly. The journey wasn't too difficult I hope," Gavin said, taking the priest's hand in his. Nakkole watched him stretch his neck as though to peer into the back of the cart, but he made no other move toward it. Instead, he asked Alec to see to his mother, then led the priest toward the keep.

She had to admit to being a bit curious to see the woman who had captured King Arrane's heart so long ago. "If the journey had been difficult," she heard the priest say, "your mother would not know it. She slept throughout our travels."

"Good, very good," Gavin said. Nakkole walked behind them. No matter how anxious she was to meet Geraldine, she was in no hurry to find out whether or not the lady would be able to see her as a faery. "I'll have you meet with Lady Nakkole before you depart. She'll need to be prepared before dealing with Mother."

"No need, Laird. I can speak with him now." Nakkole sped up her pace until she stood in front of the men, forcing them to stop their steps.

The priest's gaze traveled over her person and settled on her feet. Uncomfortable, Nakkole shifted her stance, hoping to no avail to hide her bare toes beneath the hem of her skirt. He looked as though he wished to comment on the sight of her, but Gavin blessedly did not give him the chance.

"Father Donnelly, afore you begin instructing Lady Nakkole about Mother's illness, I wanted to first ask if you might preside over a burial for Rufous this eve."

Father Donnelly's face softened. "Of course. A young lass by the name of Millicent stopped us as we arrived and told us of Rufous's death. When I heard, well . . . he was a good man. I'm sorry for your loss."

Gavin nodded and pointed to the keep. "My thanks. Shall we fill our bellies? Noon meal should be waiting by now."

The priest nodded and followed Gavin up the steps and into the keep, but Nakkole stayed put. "My laird? What of your mother? Shouldn't you like to see her first?"

Turning around to face Nakkole once more, Gavin's grin vanished. "Aye, Lady Nakkole, I would. But she's not likely to know whether I'm there or not, so a few more moments shouldn't matter."

Nakkole glanced at the cart coming through the gates. The whole situation saddened her. That such illness could be caused by a love as strong as a soul match . . . it hardly seemed fair.

She understood now all of Abunda's cautionary tales meant to prevent the White Ladies from falling in love with their trespassers.

One need to only look at poor King Arrane's withered body to see such proof of love's destructive capabilities. His youthful, strong form had dissipated into that of a gaunt elder's.

She cast another wary glance at Gavin. He spoke to the priest in a placid tone, inquiring about his mother's health. Grey Loch was not good for Nakkole's self-control. Already, by just visiting this human world, Nakkole had felt strong pulls on her emotions that had been more easily controlled in her world. Why had her mother thought such sensitivities would benefit her duties here?

So far they were naught but hindrance.

"Pardon," she said, stepping past Father Donnelly. "I'd like to meet Lady Geraldine now. Perhaps Father Donnelly and I could join you for noon meal *after* we've seen to your mother."

She looked to Gavin. He nodded and rubbed his jaw. "Very well. See her settled. Father Donnelly, I look forward to speaking with you when you're finished."

Gavin turned into the great hall, and Nakkole followed Father Donnelly up the stairs, slightly disappointed that Gavin chose not to join them. Why would a son avoid a mother so near to death? She would think he'd be eager to spend as much time with her as possible.

Alec appeared behind them carrying Geraldine, and she and Father Donnelly moved aside to let him pass. Nakkole caught only a fleeting glimpse of Geraldine's long, black-and-gray hair. Her stomach flipped, and she realized she was not fully prepared to meet the woman who should be her queine.

To allow herself a moment of preparation, she delayed following them up the stairs, instead turning to Father Donnelly. "I'd be obliged if you would tell me whatever you can about Lady Geraldine's illness."

To Nakkole's relief, he stood where he was, leaning a bit on the wall behind him. "Shortly after Laird McCain's birth, a few noticed her odd behavior. Bouts of crying that would last hours. Then, her husband claimed she'd started taking to her bed earlier and earlier until, one day, she stopped getting out of it. She stopped talking that day . . . and feeding herself."

He screwed his lips together and scrunched his brow as though trying to remember more. "When she came to the monastery, we made it a rule that she would walk with the sisters twice a day. She managed to shuffle her feet, but never said a word and always fell back into bed the moment we returned her to her room."

"So she *can* walk then?"

"Aye, but not well on her own, and it's tricky to find a time when she's awake long enough to do so." He glanced up the stairs. "As you'll come to see, she's too thin, likely malnourished. We feed her, but we can't always force her to

swallow. I must warn you, she will not eat for people she
doesn't trust, so my advice is to spend as much time with her
as possible. The sooner she is familiar with you, the better."

And when was Nakkole supposed to find time for *that*?
This woman needed true tending from a true healer. Nakkole
needed to tend to Gavin's safety. And yet, a part of her
wanted to care for Geraldine the way she obviously needed.

How was she supposed to do both?

"And no one knows what caused her crying and her illness after Gavin's birth?"

"Her family had thought she was merely lonely, grieving
the loss of her first husband, and so they sought out a new
marriage to Bruce McCain."

"Her first husband?"

Taking Nakkole by the elbow, Father Donnelly began to
lead her up the stairs once again. She fought back the twitter in her belly.

"Aye. She married a Norman of all things. Her family,
however, never met the man. But one day, Geraldine returned to them a mourning widow, a child full in her belly.
They presumed the mourning worsened with Gavin's birth.
Perhaps he reminded her of her dead husband."

A widow?

A flash of anger lit up inside Nakkole at the thought of
Geraldine proclaiming Arrane dead. The truth of it was,
she'd been married to two men at once—a sin among humans that this priest would never condone.

"Her husband, the previous Laird McCain, thought of
sending Gavin away to improve her state of mind, but
Geraldine's parents wouldn't hear of it."

"And where are *they*?"

"Deceased for many years. Before Gavin could even
learn their names."

How sad that a child had no true family to care for him—
only a father who wasn't truly his.

They had arrived at a partially opened door. It opened farther, and Alec excused himself and eased around them to
disappear down the stairs.

"Shall I introduce you to Lady Geraldine?" the priest
asked.

With a knot in her belly, Nakkole nodded. They stepped inside, and she steeled herself for what was to come.

Lady Geraldine looked nothing as Nakkole had expected. She had envisioned a hunched-over, gray-haired woman who might appear more of a hag than a widow of a powerful laird. What she found, instead, was a lady lying in peaceful slumber, her black hair, touched by the hands of time, fanned out on her pillow. Lady Geraldine's face held lines and wrinkles, but her beauty was still quite evident—even through the gauntness of her cheeks. The thin skin stretched over her cheekbones needed fattening.

"I don't wish to bother her," Nakkole whispered to Father Donnelly. The woman lying prone in the huge bed had found peaceful slumber. To disturb her seemed cruel.

"She's likely to remain sleeping for several more hours. I had hoped she'd have awakened to meet you, but once the lady succumbs to sleep, not much can wake her."

"Is she aware of her surroundings? I mean to ask if I were to talk to her, would she hear and understand me?"

"At times she seems to. Other times, it's hard to tell."

A wave of pity swept over Nakkole, but she quickly brushed it aside. "I'm sure we'll understand one another," Nakkole said, praying it would be true.

She sighed and followed Father Donnelly out of the chamber and back to the lower floor.

When they reached the great hall to join Gavin for their meal, a young girl with two tightly coiled plaits covering her ears rushed into the keep and skidded to a stop in front of the great trestle table.

"Isolde? What is it?" Gavin asked, already rising from his chair.

"The cows, my laird. There's no milk! We've been trying all morn, but not a one has given even the merest drop."

Nakkole closed her eyes and took a deep, calming breath. Drying a herd's supply of milk was a common trick used by fae. Would Elphina and her allies stop at nothing to make her task as difficult as possible?

The third cow Gavin looked over resembled the first two, from its large, glassy eyes to its dried-up udders. Gavin cursed and rose from his position on bended knee.

He had a dead, loyal friend in his chambers, a mother he wanted to know how to say good-bye to, and a healer who had captivated his thoughts since the moment he saw her dancing with the woodcutter's son. Now he had cows who offered no milk to his people.

Would nothing go his way?

A smart man would have claimed his weaknesses long ago and would have handed the title of chieftain to a more worthy man. But of all of Gavin's flaws, stubbornness and pride were among the strongest. Even if tending land and people came as naturally to him as nursing a child from his manly breast, he would not give in, nor would he succumb to the untrusting glares of his clan's people as they watched him blunder his way through yet another mundane task.

Lead an army and a clan, aye. But care for them as a good laird should—Bruce McCain had not seen to tutoring Gavin in *that*.

Closing his eyes in disgust, Gavin knelt beside the fourth beast and prayed for a more positive result.

"You won't be getting any more milk from that cow than you did from the others," the young girl standing beside him said. "If you ask me, it's the work of the gentle folk. Their magic's been abundant in the village as of late."

He shook his head and refocused his stare on the dry udders beneath Bessie. "Nonsense, lass. More likely there's something wrong with their grazing land, their water. Who tends this herd?"

"I do," the girl said. "But the other herds are just as dry."

"Millicent, get the laird a proper stool," a large woman said to the girl.

With renewed determination, Gavin took the stool from the lass and glared into the cow's eyes.

All right, Bessie. Give me a bit of milk now, else I'll be getting a good bit of meat from you for supper.

Bessie blinked and stared at him with bored, expressionless brown eyes before bowing her head and returning to her grazing. Apparently, she had not taken his threat seriously. Gavin closed his eyes and perched on the stool beside her, irritated that he had been reduced to conversing mentally with an animal.

Unsure why he should even attempt to milk a cow so obviously dry, he squeezed an udder, probably a tad too firmly as Bessie paused in her eating long enough to turn her big head around to give him a look of contempt. Resting his head on Bessie's ribs, Gavin squeezed, rolling his fingers down the teat.

Nothing. Not a single morsel pinged into the bucket below.

A cool, soft touch to his hand opened his eyes. Nakkole leaned over him, her hand sliding over his wrist to cup the fist holding Bessie's teat. Her hair fell over his shoulder, her cheek all but resting against his.

She looked at him and smiled, her gaze penetrating his. "Allow me to help, Laird?"

How sunshine could be contained in a scent, Gavin didn't know, but the smell engulfed him as he nodded. "You know about cows then?" he asked, allowing her to entwine her fingers through his and gently pull at the teat.

"Not much." She shifted, allowing him a much-too-fleeting glimpse of the curve of her breast, then lowered herself to her knees beside him. "But sometimes it helps to envision the outcome you wish for in your mind. To will it, I suppose."

Nakkole bit her lip, hoping Gavin wouldn't think her mad. But this had seemed the perfect opportunity to see if, like his father, Gavin possessed the gift of creation. To create some small thing from nothing—like milk from a dried-up udder.

"What would you have me do?" he asked her.

Nakkole thought a moment. If she explained this wrong, he could begin to doubt her sanity. "Imagine you can see what's wrong with the cow, and in your mind's eye, you can fix it." When he stared at her blankly, she added quickly, "It's an old healer's trick."

Gavin muttered something under his breath. "How's what's in my head going to matter to the cow?"

She laughed. "It's not what's in your head. It's . . ." How could she explain? Her mind searched for memories of Abunda—times she used her gift to heal, a gift she'd not shared with any of her daughters thus far.

"There are healers who use their hands," she stated. "They feel certain . . . heat around spots of illness on another body. They use that heat to sometimes force it from the flesh."

Around them, the crowd was growing restless, shifting on their feet and breaking out in whispers. Gavin looked at them, then turned back to Nakkole. "You're the healer, you do it."

What was she to say to that? The only thing she could. "But you're their laird and it will comfort them to know you aided them, not I."

Every offensive word Gavin had ever heard rolled through his brain. The crowd's restlessness was making him anxious. He was out of ideas of his own, so what harm could come from trying Nakkole's?

With a sigh, he closed his eyes once more and felt Nakkole slowly pull her hand from his. He suddenly felt very much alone, even amidst such a large crowd. It took everything within him to clear his mind for the task at hand. He pictured the inside of the udders, dry and unproductive. He thought of the drained, crackling nipples dampening with a single drop of creamy milk, the lone release moistening the tip of his finger. He strained, pumping the teat, trying to ignore the whispers of the clansmen observing from behind.

Please.

The milk drop in his mind turned to a steady stream, each pull filling his imaginary container a bit more than the last. With each squeeze, he understood more and more what Nakkole had wanted him to do. It wasn't all that different than when he led his men into battle. This use of mental pictures was a tactic he employed on the battlefield, thinking of the desired outcome in order to create his reality. Believe in success and you could attain it.

Still, focusing one's mind on the battlefield to control his

skill and movements was one thing. Forcing a cow to produce milk was completely beyond his control.

He sighed, slowly opening his eyes and trying to think of
an explanation his people would accept, one that did not in-
clude the mischief of gentle folk. The sound of gasps penetrated his consciousness before he could focus on his still
moving hands.

He looked at the pail beneath the cow, then glanced over
his shoulder to make certain he wasn't the only one who
could see the frothy liquid now filling the milk pail. When
he looked back beneath the cow, his hands froze in place. He
stumbled backward, toppling from the stool, then barely
caught himself before he could fall on his backside.

Nakkole stepped back, avoiding being knocked over by
Gavin's stumble, but she never took her gaze off of the milk
still dripping from Bessie's udders. It took every ounce of
strength within her to prevent the grin she felt inside from
spilling onto her face. King Arrane's magic had mirrored a
bit of each of those who served him. He took their strengths
and dismissed their weaknesses.

It seemed Nakkole had just seen a bit of the father in the
son, for Gavin had just used a gift owned by the White
Ladies—that of creation. He had just produced milk from a
dried-up cow, a cow plagued by faery magic. He looked up
at her, a childlike grin on his face. The excitement she had
been holding back slowly crept onto her face, and her body
began to tingle. Gavin had the power, had *used* the power.
Now all she had to do was train him to better wield it.

❦

That evening, as darkness fell around the Grey Loch keep,
Nakkole quietly closed the door to Geraldine's chamber,
confident the woman would sleep soundly throughout
Rufous's funeral. Geraldine hadn't so much as twitched in her
slumber when Nakkole had checked in on her, thereby allowing Nakkole the freedom to seek out Gavin and see how he
was feeling after the cow incident.

She suspected he'd been using some of his powers
throughout his life, but likely never considered them magi-

cal. It was very easy for nonbelievers to dismiss such things
as coincidence or lucky chance. How was she to make Gavin
believe differently?

As soon as Bessie had finished giving milk, he'd set
about his day, working with his men and making plans for
Rufous's burial. She hadn't had a chance to speak with him
since.

She found Gavin just outside the keep, his head bent over
a large barrel of water, rinsing the day's grime and sweat
from his face and hands. His chest was bare and glistening,
his plaid wrapped tightly at his waist. When he ran his wet
hands through his hair and dampened the dark strands of
black, her belly twisted in a peculiar manner. She stepped
forward so that he might see her face in the fading light.

"I checked in on Geraldine," she said, suddenly unsure
what to say to the glorious man in front of her. "She sleeps."

He nodded and offered a small grunt of acknowledgment,
then snatched his tunic from the barrel's edge and slid his
arms into the sleeves. He fastened the loose ends of his plaid
over his shoulder and used the hem to dry his hands as he
watched her in silence.

Why did he not speak?

Her throat dry, Nakkole barely managed to say, "I wanted
to see how you fared, as well. I know today was not an easy
one, and tonight will be even more difficult for you. Is there
aught you need?"

His gaze never left hers, and for a long, horrid moment,
she thought he would do nothing more than stare at her.
Finally, however, he shook his head. "You're here to care for
my mother. Not me. Save whatever drafts and concoctions
you make for her."

Gavin could hear the gruffness in his own voice and grimaced. The expression on Nakkole's lovely face was one of
concern and curiosity. She certainly didn't deserve to bear
the brunt of his frustration. It wasn't her fault that he felt the
weight of Scotland on his shoulders.

"I'm fine," he said, forcing a slight smile. "I've just a lot
on my mind at the moment."

She nodded, her bottom lip disappearing briefly inside
her mouth, then reappearing slightly plumper than it had

been before. His gaze focused on her lips, he said without thinking, "Why aren't you married, Lady Nakkole?"

His question took even him aback. What did he care about her marital status? Aye, she was a comely lady, but certainly not the sort he was meant to marry. His wife would be of Scottish blood, likely born of a clan whose alliance would help his own prosper. But as he thought on it, he did begin to wonder about his query. Such a bonnie lass with no man to claim her? Certainly she'd had many offers of marriage.

"Married, Laird?" Her light accent drifted quietly on the wind to settle in his ears. Norman, aye, but something else tinted that voice. An accent he couldn't quite place.

It wasn't until he felt the soft flesh of her cheek against his palm that he realized he'd reached out to touch her. Startled, he flinched, but did not remove his hand. His thumb stretched to brush her bottom lip, remembering how it had felt against his mouth. She was speaking, moving those lips, her tongue darting out to moisten them, but he heard not a word.

"Laird?" Nakkole's whisper was so quiet, he barely heard it. She pulled her cheek away, brought a hand up to cover the place his own had held.

He cleared his throat. "My apologies. You were saying?"

Her blink was slow and lazy. "Only that . . . the opportunity to wed has not yet been given to me." She took a step back. "I should leave you to finish readying for the funeral." Nakkole glanced up at the sky, her long, ivory neck stretching and all but calling for a kiss. Gavin was quite proud of his restraint.

"It's getting quite dark. Perhaps we should both go inside."

Wiping the sleeve of his tunic across his brow to dry the remnants of his washing, he nodded, at a loss for anything else to say—a state in which he seemed to find himself whenever Nakkole was around.

"Do you plan to attend Rufous's burial?" he asked, following her toward the keep. The raspiness had returned to his voice, but this time it was born of desire, he suspected, rather than irritation.

"If it pleases you."

"I have a peculiar feeling there is little about you that wouldn't please me, Lady Nakkole."

She stopped walking, turned to face him. "I would say the same of you, Laird, but I'm certain it wouldn't be appropriate." She closed her eyes. "Whatever it was that made us kiss at Beltane . . . it shouldn't have happened. If I have encouraged your advances, then I should try to remedy that. 'Tis the truth I'm not accustomed to being around men such as you."

Curious, Gavin raised his brow. "Men such as me?"

Her bottom lip had disappeared again, her gaze drifting away from his. "Aye. You're not at all like the men I've encountered in Normandy. At least, I mean to say, I never felt compelled to kiss them as I did you. Perhaps it's best to declare now that I never mean to do so again." Her words tumbled out like an overflowing pitcher of ale. She took a deep breath and returned her gaze to his. "I have a duty here that I mean to perform to the best of my capabilities. Whatever this attraction is, I won't be falling prey to it again."

Gavin couldn't help the smile he felt tugging on his lips. "Then you admit to being attracted to me?"

Her hands clasped onto the folds of her poorly wrapped plaid, wringing the fabric with white knuckles. "I admit that there is something about you that appeals to me, and I only admit as much in order to plea to whatever mercy you might possess. When you . . . touch me, as you did a moment ago, it's highly unfair given the short-term nature of our relationship. I would ask that you not do so in the future, for it leaves me quite . . . disturbed."

"Disturbed?" For the first time in several days, Gavin chuckled. He watched Nakkole stride to the door, turn and wait for him to follow, and never quite look him in the eye. Well, he was damned pleased to know their encounters were disturbing her because they were sure as hell disturbing him.

She was right about the unfairness of his advances, however. He had no intentions of a future with a strange woman from Normandy, and he wasn't in the habit of bedding virgins and ruining their standing in the eyes of society and the church.

But, as he walked past her into the keep and the smell of sunshine enveloped him yet again, he couldn't bring himself to promise never to touch her again, either. Such would be like promising to spend the winter bare-arsed naked—both left him feeling cold and irritated.

❧

akkole hurried up the stairs, not daring a look back at Gavin. She reached the sanctity of her chamber and collapsed onto the bed, unable to catch her breath. Her entire body trembled, and she raised a hand to once again touch her cheek as Gavin had done. What had possessed him to touch her so? She certainly hadn't used any glamour on him, and she hadn't felt enchanted, either. Nay, it had felt more like longing in her bones. And for what? A man she barely knew? A man who would one day be her king?

She had no right to have such feelings or such thoughts.

Taking deep calming breaths, she lay in the dark stillness of her chamber for several long moments. It was the sound of voices coming from below her window that finally forced her back to her feet. She smoothed the skirt of her dress, watching from the window as mourners began to spill from the cottages and keep, walking toward the cemetery. Gavin had likely already put their encounter from his mind in order to prepare for Rufous's burial. Nakkole must do the same.

She had never been to a human's burial before and wasn't quite certain what expression to wear. When one of her kind died, they were celebrated, not mourned. The female faeries wore garlands of wildflowers in their hair and buried the deceased beneath a mound of petals. The human way seemed so very different from hers, but if mimicking their actions would show Rufous the respect he obviously deserved, she would comply.

She pulled the shutters closed on her window and left her chamber to look in on Lady Geraldine one last time before going to the service. Father Donnelly had watched over the woman, keeping her company throughout the afternoon, but Nakkole knew she must accustom herself to caring for Geraldine sooner rather than later.

She opened the door to Lady Geraldine's chamber and stepped inside. Three candles lit the room from near the window. The bed curtains had been pulled closed. Father Donnelly must have already departed for the funeral, for he was nowhere about.

Fighting her nerves, Nakkole eased farther into the room. She shoved back the lacy bed hangings, revealing a slumbering Geraldine dressed in a cream-colored sleeping gown and covered in dark green blankets.

Someone would need to stand watch over the older woman while Nakkole attended Rufous's funeral. She thought of calling on Timpani for the task, but thought better of having another faery in the same room as Geraldine. It was bad enough that Nakkole would be spending much time with a woman who claimed to see her kind. She couldn't chance having her accuse others, as well.

As she tried to pull the flimsy curtain closed around the bed, she felt a cold, clammy hand grip her wrist. Gasping, Nakkole spun around to find Geraldine sitting upright in her bed, her black eyes wide and unblinking. Her lips moved with eerie speed, but the words she whispered were unclear.

With a shaking hand, Nakkole brushed her hair from her face, tucking it behind her ear, then leaned forward to better understand Geraldine. The moment Nakkole leaned close enough to feel Geraldine's breath on her ears, the woman's voice found its way back.

"You'll not be taking my son!"

A long, high-pitched scream infiltrated the chamber. Before Nakkole could react, Geraldine had reached out to her night table. She snatched the candle burning there and flung it at Nakkole. In a frenzied, dreamlike moment, Nakkole stared down at her feet and watched in horror as her dress went up in flames.

Five

G avin was only just leaving his chamber to make his way
to the cemetery when the scream came from his
mother's chamber. He barreled through her door. His heart
pounding like a dozen steeds trampling a rocky path, he
stared, transfixed by the bright orange blaze in the center of
his mother's chamber.

The smell of singed hair choked him. His eyes watered.
His vision blurred, but thankfully his mind still retained
some control over his body. He seized the large wash bowl
on the stand by the wall. With a wide swing of his arms, he
tossed the water onto the main source of fire, knowing in his
gut what even his mind refused to acknowledge.

In the midst of the smoke and fire was Nakkole.

Behind him, heavy footsteps stormed into the room, but
the task of beating the few remaining flames from Nakkole's
dress consumed his full attention.

"Sweet Mary, Gavin!" The voice belonged to Alec.
Thankfully, the man wasted no more time with words,
knowing instinctively that action was needed. Alec found a
blanket and flung it around Nakkole's body. The last flames
went out and Gavin stepped back to survey the damage.

Nakkole stared wide-eyed and openmouthed, her hands still holding a charred blanket as she beat at imaginary flames. Though the smell of burnt hair overwhelmed the room, only a finger's length of her long tresses had curled up in a black singe. What was left of her dress barely covered her thighs.

His healer was in need of healing, but she would live.

With a slow turn of her head, she stared at him, opening her mouth to speak. The color drained from her face, and she brought her hands up pleadingly, then she promptly fell to the floor in a heap.

Gavin cursed. He knelt to scoop her into his arms, but a low, eerie moan called his attention away from Nakkole's body. The chaos had made him forget about his mother. The sight of her sitting upright in bed mumbling to herself rattled his bones.

He hadn't heard his mother speak more than a few times in his entire life.

His throat closed up at the sight of Geraldine's strained expression. He fought to find his voice, then turned his attention to Alec. "Take Lady Nakkole to her chamber and fetch her lady's maid."

Alec didn't question the command. He bent, gathered Nakkole in his arms, and left Gavin alone with his mother—a position he had avoided since he was a lad. Being around a mother who couldn't comfort him had been too much for him as a child, and her impending death had never made it any easier to be around her as he'd grown into a man.

"Mother?" he whispered, not trusting the sight before him.

She seemed to truly see him for the first time. Her head tilted, as though she considered what she saw, and her gaze traveled over his person.

He stepped forward. His soul yearned to hear her forgotten voice, needed to have her speak to him, speak at all. She watched him come closer, and he thought he saw her gaze soften. But then she squeezed her eyes closed and snapped her jaw shut. Her mumbles stopped, as did her rocking. She simply lay back on the bed.

He fingered the chain around his neck that had once belonged to his mother and squeezed the charm that dangled from it. It was truly all he had left of her.

"It's all right, Mother. No one wishes you harm," he said, willing her eyes to open, dying to catch just one more glimpse into the soul he was certain still lingered behind them.

With an ache in his heart, Gavin stepped away from the bed and snuffed out the remaining candles.

What had caused her sudden outburst?

A niggling of hope snuck into the depths of his chest. Could a burst of energy mean a possible recovery after all? It was hard to feel joy, however, when such activity had harmed an innocent bystander.

Poor Nakkole. Gavin cast one last, hopeful glance at his mother, then left to enter Nakkole's chamber. Nakkole had been sent here to help heal a sick old woman, and on her first day, she had nearly been killed. With a sigh of remorse, Gavin rapped lightly on Nakkole's door, then let himself in without waiting for permission.

Timpani stood by her lady's bedside rubbing ointment on Nakkole's back. The soft moans coming from the bed were both pitiful and proud, for even a brave man would surely be howling over the touching of such tender and wounded flesh.

"Is she all right?" he asked, surprised by the harshness of his voice. It seemed the compassion he felt hadn't yet reached his throat.

Timpani turned, her long, blond plait tossed over her shoulder. "She will be. Her back and legs have been burned badly, but her hands will barely even blister."

The waves of fiery locks cascading over Nakkole's back were lifted in Timpani's hands and tucked out of the way of her wounds. A naked, feminine back should have been a welcome, if not fascinating sight to a man—especially when that back belonged to a remarkable beauty such as Nakkole—but Gavin couldn't make himself look past the violent pink blotches.

"'Tis odd that her hands didn't get the worst of it, but I suppose the blanket sheltered them a bit," he muttered.

"No time to ponder the oddities here, Laird Gavin. No

offense intended, but I could tend her more efficiently if we were left alone."

Timpani's tone was icy, but Gavin knew she was right. "Very well. Rufous's burial is awaiting me. I'll go then, and leave you to care for your lady."

But his feet didn't seem inclined to move. It took Timpani pushing at him to pry him from the room and the door closing in his face to get him moving through the corridor, downstairs, then outside. The image of Nakkole lying on her stomach, her scorched back staring accusingly at him, stayed with him until he reached the cemetery. Then, his focus turned sharply to the scene at hand, at the box holding his cherished friend's remains, and at the mourners by its side.

Mother. Dying.

Rufous. Dead.

Gavin ran his fingers through his windblown hair, pausing to pull at the roots and inflicting just enough pain to pull himself from his self-pity. His self-loathing would be buried here with Rufous this eve. It was a silent oath he made to himself, but by God, after this horrid night ended, he would begin to prove to everyone around him that he could be the great laird his stepfather had not been, the laird Rufous had tried so desperately to turn Gavin into.

He would make Rufous proud.

◆

Be glad you're not well enough to play witness to this," Timpani murmured, standing at Nakkole's window, her head turned toward the northern cemetery.

Nakkole tried to move onto her side, but the pain that came with twisting her back forced her to remain still. As long as she stayed flat on her belly, her back didn't ache so much anymore. The salve Timpani had administered with Nakkole's faery spade had done its job well, but still, her legs pained her, burning, itching, and throbbing all at once.

"If it's so horrible to watch, why do you still stand there to witness the burial?" she asked, wishing she had the strength to brush away the pesky, wild hair that incessantly tickled her nose.

"I'm not sure. Perhaps for the same reason I could not turn away when that Norman woodsman cut off his finger with his axe last spring. 'Tis not a pleasant sight, but fascinating enough to hold my interest."

"They grieve differently than we, Timpani. Be respectful of it."

"Oh, I am. I'd not be foolish enough to tell a one of them how senseless it is to fall apart as they are, all for something as inevitable as death. Why, they're all crying, save for the men who just stand there, solemn-faced."

Timpani's views were shared by most of the fae, including Nakkole herself. But humans didn't seem to be plagued with detaching themselves. Even knowing one day that a person would be taken from them, they bonded freely. It was admirable, but it was not a quality Nakkole ever hoped to possess. She'd yet to experience losing a loved one, but with King Arrane coming so close to meeting his death, she knew a twinge of what Rufous's mourners were now feeling, and she didn't welcome it at all.

"Leave them in peace, Timpani, and put more salve on my back, please. I'm beginning to feel as though I'm on fire all over again."

The bed gave way a bit, and Nakkole turned her head to see Timpani sitting beside her.

"Wonder what the devil set Lady Geraldine's mind to lighting you up so, anyway?"

At the feel of the cool salve being rubbed on the small of her back, Nakkole closed her eyes and buried her head in the pillow. In her mind, images whirled of turning and seeing Geraldine's wild eyes glaring at her with such loathing. The feel of the cold, bony hand wrapped around Nakkole's wrist.

Nakkole moaned. "She knows I'm fae, though I believe she suspects we're here to harm Gavin."

"That could prove a rather large obstacle." Timpani paused in her massaging for a brief moment, then continued on. "You don't think she'll cast suspicion on us?"

"Father Donnelly said she's been *seeing things* as of late.

Perhaps if she does see fit to speak to anyone else, they won't take her seriously."

Timpani set the jar of herbal salve on the bedside table, then leaned forward to brush Nakkole's hair from her face. "Do you think all the others she's claimed to see were truly our kind?"

Nakkole would have shrugged if she'd had the strength to do so. "I don't know. If Arrane took nothing else from his time with Geraldine, he definitely took the mortals' notion of love. I wouldn't doubt he's been notified of her every breath since she left his side."

Timpani frowned and headed for the door. "All these years," she mumbled. "That's a remarkable number of breaths."

❧

Gavin stayed beside Rufous's grave site for a long while after the other mourners had left. For a few moments, Alec had remained as well, staring at the fresh mound in silence. But then he, too, had returned to the keep. Now, rain pelted Gavin's face and hands, dampened his clothes, and drenched his hair, but he didn't move, didn't even consider finding shelter and leaving his friend to suffer his first moments beneath the earth alone.

No matter how fine a warrior Rufous had once been, or strong a man he'd continued to be, he'd never been good at solitude. In the last few months, he'd been forcing himself to spend more and more time alone, telling Gavin that a man had to face his demons before the time came to meet his maker. Still, it bothered Gavin to no end that his friend had died alone, when being alone had been his greatest fear.

Gavin lowered himself to one knee and ran a hand over the muddied earth that served as Rufous's grave. He pulled his sword from its sheath, pressed the amber-jeweled hilt to his lips, then to the ground. "Honor and brotherhood."

The people of Grey Loch owed Rufous much. He'd managed to take the home and the land Gavin's stepfather had let diminish, and had begun to make it thrive again. Rufous had been the only reason the people of Grey Loch had not completely shunned Gavin as their laird. They held little faith that the stepson of such an inattentive laird would care any more than his predecessor, but with Rufous's tutelage, they'd been willing to give Gavin a chance.

As Gavin walked back toward the keep, his feet sinking into the newly formed puddles of mud, he let out a whispered curse. What the devil was he going to do without Rufous's guidance?

Feeling eyes upon him, he glanced up at Nakkole's window and spied her lady's maid standing there, watching him. He inclined his head in greeting, then stepped into the keep, his mind overly burdened with what may come tomorrow.

◆

"He's returned," Timpani said, pulling the shutters closed. She bent and retrieved her bedroll from the corner of the room and spread it out on the floor.

Nakkole shifted on the bed, but no matter which way she positioned herself, she could not escape the raw aching in her legs. Her sister was supposed to be allowing Nakkole to sleep, but it seemed it would not be so. No matter. Nakkole couldn't fight her way through her pain long enough to drift off, anyway.

It would not do to be held up in bed much longer. Her time at Grey Loch would not permit illness or suffering of any kind.

"Is there anyone else about?" she asked, forcing her body to sit despite the screaming in her lower back.

Timpani turned back to the window and pushed the shutters open once more. After a quick glance about the grounds below, she shook her head and pulled the coverings closed again.

"Doesn't appear to be. Why? Do you sense something amiss?

"Nay, but we're going to find our mother, and it's best if we're not seen."

"We can't risk running off to the loch at this hour! It'll cause suspicion if we're spotted, and after what happened with Lady Geraldine this afternoon, I'm not thinking you should be calling more attention to yourself."

"If we don't go, we won't be here long enough for it to matter whether or not we're caught. My legs won't allow me to get around as I need to. Why should Gavin keep an invalid around to care for another of the same kind?"

Timpani sighed and squeezed her eyes shut. "And how do you suppose we get there? You're barely able to move, let alone walk such a distance."

Nakkole smiled, pleased that she'd finally managed to coax her mind into thinking ahead. "Call for Beanie. She'll get me there."

After a long, drawn-out blink of her eyes and a quick nod, Timpani left the chamber and disappeared from Nakkole's sight. A few moments later, she returned with Beanie following close behind, the top knot on her head barely visible over the side of Nakkole's bed.

"You're needin' to get somewhere in a flash?" Beanie said, stretching onto her toes to peer up at Nakkole.

"Please," Nakkole answered. "To the loch."

"You're riskin' a lot by disappearing now."

"I'm risking a lot by staying. Will you take me?"

Beanie nodded and held out her hand. "Hang on tight, me gel. The first time's likely to make you a bit sick."

Nakkole raised her arm and slipped her hand into Beanie's tiny one. For such a small woman, the house faery had a grip that rivaled an ogre's, and Nakkole couldn't stop her astonishment as the woman pulled her toward her stout body. Then, Beanie reached out with her other hand and did the same to Timpani.

"Close your eyes," Beanie said. "Now, take one another's hand and let us form a circle. Good . . . good."

When Nakkole next dared to pry open one eye, she was surprised to find herself floating above the rush-covered floor in her chamber. A thin, golden sphere encircled them like a hollow moon. They were inside Beanie's bubble. She glanced down at her hands. They looked normal enough, but everything outside the haze of the bubble loomed over her like enormous fortresses. Her bed had become a sprawling plain below her, the door a gigantic, smooth-faced cliff. Off balance by the sudden change in size of nearly everything around her, she squeezed her eyes shut again and clutched her stomach.

The bubble jerked and Nakkole gasped, her eyes popping open to find the sphere had swerved to the other side of the room. From this distance, her window across the chamber looked at least the size of the stables.

She glanced at Timpani, whose eyes were still squeezed shut, then at Beanie, whose gaze darted about the room. In a flash, they rushed toward the wall above the closed shutters. Nakkole braced herself for impact. Closer, closer, the wall came at them. Nakkole bit into her lower lip. She opened her mouth to yelp, but no sound emitted. Higher they rose. A hole the size of a human eye appeared in a crack in the stone. The threesome slipped through the hole as though it were a normal-sized doorway, and Nakkole found herself floating high above the ground.

They breezed over a copse of trees, darted down among the leaves and reappeared above a small dirt path. A rabbit darted across the trail. They swerved right, then sharply left, then right once more between an oak and a holly tree, each quick movement of the bubble making Nakkole cry out in agony. Finally, they stopped moving just in front of a great lake as still as a looking glass.

Suddenly, Nakkole could feel the cool grass beneath her bare feet and the burden of her weight on her aching legs. She shook her head, realizing Beanie had released her, then, unable to stand alone, she crumpled to the ground.

"What an . . . odd sensation," she muttered, twisting so that her weight didn't sit directly on her burned thighs.

Timpani groaned and eased onto the grass beside Nakkole. "I feel a little woozy."

Nakkole smiled. "Just be glad you kept her eyes shut. I thought my heart would stop when we nearly rammed through the wall."

Beanie tsked and adjusted the tiny cap on her head. "We did no such thing. You only felt as though you were your normal size, but once we left the ground we were no bigger than a wee pearl."

Nakkole never failed to be amazed by the different sort of

magic possessed by other faeries. While she'd seen Beanie in her twinkling form, she had never considered what the view of their world looked like from within.

"Amazing," she said, her voice breathy. "Truly amazing."

Beanie brushed off her skirts, though not a speck of dirt marred them, and grinned with pink, pride-stained cheeks. "I think so. Now, let's do what you came here for, me gel, and be gone before someone notices you're missin'."

❧

Gavin's fist stayed positioned in front of Nakkole's chamber door for a long moment as he considered knocking. He didn't wish to disturb her, but his conscience needed to make certain she was faring well.

He lowered his hand. He should let her sleep. She needed to heal. As it was, she may not be feeling well enough to resume her duties for some time. Interrupting her rest would not help her recovery along.

He slid his palm down the rough, oak door until it curled over the handle. He would crack open the door and check if she was sleeping. If he found her to be, he would leave her to it. If not, he'd see how she felt and begin trying to apologize for his mother's outburst.

He pushed, and with a low squeak, the door opened just enough for him to poke his head through. No light penetrated the chamber. He couldn't see a thing. Cursing, he knew she must be asleep. He should turn and leave.

He stepped farther into the room, his ears alert for the sound of her breathing but found only eerie quiet instead. He should *definitely* leave. His feet didn't seem to agree. They continued moving forward as though with a mind of their own, until finally, he stood at the foot of her bed, staring with incredulity at the sight before him.

The woman who had just been nearly burned to death was gone.

Six

⁓

With her weight balanced between Timpani and Beanie, Nakkole allowed herself to be lowered into the wonderfully cold lake water. All at once, the water both relieved the pain of her burns and stung as though it penetrated the blisters on her naked skin to course through the blood in her legs.

Desperate to focus on the relief rather than the pain, she sucked air through her teeth. Behind her, Timpani whispered to Beanie to step back and give Nakkole solitude to summon the White Lady queine.

"Wait." Nakkole glanced back at the pair standing on the shore. "Beanie, please take Timpani back to Grey Loch. I feel uneasy having Laird Gavin left unattended. You can come back in a bit to retrieve me."

Neither faery protested, realizing, Nakkole was sure, that Gavin's safety was far more important than her own.

Finally alone with the night and with the chilled, calm waters, Nakkole grimaced against the pain in her legs and leaned backward. The lake seeped into her hair, saturating it with its beautiful, graceful body. She brought her hands up and curled the ends of her long hair around her fingers, breaking off the remaining singed strands.

Then, she stared into the water and focused on summoning her mother. The beckoning required all her attention, which was quite a feat considering the many sensations demanding it now. With concentrated effort, she reached her arms out in front of her, laying them flat against the smooth, calm surface of the water, then opened her palms, letting them soak up the elemental strength from which her faery powers had been born.

She moved her arms outward, pushing the water away from her to banish any negative forces that might have lingered there, then changed their direction to beckon Abunda's spirit to this place.

Already she could feel the healing powers of the water, reviving her with much-needed strength. Still, she needed Abunda to bring a more powerful healing to the burns on Nakkole's body, and there wasn't much time left before the sun would awaken and Nakkole would be expected back in her chamber.

She straightened and lowered herself onto her knees, the sandy bottom of the lake chafing her raw skin. With outstretched arms, she lifted her hands, palms up, to the surface, grasping a small puddle in each fist, then let the small droplets rain from her flesh and onto the skin of the water.

"Queine of the passages, queine of the springs, show yourself, your powers bring. Night's cool air and Scottish shores, come so I may be restored."

A long moment passed, long enough that Nakkole feared her plea had not been heard, but then the waters around her rippled, lapping at Nakkole's shoulders and chin. A gust of wind picked up a few scattered leaves that had fallen on the shore and sent them into a slight whirlwind until they landed delicately around Nakkole. She reached for one, turning the soft greenery in her fingers and waited for Abunda to show herself.

"I had so hoped you wouldn't be requiring my assistance this early in your mission, Nakkole. I was at Arrane's palace when you beckoned me."

Nakkole dropped the leaf and darted her gaze about the

watery surface. Sure enough, Abunda's image appeared just a foot or so away. Nakkole wanted to sag with relief, but stayed perfectly still so as not to disrupt the faint reflection in the lake.

"I've been injured," she whispered. "And I'm afraid my duties will suffer if I'm not tended to straight away."

Abunda's reflection glimmered beneath the moonlight, worry rippled her brow. "What's happened?"

"Prince Gavin's mother is what happened. She tried to kill me."

As Nakkole explained all that had transpired in the last few days—Rufous, the dry cows, Geraldine's arrival, and the catastrophe of tonight's events—Abunda's magic worked on her raw leg burns. The warmth made it difficult not to fall asleep, but Nakkole forced her eyes wide open.

"I suspect you're right," Abunda said when Nakkole finished speaking. "The maras have been about. This man, Rufous, seemed to have been in the wrong place at the wrong time. Lucky we are that Prince Gavin is still among us. Still, I worry about Lady Geraldine. Arrane told me she wasn't well, but he failed to mention that my daughters might be in danger."

Nakkole sighed. "Well, I admit she took me by surprise. How someone so frail could move so quickly is beyond my understanding."

"Roll over, love, and float on your stomach. Let me work the burns on the front of your thighs."

Nakkole did as she was told. "It won't happen again. Now that I know what she's capable of, I'll be better guarded against her. I think she only wishes to protect her son. If I can show her that my goal is the same, perhaps she'll come to trust me."

"And how do you plan to do that?"

From her position, Nakkole could no longer see Abunda's reflection. "I'll think of something."

The warm healing moved from her upper thighs to her lower belly, a place barely touched by flames, but pained just the same.

"Very well, I trust you'll succeed," came Abunda's voice.

"Now tell me more about this incident with the cows. What powers, exactly, did you see from the prince?"

"Ours. 'Twas exactly as it would have happened had it been my hands upon the beast's teat. Gavin produced what didn't exist, and yet exactly what he needed so desperately."

"Ah, then we've seen the power of the White Ladies. I imagine it won't be long before the other sorts of magic begin showing themselves in him."

Nakkole opened her mouth to mention that she was nearly certain she'd also witnessed a bit of Gavin's ability to produce glamour, but thought better of it. If Abunda suspected that she'd fallen under Gavin's charms for even a moment, she wouldn't allow her to continue on at Grey Loch. And Nakkole wanted to prove herself by guiding Gavin into becoming the finest faery king ever to reign. Returning to Normandy with naught but failure to show for her efforts would bring her no respect, as well as, she assumed, a great disdain from her king.

"We've seen him create," she heard Abunda say. "Soon, I'm sure, we'll see his ability to destroy, communicate, and most important, to control. I suspect he's been using them all along without knowing so. Having so many fae around him will undoubtedly make those powers surface more readily. When you return to him, find ways to bring these qualities to his surface, but focus on his ability to control objects with his will. It's bound to be his strength, just as it is Arrane's. It is that ability that is most likely to aid him when the time to fight—"

The warmth left Nakkole's lower belly with the strength of a dam bursting.

Abunda was gone.

The apparition of the queine rarely lasted much longer than a few moments, for it required the most powerful source of her energy. But the visit had been long enough to leave Nakkole feeling somewhat normal, if not a bit shaky.

She lowered her feet to the sandy bottom of the lake, thinking over Abunda's orders.

Find Gavin's source of control and nurture it. Surely, even Nakkole could do that much.

In the amazingly wide berth of Beanie's tiny bubble, Nakkole traveled back toward her chamber with her two companions, watching the keep grow nearer through a dizzying haze. She could no longer feel the aches in her thighs and belly, though upon occasion her lower back still stung with swift movement. Abunda hadn't the time to complete the healing there, but at least the most severe of Nakkole's wounds had been tended. Come morn, she would be able to resume her duties as Lady Geraldine's caretaker and Gavin's secret mentor.

The healing had drained her of what little strength she'd managed to hold on to, however, so thinking of ways to fulfill both duties would simply have to wait until her mind was as fit as Abunda had made Nakkole's body. She feared, however, that it would take more than one evening's sleep to restore her mind. She missed her leisurely naps in Normandy, missed her lazy afternoons. Her body now begged for sleep, and had there been a place to lay her head inside Beanie's golden bubble, Nakkole would have sought it out.

The moment they flickered through the same tiny hole in Nakkole's chamber from which they had departed, however, Nakkole knew sleep would not be quick in coming. Trouble paced the floor in front of the window, its name being Gavin McCain.

Beanie darted their transport over Gavin's head, then down toward the floor and out of the chamber from beneath the door. A moment later, Nakkole found herself on unsteady feet at the end of the corridor, an equally unsteady Timpani by her side. Beanie's twinkling effervescence danced in front of them for a moment in a quick "good eve," then promptly darted away.

"Don't think I've ever missed walking on these two feet more," Timpani murmured, bracing her swaying body against the wall.

"I'm not certain my vision will ever be the same," Nakkole whispered back.

"He's angry. Did you see how angry he was?"

At Timpani's abrupt change of topic, Nakkole jerked away from her side of the wall and shook her head to clear the blur from her eyes. "Gavin?"

"*Oui.* How will you explain your absence?"

"With as much of the truth as poss—"

"Where the devil have you been?"

Gavin's booming voice echoed in Nakkole's ears. She winced and leaned once more against her side of the wall. Gavin stood, half of him in her chamber, half of him in the hall, his glare so fiery it nearly set the corridor aglow.

"I asked you a question, Lady Nakkole. Last I saw you, you were horribly wounded and prone in your bed. My men and I searched all of Grey Loch for you and found nothing." His menacing stare narrowed, and he stepped fully into the corridor. "Now I find you standing on legs that shouldn't be fit for standing, at the top of the stairs, which implies you've been down them."

A bit of anger mingled with Nakkole's extreme weariness. She clinched her jaw, irked to have been spoken to as if she were naught more than a mischievous gnome. "You asked for a healer, and 'tis what you've received. Think you I should save all the healing for your mother and refuse any for myself? If so, how am I to tend her while I, as you so delicately put it, lay horribly wounded and prone in my bed?" She matched his glare, uncertain whether she was more angered that he hadn't shown any relief to see her healed, or that he had ruined her reunion with her soft bed. Her eyes burned with need for rest. This was not a conversation she wanted to hold at the moment. "If you'll excuse me, all this healing will be for naught if I don't rest now."

Silently pleading for assistance, she glanced at Timpani.

Thankfully, Timpani complied and tucked her arm around Nakkole's waist. "Let me help you prepare for bed, my lady."

They walked entwined toward Gavin, but he seem disinclined to move out of their way.

Exasperated, Nakkole closed her eyes. The relief to her dry, tired eyes stung, but she welcomed it. "Please move," she whispered. "We can discuss this in the morn if you'll only let me sleep now."

She opened her eyes to find his steely gray gaze settled upon her face, his features unrelenting in their tautness. "I'll allow you rest after you've answered me one question."

Even as she lowered her head toward Timpani's supportive shoulder, Nakkole nodded. "Anything. Just let me rest."

Timpani tried to intervene. "Can't you see, Laird, that she'll not get well until she—"

Gavin ignored her. "Where were you? My men hunted everywhere."

His angry stare turned to one of suspicion. A wave of queasiness pushed her insides toward her throat. He knew something wasn't as it seemed. She could sense it in the way he regarded her, in the firm set of his jaw.

Knowing she was too tired to tell lies and expect to remember them come morn, Nakkole sighed and told him as much of the truth as possible. "Timpani accompanied me to the loch. I didn't wish to disturb the keep with a request for a bath, and the salve Timpani used on my burns required me to soak."

Gavin scoffed. "You expect me to believe you rode on horseback with your wounds? Or that you walked? My lady, forgive my disbelief, but I've had men with far less damage done to them by fire who could not move from their beds for a fortnight or more."

"Then it is a pity your men did not have Lady Nakkole to tend their wounds, for surely they would not have acted so pitifully," Timpani said.

Nakkole had difficulty hiding her smile of pleasure at her sister's defensiveness on her behalf. With her head still upon Timpani's shoulder, she sent her a grateful glance even though she knew her sister couldn't see it.

"Aye," Gavin murmured. "Perhaps it is."

Still he did not move from their path.

"A numbing salve allowed her a small measure of ease from her pain, my laird. Long enough to travel to the loch and back," Timpani continued. "'Tis a clever salve that you're welcome to sample whenever your aches become too much to bear, if you do not believe me."

Again, Gavin scoffed, but this time, he said nothing.

Nakkole lifted her head from Timpani's shoulder and raised her brow at Gavin. "May I rest now?"

"One last thing, then you may sleep until your heart's content. I'll even inform the servants that you are not to be awakened."

His lack of concern for her welfare chipped away at her patience. Only reminding herself that he was her future king allowed her to hold her tongue against a sharp retort.

"If you were bathing in the loch," he started, "why is your hair as dry as my own?"

Nakkole gasped and brought a hand up to touch her dry locks. She had not considered her hair. As always, while she'd lingered in the water, her hair had been as saturated as any creature's. But, as with all White Ladies, it dried moments after stepping out of the lake.

Obviously frustrated, or perhaps as unnerved by Gavin's question as Nakkole, Timpani grasped Nakkole's waist tighter and pulled her toward Gavin, nearly knocking him down in order to get past him. Somehow, Timpani managed to push past his barricade and into her chamber. Before she shut the door in her future king's face, however, Nakkole stuck her head back into the hallway.

"'Tis called a ribbon, my laird," she said. "'Tis a clever little device that a lady may use to tie up her hair."

Timpani gasped and promptly shut the door. Together, they slumped against it. Once the sound of Gavin's footsteps stomping away could be heard, Timpani pushed herself from the door and pulled down the blankets on Nakkole's bed.

"Thank you," Nakkole said, wobbling toward the bed, then sliding beneath the covers. She turned onto her side to stare at her sister. "I seem to be mucking up this whole task."

"You've been through an ordeal, Nakkole. Try to be more kind to yourself." Timpani yawned. "Sleep well. I'll stand guard over Gavin this night."

Nakkole allowed her eyes to close. Her last thoughts before sleep consumed her were of how very close she'd come to aiding the destruction of the good magic in the world. Queine Elphina and her maras were probably laughing with glee that it was she who had been sent to stop their attempts to overthrow Arrane. After all, who better to have against them than a bumbling fool like Nakkole?

❧

Gavin kicked open his chamber door, both angered at himself and at Nakkole. He'd gone to her room to try to convince her to stay on and help his mother. Instead, he'd treated her like a criminal, even refused her the rest her body needed to heal. If she stayed even one more day, he'd be damned surprised. He'd have to make amends come morn or risk having her walk away, and that simply couldn't happen. Geraldine needed her care, and damnit, Gavin didn't *want* Nakkole to go.

He liked her.

A lot.

But he couldn't quite stop his anger with her, either. It wasn't that he didn't believe her story—at least most of it, anyway. But some of the details just didn't make sense. He'd dealt with many healers in his lifetime, as had most of the men with whom he fought on the battlefields. None had ever produced a salve of any kind that could do the things Nakkole claimed hers could. She shouldn't have been walking yet, let alone traveling the good distance from here to the loch.

He lay back on his bed, pinching the bridge of his nose and grinding his teeth against the throb in his temples. There was something different about her, and if he believed in such things, something enchanting about her that could make him believe nearly everything that came out her mouth. He had a feeling this pain in his head wouldn't be cured by some salve Nakkole possessed. In fact, he'd be willing to stake his life that he wouldn't find relief from it as long as Lady Nakkole of White Waters resided at Grey Loch.

Seven

～

The Desolate Caves of the Otherworld

A queasy knot of frustration and intolerance roiled in Elphina's belly. She quietly pushed closed the heavy door to her chamber and turned with a false calm to face the mara chief who'd awakened Elphina moments ago with news that would cost him his life.

The moment her gaze fixed upon the creature, he fell to his knees, pressing his hairy red brow to the dirt floor.

"We did as you bade us, Majesty," he croaked.

"Is that so?" Elphina circled the small chief and, when she arrived behind him, placed the toe of her boot against his backside and shoved, sending him sprawling onto his bare belly. "Why, then, is my brother still alive?"

The mara didn't dare move from his supine position. He merely rolled his mouth away from the dirt in order to answer his queine. "We thought we'd done right, Majesty. The man we killed . . . he wore the laird's brooch, as you'd told us was customary."

"You killed a decrepit old man, you foolish gnat. What would ever make you think such a person could be Prince Gavin?"

"Time there," he whimpered, "it's not the same. We

thought perhaps his world had not been so generous—we were not shown what your brother looked like, Majesty. Please . . . be merciful."

"Merciful, indeed."

Elphina lifted her foot and pressed her boot to the creature's cheek, then stomped down until she felt his skull crunch like kindling. "Your dinner, Rancor," she said to her raven, opening the door to her cage. "Pick him clean and I'll have Lucette tidy up when you're full."

Rancor shuddered in delight, nipped Elphina's finger lovingly, then drifted to her feast on the floor. Elphina watched with morbid curiosity for a few moments before changing her bloody boots and opening the door to call for her mother.

Gavin was still alive. The maras had failed her.

It was time to call forth the banshees.

Scotland

The next evening, Gavin tugged on his tunic and wrapped his plaid about him, belting it at his hips. He then left his chamber with determination to seek out Nakkole. He hadn't had time to check in on her this afternoon, but he'd been told she'd stayed in her chamber, requesting meals to be brought to her there.

On his way to find Nakkole, however, the pull to see his mother drew him to her chamber. He peered into her room, opening his mouth to call out a quiet, *"Mother,"* but stopped before the word reached his tongue. The profile of her sleeping face looked so serene, so beautiful. In the time she'd lived at the abbey, he'd almost forgotten what she looked like.

Look at me, Mother.

He hadn't truly expected her to hear his silent plea, but the familiar hollowness in his chest he'd carried around as a lad returned. He shut the door to her chamber *and* to the painful memory of a child in need of his mother.

Swallowing back his frustration, he resumed his mission to find Nakkole. He almost expected to find her chamber empty once more, but on his second knock, Timpani opened the door to him and stepped out of his way to allow him entrance into Nakkole's chamber.

"Good eve to you both," he muttered, glancing about the dark room and spotting Nakkole sitting up in the bed. "How are your wounds faring?"

Nakkole, with her flaming red-gold hair fanned out about the pillows behind her, looked a vision in her white nightdress. Gavin's blood wasted no time in stirring. She smiled at him, raising the heat in his body enough to dry the remaining droplets of bathwater from his skin.

He swallowed.

"I'm feeling much better. I should be up and about soon enough," Nakkole said, adjusting herself on the bed so that a long lock of her hair fell to cover her bosom.

"Pardon me, my lady, Laird. I need to fetch milady fresh water," Timpani said.

Gavin blinked. A lady's maid knowingly leaving her mistress alone with a man? Odd, but advantageous for him. "Good night to you, Timpani," he said and watched her disappear down the hall.

A long moment of silence filled the space between Gavin and Nakkole. Finally, he said, "Father Donnelly gave one of the maids, Nettie, instructions on how to care for my mother while you're healing. She wished for me to relay to you that Mother has had no more outbursts."

Nakkole smiled and shifted with obvious effort. "Please give her my thanks."

Gavin continued, "I also wanted to apologize for speaking so harshly last eve."

"Thank you, but I feel it is I who should have been the first to apologize."

Her voice was aught more than a whisper, and yet he felt as though he could nearly feel her breath upon his ear.

"You sent for me so I might care for your mother, and I feel as though I've done little more than lie in this chamber since I arrived."

It took all of Gavin's strength to focus on Nakkole's words. Seeing her lying in her bed, even wounded, he could not keep his imagination reined in. He could focus only on her wide eyes, her warm glow, her full, soft mouth, which he had experienced during one of the most thrilling kisses of his life.

"Are you all right, Laird?" Somehow, she was out of her bed and standing before him. Then, she was pressing her palm firmly against his brow. The position of her body gave him a clear view of her generous bosom, white and lush.

He was sweating. He was hard. And God help him, he wanted to ignore her recent injury and claim what he'd desired since he first met her. Having her place a tender, soothing hand on his brow nearly undid him. When was the last time a woman had cared enough to do so?

"Tired, I believe," he managed. "Forgive me . . . but I can't remember why I sought you out."

"I'm sure it will come to you." As she turned away from him, she winced.

"Are you all right?" he whispered.

Nodding, she bit her lip and eased onto her bed. "Timpani forgot to apply my salve before she left. I'll be fine in a moment."

A sudden, painfully erotic image of Nakkole baring her back and thighs to him flashed through Gavin's mind. He imagined spreading his hands across her thin waist, feeling her flesh against his palm.

He swallowed hard, his breathing labored. "Where is the salve? It is the least I can do."

The offer did not seem to shock her as it would have any other woman. She merely retrieved a small jar from her night table and handed it to him.

"My thanks," she said, her smile genuinely unembarrassed.

When Nakkole turned her back to him and began to shove her night shift off her shoulders, baring her slender, red back, he nearly dropped the salve. "Lie down."

She did, rolling slowly onto her belly to allow him access to her wounds. He was surprised by the lack of blistering upon her back. After what she had endured, the faint red markings should have been screaming with injury, but Nakkole looked only as though she'd been in the sun for far too long.

He eased beside her on the bed and opened the tiny jar.

The bitter scent of herbs assaulted him at once. Grimacing, he scooped a fingerful of the gooey salve onto his palm and braced himself for the feel of her in his hands.

Her satiny skin was heavenly.

Nakkole took a deep breath, sucking the air through her teeth. Lord, that he could be any more insensitive did not seem likely. Here he was, lusting after her, and couldn't even think to warn her of the cold salve.

"It's cold," he said stupidly. He grimaced and rubbed the next bit of salve between his hands before applying it. "This should be a bit warmer."

Nakkole didn't wince or shrug away. Instead, she moaned and buried her face in the pillow. The blood stirred in Gavin's loins once again. He couldn't help himself. He simply had to taste her. Slowly, he bent forward and placed one soft, feathery kiss over the worst of her burns. Nakkole's head snapped up and she looked at him from over her shoulder.

Nakkole wriggled a bit, raising her head from her pillow. "My lord? What are you—"

Guilty, Gavin jerked upright, but he would offer no apologies. The feel of her skin on his mouth had been punishment enough, for he would not likely find comfort in his own body again for the remainder of the night.

"I'm finished," he said, closing the jar and placing it on her night table. "It would be best if Timpani applied it to your thighs."

He could see himself lowering his head once more to the tender flesh of her upper legs, so very close to the treasure he knew was hidden there. Should she allow him to tend those wounds, it would be a temptation he was not strong enough to deny himself. If he was to be honorable, he must leave her to heal without seducing her.

"Laird Gavin," she whispered. Was that arousal in her voice?

A loud, intake of air expanded Gavin's chest, and he snapped his head up and stared Nakkole in the eye.

"Rest now. I'll send for Timpani."

Before she could utter another word, he stood and left her chamber. He paused outside her closed door for a long mo-

ment, seeking composure. Slowly, his blood cooled and he
managed to wipe the taste of her from his mouth, sweetness
and herbs combined. With a soft groan, he pushed himself
away from the door and turned to find her lady's maid.

❧

Two days later, with only a few aches remaining on her
lower back thanks to the faery ointment Timpani had
been applying, Nakkole was faced with yet another burn.
She'd only just set a bowl of broth on Geraldine's bedside
table when the older woman slapped it with her fist, sending
the contents all over Nakkole's bodice, straight through to her
breasts.

After a long night of watching Gavin while he slept, she
was in no mood for another ordeal with Geraldine McCain.

"Lady McCain," she said through gritted teeth, fully prepared to give the woman the set down she deserved. But the
woman's eyes were closed, and she was once again sighing
the serene sounds of slumber. "Lady Geraldine?"

Geraldine's eyelids fluttered, but she made no other sign
that she'd heard Nakkole. Nakkole leaned in closer, careful
not to put herself in harm's way, and whispered, "If you can
hear me, Your Majesty . . . and yes, I know you're King
Arrane's wife, and my queine. I wish to put your mind at
ease. I'm not here to hurt your son. I'm here to help him."

Geraldine didn't so much as twitch.

Sighing, Nakkole gathered Geraldine's supper. What little broth was left in the bowl now was as cool as the broth
clinging to her chest. She left the chamber as quietly as possible, and closed the door behind her.

"You should not be up and about."

Nakkole gasped at Gavin's sudden appearance. The man
moved like a cat. Quiet and purposeful. Though both expressions could describe the man as a whole.

"I'm feeling much better," she said. "It is time for me to
resume my duties, at least those that do not require much
bending."

He stared at her as if she were a stranger. In truth, she felt
a bit like one. She had not seen nor heard from Gavin since

he'd tended her wounds. The uncertainty as to what kept him gone weighed on her, for she could not escape the agonizing memory of his lips upon her back. Did he regret his bold action? Should she be backing away from him coyly now that they'd partaken in such closeness on several occasions?

How did a human lady behave in such a circumstance?

"She wasn't awake?"

She sighed. "Only for a moment."

"What happened to your . . ." He pointed at her bodice.

Nakkole considered telling him the truth but thought better of it. The man had enough on his mind already. "I'm a bit ungraceful, I'm afraid."

Nakkole took advantage of the shadowed hallway to drink in the sight of him. His plaid hung over his shoulder and across his chest. The gray and green colors of the fabric matched the flecks she knew tinted his eyes. A belt cinched the plaid over a loose, white shirt, emphasizing his broad shoulders and narrow waist.

He was so much larger than any male faery she'd ever met, and his size aroused her curiosity in every way. She'd always felt dainty and feminine. It was in the White Ladies' nature to embrace their sexuality without ever acting upon their urges. Yet this human-faery who sometimes stared at her as though she were a cup of creamy milk to be savored, made her feel more delectable and . . . seductive than any human she'd ever encountered in her mountains had.

Her throat dried. She brought her gaze to his mouth and noticed it moving.

"Are you all right? You look a bit faint," he said.

Nakkole shook her head, shamed by the path of her thoughts. She'd done nothing as of yet to help this man reach his potential as the future king of Norman faeries. And now she allowed these dangerous, useless thoughts of him to fill her mind when her efforts would be much better placed elsewhere.

"Forgive me," she whispered. "I'm still not completely well."

Her back *did* still pain her.

"I'm still amazed that you are up and about at all." He stepped closer. The light from the sconce hanging on the wall shone on his eyes. They were narrowed, and his brow grooved with what looked to be worry. "Nakkole . . . Did she . . . did my mother speak again?"

"Nay . . ." She stopped, realizing that her words were not those he wished to hear. "I'm sorry."

He took on the appearance of a child, of a lost boy. Abunda had always claimed Nakkole was too humanlike for her own good, and now, in a time when she could not afford the weakness caring brought, she could not prevent it from developing for Gavin.

He closed his eyes and reopened them swiftly, the look of sorrow and distress gone so quickly, Nakkole wasn't sure she hadn't imagined it. Before she could stop herself, she reached up and cupped his cheek in her hand and rubbed his lashes with her thumb. He leaned into her touch. His eyes closed again briefly and reopened to stare intensely into her own.

"I will do all I can for both you and your mother," she whispered.

She dropped her hand to his throat and felt it rise in a deep swallow. His stare never broke from hers, but his head moved closer. The same numb feeling that had overcome her at the Beltane festival wove through her mind, pushing thoughts of escape into hiding.

He dropped his head closer still until she could feel his breath upon her nose, warming her even more thoroughly than the broth on her breasts had been able to. It grew more and more difficult to find room in her chest to breathe.

His hand brushed the hair off her shoulder, then moved to cup the back of her neck, and then he kissed her.

Eight

~

The corridor outside Geraldine's chamber suddenly felt very small, and Gavin's hand on the back of Nakkole's neck felt so very powerful. She awaited his kiss, knew it was forthcoming. Closing her eyes in anticipation, Nakkole stretched to the tip of her toes and parted her lips. A moment later, Gavin dragged his bottom lip across hers.

The kiss broke. Though it had been sweet and gentle and painfully quick, Nakkole lost what strength she'd possessed in her legs. The weight of his forehead pressed against hers nearly forced her backward, but she tightened her grip on his shoulders to keep her balance.

"You taste like spring rain."

Spring rain? Nakkole smiled. What else could a White Lady possibly taste like?

"Well, if I am like spring rain, then you must definitely be a thunderstorm."

"I am assuredly a thunderstorm, Nakkole, one you should be wary of being stranded in."

The implications of his words sent shivers down her spine. She pulled away, trying to regain her composure. If she didn't find solitude soon, she would surely melt into a puddle at Gavin's feet.

Being this close to him was wrong. He was her prince, her future king. She could not be with him the way she so wanted. Sweet Avalon, should King Arrane ever discover she had even kissed his royal son, she would be rightfully punished.

She would be spending a large amount of time in Gavin's presence, and now that her wounds were nearly fully healed, she would begin working to discover his powers. Somehow, she would have to find a way to put her longing for him behind her in order to do her duty here.

"Forgive me," she whispered. "It's time for Timpani to rub more salve onto my wounds."

The look of teasing contentment on his face was replaced by the same solemn stare he'd possessed when he'd asked about his mother's welfare. He gave a curt nod and released his hold on her neck, then stepped back to give her room to maneuver around him. "My apologies for keeping you."

She stepped past Gavin, loathing herself for being the cause of his gloom, but she had no choice.

The next day, Nakkole clutched a small basket and walked downstairs, a plan to kill two birds with one afternoon stroll lifting her mood. Father Donnelly had said Geraldine needed to take walks occasionally, and what better day than today? She would take Geraldine on her walk, and Gavin would accompany them, giving Nakkole a chance to ply him for information regarding the use of magic in his lifetime. She'd spent the whole of last night thinking up ways to convince him to tell her about how his nickname, Gavin the Immortal, came to be, and hoped she was right in believing a lot of it had to do with his ability to control his weapon and that of his enemies.

When she approached Gavin with her request to take his mother for a stroll to collect herbs, she doubted he would deny her. Geraldine would require a strong body to lean on, and given Nakkole's recent wounds, he would surely see that she required his assistance. It bothered her a good deal that she'd yet to see the man spend any time with his sick mother. If her plan worked, he would have no choice but to do so today.

She headed toward the stables where she'd seen Gavin from her chamber window earlier. Finding the grounds around the stables deserted, she glanced around the open fields. She collided with a rock-hard form and would have fallen on her backside had a hand not reached out to steady her.

"Oh!" she gasped, then looked up at the solid wall of Gavin's chest.

His fist curled around her upper arm, yanking her to him. She regained her balance and reluctantly stepped away from him.

"And where were you running off to in such a hurry?" he asked.

"Wha—oh, oh. Herbs. I used a large portion of my supply on my burns. I'll be needing more." She bit her lip, uneasy now that the time had come to ask him to spend an afternoon tending to his mother. "I thought a stroll to collect them would be a good opportunity to take your mother outdoors, as Father Donnelly instructed."

He studied her, his mouth parting as though there was something he wanted to say. Hesitating, she could sense he changed his mind about his choice of topic, and he said, instead, "You mean to take my mother into the forest . . . alone?"

"Nay. My body is in no condition to offer the support she'll need. 'Tis why I've come to find you. I was hoping you could accompany us, Laird."

He turned his back to her, making his way back inside the stables. "I'll ask Alec if he's available to escort you. I've too much to do."

Nakkole hurried after him. "But she's *your* mother, not Alec's." Her mind was working quickly, taken aback at his offer to find a replacement. She hadn't counted on that. "Are you afraid of her?" The question sprang forth without much thought, but now that it had been asked, she realized she truly wanted the answer.

Gavin spun around, his face contorted in a grimace. "Of course not."

"Then why have I not yet seen you sit with her? What is it about her that makes it so you can't stand to be near her?"

Gavin could hear the blood pounding in his ears, Nakkole's accusation hitting him too close to the heart. He wasn't afraid of his mother, but he was certainly afraid of how he felt each time he dared to approach her. He couldn't very well admit that it was easier for him to think of her as dead already than to continue hoping she'd one day be able to call him *son*.

He started to state once again that he'd call for Alec's assistance, but the look in Nakkole's eyes challenged him. It was as though she was daring him to do as she asked.

An afternoon with his mother. Could he manage it? He'd never backed down from a challenge in his life, but this time, he was sorely tempted.

"One hour," he muttered. "That is all I can spare."

Her smile lit up her entire face. "Wonderful. She's awake, so you won't be disturbing her. I'll wait for the both of you here."

❧

The walk to his mother's chamber seemed to take an eternity, yet his arrival came all too soon. He found Geraldine lying on her side, her blank gaze focused on the doorway. She didn't seem to notice his appearance. Hell, she barely blinked at all.

"We're going for a walk, Mother," he said, the silence of the chamber awkward. "I'm going to pick you up, so don't be startled."

Finally, she blinked, her gaze settling over his face. She wore no expression, no sign of recognition for her only child. He leaned over her, scooping her thin body into his arms. He gathered the blanket from her bed and wrapped it over her. She lay limply in his arms, forcing him to hold her more closely than was comfortable as he made his way downstairs. He found Nakkole where he'd left her and gently set Geraldine on her feet, securing the blanket around her shoulders.

"We want you to walk, Geraldine. Can you do that?" Nakkole asked, sliding Geraldine's right arm over her shoulder. Gavin did the same to her left arm, and together they waited for some sign of understanding from Geraldine.

She gave it with a slight shuffle of her feet.

"See there?" Nakkole smiled up at Gavin. "She understands us perfectly well."

Feeling as though he had stones shackled to his ankle, Gavin stepped into the forest, his mother's weight heavy against his side.

When they'd walked far enough into the trees that the sounds of the village were no longer as clear, he stopped, withdrew the blanket from his mother's shoulders, and spread it on the ground. He lowered her onto it, where she collapsed onto her side and shut her eyes.

"She needs a rest," he said. "How far must we walk to find these herbs of yours?"

Nakkole glanced around the area to their right, searching for something that might qualify as a healing herb. She knew nothing of what the humans used for remedy, but thankfully, she knew her plants well. Perhaps people used the same sort her own kind employed. Gavin should not become suspicious of anything she might say. Spotting a patch of heather growing wild across a small clearing alongside their trail, Nakkole pointed and stepped over a log in her way.

"I'll be needing some of this," she said, setting her basket on the ground.

She felt him kneel beside her and watched his strong, long arm reach in front of her and pluck a tiny purple flower from its bed.

Purposefully, she set to arranging the sprigs in her basket, glancing about for anything else she might pluck. She cast Gavin a wary glance. He knelt beside her, no look of suspicion on his face. He appeared more restful than she'd seen him yet, his furrowed brows now released in nice, taut flesh.

What a beautiful, glorious man.

She pondered how best to question him about his nickname when a bright yellow flash moved to her left. She caught a glimpse of it from the corner of her eye. At first glance, it appeared to be a butterfly, but Nakkole well knew that it was likely a pixie. The faeries that most humans tended to think of resembled butterflies at a quick glance, small and fluttering. If one looked closely at the head, however, they might notice a tiny, human face with glittering eyes and a mischievous smile.

Nakkole gingerly lay her last bundle of heather in the basket and watched the butterfly dance upon the heart-shaped foliage of bluebells. Her apprehension flared. She could take no chances that this little winged creature might hear their conversation. The maras had turned many a light fae into dark. This pixie could very well be one of them.

In a swift motion, she leaned onto her knee, stretched forward, then fisted the fluttering insect in her hand. Its wings beat ferociously against her closed palm. Slowly, unwilling to allow its escape until she'd inspected it thoroughly, she opened two fingers and peered inside. Two small antennae wiggled free, followed by a little, black furry face. A butterfly through and through.

"What have you caught?" Gavin asked, scooting closer to peer over her shoulder.

"A butterfly. Quite a beauty, too."

She opened her palm, ready to release the poor thing back to freedom, but it lay crumpled there, its left wing torn straight down the center. A retched sickness roiled in Nakkole's belly. She'd killed a creature of nature and beauty and innocence. Distress wouldn't have filled her more had she just delivered a fatal blow to a faery child.

The feel of Gavin's thumb lightly brushing away the first tear she'd shed in years brought her face up. "Nakkole?"

She blinked, unwilling to fall apart over something she couldn't possibly explain to him, and held out her hand. While her power to create was mighty, she could not bring back what she'd taken from this gift of nature.

"It's dying. I've killed it. I—I didn't mean to."

Gavin's gaze dropped to her outstretched hand, and gently, he scooped the butterfly into his own. "'Tis nothing to cry over, Nakkole. Aye, it is beautiful, but 'tis just a wee critter."

"Every life should be celebrated, Laird. My people do not destroy what Mother Nature has so generously given us." She choked back a sob and watched his long, tanned fingers curl over the tiny winged body. Natural death was honored by her kind. This sort of murder, accidental or not, was a tragedy.

Gavin tightened his fist, thinking it better to quicken the butterfly's death rather than let it suffer with its broken wing and be eaten alive by a predator. But when the soft fluttering slowly stilled in his hand, a sorrow overwhelmed him that seemed extremely foolish. He'd killed many times in battle, humans of flesh and blood, with sons and mothers who would grieve for their loss of life. And yet, this small creature who he killed only out of mercy affected him as none of those men ever had.

"'Tis not you who has killed her, Nakkole," he whispered, surprised to find his voice raspy. "'Tis I. She'll feel no pain now."

He watched Nakkole's eyes widen and her mouth open, then he dropped his stare to the motionless butterfly. It lived no more, and yet the bounty of its beauty seemed more alive than aught he'd ever seen. Closing his eyes, his mind struggled to grasp an image that pulled at him, beckoned him to recall it.

When next he opened his eyes, he no longer sat with Nakkole in a forest clearing, but with a tall, dark man in a meadow of larkspur and clovers. Gavin looked up with a child's eyes and reached out with a child's hand, holding a butterfly in his small fist. The image filled him as would a living thing, so strongly that it didn't feel at all like a dream, but more like a memory.

"He's dead, Father. I didn't mean to kill him. I only wanted a better look," Gavin said in the voice of a young lad.

Father. And yet this man was not Bruce McCain—the only person even close to resembling such a figure in Gavin's life.

The dark man kneeled down in front of him, his black, kind eyes filled with caring. "I know you didn't mean it, my son. But don't let your grief overwhelm you. There's something good to come of it, Gavin. 'Tis time we finished the lesson we've been working on."

"I—I can't, Father. You do it. I'm not yet strong enough."

"You can. You will. Close your eyes, Gavin." The man placed a large hand over Gavin's eyes, casting the vision into darkness. "Now, close your fist."

Gavin did so, the silky wings cold against his tiny hand. His throat began to burn, but he wouldn't cry. His father wouldn't want him to cry. He'd want him to be strong, to succeed at this secret lesson as he hadn't been able to before.

"Now," the man said. "Concentrate, my boy. Create life."

His eyes squeezed tightly shut, he brought a million of his youthful wishes to mind and focused them all on the lifeless creature in his puny fist. He found his yearning for his very own horse, then cast it from his wishes. *The butterfly must live.* The desire for sweetmeats that he'd begged the monastery cook for, he no longer wanted. *The butterfly must live.* A dozen other wishes were banished from his mind until the only one in existence was that for mercy for the small butterfly his curiosity had killed.

"Create life, Gavin. Focus, and create life."

"I cannot!"

"You can."

Forcing back the tears burning his closed eyes, Gavin searched out the vault of magic his father had sworn lived in their bodies, just beneath their hearts. He found it. He found it and nearly turned himself inside out trying to burrow his way deeper into the reserve. The butterfly began to warm slowly, and a tingling shot down Gavin's arm and into his fingers.

"Create life," he whispered. "Create life. Create life."

Slowly, he opened his eyes. The blue-and-green wings began to flutter and the butterfly slowly picked itself up and stood as though in a daze, in the center of Gavin's hand.

Smiling, and unable to stop his joyful tears, Gavin thrust out his hand, willing the insect to fly away.

"Create life!" he shouted at the top of his lungs.

The butterfly rocked slowly, then flew from his palm and into the misty air. When it vanished, Gavin could no longer see the man. Instead, he saw Nakkole watching him quizzically.

He blinked, nauseated and uncertain of his sanity. It couldn't have been a dream. Dreams weren't so vivid. It was more as though he remembered the scene. As though it were a memory. But how was that possible? And yet, now his mind recalled his secret visits with the man in the vision—visits he'd been told to keep to himself for fear of upsetting Geraldine. *His father*. He did have memories of him, after all. But magic? The brief leap of joy his heart attempted to take fell short as the uneasiness of what the memory had implied came over him.

"Sweet Avalon!"

Nakkole's gasp pulled Gavin from his foggy thoughts. "I'm sorry, Nakkole. I have no idea—"

"Look, Gavin!"

He followed her stare to his hand. The butterfly that had lay dead in his hand a moment ago now wiggled with new-found life. He searched his mind for possible answers. Had it ever been truly dead? Of course not. It couldn't have been.

"You gave it back its life," Nakkole whispered. She sounded so calm, as though none of this was odd to her in the least.

"Don't be foolish. Of course I didn't. I had hoped to put it out of its misery, but apparently I didn't squeeze hard enough."

Her eyes widened at his bluntness, but he didn't care about her shock. He needed to find an explanation that made more sense than what he was beginning to believe had just happened.

God help him, he did *not* believe in magic!

He stood, searching for a surface on which to lay the still-wounded creature. "It wasn't dead."

"Where did you go when you held it?" she asked, her voice calm and low. "Who did you speak to so clearly? And why, when you chanted the words *create life* did the butterfly begin to move once more in your hand when only moments ago it couldn't move at all?"

She had heard him? Had he spoken his memory aloud?

"With the exception of siring a child, I've no ability to create life. Come, it's time to return home."

He lay the butterfly on a small rock and watched it struggle on its side. Not wanting Nakkole to see his trembling hands, he quickly shoved them in the folds of his plaid.

God, but he'd been certain the butterfly had been dead.

"Fine. We'll go. But answer me this. You saw as well as I that its wing was torn straight down the center. If your words did nothing, then why is its wing fully healed?"

Gavin didn't answer her, couldn't answer her. Instead, he moved to retrieve her basket of herbs. When he glanced back at the butterfly, to his horror, the creature wobbled on tiny legs, then flittered off, disappearing behind a copse of oak trees.

"Create life," he muttered, handing Nakkole her basket and turning to gather his mother in order to return home. "Nonsense."

He froze. Geraldine was already on her feet, standing unsupported, and staring directly at Nakkole with clear, healthy eyes. "White Lady," she whispered, a smile spreading onto her face. "Home."

Nine

~

Gavin couldn't move. Couldn't breathe. Here was his mother standing and speaking just a few feet away, and he could do naught but stare.

"Mother?" he asked.

But as quickly as it had come, the coherent look in her eyes faded, blurred again by a blank stare, and she began to teeter on her feet. Gavin rushed forward, barely catching her before she hit the ground in a cold sleep.

His heart falling to his toes, he scooped her up and turned on trembling legs to face Nakkole. "What did she mean, White Lady? What just happened?"

Nakkole's face was pale, her mouth parted slightly. She shook her head, as confused, it seemed, as Gavin. "I—I'm not certain."

As though snapping out of a daze, she shook herself and hurried to gather the blanket. "Come, let's get her home. Perhaps this stroll was too much for her."

Nakkole fixed her gaze on Gavin's back, matching his hurried stride along the trail. She clutched the pitiful weed-filled basket in her fist, desperately wishing for a chance to escape undetected to the lake where she might summon

Abunda. Seeing Gavin's reaction to his power had left
Nakkole more than a little distressed. She'd expected baffle-
ment, confusion, even anger if he'd expected magic had
aught to do with the insect's recovery. But she had not expected the absolute fear that had darkened his features.

Nor had she expected Geraldine's sudden coherency. The
fact that she'd named Nakkole as a White Lady had left her
far more than shaken.

She had absolutely no idea what she should do next. She
desperately needed Abunda's council.

"Gavin," she called. "Please wait. If you'll only speak to
me . . ."

But he continued on, not sparing her even the slightest
glance.

He must be told. He must know the truth about his sire
and his destiny. Showing Gavin his powers without offering
an explanation for them was simply cruel. While Timpani
and Abunda would have no difficulty distancing themselves
from Gavin's agony, Nakkole could not. How could she
when she'd seen for herself his innocent awe at recalling his
memories of a father he never remembered knowing?

"I know you didn't mean it, my son." When Gavin had
spoken those words aloud, his voice had eerily turned into
Arrane's. It was as though he had not only remembered, but
had relived the event, and Arrane had been within him
throughout.

And that, perhaps, was what bothered her most.
According the Abunda, Gavin had been taken from Arrane
before birth. How was it even possible that Gavin should
have any memories of his father at all?

❧

Gavin stared down at Geraldine, his eyelids growing heavy
with the need to sleep. He'd been sitting in this chair for
nearly an hour, watching his mother sleep, praying she might
waken and speak again. He wanted her to glance at him with
the same pleasure with which she'd stared at Nakkole.

But Geraldine did nothing to raise his hopes. It seemed
she kept saving her lucid moments for Nakkole only.

He stood, making up his mind to bring Nakkole here. Perhaps then Geraldine would wake up and notice him.

But when he entered the dining hall where his men were now supping, there was no sign of her.

"Where's Lady Nakkole?" he asked Timpani. She was seated away from the crowd, save for Alec and another clansman, and quietly cutting into her meal.

Timpani's stomach knotted. She'd been awaiting that question ever since Nakkole had left several moments ago. "She's had a long, tiring day, my laird. She wished for a swim before retiring."

It was as close to the truth as Timpani's duty would allow her to speak. Nakkole had foolishly, in Timpani's mind, gone to seek Abunda once more. She hadn't wanted to chance disappearing in Beanie's bubble again, however, and had asked Timpani to state the story she now told.

If Nakkole had her way and told Gavin the truth of it all now, it would very likely put an obstacle in their path that they would not be able to cross. He'd throw them out and leave himself, and the Norman faeries, open for an insurmountable attack by Elphina's army.

Timpani could only hope Abunda would refuse Nakkole her wish.

"She should not be swimming alone this time of eve," Gavin said, slamming down his tankard.

Nay, she should not, indeed.

Timpani stilled her tongue with a swallow of warm milk, then offered Gavin a smile. "She's well capable of tending herself, my laird. No harm will come to her, you have my word."

He raised a brow and finally sought her face with his stare. "I suppose you believe it is not my place to worry over her welfare, but I can assure you, you are wrong. She is under my protection while she remains at Grey Loch."

"And I can assure *you* that none have ever had such need to enfold Nakkole in their mighty shields."

A flash of doubt flared in Gavin's eyes. For a moment, Timpani wished she hadn't said anything. This man might seem like a mere human man now, but he was her prince and was soon to be her king. She could only hope he didn't hold on to anger very long.

"My pardon, my laird. I'm just not accustomed to the strict watch the men of Scotland seem to keep on their women. Where we come from, women enjoy much the same liberties as men."

"Is that so?" A faint smile lifted his mouth into an amused curve. "Has Normandy changed so in the short time since I traveled there? Surely, you exaggerate, Timpani."

Timpani flinched. She'd had no knowledge of his ever being in Normandy. Of course, he *would* believe she spoke of Normandy and not the magical world within it.

She could only shrug. "Perhaps, but only a bit. 'Tis true enough that Nakkole and I have never been restricted because of our gender."

"Well, for my own peace of mind, I think I'll ride out and see how she fares."

"Nay!" Timpani jumped up, resulting in grunts from the men who shared her dining bench. "If it will make you feel better, I shall go myself."

Oh, but if he saw Nakkole speaking to a watery reflection of Abunda—

Timpani shuddered.

"And have two fair ladies alone in such a place? Think me completely green, Timpani? Tell me exactly what is going on or I'll bloody well find out myself."

Timpani swallowed, damning Nakkole's weak nature. Her mind bustled with thoughts that might keep Gavin at the keep.

When he turned to leave, she stood and shouted, "Her burns, my laird!"

He turned to look at her, his eyes narrowed.

Timpani hurried to continue. "She didn't wish you to know they still pained her."

Gavin swore and turned away. Before she could think of another way to stop him, he was gone.

Avalon help them if he witnessed Nakkole speaking to Abunda. Her heart pounding, she hurried to find Beanie in the kitchens, hoping the faery could warn Nakkole while

Timpani followed their prince to make certain he remained safe.

When she saw no one else in the kitchens, she let herself catch her breath.

"Beanie!" she called, spying the house faery crouched in the corner of the small pantry, dipping her thumb in the cream. "We must hurry . . ."

❧

"If you won't respect Gavin, the man, enough to tell him the truth, then perhaps you should consider that he is also Gavin, your prince and future king," Nakkole said, fighting her temper with every bit of control she possessed—which at the moment was nearly none.

The sound of Gavin's voice becoming that of a young lad continually played in her head. A boy with his father. A father with his son. It wasn't until this afternoon that she'd fully realized the sort of pain Gavin must have been carrying with him all these years. And for him not to even recall ever *meeting* his own father was all the more saddening.

She held the gift of their possible reunion in her hands. But what was she to do with it? Defy her mother? Her king?

"We sent you here to determine when he was ready to know the truth," Abunda hissed. "But you are wrong to believe that time is now. Wanting to soothe old wounds and reunite father and son is not reason enough to chance losing his trust so soon!"

"Not reason eno—"

"Nakkole." Abunda's voice was stiff and stern, her watery reflection glowering. "I will not repeat myself again. Return to Grey Loch but say nothing of this to Prince Gavin. He *will* cast you out; will likely think you mad."

"He'll think me mad no matter *when* I tell him."

"Aye, but by then, you'll know more about his powers. Do not tell him anything until you've seen all he can do."

"But—"

"I warn you, should you go against me on this, you will be brought back immediately. And while that might not sound so horrible, you may believe I won't be so generous as to your placement here."

Abunda's watery reflection rippled, her dark eyes turning a murky black in anger. Nakkole braced herself to continue her argument. Gavin would be their king. 'Twas he who deserved her strongest loyalty just now.

"Very well!" Nakkole shouted at her mother for the first time in her life. "I will let the matter rest." *For now.* "But I need to know something afore you disappear. Gavin had a memory of Arrane. How is that possible when Gavin was taken before he was even born?"

The anger flickered from Abunda's eyes, and her reflection shook its head. "I was afraid this might happen. Often, when Gavin was a child, Arrane would visit him away from the keep when he played alone in the forest. No one ever knew. Gavin's memories are real enough, but might very well cause us problems if he begins to suspect before we are ready to—"

"Nakkole!" Nakkole spun around to find Beanie bolting from the trees. She stopped with a jerk, gave a quick curtsy to Abunda's refection, then turned back to Nakkole. "Prince Gavin . . ." she said breathlessly. "He comes. Must go . . . back."

"Wha—"

"Hurry. We'll be using me bubble."

Gasping, Nakkole bent to gather her discarded boots. "I must go, Mother."

The image faded on the surface, becoming one with the water, then nothing at all.

Nakkole placed her hand in Beanie's ready to depart before Gavin could find them here, but the steady sound of footsteps stopped them. Not the sound of a human, but of an animal. It trampled leaves to Nakkole's left, and she turned to face it, her body instantly alert.

The bloody glow of its eyes shimmered in the moonlight. It paced, staring at Nakkole as though trying to communicate. Barguest. He'd come again. But whose stolen life was he foretelling this time?

Nakkole shuddered and glanced at Beanie, who looked as

worried as she. "Please tell me you were wrong. Gavin is not coming here for me . . . alone," she whispered.

Beanie held out her hand. "Come!" she shouted. "We must hurry."

Ten

~

As Beanie's bubble raced above the forest trees, Nakkole caught a glimpse of Timpani dashing into the open fields of Grey Loch. The panicked expression on her face squeezed Nakkole's chest with worry.

"Let me out, Beanie."

The bubble burst and Nakkole fell to her backside just paces away from her sister. "What has happened?"

Timpani glanced down at Nakkole, her cheeks flushed and her chest heaving to catch a deep breath. "I . . . was with him. Following him . . . to keep him . . . safe." She sucked in a deep gulp of air. "He went into the stables and . . . I couldn't keep up with his steed."

Behind her, Nakkole could hear, even feel, Barguest's contemptible presence. But when she chanced a glance over her shoulder, she could no longer see his dark form through all the brush and bramble, though she thought she saw the quick flash of his red-yellow eyes. She guided her feet easily around rocks and over fallen trees, all the while searching fruitlessly for any sign of Gavin's approaching form.

"I do not see him!" she called to Timpani.

Timpani ducked under a low branch and leaped over a

bush. "I see no one, but hurry. Barguest never brings false news."

So . . . Timpani had seen Barguest, too.

Last time, it had been Rufous's death the hellhound had foreshadowed. Who was at risk of meeting their maker now?

"I'll drift above and see if I can spot 'im," Beanie said. In the next instant, she was naught more than a speck of dust hovering overhead.

As they approached the clearing, Nakkole dared to slow slightly, her gaze darting nervously about the open field. Ahead of her, she saw him. He charged toward them on a great, black horse. Gavin.

Nakkole swallowed her growing fear. "Run," she whispered to Timpani. "We must keep him away from these trees. Keep him in the open where we can see all around us."

Timpani nodded, her chest heaving with weighty breaths. Before hurrying off again, however, Nakkole puffed out her chest, brought her fingers to her mouth, and let out Arrane's battle cry—a long, piercing whistle, followed by three short trill ones. The signal had been made, and in a few moments, the rest of Abunda's hidden army would flee from their stations and gather around their prince. Nakkole only hoped more than Beanie would hear it.

Together, Nakkole and Timpani ran toward the galloping destrier. Slowly, the horse stopped in the center of the field. A loud screech penetrated the air, and the horse reared, flailing its legs. Another screech sounded, then a third, bringing Gavin's hands to his ears.

Before Timpani and Nakkole could reach him, a large, black figure swooped down from the trees and knocked Gavin from his horse. The horse reared, nearly stomping Gavin's body as it landed on all fours once again, then bolted toward the stables, leaving Gavin alone in the wide open field.

With a scream, Nakkole forced herself to run faster. She threw herself across Gavin's prone body, shielding him as a gush of wind whipped over her back.

Timpani fell to the ground beside her. Together they searched for signs of injury on the still unmoving prince.

Another screech pained Nakkole's ears, but when she glanced around she could see naught but dark shadows.

"He has hurt his head," Timpani said.

Nodding, Nakkole's fear eased a bit with the slow, steady rise and fall of Gavin's chest. "That noise, Timpani. It sounds like . . . but, it can't be—"

"It is. Smell the air, Nakkole. 'Tis a banshee if ever I smelled and heard one."

Nakkole sniffed and caught the faint aroma of rotting refuse. She spun around, searching the dark trees for any sign of the vile creatures. She could see nothing. "We must get him inside."

"I'll be takin' him in." Beanie's voice appeared as suddenly as her tiny body. "Move away now and I'll get him safely inside."

Nakkole swallowed, rolled the rest of the way off Gavin's body, and looked around. Was this all her summoning had brought them? Beanie? She could not possibly be the only other guardian sent here besides Timpani and Nakkole. Abunda would have sent more . . . would she not?

Blinking, Nakkole nodded, but the shadow of another figure running from the keep hurried her movements. "Take him, Beanie. We have an uninvited guest."

It was Gavin's man, Alec, and he already had his sword unsheathed, a look of fury on his face. In the next instant, Gavin and Beanie were gone.

Alec raised the sword and Timpani squealed, rolling away from Nakkole. He was aiming right at them. But to Nakkole's surprise, he dropped the sword at her feet, tossed down yet another, and pulled a third from the sheath on his hip.

"Arm yourselves. The banshees come closer."

Nakkole did not question how he knew of the banshees. Instead, she seized one of the large, heavy swords at her side. She had to stand before she could even lift the weapon, and when she did, it weighed her down. Still, when a loud screech ripped past her ear, her fear allowed her to swing around and raise the sword, splitting the attacking banshee in two. It disintegrated at her feet, a pile of ashes already blowing away in the wind.

"Inside!" Alec yelled, grabbing Timpani by the arm and heaving her to her feet. "Go!"

Nakkole turned to do just that, but noticed Alec made no move to get himself to safety. She couldn't leave him here to fight an unknown number alone.

When Nakkole did not move to follow her, Timpani grabbed her by the arm and began pulling her toward the keep. "He is not our concern, Nakkole. Our concern is already wounded inside!"

Of course, Timpani was right, but she couldn't simply leave Alec here to be terrorized and killed. Already the horrible wails were causing his confusion. She could see it plainly on his face. Though he was still armed, his free hand was cupping one ear, and he wore a pained expression as the wails grew louder and more shrill.

"Go, then!" Nakkole shouted to be heard. "I'll not leave him."

"Don't be foolish! We must protect our prince," Timpani yelled, then she pivoted and dashed toward the keep, leaving Nakkole and Alec alone in the night.

Nakkole approached Alec and touched his forearm. "We cannot think to fight these alone. We do not know their numbers!"

He looked down at her. His large brown eyes widened in confusion. His hands gripped his ears while he shook his head. "Arrane will not forgive me if harm comes to his son."

Her heart stopped. Her mouth fell open. The wind howled. A drop of rain splattered on Nakkole's nose and trickled down her mouth.

"Arrane?"

Alec rolled his eyes and pushed Nakkole behind him, shielding her with his body. She turned so they were back-to-back, protecting one another, even though her mind had gone completely numb. Alec was one of Arrane's.

She had no more time to ponder his words, however, for ahead of her, three banshees flew over the keep and toward her, their bared fangs yellow in the moonlight. The screeches came in quick succession now, growing closer in an ominous parade of echoes.

Behind her, a gust of wind ripped through her hair, burning her ear. A curse sounded from Alec, then a whack and a gush of air. She glanced up at him from over her shoulder. A large, withered form seemed fastened to Alec's body, his face no longer visible as the ghostly invader latched on to him. Gray, stringy hair fell out around the torn, filthy garments cloaking it. Nakkole watched in horror as Alec's arms flailed wildly, then struggled to push the creature from his face. The banshee seemed fixed on Alec's face . . . horrible sounds of feasting mixed with the poor man's screams.

Nakkole raised the sword in her hand, but it was so heavy her movements were slow and cumbersome. She couldn't very well pierce the banshee, for she would have little control over the heavy weapon and could injure Alec, as well.

Finally, with a swipe of his arm, Alec dislodged the banshee from his body, and Nakkole summoned every bit of her strength to raise the sword above her shoulder and slice it through the banshee's middle. It cried out and shattered into a thousand tiny bits of dust.

Gasping for breath, Alec grabbed Nakkole by the arm and dragged her toward the keep. A chunk of flesh had been torn from his cheek and his plaid had been ripped, but he would live.

❧

Gavin swatted at his face for the third time, but the pesky golden insect bounced around his head as though at play. He scowled, backed away from the cellar door, then tried once more to kick the blasted thing open. When he'd awakened to find himself alone in the cellar, it had taken him a while to remember what had happened, what had made his head throb like the devil.

An attack. But by what? And how had he gotten to the cellar?

He rubbed the back of his head, recalling the dark shadow that had knocked him from his horse. For the third time, he tried the cellar door. It still would not budge.

"Blasted door." He'd never known it to stick like this before.

Not a moment after he said the words, the large cellar

door creaked open. The flittering golden insect escaped, and Gavin followed. Timpani stood just outside the door, a worried expression on her face.

"You are all right?" she whispered, her hand pressing to his brow like a worried mother's.

Gavin scowled and brushed her away. "I am fine. What the devil happened? I saw you and Nakkole fleeing from the forest, and then . . . and then I don't know what happened."

Blinking, Timpani stepped back, allowing him to pass up the stairs. "Wild animals, we think. Your man Alec was attacked as well, but he needs only a bit of stitching to be as well as before."

Wild animals? Gavin closed his eyes and prayed for the pounding in his head to cease. It did, so suddenly he became woozy with relief. "What sort of wild animal flies through the air like that? Where's Alec?"

"Your men took him upstairs to a vacant chamber in the north wing. I was on my way to tend him when I heard noises from in here."

Gavin glanced at Timpani. He wanted to ask how he'd ended up in the cellar, but did not dare. His mind was muddled with questions he did, yet did not, want answers to. Something in his blood told him he would not like the answers.

Instead, he asked only the simplest one he could find. "Why do you tend Alec? Nakkole is our healer. Find her. Send her to Alec at once. I'll speak with her once she arrives."

He didn't await a reply. Instead, he dashed through the hall and up the north stairs to the three empty chambers kept ready for guests. Damnation.

He found Alec sprawled on the bed in the first vacant chamber, his hand cupping his cheek. Two of their clansmen, Robert and Markham, stood by the bedside wearing equally wary expressions.

When Gavin stepped inside, Markham drew a trembling hand through his white-blond hair and frowned. "We've washed most o' the blood from 'is face, Laird Gavin, but the wound still 'asn't ceased its flowing as yet."

Gavin nodded and allowed Robert to step out of the way

before he approached Alec's side. When Alec lowered his hand, a large, gaping wound glared up at them from his cheek, nearly leaving the bone visible. Flinching, Gavin swore and pressed his hand to his friend's brow. Warm, clammy flesh greeted his palm.

"What sort of creature inflicted such a wound?" he asked.

Alec shrugged. "It was dark. I heard the wails, but afore I could open the blasted door to get outside, you had already been knocked unconscious," Alec said. "I, too, was attacked before Nakkole or I could see what came at us."

Alec's gaze darted toward the dark corner of the room. Gavin's followed, spying Nakkole standing in the shadows. In her hand, she held her herb pouch, and she would not look at Gavin. The sight of her, well and in one piece, calmed Gavin a bit. Anything could have happened to her. Odd that it had been worry for her safety at the loch that had driven him out into the night, yet he had been the one injured. Not she.

When Nakkole finally spoke, her voice trembled but she stared him in the eye. "Alec has the right of it," she said. "It all happened too quickly to get a good glimpse at our attackers."

Timpani appeared in the doorway and hurried over to Nakkole. She took the pouch from Nakkole's hands. "Tend Laird Gavin, my lady. I'll see to this man's wounds."

Nodding, Nakkole stepped into the light and focused on Alec. "Alec," she whispered. "Thank you."

Alec gave a curt nod, then focused on Timpani who eased herself onto the edge of his bed.

Swearing beneath his breath, Gavin seized Nakkole by the arm and dragged her from the room. He wanted answers, and now that it looked as though Alec was faring well considering his wound, Gavin would seek his answers from Nakkole.

He guided her through the keep, toward his chamber, slamming the door shut before she could so much as react to his bullying. "Know you how I got to be in the cellar, Lady Nakkole?"

Without looking him in the eye, she wandered farther into

his chamber, keeping her back to him. "I believe Alec called for assistance and asked them to get you to safety."

So they put him in the *cellar*?

"Of all the witless, doltish—they got me to safety but left two women on the field being attacked?"

Gavin's tirade was cut short by Nakkole's quick pivot to face him. It was the first real glimpse he'd taken of her dishevelment. Leaves clung to her wild, tangled hair and torn plaid. Blood stained the garment and splattered her cheek. Alec's blood. Good God, he *hoped* it was Alec's blood. How close had she been to whatever had done this?

"Are you all right? Have you been hurt?" The questions sounded foolishly tardy, even to him.

She waved off his concern. "Let me tend your head, and when I'm done, I can try to answer your questions."

Before he could respond, Nakkole all but shoved him onto the bed. Immediately, she sat beside him and placed her hand upon his brow.

"I'm fine," he muttered, though in truth her touch bothered him greatly. She was in his chamber, on his bed. God help him, the horrid events of this night were fading fast from his mind as more pleasurable thoughts began to consume him.

He thought of their kiss, of her skin beneath his palm when he'd tended her burns. Thoughts of Alec and wild creatures were banished in that moment, for all he could see was Nakkole's pleading gaze, her soft, partially opened mouth.

Now that the threat of danger had passed, the energy within him seemed to pool into a frenzied lust, as though it sought a new form of release.

Damn, but he was tired. He wanted to sleep, but wanted even more to pull Nakkole into his arms and have his way with her.

Nakkole watched Gavin's eyes. She knew the endless questions he wanted answered, but recognized now that his thoughts had turned toward her, just as her own had turned toward him. Something seemed to happen each time they were alone together. It was almost as if they'd both unwittingly used their glamour upon one another, filling the chamber with such magic as to cause her to lose her senses.

The world around them seemed forgotten. Enchantment and attraction was all that consumed Nakkole now, and she saw it as a blessing, for whatever happened in this moment would delay the inevitable questions from Gavin.

She watched his face sway closer to her own and gave no thought to backing away. It was wrong. She should flee. But she couldn't, for she wanted his kiss so badly, wanted to experience again what they'd shared on Beltane Eve. He could have died tonight. He could have perished and she never would have been given this chance to know him so intimately. How could she deny herself this pleasurable act when she'd just faced losing the opportunity forever?

Her desire for this man, this future king, overwhelmed her, and she could no longer control the impulse to touch him. Her mind raced. She knew she should leave now that she'd made certain he was well.

But one touch . . . surely one touch would cause no one any harm. She simply had to know if his flesh was as warm and smooth as it looked. And though it shamed her to admit it, she wanted to see the rest of him, those forbidden parts hiding beneath his plaid.

Her hand shook, but she raised it slowly, wanting to touch his cheek. He moved, however, lying back on the bed, his hand pillowing his head. With his other, he reached for her, pulled her down on top of him, and when she wiggled to better reach his face for a kiss, she watched his eyes slowly close.

Gavin's heart pounded as he waited for the feel of Nakkole's mouth on his. He slowly opened his eyes. At the sight of her tongue flickering over her pale pink lips, Gavin grew rigid beneath his plaid. His belly rose and fell in rapid succession beneath her body. She dragged her bottom lip over both of his and released a soft moan.

Slowly, her eyes flickered open and met his stare. "I shouldn't be here . . . like this."

She rolled off of him, her hair tickling his chest.

"Nay," he said, pushing himself up to lie on his side. "You probably shouldn't be. But . . . do you *wish* to be?"

"It was wrong of me to ever begin such a thing," she said, her voice quivering. "Wrong for reasons you can't begin to understand."

Gavin adjusted himself on the bed, pulling her closer so that she was forced to sit on the edge of the mattress. Her hair fell over her face, covering her left eye and drawing a disturbing amount of his attention to her full lips.

"Answer me. Do you *wish* to be here with me now?"

She nodded, her eyes glassy with both passion and tears.

"Then that is all that matters to me."

His hand released her wrist and cupped the back of her neck, drawing her toward him.

Nakkole watched in fascination as Gavin's lips grew closer, damp and parted and calling to her own like the sirens of the seas. The air grew thick, making it difficult to breathe, but Nakkole inhaled, instead, the desire radiating from Gavin's eyes, breathing it in like a life force that promised a better tomorrow. She needed those eyes, those lips, just as she needed the water and the rain, and here he offered it to her freely.

How could she possibly refuse what her body needed to survive?

Her taut neck relaxed in his hand. She allowed herself to be pulled even closer, until his lips pressed against hers again, and her breasts and his chest were separated only by the thin fabric of her gown. He pulled her bottom lip into his mouth, suckling a bit before releasing it, then coaxed her mouth open farther with his warm, sweet tongue.

Nakkole moaned and leaned on her elbow to allow herself better access. They lay side by side, and slowly, Gavin's hand left her neck and traveled down her back. It moved over her buttock and stilled on the back of her thigh. He lifted her leg, draping it over his atop the blanket. The fabric of her skirt lifted and she could feel his palm on her bare leg. She shivered with delight.

All thoughts of pulling away were forever gone. She was not strong enough to deny herself this one thing she wanted above all others. The seductress in her emerged—not to play havoc with this man, but to fulfill her own desires. Slowly, she rolled herself until she'd forced Gavin onto his back and she straddled his hips.

Gavin stared up at Nakkole, barely able to make out her features through the desire clouding his vision. Nakkole looked a sorceress, sitting astride him with her hair unbound and wild. She reached for the hem of her gown and slowly pulled it over her head. His heart stopped beating, but his blood increased its flow. Her milky white skin glowed, shimmered, in the faint light. He drank in the sight of her flat belly, her full breasts tipped with small, pink buds that would taste so succulent.

As he reached out to touch her, his hand trembled, but his eyes fastened on the thatch of curls nestled at the juncture of her thighs. It was like staring at the gates of heaven.

"You're beautiful," he managed, still amazed at her boldness.

Nakkole smiled and shifted her weight, pulling the blanket from his hips, then nestling both of their bodies beneath the covers. She placed a soft kiss on his chin, then sat up and fastened her eyes on the length of him, swollen and hard with need. Her wide eyes told him this was a new sight for her, but still she didn't seem embarrassed or frightened. Instead, she traced the sensitive, tight flesh with her finger, pausing for a long, torturous moment at the tip.

Gavin groaned and shot forward, wrapping his arms around her waist. If she touched him in such a manner again, he'd not last long enough to see what the inside of heaven looked like.

Nakkole draped her legs around him, locking her ankles together behind him, then kissed him with such hunger he thought it might actually match his own. With one fist wrapped around her hair, he let the other maneuver its way to her breast. He cupped it, softly gliding his thumb across the hard peak, feeling her moan into his mouth.

Her hips began to wiggle, dampening him with her desire. He couldn't take much more. Had she any idea what she was doing to him?

Wanting to still her movements, he released her hair and found with his finger the spot between her legs that would bring her the most pleasure. When he stroked it, she jerked away from their kiss and threw her head back. Her hips rocked faster and he could nearly feel her body preparing to peak. As she drew closer to her climax, he suckled her breasts. Her back arched, granting him better access.

"Gavin!" She gasped and brought her head up to stare him in the eye. "I can't . . . I cannot hold myself up any longer."

He needed no further prodding. Keeping his palm firmly cupped against her wetness, he rolled them over and lay atop her.

Nakkole thought she might die. She felt so close to something so wonderfully unexplainable and knew not how to get there. She closed her eyes, and Gavin resumed his sweet torture of her body. Drifting closer and closer to that place just out of reach, she bit down on her lip and broke through the surface of the paradise that beckoned her.

She screamed his name and bucked against him. While shudders ripped through her tingling body, she still wanted more.

Gavin withdrew his hand and held his weight above her. She nearly cried out again, but this time in protest to the absence of his body on hers. She stared at him, his eyes wild and dark, then allowed herself to sink deeper into the mattress, knowing he was not yet done.

"Show me," she whispered. "Show me what's to follow."

She watched his chest heave and he reached between their bodies. A moment later, she felt the hardness of him that had so fascinated her earlier pressing against her sensitive flesh. Her mind grasped what was to come and she was prepared to beg for it.

"Please."

Gavin braced himself and, armored only in his lust and need for the woman beneath him, broke through those gates of heaven and sought desperately for the redemption he could find only there.

He felt her maidenhead straining against him. He stilled himself, anxious to feel all of her completely, but just as anxious to cause her no unnecessary pain. Closing his eyes, he prayed for patience, but more so, he prayed for a painless, pleasurable experience for Nakkole. Her nails bit into his shoulders, piercing his thoughts as a blade of grass might burst a bubble, and he focused on the need filling her eyes. She wanted this. There would be no pain.

"I'm sorry," he whispered, then surged forward, breaking the remaining proof that told of her inexperience. She was innocent no longer.

Nakkole didn't cry out, didn't whimper. Instead, she tightened her grip on him and raised her hips to match his rhythm. Her passion intensified his own, and he found himself building quicker and quicker toward ecstasy. She met him there, he could see it in her eyes.

His yearning was not his alone to bear, for she shared it with him, and soared with him, until both collapsed in the other's arms, spent and fulfilled.

Eleven

~

Timpani retrieved a small square of linen from the bed-side table, reached into the folds of her skirt, and pulled out the faery spade Nakkole had used on her burns. After wiping the magical, blessed spade clean, she sprinkled a few drops of the bottled liquid onto the spade's tip. Ointment that fae healers used to mend those possessing no magic. It shimmered, lighting up the chamber with a soft, white glow.

Alec's eyes widened, and he leaned closer for a better look. Gasping, he stared at the glimmering spade.

"Is that the Ointment? Do not think to touch me with that—"

"What are you, exactly? You are not a mere man, are you?" Timpani interrupted Alec's refusal with a thrust of the spade, hoping her actions were at least a bit threatening.

"Aye, I am a mere man, but you are no mere woman, White Lady."

Timpani dropped the spade and nearly dropped the Ointment as well.

"Who *are* you?" she repeated.

"I am not here to hinder your efforts to return Gavin to his father, Timpani. I am here only to aid him, as I have always done. I am, and have been since childhood, Gavin's guardian."

Relief washed through Timpani, and she bent to retrieve the spade from beneath the bed. So, *this* was the man Arrane had sent to his son, the longtime guardian Abunda had spoken of.

"Then you are human, but gifted with the Sight? By Arrane?"

"Aye. He found me as a child, no family of my own. Arrane and Gavin are my only family, and so I protect them as I would a true brother and father."

"Then I thank you." Timpani reapplied the Ointment to the salve and eased onto the side of Alec's bed. "You already possess the Sight, Alec. Let me tend the wound with the Ointment. As long as I don't apply too much, only good should come of it."

She hoped she spoke truth. One never knew how a human would react to it, whether the magic would simply seep into the wound or into the whole of the body.

Timpani lifted the spade and moved the smooth surface over Alec's face. He reached out and seized her wrist. "Wait," he whispered. "What if my body drinks it in? What if it doesn't stop its flow before—"

"Shall we play 'what if' all evening, or shall we begin healing you before Gavin charges back in here and catches us in the process? That won't be too easy to explain."

Watching the mystical steam rise from beneath the spade, Timpani tried not to stare into Alec's intense gaze. A hiss sounded from Alec's wound, and the raw, torn flesh began to move, one ripped side reaching for the other with invisible fingers. Timpani removed the spade before the seams could seal, but already the bone was no longer visible in Alec's cheek. The redness remained, as well as the blood, but the injury was no longer so gaping in size.

"I shan't risk any more than that. The wound is cleaned and you will live, but to have it heal completely would be unexplainable. Here." Timpani took the square of linen from her lap and dipped it into the washbowl on the table. "Hold the water to the wound."

Without another word, Timpani rose and clasped her

hands together. The truth of the matter was that her hands were trembling, and she had no desire for Alec to notice. She paced the room, uneasy with the silence now hovering between them. She could only hope that her quick withdrawal of the spade prevented the Ointment from seeping too far into Alec's system. While they could use all the allies they could find, she didn't think Abunda or King Arrane would look kindly on her if she turned Gavin's guardian into something magical. Since she could have no way of knowing from which sort the Ointment had been made, she could only speculate as to what sort of magical being that might be.

She grimaced. Abunda's favorite source for the Ointment normally came from the tears of the Norman pixies. Of all the outcomes possible, having Alec transform into a pixie would be one of the worst and most unexplainable. The image nearly made her laugh. Alec was not a small man, and though not as large as Gavin, the thought of his becoming so very like a butterfly was quite the illustration.

Though probably due more to weariness and worry than amusement, Timpani's bubble of laughter erupted in a long, drawn-out burst of giggles. The look of disbelief on Alec's face forced her to try and regain control over herself, but the task was a difficult one.

Sweet Avalon, what was wrong with her? Poor Alec lay here wounded, and the thought of his becoming a pixie had her senseless with laughter.

"I've seen madness inflict humans, Timpani, but never a faery."

"I-I'm sorry," Timpani said, holding her side. "I don't know what's come over me."

"I should think you're only tired. Go on to bed now. I am fine."

Finally finding her wits, Timpani stilled her laughter and shook her head. "I'll find a bedroll and bring it in here. Someone should be here in case . . . in case the effects of the Ointment aren't of the desirable sort. Gavin would be suspicious if I didn't stay by your side in Nakkole's absence. And as she's likely to spend the evening watching over our prince . . . I'm staying put."

And in truth, he fascinated her. Here, finally, was a human who seemed neither cowardly nor imbecilic.

"Very well. Have the bedroll brought up." Alec moved onto his side, his wound facing the ceiling.

With a heavy sigh at his dismissal, Timpani left to do just that. As she entered the corridor, another thought worried her, pushing all others aside.

How many more would Elphina send to kill her own half brother?

And how would Nakkole and Timpani keep him alive long enough to teach him to fight them?

❧

I never imagined it could feel so wonderful," Nakkole said, burying her face in the crook of Gavin's neck.

He sighed, knowing he was probably crushing her, but was unable to move his body. His bed had never been more comfortable.

"Neither had I."

She chuckled, her breasts rubbing against his chest. His blood stirred again.

"I think this was not as new to you as it was to me. Surely you knew how grand it could be," she whispered.

Never had it been *this* grand. He contemplated telling her so. If he should admit how satiated she'd made him, how completely content he would be if he never knew the touch of another woman, he'd likely be setting up both himself and Nakkole for heartbreaking disappointment. This would never last, this contentment. It was not, after all, as though they held a deep affection for one another. They had been merely unable to fight their mutual attraction any longer.

Gavin's people needed him. They needed a laird who would marry to better their clan, perhaps allying them with another, greater laird with a union between the two.

A life with Nakkole? Impossible. Even if he did want her more than any woman he'd ever had, there was no emotion here beyond lust, certainly nothing powerful enough to make him think it could last.

She pulled at the chain around his neck and palmed the

small stone dangling from it. He'd found it in the loch when
he'd first learned to swim and had gifted it to his mother.
When Geraldine had gone to the abbey to live, he'd taken it
back, telling himself she wouldn't even know it was missing,
but the truth was, it was a memory he wanted to hold on to,
unsure whether he would ever see his mother alive again.

"What's this?" she asked, rolling the stone over his chin.

He pulled the chain away, unwilling to share the pathetic
part of him that had clung so desperately to a mother who
hadn't known he'd existed. "Nothing."

"You're too quiet. Tell me what you're thinking,"
Nakkole said, caressing his cheek with her fingertips.

He nuzzled the crook of her neck with his nose. "I am
thinking that time is such a fleeting thing . . ."

Gently, she maneuvered herself from his arms and
pushed herself to her feet. Her naked body cloaked in naught
but early morning shadows, she reached for her clothing and
shook her head. "*Oui*. Time is often an ugly word."

She pulled her gown over her body. Gavin watched her,
his arms suddenly aching with emptiness. Seeking to change
the topic, he rolled to his side and said, "Will Alec be all
right?"

"I'm sure your friend will be up and about soon enough,"
she murmured. "I shouldn't have neglected him this long."

She straightened the dress and bent down to lay a feathery soft kiss on his forehead. When she turned to leave, he
grabbed her wrist and pulled her back onto the bed. Quickly,
he smothered her protest with a searing kiss.

Nakkole's insides churned with building need. Once with
Gavin was never to be enough, and if things were different,
if his life wasn't in her hands and he weren't destined to become her king, she would have given up everything she held
dear just to linger at his side long enough to have him make
her feel as perfect as he had moments ago.

But life had a way of interfering with the simplest of
dreams. Her kingdom needed her now. Her own needs would
have to wait. No matter what Abunda said, Gavin *had* to
know the truth. Elphina was growing more aggressive by the
day, and if tonight's attack was anything to go by, Gavin's
life was in dire jeopardy.

She pulled her head back and stared into the pool of gray in his eyes. How could she feel so strongly about a man she had known so briefly? And more important, how could she feel so strongly about a man she was lying to with every breath?

Twelve

～

Nakkole sat in silence the next morning, her chest tight with uncertainty. Everything had changed the moment she'd submitted to her need to make love with Gavin. She'd taken a foolish risk by opening her heart and body to him so readily. She could be outcast by her king and people for daring such intimacy with their prince. She could be carrying his child. She could, and likely would, end up with a broken heart. Even if Gavin chose not to claim the throne when it was his time to do so, he would likely return here, to Grey Loch and the humans he was charged with. She could no more be a human wife for him than she could be a faery queine.

But what concerned her most was what their lovemaking meant for Gavin. She'd taken her charade one step further, no longer able to claim she was only a small part in the plot to get him back to the Otherworld. She'd now become the main deceiver, for certainly he would forgive those he barely knew before forgiving the woman who'd allowed him to be so intimate with her.

He had to know the truth, *now*, and she had to be the one

to tell him. Otherwise, there was no chance of saving him from the hurt of deceit.

But how was she to divulge the truth without him thinking her insane?

The knot in her stomach tightened at the thought of defying her mother. She would be punished for telling him now, before Abunda thought him ready. But wasn't that why they'd sent Nakkole here? To sense when the best time to reveal the truth to Gavin might be?

Her confidence building, Nakkole slid out of her bed and wrapped her plaid messily over her body. Her mother and king had sent her here to do a duty, and by Avalon, Nakkole meant to do it. They'd wanted her to be gentle with the truth . . . well, if she waited a day longer, there would be no gentleness left in the truth at all.

She froze at the doorway, sickened by her predicament. What if he believed bedding him was part of their ploy to gain his agreement? And that was only a problem if he believed her at all. She would need help revealing the truth to Gavin, and she needed a clever way to make him believe.

Making her way down the corridor, she stopped at Alec's door, hoping she'd find Timpani inside. Alec was more than he appeared to be—of that much Nakkole was certain. The events of the previous night proved it, and she planned to find out the truth. Perhaps he would be a help in sorting out this mess with Gavin. She knew he was human, as there'd been no sign of fae in his eyes, and perhaps another human was exactly what Gavin would need to believe the strange tale Nakkole was about to tell him.

❧

"I wish to show you something."

Gavin lifted his head from his pillow and smiled at the sight of Nakkole standing in his doorway, a plaid barely covering her breasts and legs. She stood with her hands fisted at her sides, a soft smile on her face. The smile seemed strained, however, and now that he really looked at her, her face was pale and her brow was furrowed.

She was not the serene Nakkole she'd been last night.

Curious, he dragged himself out of the bed and set about dressing, keeping careful watch upon her. Was she about to tell him last night had been a mistake? God, he hoped not. True, he had his own worries over what had happened between them. He couldn't marry a Norman lass, not when his clan needed him to wed someone who would ensure them a strong alliance. But he could have gotten Nakkole with child, and then what? Was he to walk away? Who was he to hurt? His clan or Nakkole?

Neither sat well with him.

The euphoria he'd awakened with burst like a bubble as he fastened his plaid over his shoulder. "What have you to show me?" he asked, forcing a pleasant tone.

"Please," she said quietly and pointed to the bed. "Sit."

He did as she asked, the forboding feeling within him swelling all the more. "Very well, I'm sitting." His gaze fell to her fisted hands. "Show me."

Nakkole took a small step into the chamber, her damned bottom lip once again gone from view. She exhaled deeply, took a few more steps, then sat beside him. "I must ask you something first."

He watched her, watched those closed fists as though a snake might emerge from the cracks between her fingers. Whatever was on her mind, he wasn't sure he wanted to know.

"Do you believe in magic, Gavin?"

His laugh was far too loud, even to him, but God save him, the question seemed so ludicrous after all his worry. "I enjoy a good magic trick at the festivals, aye."

She smiled, the light not quite reaching her eyes. "Nay, not tricks, but *real* magic."

Gavin sobered, wishing she'd given him time to fully waken before coming to him with this sort of questioning. "Then, nay, I do not."

Nodding, Nakkole's gaze drifted to his, a look of pleading deep within her eyes that made him tense all over again. "What about Bessie? Do you believe it was magic that allowed you to milk her when she had no milk to give?"

Becoming slightly annoyed now and disappointed that she had not come to him in tenderness after their incredible night of lovemaking, Gavin shook his head. "I just said I do not believe in magic. Why do you ask me this?"

"How do you explain what you did with Bessie if it was not magic?" she asked him, completely disregarding his own question.

"Sheer will."

"Ah." This time, her smile was true. "So Bessie felt your will to produce milk and she complied?"

"Nakkole, I'm hungry and still slightly tired. Whatever it is you've come to speak to me about, please get to it. You said you had something to show me. What is it?"

She suckled her lip and glanced down at her hands. "Will you watch without saying a word?"

Gavin ground his thumb into his left eye, wiping away the last remnants of sleep. He yawned and nodded.

Nakkole opened her palm to reveal a plain, gray stone no bigger than a beetle's shell. Other than a speck of black on its top, he could see nothing remarkable about the stone. He opened his mouth to say as much, but remembered his vow of silence and held his tongue.

"Watch," she whispered, then closed her fingers around the stone once again. She closed her eyes, her mouth opening. "Create gold."

She repeated the words over and over, making Gavin shift uncomfortably on the bed. She was speaking words such as he had when he'd held the butterfly in the forest. Was she mocking him?

Then, she uncurled her fingers and held her hand out to him. No stone sat in her palm any longer. Instead, a small golden nugget glinted up at him in the morning light. He swallowed, unsure how he was meant to react.

"Fancy trick, that." He glanced at her other hand, certain she'd managed to exchange the pebble for the gold. "Where's the stone?"

"This *is* the stone, Gavin. I turned it to gold."

"Funny," he drolled. "Lemme see your other hand."

She opened it to reveal . . . nothing. He turned her hand over, searching for the secret of her trick. "I'm impressed," he said when he found no sign of the gray rock.

"I know you don't want to believe this was real, Gavin,

but I only did to that rock what you did to Bessie, what you did to the butterfly in the forest."

"Willed it?"

"Aye." She slid the gold into his hand. "With magic."

His laugh escaped from his nose, sounding more like a snort than a chuckle. He reached for his boots, unwilling to waste more time on her magic tricks, but Nakkole grabbed his wrist with an astonishingly strong grip. "I'm not finished."

Anger slowly ate away his irritation. This was not how'd he'd envisioned spending the morning after bedding the woman. "Well, I am."

He pushed himself off the bed and slid his feet into his boots, not bothering to lace them. He wasn't quite certain why this topic was bothering him so much, but he suddenly felt as though an army of ants had invaded his intestines, and he wanted out of this chamber.

"Gavin, wait!" Nakkole leaped from the bed and closed the chamber door as though she thought she might be able to keep him from leaving. "Those memories," she started, leaning against the door, "of the man who taught you to bring life back to that butterfly . . . the man you called Father . . . they really happened, Gavin. And after the attack last eve, I can't afford to wait any longer for you to hear the truth!"

He was completely unable to do aught but stare at her. "You're mad."

"Perhaps." She closed her eyes and heaved a weary sigh. "But I am also speaking only truth to you. The *things* that attacked last night were targeting *you*."

"Timpani said they were wild animals. Wild animals do not strategize in the way you speak of, Nakkole."

Nakkole reached out to take Gavin's hand, fighting the urge to flee from this conversation and allow someone else to do it. She couldn't. This was *her* duty. She must see it through. "You need to know why I am here."

The corner of his mouth lifted into a wry grin. "King James sent you here to care for my mother."

Sweet Avalon, this was difficult. "Nay. I'm not."

She swallowed and stepped away, uncertain how he

would take her confession. Already, he'd dimissed her powers as silly trickery. Now, his eyes darkened. His grin faded.

She walked to the window and prayed he wouldn't leave
before she could finish her task. Pushing open the shutters,
she reached her hands outside and began beckoning the dew
into her palms. "The truth is, I was sent by my king, not
yours."

She wasn't certain he'd heard her. She turned to face him,
sprinkling the tiny drops onto her feet. He was staring at her,
his eyes narrowed, his face contorted in confusion. "I didn't
come to help your mother. I came to help *you*."

The dew turned to vapor, cloaking her feet, her calves,
her thighs.

"What the—"

"Gavin, look at me. What you see is what I'm trying to
explain."

He reached out, swiping at the fog engulfing her as
though he'd suspected it wasn't real. "I don't—"

Licking her lips, Nakkole felt the coolness shroud her
belly and her breasts. "The butterfly, Gavin. You brought it
back to life. That is one of your abilities. This"—she ran her
hand down her body—"is one of mine."

Suddenly, she felt more exposed than she had when he'd
stared at her naked body the night before. She took advantage of his state of bewilderment and summoned the fog to
fully engulf her. To prove her body was no longer solid, she
drifted up, off the floor, then under the bed, coming back to
wrap her cloaked self fully around Gavin.

He hissed and stepped back as though burned, his eyes
blaring with . . . fury. The fog cloak fell away, leaving
Nakkole standing before Gavin wearing nothing but her
fears. Uncomfortable with her nakedness for the first time in
her life, she summoned the White Lady garb she hadn't
donned since arriving in Scotland.

Gavin's hand moved so quickly, she thought he meant to
strike her. Instead, he seized the hilt of his sword that had
lain propped against the bed, the veins in his arms pressed
violently against his skin as he rubbed the amber jewel in the
hilt of the weapon.

"Devilry," he whispered, his gaze darting frantically

about her body. "I don't know what the hell you are, but I want you gone from McCain lands."

His long, powerful strides forced her to run to keep pace with him, but he did not look back.

"I'm here to help you, Gavin. Please. You're in danger." What in Avalon's name had she done? "Please, Gavin, listen to me. Your father sent me—"

In the next instant, the cold, sharp tip of Gavin's sword was pressed against her breast, and his hot breath was burning her cheek. "My father? My father died before I was even born—"

"Nay. He didn't." Carefully, Nakkole pushed away the blade. "But he could very well die soon if you don't listen to me. They told me not to tell you, but I believed you should know, thought you deserved to know the truth!"

His face offered her no reaction. He simply stared at her with hatred in his eyes. The pain of that stare cut far more deeply than any sword could have, and Nakkole nearly lost her will to continue.

But it was the hope she thought she saw amidst that hatred that spurred her on. "You are a prince, Gavin. Destined to rule your father's kingdom. Not a country, but an entire world of magic that you refuse to believe in. You also have a sister, mothered by a succubus named Lucette.

"They're after your throne, and should they win it, life as we all know it will forever be destroyed."

Gavin gripped her arm and squeezed tightly, then flung her away with disgust. "You're not welcome here any longer. I'll not have you anywhere near this place, near my mother."

Then, he turned and marched away, leaving Nakkole too dazed to do aught but let him go.

When he reached the door and flung it open, however, Alec stepped in his path. He and Timpani had been in the corridor, awaiting the right time to show themselves should Nakkole have need. She'd been hoping their interference wouldn't be nessesary, but just now, was extrememly pleased to see them. Timpani had told her about Alec's true reason for residing at Grey Loch, and Nakkole suspected that, if anyone could get through to Gavin, it would be him.

"She speaks the truth, Gavin," Alec said, his face grim.

He put a hand on Gavin's shoulder, gently guiding him back into the chamber. Timpani followed, shutting the door behind her. "'Tis because of your father, the king, that I first came to you as a child. I was to be his eyes and report to him about your life. It was I who told him when you were playing in the forest alone, making it safe for him to come visit with you."

Gavin shrugged off his friend's touch with a violent swing of his arm. "I don't know what the hell is going on here, but I'm done with it. Do you understand?" He tried to push past Alec, but Alec wouldn't budge.

When Gavin brought a fist up, Nakkole gasped. It swung out at Alec's jaw, but Alec ducked. "Look at me, friend." His chest heaving, Alec pulled at the bandage on his cheek. "You saw my wound—clear to the bone. What else but magic could have healed it so quickly?"

The bandage came free, revealing a dark red cut on his cheek. But it looked no deeper than a scratch, and certainly wasn't as dire as it had been just the night before. Gavin shouted a curse and thrust his sword forward, using the sharp point to nudge Alec from his path.

"I'm leaving this chamber, and when I come back, I expect the lot of you gone." He turned to Alec. "Them, I barely know. But you? What the devil are you pulling, Alec?"

He didn't give Alec time to respond. He stormed from the chamber, looking as though he meant to cut through any who tried to stop him this time. His reference to Nakkole as a near stranger cut, but she swallowed her hurt and tried to follow Gavin. Alec stopped her at the doorway.

"I'll follow him to make certain he remains safe, but you must find a way to speak to your mother, tell her of what's happening. We might have no choice but to force Gavin into your world now that he's been told. I doubt he'll come willingly."

It was obvious to Nakkole that Alec did not agree with her choice to tell Gavin the truth, but she had to stand by her decision. Better he started accepting the truth now rather than when the heat of battle was upon them all.

"Keep him safe," she whispered, then turned to Timpani. "Come. We go to the loch."

Thirteen

～

Gavin rested his head on his arms, which dangled over his bent knee. He'd found this secluded spot in the forest, certain that if Nakkole or Alec was foolish enough to seek him out, he would hear their approach before they could find him.

He didn't know which hurt more—his mind or his heart. Nakkole's strange lies had muddled his brain, but he'd given a tiny bit of himself to her and now that bit was gone forever.

And Alec! Why would *he* say such things? He wanted nothing to do with either of them just now, mayhap forever.

And yet, the thought of never seeing Nakkole again was a dagger through his soul. He liked her. Cared for her.

A prince. Bah.

A twig snapped from behind him. He turned to find Alec framed by two large Scottish pines. "Leave now, Alec. This is one time in my life I don't wish you near me."

Alec opened his mouth to speak, but the sound of two low *wooshes* silenced him. He fell to the ground before Gavin could feel the sharp sting in his own shoulder. Then, he knew of nothing but darkness.

Nakkole knelt by the loch, preparing to summon her mother and very afraid to do so. Avalon save her, she was every kind of fool. She'd been so certain it was time to tell all to Gavin. No matter that Abunda and Arrane seemed to think Gavin was unable to cope with the truth, Nakkole thought the man to be stronger than any of them had thought—thought perhaps their refusal had been a test to see if she'd truly be able to feel when the right time had come for Gavin to hear what he needed to be told.

Her error in judgment might very well grant Elphina the throne she so wanted.

She caught a glimpse of herself in the water, dressed in the shimmering, nearly translucent gown of the White Ladies. She missed home desperately, but the thought of leaving Grey Loch as Gavin demanded brought a painful ache to her chest. What was she to do?

"Best to get it over with," Timpani said, kneeling beside her.

Nakkole took a deep breath and ran her hand over the surface of the loch, but before she could begin her summons, Alec's voice screamed through the trees.

"He's gone!"

Nakkole's breath caught in her throat. She prayed her instincts were wrong, and yet knew they weren't. "Wh-who's gone, Alec?"

His breathing heavy, Alec collapsed against a tree, clutching his arm. "Who do you think? Gavin is gone. They shot me with an elf bolt, and when I'd awakened, he was gone."

She was going to be ill.

"I found this far from where I last saw him." He reached into the folds of his plaid and pulled out a dagger. "It's Gavin's. Hopefully, he still has the sword. I could not find it."

"Wh-where exactly did you find it?" Nakkole seized it from him, studying it as though it might speak the secrets of Gavin's whereabouts.

"Near a glowing ring of toadstools. The gates of Elfame have been opened," Alec continued. "I cannot go after him without you . . . I need a faery with me to enter the gates. I came to find you, to find any others you may have here. We must leave at once."

Nakkole's legs went numb, but her mind came alive. She turned to find Timpani behind her, her face the color of snow. "Timpani, go fetch Beanie."

"We do not have time!"

Glaring at Timpani, Nakkole pointed toward the keep. "Go. *Now*. Meet me back here, and bring Beanie with you."

Timpani opened her mouth to refuse again, then quickly shut it and turned to do as Nakkole commanded. Nakkole quickly pivoted to follow Alec out of the forest.

As they reached the fields of Grey Loch, Alec approached a group of Gavin's men who'd just begun their morning exercises. "Robert, find Markham and two others best skilled with their swords."

Soon, Robert returned, ushering three other men from the barracks. Concentrating on using more of her powers than she'd ever had to before, she sent out her glamour and called out to them.

"Are you ready then?" she asked sweetly.

All five of the men nodded in turn.

Alec, however, scowled. "They'll need their wits about them. Why would you enchant them and hinder their abilities?"

"Would you willingly leap into a faery ring? Better my glamour hinder them than the fear and disbelief of what they face. Once they've had time to believe, Timpani or I will disenchant them."

Alec gave a curt nod and turned his attention to the men. "Don your hauberks, but naught else over your clothes. You'll have need to move quickly and silently where we are going. Bring only your shields, bows, and swords."

She thought of asking him to fetch spare bows for her and Timpani, and quickly changed her mind. She and Timpani were excellent with the weapons, but faery bows were much lighter, much different than those of the humans. Any Alec would bring her would be useless in her hands.

While she tried to think of a plan, the men rushed to find the items Alec had instructed them to bring.

The confusion inside of her was overwhelming. How could she be certain this wasn't a trick? What if Elphina meant for them to enter Elfame and leave Gavin completely unguarded here in the human realm where he was most vulnerable? And if it was all true, in fact, why would they take Gavin under rather than attacking him where his powers were still unlearned? Surely they realized that the entrance to the Otherworld would give Gavin's abilities so much more power, would make him so much more difficult to kill.

She needed answers.

"Alec!" she called. "I must go ahead to the lake."

Set on pulling his hauberk over his head, Alec grunted agreement.

Satisfied they would follow shortly, she ran to the lake with every bit of speed her legs would allow.

When she arrived, she had no need to beckon anyone. A face as big as a moon's reflection stared at her from the rippled surface. Nakkole stopped her running abruptly, sliding in the slippery mud, and landing hard on her bottom.

It wasn't Abunda's face who stared back at her. It was her king . . . Arrane.

Fourteen

~~~~

"Y our Majesty!" Nakkole gasped, glad to already be sitting on the muddy earth. Her legs shook with fear for Gavin's safety, but it was the look of condemnation simmering in Arrane's eyes that rendered her immobile.

"I had hoped your sensitivity would feel the right moment to tell Gavin the truth, but you were as blunt with that knowledge as your sisters would have been. You have allowed my son, my *hope*, to be stolen from your watch."

Arrane's silver hair flowed around his reflection, as real as the leaves circling around Nakkole's knees. Never had Abunda appeared so real during a summons. Nakkole shivered.

"I know I've done wrong," she whispered. "Please, tell me how to make this right."

"Come into the water."

Nakkole's legs wouldn't allow her to obey. The image of her being pulled under the rippling current, held down with Arrane's wrath, washed through her mind. "Please, Your Majesty. Let me go after him. It's not too late."

"Come into the water, *now*."

As if by magic, her body pushed itself off of the muddy

bank and slid into the cool depths of Grey Loch. She kept her gaze on Arrane's face, watching his expression soften only a bit as his hair and beard reached out to encircle her waist. Warmth coursed through her body, tingling her arms, legs, and finally her belly.

"You have the Bean-Tighe with you still?" Arrane asked, his beard curling around her neck with an ominous warning.

She nodded, feeling her body relax in the cradle of Arrane's hold. Soothing. So very soothing. Suddenly, she wanted naught more than to sleep until eternity.

"*Oui,*" she said, her eyes closing. "Beanie comes with the others to the gates of Elfame."

"No longer. She is to transport you here to the Isle of Arran as quickly as possible. Timpani and Alec will lead the others through Elfame after Gavin."

Nakkole snapped out of her daze. "Your Majesty, I know I failed you, but please, do not lose all faith—"

Arrane's beard snaked up her face, then released its hold on her body, and she floated toward the shore.

"You will obey me."

Nakkole jerked. Never before had she heard her king so angry, so determined.

Planting her feet on the sandy lake floor, she turned back to see Arrane's reflection growing smaller, bit by bit.

Shouts and yells sounded from the thick copse beyond the forest trail. Nakkole glanced back, her mind still struggling to come fully awake.

"Please, Your Majesty. Allow me to lead the others!"

"I'll expect to see you and Beanie in the Isle of Arran in one day's time, Nakkole. Alec already knows what's expected of him . . . he's been preparing for this battle his whole life."

Nakkole sobbed, knowing she would pay a price of the highest order when she disobeyed her king, but she had no other choice. She would not leave Gavin to those who had taken him. She would not leave her duties here, or her feelings for her prince, behind.

Arrane's reflection glided over the lake until it peered at her from only a few feet away. "You think of defying me?"

His dark eyes glistened, eerily calm and yet aflame all at

once. Nakkole swallowed, awaiting his punishment for her disobedient thoughts.

"It seems you cannot be trusted," Arrane said, his beard coiling around her head like a crown of fur. Slowly, she felt her need for sleep returning, and no matter how she fought against it, her eyes would not remain open. "Sleep now, and when you awaken, you'll be here, at the Isle."

Nakkole opened her mouth to protest, but found it covered with Arrane's hair.

As she drifted closer to sleep, Nakkole smiled, contentment filling her with Arrane's sweet hold.

◆

Geraldine McCain knew the instant King Arrane began to form solid bits of himself nearby. She didn't know where he was, or why he was so close, but the very fact that she was capable of climbing out of bed to search the skies from her chamber window was proof that some part of him was close. It wasn't much, but a morsel of time and pining fell from her old bones, allowing her the use of her body and mind as she hadn't been able to in so many years. Her heart pounded with such life as it had not known in so long.

Arrane.

She could feel him. His presence beckoned her like the shore to the sea at eve-tide.

Her eyes strained against the thick fog settling over the forest trees. Swirls of mist rose and gathered before her, creating shapes that made her—not for the first time in her life—doubt her sanity. Could the small droplets of vapor truly have created Arrane's image, or were her eyes playing tricks on her?

"Arrane?" she called out with her mind, unable to form the words upon her lips.

She wanted to run from her chamber toward the loch and search for her love, but this miracle was not so large as to allow her to do so.

Why was he here? Why now, after all these years did he come to Scotland? She remember a few times . . . how long ago she couldn't be sure . . . when she'd been certain he'd been close by. In those rare moments, she'd felt as strong as she had as a young girl. But one day, they'd stopped. Now, suddenly, that feeling had returned, though far weaker than her prior experiences.

Can you hear me, Arrane? Why are you here?

She shuddered. *Gavin.* Why would Arrane come now, unless danger had invaded this place? He would come for Gavin. He would have no use for the woman who had abandoned him, who had taken his child and had doubted her husband's ability to protect them from harm.

Two small figures bounded across the open field, both being of fae blood. She could see the magic in them thanks to the Ointment her dear pixie friend, Pila, had been applying to her eyes all these years. Before she'd fallen too ill to speak often, she'd made Pila promise to apply the magic to her eyes every day, for she'd wanted to remain aware of any magical beings in her presence. She wanted to know if her son was ever in danger.

Geraldine tried to grip the windowsill in order to lean farther out the window, but her fingers were too weak. Where was the White Lady who'd been caring for her? She knew from the day Gavin had brought that butterfly back to life that her new healer was a White Lady, and oh, how relieved she'd been. Only Arrane would have sent such a guardian here, to Grey Loch.

Geraldine watched, then glanced back up at the mist she thought carried Arrane's features. It was gone. She sighed and placed a hand to her heart, wishing she could soothe the pain growing there. It did not relent, but steadily spread throughout the rest of her body. The hated weakness slowly returned to her aging bones, and she knew at once Arrane was returning to his home, leaving her body to continue dying in his absence.

Alec dashed out of the armory, followed by four other men. Seeing Alec running in such a panic alerted her.

Gavin's protector.

Something was not right. But from her window so high above them, she could hear nothing.

Panic gripped her heart and made her bones ache.

*Arrane! Hear me now! I am begging you . . . find a way to
bring me home. I must know that my son, our son, is safe.*

❧

Timpani watched as Alec adjusted the sword at his hip.
She glanced over Robert and Markham's armed bodies,
satisfied they looked capable of defending themselves and as-
sisting along the arduous journey ahead.

Two other identically clad men stood with Robert and
Markham, and though Timpani recognized them, her deal-
ings with Gavin's men had been limited to only Alec,
Robert, and Markham thus far.

"Who are these men?" she asked, eyeing them carefully.

Robert pointed to the man closest him. He was overly
large with long, tangled brown hair and a barrel chest that
looked solid and strong. "This be Brock, and there's Luke."

The one named Luke looked no more than a young man
of sixteen or seventeen summers. Timpani swallowed hard
against the thought of sending such a skinny boy into the
battles that may await them.

The others looked strong enough to handle just about
anything. But were their minds as capable of understanding?
She could see remnants of glamour glimmering on their
flesh, but it would not hold long. Understanding that
Nakkole had done what was necessary to gain their accep-
tance thus far, Timpani knew she could not enchant them
again so soon without risk of overwhelming their senses and
making them useless in Elfame.

"We must hurry," Alec said, beside her.

"I would ask a favor of Luke." Timpani sent a pleading
look for silence at Alec, then cast a warm, beseeching smile
toward the skinny, young man. "Someone needs to remain
behind to watch over Lady Geraldine. Should something
happen to her, it will only weaken Arrane further. My wish
is for Luke to stay and guard her."

While her words were not lies, they were also not the
whole truth. She could not take this boy with them in good
conscience. He wasn't seasoned with war and bloodshed,

and Avalon help them, there was bound to be plenty of both where they were going.

She could have sworn she saw relief flicker in Luke's eyes. He looked at Alec for approval, and Timpani took no offense. Alec was his commander in Gavin's presence, not Timpani.

After a quick glance at Timpani, Alec nodded to Luke. "Stay."

Then, he pulled Timpani's arm leading her away from the group. "Nakkole enchanted the lot of them to make their journey easier to understand. Disenchant Luke. I can give him orders in Gavin's place, but he must be loyal to me, not to Nakkole. He will obey what I tell him with a clear mind."

Without saying a word, Timpani closed her eyes and retrieved the webs of glamour Nakkole had cast over Luke, bringing them into herself where it found no place to live, for it had not come from her body, but from Nakkole's. Instead, Timpani's fae eyes watched the thin, silk web fall to the grass at her feet.

"Protect Lady Geraldine with your life, Luke," Alec said.

"Aye, Alec. You've my word." Luke bowed his head, but Timpani could see his shoulders sagging with relief.

"Come then. The rest of us leave now." Alec adjusted his bow and once again, taking Timpani's elbow in his hand, pulled her along toward the forest.

They were off, and Avalon help her, Timpani was thrilled to be going home.

The sharp, piercing pain in Gavin's shoulder awakened him, forcing him to bolt upright from the hard earth he'd been sprawled upon. Bringing his hand up to clutch the small, pebble-sized hole in the flesh of his shoulder, he closed his eyes tightly, then reopened them. Still, naught but darkness greeted him.

Where the devil was he? It felt like some sort of cave, but he did not feel enclosed. His head was pounding, more from the frustration of trying to remember than from the dull pain at the back of his skull.

Nakkole . . . her outrageous tales. He'd been furious with her. It seemed all of that had occurred only moments ago, but he had no true knowledge of how long he'd lain sleeping here. And Alec. He'd seen Alec in the forest. Something had happened . . . then, he remembered naught else.

Fumbling, he felt for his sword with one hand while trying to pull himself to his feet with the other. His sword was gone. Quickly, he felt around the inside of his plaid for the dirk he kept there. The small knife was gone as well.

Gavin cursed. He had to get out of this darkness. Had to find light to help clear his mind. He looked over his shoulder and squinted into the shadows. Not even the faintest light glowed from that way. But ahead of him, barely visible, a tiny glow of yellow radiated, beckoning him toward it. He could not bear the thought of heading farther into darkness, and since he had no way of knowing from which direction he had come, he chose the path that led to light.

As he stepped forward, clutching the dirt and stone wall for support, a giggle tinkled from somewhere above him. Gavin flinched and ducked out of the way, feeling a light breeze brush his ear. A shiver ran down his spine, but he kept moving . . . moving toward the light.

Again, the giggle.

"Who are you?" he bellowed, his voice bouncing off the walls and ricocheting right back at him, burdening the pain in his head all the more.

He heard a soft, singsong voice—nay, *voices*. What were they saying?

He followed their sound, but now they seemed to be coming from above, behind, and before him.

Then, it was as though one of the voices sat on his shoulder, and he could hear it clearly. "We got you, we got you. King Arrane shall die away and the Dark King will take his place, and Prince Gavin will know his fate. We got you, we got you."

More giggles, this time coming from all around him, like a cocoon of laughter that was neither cheery or kind, but eerie and cruel.

"Tsk, tsk. He bleeds, he bleeds. Queine Elphina will not

like his blood spilling before his death. It will weaken his spirit. Clean him, clean him."

Suddenly, a sphere of light lit up around Gavin and he could see a dozen small yellowish creatures clinging to the walls and ceiling around him with long, *very* long, thin arms. Gavin found himself fascinated by their large, flat feet the size of large lily pads, which was all the more odd since their bodies were no bigger than Gavin's hand.

His head swam with dizziness. One of the creatures dangled off the wall in front of him, staring him in the eye, and Gavin had to grip the wall tighter in order to keep himself upright.

"Pech," he whispered. "You are a pech."

The odd being glared to its right. "Told you, told you! You shouldn't have shot him with the elf bolt. You don't know how to use it right and now look what's happened. He can see us for what we are, what we are."

An elf bolt? That explained the small hole in his shoulder. As well as the dizziness. Magical creatures. Peches. God help him, he was losing his mind. How did he even know of such things to imagine them? He couldn't recall ever hearing of anything such as a pech, and yet, when he looked upon the odd creature, he knew that they lived in the lowlands, burrowed underground in caves such as this. He knew they feasted on the fungi that grew in such dark, dank places. But he also knew that they were not born cruel creatures, either. Why then, were these peches looking at him as though they would love naught more than to kill him?

He raised his arm and swatted the pech in front of him, but the creature's tight grip on the wall kept it balanced.

"Queine Elphina will not be happy, not be happy," another small voice said from beside Gavin.

"I had no choice, no choice!" yet another voice called. "It got him here, didn't it? Queine Elphina will be glad, glad, glad."

"If you don't wish to be squashed like the pests you are, I suggest you direct me from here and leave me be," Gavin said, his throat dry and burning for water.

Cackles, soft and far more eerie than their previous giggles, sounded throughout the small crowd. "Hard to squash what you can't see, can't see!"

The sphere of light vanished, leaving Gavin once again in the darkness that had so chilled him earlier. Groaning, he pushed forward, toward that one small glowing light far away. He needed to see, needed some way to gain his bearings. Between the odd little creatures now yanking on his hair, the loose stones catching beneath his boots, and the horrible ache in his shoulder, Gavin knew he'd likely lose his mind if left in this darkness much longer.

"Let me see!" he shouted, slamming his fist into a soft spot on the wall.

A muffled yelp cried out and something sticky and warm coated Gavin's hand. He paid no more attention to it, focusing instead on squinting into the utter darkness, straining to see. "Let me see!"

Suddenly, the darkness around him dissipated, and though no light came forth, Gavin found himself able to see into the darkness. The peches had become silver shadows he could easily make out, even if he could not distinguish their tiny features. Pebbles glowed with white silhouettes, and the path ahead of him looked lit with moonlight.

"Tookan!" a pech cried out. "He's killed Tookan!"

Gavin looked around, his gaze finally settling on his sticky hand.

There, between his fist and the wall, lay a limp pech. Gavin's fist had plunged into the wee creature's belly.

Squashed.

Whispers began to echo around him, growing louder even as Gavin struggled to free his hand from the pech's middle. "His powers control his eyes, his eyes! Flee! His powers soon will grow stronger, stronger!"

Powers? Controlling his eyes? Why, of course he controlled his eyes. His gaze darted around. He finally freed his fist and began his pursuit of the flame in the distance once more. Before he took even two full steps, a sharp pain stabbed his wounded shoulder and he found himself falling to the hard floor, his mind already growing hazy.

Rolling onto his back, Gavin stared up at an angry pech dangling above him from the ceiling. In its hand, the pech held a bright yellow staff. The staff glowed and smoke rippled from its jagged tip.

An elf bolt. How and why would he recognize such a thing?

He didn't have much time to ponder.

"*This* is for Tookan, Tookan! His death means your death. Prince or nay! Prince or nay!" The staff began to glow with power, and the pech pointed the elf bolt directly at Gavin's heart.

Fifteen

~

The Desolate Caves of the Otherworld

Triumph.

Finally, Elphina had won a small battle in her war with her father, and it came in the priceless package of her loathsome brother, Gavin. Her army had done something right for a change. Gavin was in the Otherworld.

Helpless, likely confused, and soon to be at Elphina's mercy.

"The peches, of all the creatures," she mused, barely containing the glee in her voice. "They've done well."

Lucette eased into the gilded chair beside Elphina's throne and clapped her hands together, summoning a nearby succubus toting a tray topped with two goblets of bluebell wine. Elphina helped herself to a goblet and drank a hardy gulp of the bitter, potent liquid.

"I suspect they'll bring him soon," Lucette said. "The pech who brought me the message claimed the others are having a difficult time carrying him. It seems your brother has inherited your father's impressive size."

Elphina eyed her mother with suspicion, loathing the longing she saw on her face. She considered reminding Lucette that Arrane had only bedded her once because dark magic had seduced him to do so, and that she had no chance of his ever falling for such trickery again. But she held her tongue. Let the old hag have her fantasies. They were all she'd ever be granted.

"You're certain they told the truth? They could have been lying about bringing Gavin into our world so that I wouldn't smash their skulls."

Lucette glanced up and, once again, clapped her hands, this time bringing forth a pech from the throne room's doorway. His large, lily-pad-shaped feet stumbled as he dragged something behind him. When he finally reached the stone dais, he thrust the object forward and bowed his head in reverence to his queine.

A flash of silver glinted across the sapphire jewels of Elphina's throne, causing Rancor, who was perched just behind her left ear, to twitter with excitement. Unimpressed, Elphina simply stared at the offering.

"What need have I of a sword?" she asked the pech, reaching out to take the weapon with both hands.

Without looking at her, the pech mumbled, "It's your brother's sword, Majesty. Proof it is that we've brought him here, brought him here."

Elphina turned the weapon carefully in her hands, looking for anything remarkable. There was nothing that she could see. Metal and silver and a large amber stone centered in the hilt. "This sword could belong to anybody," she muttered, passing it into Lucette's hands.

"It is *his*," the pech protested in a panicked, screeching voice. "I swear it, swear it, swear it, Majesty."

With a sigh of irritation, Elphina motioned for him to stand. "Be gone. Find your brothers and help them bring Gavin to me. And if you would like to continue living, I suggest you be back here by tomorrow morn."

Krion save her, if she was forced to kill many more of her underlings, her already minuscule army would be nonexistent.

Her gaze flickered to the clay and stone tomb across the chamber where the Dark King, Krion, was bound. If he'd been awake, his powers of destruction would have already won her battles for her. The only other being with such power was Arrane.

And perhaps, Gavin.

She frowned at that thought. Which of their father's powers *did* her brother possess?

She hadn't truly worried for her life since her succubus blood would protect her from any man wishing to do her harm, but a tickle in the pit of her stomach made her wonder if, perhaps, she had overlooked something that might lead to her defeat.

Nonsense. All she needed to do was locate the Orb of Knowledge, the Orb of Creation, then steal the Orb of Truth from Arrane. With the Master Trinity, she'd awaken Krion and together they'd destroy Arrane.

But first, she would prepare to meet, and kill, her *beloved* brother.

❧

Timpani slid to a halt on the muddy bank of the lake, the sight of Abunda's image causing her to gasp and clutch Alec's arm to steady herself. Behind her, Robert, Markham, and Brock cursed, and she heard the distinct sound of their swords being unsheathed.

"Mother," Timpani whispered.

She swallowed, turning her gaze back to Abunda. Then, she noticed Nakkole's limp body lying behind tall reeds, and all thought of propriety fled.

"Nakkole!" Timpani leapt to her feet, stumbling to reach her sister's side. "What's happened? What's happened to Nakkole?"

"She is fine. And Arrane will see that she remains so until the full of this battle has been won. Is the Bean-Tighe with you now?"

Timpani pressed her cheek against Nakkole's chest, relieved to feel the steady rise and fall of shallow breaths.

Beanie burst from her bubble, approached Abunda's reflection, and bowed her head. "I am here for whatever purpose you may have, Queine Abunda."

Shaking Nakkole's shoulders in hopes of waking her, Timpani sobbed, angered at their mother's lack of concern.

"Cease your worry, Timpani. She sleeps because Arrane commanded it." Abunda's voice was soothing, calming. "Bean-Tighe, your globe is the quickest way to return Nakkole to the Isle of Arran. I cannot take her with me, as you know, for I am not truly here. Take her, Bean-Tighe, and bring her safely to Arrane at once."

"What is wrong with her?" Timpani demanded. "Why does she sleep?"

Beanie darted a desperate glance up at Timpani. "Don't be questioning your mother, me gel. She'll not be leading you astray."

"No, I would not." Abunda turned and beckoned Beanie. "Take her to Arrane at once. The six of you will go after his son. The Orb of Truth has shown King Arrane that the prince has been taken toward the dwarf mines at the borders of Elfame and Annwyn. I'm certain they intend to travel through Annwyn to reach the mist gates of Normandy. They'll not attack our kingdom until they've taken him to the Desolate Caves and delivered him to their queine."

Swallowing hard, Timpani stood and pointed at Beanie. "Go now," she commanded. "Alec, make sure your men are ready. We leave at once."

"Timpani," Abunda called out, her reflection already beginning its drift back to its home. "Be careful when you find our prince. His powers will be stronger in the Otherworld. He will not yet know how to control or use them. He could very well be a danger to the lot of you."

✦

Nakkole moaned and rolled to her side. Her body was awakening, but her mind demanded all efforts to wake be stopped, for she did not want to lose this warm feeling of calm. Her eyes were locked closed and through no power of her own could she open them.

A faint humming penetrated her comforting silence and she focused all of her strength on prying one lid open. A filmy, familiar golden glow greeted her eyes, hanging around her like a foggy mist.

Through the golden fog, she could see the faint outline of Beanie's body, pressed against a darker shade of gold.

The bubble. She was in Beanie's bubble.

In quick succession, flashes of memory assaulted Nakkole. The loch, Arrane . . . Gavin!

She sat up, the quick movement making her already foggy mind whirl. "Beanie. Stop. This instant. Stop."

Beanie glanced back at Nakkole from over her small shoulder, her brown eyes as regretful as her sagging shoulders.

"I have orders from your mother that must precede yours."

Turning back around, Beanie pressed against the bubble once more, leaning a bit to the right. The movement caused the bubble to turn in the same direction, jarring Nakkole so that her head hit the soft pillow of silk lining the orb.

"I will not abandon my duties to our prince, Beanie. Stop this globe at once and let me free."

Refusing to look at Nakkole, Beanie steered the bubble to the left. Through the transparent walls, Nakkole watched as they zoomed over a tall tree, through its branches, then lower to the ground.

"'Tis your duty to obey your *king*. Feelings of duty are no longer what bind you to our bonnie prince, methinks."

Nakkole's stomach dropped as they plummeted quickly toward the ground only to ascend above the forest once more. Sensing she would gain no compliance from the Bean-Tighe, she swiped at the swirling gold mist draping over her, found her footing, and moved to stand beside Beanie at the front of the bubble. Instantly, she realized her mistake when she saw the view from such a position. The world below looked oddly out of proportion, the things closest appearing distorted, while the things farthest appearing quite normal.

She stumbled backward, quite willing to let Beanie navigate the odd transport without Nakkole being witness to the act. "How long have I been under Arrane's enchantment?"

"Not so long now. 'Tis only a while past twilight. We'll be at the Isle some time after daybreak."

Twilight. All Otherworld gates would close come midnight, unable to be opened again until midday. She had to convince Beanie to set her free, else all would be lost to the curses of the portals.

Nakkole leaned her back on the bubble's lining, thinking of something she could say to convince Beanie of what must be done. A loud slapping noise, then an eerie *whoosh*, froze her thoughts.

Their rapid ascent ceased without warning. The bubble spiraled out of control. It rolled, sending Nakkole into Beanie. They bounced off of the resilient lining, then tumbled around the small sphere, arms and legs flailing about in wild frenzy to steady themselves. Beanie's hand lashed out and struck Nakkole across the cheek. She barely had time to gasp before her own foot flew out from under her and knocked against Beanie's chin.

Nakkole tasted blood, which seemed odd because there was nothing hard in their confines that could have inflicted such damage, then realized she'd bitten her tongue and her bottom lip.

"Wh-what is this, Beanie? What has happened?"

"An arrow." Beanie pulled herself to her knees, her fists clutching a tiny golden arrow the size of a quill. Light radiated from it, its ends glittering with a shimmering dust. "Faery bow. A leak, we have."

The orb spun again, sending them to what had been the roof only a moment ago. Against her cheek, a cool brush of wind suckled Nakkole's flesh. Once the bubble steadied itself enough, she pushed herself up on her arms and saw the tiny hole that had caused the air to escape. Already, the sphere had begun to shrink, forcing Nakkole and Beanie to lie huddled together. Pressing her face against the wall, Nakkole peered at the rapidly approaching grass. Three dark shadows darted across the open field below, disappearing behind the bordering trees.

Assassins. Queine Elphina's army.

Gasping, Nakkole braced herself for another tumble, her body numb as her mind reeled at the good fortune the creepy

little beings had thrown her way. Her hopefulness to find
Gavin had been answered, albeit not in the manner she
would have preferred. If she and Beanie survived the thun-
dering fall, she would be able to find another entrance to the
Otherworld. Locating one should not prove too difficult.

A whistle sounded, and another *whoosh* followed.
Another small faery arrow fell from the top of the sphere and
landed at her feet. She grabbed it, clutching it with trembling
fingers. The bubble was descending so quickly now, they
would collide with ground in only a moment. She doubted
very much that the thin walls would be protection enough
against the impending collision.

Closing her eyes tightly, she bit her lip and braced herself
for landing. She focused on recalling Gavin's face in her
mind, concentrating on the beauty of it, and realized that
Beanie had been right. Nakkole wanted to save him now for
more reasons than just her duty. She wanted to save him because in not doing so, she risked never seeing him again.

No more.

Kings, magic, evil be damned. Her loyalty now lay in
only herself and in Gavin, and by Avalon, she would keep
them both alive long enough to know the feel of each other
once more.

❧

Gavin's roar echoed throughout the winding tunnel. His
fury grew like a wildfire in his belly, but no matter his
strength and rage, he could not break free of the silken web
binding him to the large creature carrying him along the rocky
path.

Pebbles and sharp stones bit at his flesh, and the creature
toting him turned, causing Gavin's face to slam into the rock
wall to his left. *"Oomph."*

"Quiet," the massive creature whispered. "You waken
Orago."

For such a large being, his ability to speak so softly unnerved Gavin. Where had he come from? The last thing
Gavin remembered was that horrid little pech shooting that
elf bolt into his chest. When he'd awakened, he'd found him-

self strapped to this . . . giant's? . . . troll's? . . . back like a
child on a mother. His feet didn't touch the ground. He
merely dangled like a babe, feeling useless and utterly helpless.

"Who are you?" he said, not bothering to quiet his voice,
not fearing the awakening of Orago, whoever that may be.

Several more stones fell from the ceiling, one pelting
Gavin in the center of his head. He cursed, angered all the
more by his inability to rub the now-sensitive spot.

"Me Dulcee. Shhh, now. Don't want Orago mad."

The creature started walking once more, the tunnel growing more and more alight the farther they traveled. Gavin
could now see his bindings did indeed look to be silk. Why
then could he not break them?

"Who is Orago? Where are you taking me?"

"Orago big brother. Mean brother. We go to Annwyn
now, get far away."

Big brother? Gavin winced. He'd never seen a creature as
large as Dulcee in his life. Who could possibly be bigger?
Did he mean older?

"What is Annwyn? I belong in Scotland. Where are we?"

"Me not warn you again. Hush. Scotland up. We down.
Annwyn down. Me take you to Annwyn."

Gavin glanced around, looking for some manner of escape, but found none. First peches. Now Dulcee—whatever
he was. What the devil was going on? It was as though he
was stuck in a dream he couldn't escape, a dream he wanted
to wake from *now*.

Clearing his throat, he fought for calm, fought the frustration that caused his vision to blur. "And . . . what do you
plan to do with me in Annwyn?"

Did he really wish to know?

"Give time to run."

"From Orga?"

"Orago. From Orago and queine."

"Queen?" Gavin shut his eyes, overwhelmed with questions. However, this thing toting him around like a grain
sack was not very forthcoming with answers. Nay, he only
added to the confusion clouding Gavin's mind. "Put me
down."

"You too slow. Dulcee carry you."

A rush of anger at his helpless position soared through Gavin. His skin tingled. His fingers trembled beneath the binding web. "Destroy these bonds and put me down!"

In an instant, he was lying on the dirt path, his mouth full of grit, his limbs numb from having been bound for so long. Blood trickled from his brow, obscuring his sight, and around him he felt the puddle of the silken threads that had held him prisoner. He felt for his sword, then remembered it had been taken by the peches.

Standing on shaking legs, he stepped away from Dulcee, holding up his hand as if to ward him off. "What are you, Dulcee? Are you friend to the peches?"

As though just realizing his prisoner was no longer strapped to his back, Dulcee spun around and frowned. "You sneaky prince. You die soon if not hurry."

"Die? By whose hand? Yours?"

Dulcee shook his head, his eyes focused on his large, hairy feet. His skin looked yellow, and when Gavin wiped the blood from his eyes, he could see fine, dark hair protruding from Dulcee's head and ears—ears as long as his enormous head.

"Everybody thinks Dulcee bad. Orago bad. Me good. Take you to Arrane, to keep you safe. Me eat peches who would take you to Orago. They tried shoot your heart. Dulcee ate them. They no shoot elf bolt."

Ate the peches? Gavin's stomach rolled. "Who is Arrane? And how is he to keep me safe?"

In his whole life, Gavin had never required a protector, though he had relied upon Alec's skill with a sword more times than he could count to save his hide—something he'd thought Alec had done out of brotherly loyalty. Now that he knew Alec had been sent to him on someone else's orders, he wasn't so sure.

Gavin the Immortal.

Gavin the Insane.

He shook his head to clear his thoughts. "Who is Arrane?" he repeated.

The creature's eyes widened. "You not know? Arrane your father."

Sixteen

~

The impact was hard and sudden. Nakkole's head knocked against the surprisingly hard knee of the small house faery, then jarred to the left to bounce lightly off the thin bubble lining. The sphere bounded off the ground, spun, then landed once more, throwing Beanie onto Nakkole's prone body, pounding the last little bit of air from her lungs.

"Hold on, me dear. We're low enough now to leave the bubble," Beanie said, her breath hot against Nakkole's cheek.

A loud popping noise burst near Nakkole's ear, and suddenly Beanie's small body was its normal size, sprawled atop Nakkole's average frame. The added weight gave loose a *whoosh* of air from Nakkole, but she sagged with relief as Beanie rolled off of her. Around her, the golden fog was gone, replaced by an abundance of greenery.

Wasting no time, Nakkole pulled herself to her feet, struggling to ignore the spinning earth and her bruised body. She could feel a nearby source of water beckoning her, and she almost cried with relief.

"How long before you can repair this bubble?" she asked Beanie, who was still struggling to stand. Nakkole offered a hand, and Beanie clasped it, pulling herself up and shaking her head as if to clear it.

"I've had this bubble for more than two summers. Took me three days to weave me magic into it. Now look what they've gone and done. Ruined it, they did. King Arrane will be sorely mad."

"I am sorry, Beanie, but I cannot sit here and wait for it to be repaired when our prince is in trouble. Work as quickly as you can, then come for me in the Otherworld. Perhaps by then, I will have been successful in finding Gavin and you may carry us both back to Arrane."

"But—"

Nakkole gave her no time to argue. "Here, take this in case trouble finds you."

She thrust the arrow she'd plucked from the bubble into Beanie's hands, then turned and followed the beckoning water until she found a very narrow stream rippling between two large stones. It would hardly cover her whole body, but it was better than naught.

She sank into the icy stream, her body exhilarated over its familiar caress as her White Lady garb fell away. These waters led to a shimmering lake in Annwyn below these grounds. There should be a portal close by, but since none led directly to sweet Annwyn, she'd still have to begin her journey in Elfame. If luck was granted her, she'd find a gate near the borders of the two Otherworlds, and would not be forced to spend too much time in the dark caverns of the horrid Elfame.

Shuddering at the thought, she lay her head back in the water and let it wash away the last remnants of Arrane's sleeping enchantment.

Feeling more like her self and more certain now of her duties to her prince than ever before, she hurried from the water and waited only a moment for her clothing to reappear before she went in search of her path. She found it near a cluster of bluebells, then ran through a copse of evergreens and down a path lined on either side with small pebbles, her body already dried by the time she found what she'd been hunting.

The perfect ring of toadstools. From the ring's center, a white vapor danced and played, calling her home at last.

Before she could take a step toward her passage into the Otherworld, a loud whizzing flitted past her ear. She followed its path with her gaze, watching as a small golden arrow—the same sort that had burst Beanie's sphere—lodged itself in an oak just in front of her.

She dashed behind the tree, carefully looking about for her attackers. With one hand, she felt for the arrow and pulled until it was free. She could still make it to the portal before midnight, but then, so could her pursuers. Her visibility would be much better here than in the dark tunnels of Elfame.

Bending slightly, careful to keep cover behind the oak, she beckoned the droplets of water clinging to the grass at her feet, no doubt left there by the vapor emitted from the faery ring. The small bits of water danced into her hand, and she made haste to turn them into a shielding fog. Let them try to find her now.

"I smell her," a small, cackling voice said from somewhere in the thick of the trees in front of her. "She didn't enter the portal. I watched. She's here somewhere."

A tiny, infant-sized being leaped down from the tree just a bit away. Its body was covered from head to toe in downy red hair, its yellow, gaping teeth glowing bright in the forest's shadows.

The maras.

"Get her! She'll try to save her prince!"

One of the maras lifted its bow in her general direction. Her means of protection was as clear to her as her way home. She had no way of knowing how many maras surrounded her now, but if she could just get her hands on that bow . . .

The single mara walked closer to her, and Nakkole held her breath. One more step. One more.

When the creature was within reach, she palmed the arrow she'd retrieved from the oak trunk, and plunged it into the mara's eye. It let out a screech so loud, so eerie, it nearly made her forget what she must do. She stood frozen by the sight of the ooze seeping from his pierced eye, yellow and thick. Somehow, she pushed past the horrible sound, knowing she had only a moment before this mara's companions would come racing to finish her off.

She seized the faery bow from the mara's open hand. Its body fell to the ground. The magic bow quickly adjusted itself to its user's size, and she slung it over her shoulder. She bent to scoop up the quiver of arrows and raced around the oak. As she shook off her fog cloak, four more maras rushed down the pathway toward her. Sucking in as much air as she could hold, she pictured Gavin's face, mustered up her courage, and leaped into the center of the mushrooms into darkness.

The Palace of Arran

King Arrane was inspired by his quick visit with Nakkole. His body drained and tired beyond imagining, he still managed to smile as he sat upon his throne, his attendant, Balaster, standing near with a fresh pitcher of water. The Bean-Tighe Arrane had sent to Grey Loch would be the quickest transport to bring Nakkole to his isle, and there were other house faeries just as handy.

"Balaster," he said, lifting his goblet for the young, handsome elf to refill. "Call forth the sister of the Bean-Tighe, Beanie. Summon her here. I wish to speak with her straight away."

Balaster topped off Arrane's goblet and nodded, swept into a low bow, then hurried from the chamber where he would send word amongst the pixies that Arrane had requested such a meeting. The Bean-Tighe's sister would be here shortly.

Arrane closed his eyes and waited, reliving the gifts given to him this day. Nakkole . . . what a surprise he'd found when he'd held her in his arms. But the true gift had come in the form of a request—a request he'd waited more than thirty years to grant.

Geraldine, his queine, wished to return to him.

Until she asked it of him, he'd vowed not to bring her here. Now . . . she was coming home. He would send the

Bean-Tighe's sister to gather his queine, and in a few short days, his palace would be full of love and life once again.

That he would likely die shortly after he found Geraldine again was of no consequence. A man who died happy was the man to be envied.

King Arrane would be envied by all.

＊

The name Arrane had rung familiar to Gavin, though he didn't know why. He stared at Dulcee for a long moment, disgusted and awed by the sight of the large creature. The cave was not as dark as it had been for the cursed amount of time he'd been kept here, but the eerie shadows still played ominously across Dulcee's features. Did he even have a nose? Gavin couldn't tell.

He shook his head, desperate to create a single coherent thought. *Arrane your father.*

Then, as quickly as it had formed, the knot in his stomach eased and relief washed through him. Dulcee had mistaken him for someone else. It was the only explanation.

"I am not the man you seek, Dulcee. I am Laird Gavin McCain of Grey Loch. I don't ken anyone named Arrane. Now, if you'll just allow me to pass, I'll leave you to find the poor soul you truly seek."

Dulcee's laughter was abrupt, so loud it throbbed in Gavin's ears. Then, the giant beast covered his mouth with a hand as large as Gavin's full head, his eyes wide as he glanced quickly around the cave.

"You make me loud. We go now."

Before Gavin could prepare himself, Dulcee plucked him from the ground and slung him over his shoulder. Though the beast's stride was not hurried, the breadth of his sizable steps made Gavin's head spin, feeling as though he flew threw the air at an unstoppable speed.

"Put . . . me . . . down!" Gavin said, his breath coming in gasps as Dulcee's shoulder jabbed him in the stomach with each step.

"You cause much trouble. Me try save you, you get Dulcee caught."

Gavin lashed out with his feet. He may as well have been striking at a stone wall. He opened his mouth to further protest, but he inhaled the most obnoxious odor he'd ever experienced in his life and choked.

The coughing was intense, made worse by the pressure of Dulcee's shoulder in his stomach. Dulcee must have sensed Gavin's distress, for he stopped his brisk stride and pulled Gavin from his shoulder by the back of his plaid, then set him unsteadily on his feet.

"What is that . . . smell?" Gavin said, when he finally managed to find his breath.

"Dwarf filth. We come to dwarf mines. Annwyn is on other side."

Dwarves? Peches, Dulcee. Gavin thought he might scream for the confusion within him.

"I don't believe in dwarves. I don't believe in peches. Hell, I don't even ken what the hell you are, Dulcee, but I do not believe in you, either! What is happening?"

Gavin's knees shook with nervousness for the first time in his life. This had to be some horrid dream. Surely this could not be real. Soon, he would open his eyes and find himself still lying in bed with Nakkole, swimming in the aftermath of their night of lovemaking.

"Ogre. Me ogre." Dulcee held out his hands, as though ready to snatch Gavin up again if he chose to run at that bit of information. "Good ogre. Me likes Arrane. No likes Elph Queine."

Ogres . . . Gavin's head swam. He was forced to bend over his knees to find any breathable air away from the foul stench.

"Elf queen?"

Dulcee nodded. "Your sister . . . one White Lady supposed to save you from."

"What is a White Lady?" he asked instead. But before Dulcee could answer, Gavin found his mind already knew. "White Ladies are the guardian fae of the Norman waters," he mumbled, baffled at how he knew such. "They cloak themselves with fog and seduce travelers in order to find their true nature."

Just as Nakkole had seduced *him*. Nakkole was a White Lady.

Heaven help him. Nakkole's face flashed through his mind, her tangled, gold-red curls spread over his bed, her naked body writhing above him as they came together so perfectly. He thought of their odd meeting, their spectacular kiss on Beltane. The forest and that haunting butterfly who had come back to life simply because Gavin had willed it so.

It was all . . . true. The whole horrid tale of his mother marrying a fae king. Dear God, help him.

"You remembering now. Believing. It's good." Dulcee returned to his full height and patted Gavin's shoulder. The gesture sent a shooting pain through his wound and made him crumple to the ground. "Sorry. Forgot elf bolt hole."

Gavin remained on the ground, unable to move.

Nakkole had betrayed him. Lied to him. Nay. She'd told him the truth, and he hadn't believed her. He couldn't be angry with her for that.

But he could damn well hate her for manipulating him by using his desire for her to win his trust.

A White Lady who sought out the true nature of others. Well, now he knew *her* true nature and he didn't like it at all. He thought back to the magical night he'd spent in her arms and distinctly remembered the barrier of her maidenhead. Had that too been trickery? His chest tightened painfully. Mixed emotions played havoc with his heart. Guilt over calling her liar and anger at having been used. Both unsettled him.

And Alec. What was Gavin to make of his friend's part in all of this?

Unsure what else to do or say, Gavin looked up at Dulcee. "How do you know I mated with a White Lady?"

"Dulcee smell White Lady on you. You stink of her," Dulcee said. "Come. Orago no sleep much longer. We safer in mines, safest in Annwyn. We rest in Annwyn and Dulcee answer more questions."

Gavin didn't want to move from his prone position on the ground. Let him lie here and rot, for this was either an unescapable dream or the largest truth he didn't wish to know.

akkole moved through the dark caves of Elfame, noting the small bones that littered the ground along the way. Blood trailed down the pathway, and she wished the faint light coming from the other end would simply fade completely. She had no wish to see where she was going if this was what was to greet her. She had never traveled through Elfame, but she'd grown up on stories of the horrid place and was not at all happy to be here now.

Her throat ached to call out Gavin's name, but doing such would lead only to disaster. She had no way of knowing what other sort of creatures awaited her in the cave, nor did she have any knowledge of how far Gavin may have traveled during the time of their separation. She could tell, however, by the vines covering the cave walls, that she was closer to the entrance of Annwyn than that of Elfame. For that, at least, she was grateful.

She heard what sounded like heavy breathing. Was it hers? Nay. Nakkole pressed a hand to her heart and continued on, her steps silent as she listened intently about her.

Crunch.

Well, there was no mistaking that noise, and it hadn't come from her. The hairs on the back of her neck stood at attention and those along her arms prickled with unease. Slowly, never pausing in her steps, she reached for the faery bow strapped to her shoulder and pulled an arrow from the quiver. Even as her fingers slid the arrow from the leather bag, she felt a new one appear in its place.

She would not stop until she heard another noise, and her body was tense with listening. Was that a swallow she heard? Her own heart beat so loudly, she could not detect anything other than the steady *boom-boom* that pounded in her chest and ears.

The flame burning on the wall ahead danced and cast shadows along the darkness. She followed it, her grip so taut, she nearly snapped her arrow in two.

In front of her, she heard the faint sound of whispering.

As she rounded the corner near the flame, a large shadow paired with a smaller took an eerie presence against the far wall. Readjusting her bow, she centered the arrow inside it, pulling tight on the cord that would send the arrow flying at her command. She slowed her steps, but did not stop, aiming the arrow at the larger shadow, her hand aching to release the arrow the moment the shadow revealed its owner.

Behind her, another sound divided Nakkole's attention. She swung around, let loose the arrow in the direction of the crunch, then shoved herself up against the wall as a howl so loud she thought her ears might bleed filled the echoing tunnel.

Casting a fevered glance at the shadows along the way, she panicked when she saw they were no longer there. Certainly, they would only be larger had they come to investigate the howl. Perhaps they had fled?

Swallowing back her fear and steering her trembling legs, she investigated her kill. She took only two steps backward when she nearly tripped over a prone body. The trembling worsened when she realized how very close her stalker had been. Pulling out another arrow, she pointed it toward her feet, unsure whether the blow had been fatal. Keeping careful aim, she ran her bare foot along the body. She recoiled at the feel of downy hair that covered the creature from head to toe.

She couldn't be certain, but it felt like mara skin—slick with fine hair—which would be very likely had one of the buggers followed her in through the faery ring.

The need to cry nearly got the better of her. Even if she pushed on toward Annwyn now, she had no way of knowing whether Gavin was there. How was she to know he wasn't being held in an ogre prison, or lying unconscious somewhere behind her? Worse, she had no way of knowing if he was even still alive.

At the moment, she felt nothing but pure, hopeless dread.

❧

See? You no listen to me, we get caught." Dulcee glared at Gavin, pushing him along the tunnel, away from the strange howl that had nearly shaken Gavin's bones right out of his body.

It had taken all of Gavin's strength to pull himself off the ground and follow Dulcee away from the noise. He had no strength left, and no fear, either. His entire life had been a lie, from his birth to his infatuation with Nakkole. Where was the sorrow in losing a life that had not truly existed anyway?

His hand itched for his sword, and knowing he would not find it at his side angered him all the more. He longed to drive his blade through the belly of the next to cross his path, ached to feel the solid crunch of bone beneath his fist. He wanted destruction, and blood, and a fight to the death.

"You move slow," Dulcee said, stooping and reaching for Gavin. "Me carry."

"Touch me," Gavin replied through clenched teeth, "and I shall tear your hand from your body."

Dulcee pulled back, staring with wide eyes at his hands. "You no like Dulcee. No one like Dulcee. Dulcee dumb. Dulcee ugly. Thought Arrane son different."

Gavin had no room for remorse in his heart, for anger and frustration filled it to capacity. "Just take me from here. Take me to this Arrane you speak of, and you'll be free to part with my cruel company."

With narrowed eyes, Dulcee glared at him. "You wrong. I free to leave you now. Find own way, Arrane son. I go now. You die, not Dulcee fault."

Gavin opened his mouth to protest, but Dulcee was gone before he could say a word. For such a large beast, the ogre moved with alarming speed. Gavin watched Dulcee's shadow disappear around the corner from which they'd come.

Suddenly, being alone didn't seem so wonderful. Dread and panic at being in an unknown place, unarmed and a bit dazed, he regretted his harsh words to the ogre.

"You miss me?" Dulcee's voice said from behind Gavin.

Gavin looked up and saw Dulcee's big head staring down at him. He couldn't tell if the ogre was grinning or frowning, but he could see Dulcee's outstretched hand offering Gavin assistance to his feet. He accepted.

"You not nice, but I not leave Arrane son die here. Come. Dwarf mine through there." Dulcee pointed with one hand toward a hole at the bottom of the cave wall, barely big enough for Gavin to fit through, and pulled Gavin to his feet with the other.

"I'm sorry, Dulcee. I don't know you, but I know you don't deserve to be treated poorly by a man you've done naught to but try to help."

Dulcee did smile then, showing the largest, roundest teeth Gavin had ever seen. "Maybe you not so mean." Then, he laughed quietly and shook his head. "Tear my hand from body. No sword, no axe. You brave, stupid man."

It was hard to contradict that simple truth.

"I might be stupid, Dulcee, but I can't see you being too wise, either, if you expect to fit in that hole. My shoulders will barely pass through there. How do you expect to do it?"

The ogre smiled and his expression softened, his yellowish face alight in the glow of the fire. "You get me through."

It was Gavin's turn to laugh. "And how am I to do that?"

"You broke web on my back when you wanted free. You do same here."

He thought of the sticky bonds that had strapped him to Dulcee's back when he'd first awakened, about his anger at feeling so helpless, and about falling free of the binds, the web falling to the ground around him. At the time, he hadn't given it much thought. Perhaps his struggle had been enough to weaken the bonds. But he couldn't forget how very firm and strong those binds had been. They wouldn't have simply broken.

"How—I don't understand."

"Not your fault. White Lady supposed to teach you powers, but peches come and take you too soon."

White Lady. Nakkole. Despite his fear that she had used him, he prayed she was still safe at Grey Loch.

"The butterfly. I brought it back to life, didn't I?"

Dulcee looked puzzled and shrugged his shoulders. "Don't know butterfly. You can give life, though, yes. Can't remember . . . create? Destroy? Two more." Dulcee held up one fat finger. "Can't remember others. But you destroy wall, we go through."

"Create and destroy? And you're telling me I have these powers as well as two others?"

"Create, destroy, control, and communication," said a familiar voice from behind them.

Nakkole.

Seventeen

~

He was safe. *Gavin was safe.* Nakkole wanted to run to him, to check him for wounds, to beg forgiveness for blurting out the truth of his life so brutally. Instead, she forced her heart to slow and aimed her bow directly at the ogre's face. Her breathing had calmed since she'd first found Gavin at this fork in Elfame's caverns, but the sight of the beast standing so close to her prince made the arrow in her hand tremble.

"Step back," she commanded the ogre, taking a wary step closer. "Gavin, come to me."

"Lower the bow, Nakkole, 'fore your hurt yourself. Dulcee is my . . . well, he means no harm."

Nakkole dared a glance at Gavin and grimaced when she saw the look of anger cast within the gray depths staring back at her.

She swallowed the knot in her throat and took yet another step toward Gavin and the beast. "Ogres aren't to be trusted, Gavin. They are fickle creatures, at best."

Gavin swallowed, his eyes looking less angry than hurt. "You would know much about fickle creatures, wouldn't you? You, who entered my home under the shelter of a lie, laid in my arms, and pretended to want me in order to gain my trust?"

Seeing that Gavin had no intention of stepping away from the ogre, she slowly lowered the bow to her side. Angst over having been the one to hurt him so badly ripped through her heart and weakened her knees.

She reached out a hand, needing to touch him, to soothe him. "I never pretended," she whispered. "My attraction to you was never a lie."

He turned his head away from her hand, his stony glare told her any touch of hers was no longer welcome.

"You lied to me about who you were . . . *what* you were."

"I tried to tell you! You wouldn't believe me."

"*After* you crept into my bed."

Her heart heavy, she lifted her chin a tad higher. "What would you have had me do? Knock on your door, announce my fae heritage, and tell you of yours? Should I have told you that your sister had her sights set on killing you, or that your father is a fae king?"

He stood blissfully silent for a long moment. She no longer wanted to be the one telling the truths. She wanted to be the one he turned to for comfort, not the one on whom he cast the blame.

His blank stare quickly refocused on her, his mouth contorted into a furious twist. "There were several opportunities for you to give me the truths I deserved! The butterfly. You could have told me then, when you saw me struggling to understand what had happened." He hesitated, then slowly shook his head. "The dry cow. I created its milk, didn't I? What else? What else don't I know of?"

Nakkole closed her eyes, knowing they would be better off continuing on their way, but understanding that Gavin wouldn't agree to follow her anywhere until he had some of the answers he sought.

She hated the confusion she saw in his eyes, the self-doubt.

Chuckling, Gavin clutched his head. "The fae my mother claimed to see recently weren't really part of her sickness, were they?"

His eyes and motions were those of a man on the brink of

either an awful fit of temper or a bout of madness. The flames on the wall reflected eerily in Gavin's eyes, giving him the look of a devil, a demon.

"They were sent from Arrane. He loves her greatly, Gavin. He has never left her unguarded."

"Loved her? Oh, and a fine love it is when you abandon your lover and your child and go about your merry way. What a fine, outstanding man my father is!"

"*Oui*. He is. He wasn't only your mother's lover. He was her husband, and he loved her dearly. He didn't abandon Geraldine. She abandoned him."

"He getting mad," the ogre said. "You put anger at wall, not at White Lady. We can go to mines."

"He's right, Gavin. I know you are all but overflowing with questions, and I promise to answer all I know. But, for now, we must be on our way. Elfame is not safe for those of good magic. Let us get to the dwarf mines, and when we are safely in the light, you will have your answers."

Gavin spun, facing Dulcee, and let out a devastating roar. The wall around the tiny hole collapsed, sending rock and debris flying toward them. Dulcee stepped in front of Gavin, swooped him up, then gathered Nakkole in his big arms. He turned his back away from the destruction, shielding them with his big, scarred body.

After a moment, silence filled the cave and Dulcee placed Nakkole and Gavin back on their feet. "We go now. Too loud. Ogaro come looking."

"Ogaro?" Nakkole asked, stepping toward the light coming from the dwarf mines.

"His big, evil brother." Gavin grabbed Nakkole by the arm and turned her to face him. He closed his eyes and exhaled so deeply, his breath brushed her hair from her cheeks. "I'm pleased to see you unharmed, Nakkole, but we're not done. If you plan on evading my questions, you're sorely mistaken."

Nakkole sighed, wishing she could gather the courage to cast her glamour upon Gavin if only just to stop his look of hurt from shooting piercing wounds in her heart. But she would chance no such thing. If Gavin were to survive this journey to the Isle of Arran, he would need all his wits about him to defend himself. She supposed his confession of not wishing her harm would have to do for now.

"I wish to evade nothing. Let us go as far as we can away from Elfame, and when we rest for the night, you will have your answers."

He didn't seem to hear her. He ran his hands along the sharp edges of the newly formed entrance to the dwarf mines. "So, this is my power to destroy?" he asked, more to Dulcee than to Nakkole.

She had a feeling he would do as little speaking to *her* as was possible. The thought saddened her tremendously.

"Destroy, yes. We go a little ways and show you control."

The twosome stepped through the wall and Nakkole hurried to catch them. "He only needs to practice control. I believe he's been using it for years."

Gavin glanced at her from over his shoulder. He didn't deny her words, but his silence hurt all the same. She knew he was dying to ask what she meant, but if it meant speaking to her just now, he would probably choose ignorance over answers.

The farther they traveled into the tunnels of the dwarves, the lighter it became. The dwarves had lit rush at every turn of the path, both on the ceiling and the floor. Cobwebs became a nuisance, but a quick brush of the hand removed them easily enough. Dulcee was forced to walk at an angle, his head bent low to keep from knocking it overhead. She still wasn't sure what to think of the beast. Ogres were notoriously untrustworthy, but not deceitful. One could normally tell their purpose upon first sight. She'd never heard of, nor met, a friendly one, which made Dulcee all the more frightening. Was he smarter than his fellow ogres, realizing it would be easier to harm the prince if Gavin trusted him first?

Dulcee's head banged against a lit rush, sending embers showering over him. "Pretty fire."

Nakkole fought back a smile. He was not worthy of her trepidation. He had the mind of a child, and she had seen as much when he'd looked at her in Elfame. She found herself smiling as Dulcee lifted an ember from his shoulder and tossed it in the air. He watched with an odd grin as the tiny red dot flitted toward the ground.

As they walked in silence, she found herself with little to focus on other than the ache in her head. The crash had left her battered and bruised, and now that things had calmed for the moment, it seemed she hurt all the more. She touched her brow with a single finger, flinching when she felt the bubblelike knot forming there. For such a round woman, Beanie certainly had hard, bony knees.

"You all right, White Lady?" Dulcee asked from over his shoulder. "Me carry you if you tired."

She smiled, hoping she wasn't proven wrong in her assessment of him. After all, Gavin trusted Dulcee. That had to count for something.

He trusted you as well. What a bad bit of judgment that proved to be.

Nakkole pushed back the thoughts and shook her head. "I'm fine, Dulcee. Thank you for wishing to help."

As she made quick, darting glances over her shoulder, her head ached. The mara she had slain in Elfame could soon be followed by many others. Some would be too frightened to enter Sanddine, the dwarf mines, as dwarves frequently made meals of the little night terrors. Others, however would be brave enough to chance any such danger to catch their prince.

Why hadn't those who'd taken Gavin killed him when they'd had him alone and defenseless? The question still baffled her as she followed behind Dulcee. Why pull him into Elfame where his powers would come to him whether he was trained with them or not? Why not kill him by the loch, where it could be done quickly and without fuss?

The only answer she could fathom was that Elphina's army had been instructed to bring the prince to their queine alive. This, of course, was far more frightening to Nakkole than a quick death for Gavin, for it meant Elphina would have the opportunity to use the maras to steal the part of Gavin's soul that was human and turn him into whatever sort of fully fae being she desired. His powers would have then belonged to the dark side.

"I need to rest," Gavin whispered, his breathy tone giving Nakkole new cause to worry.

One glance at him told Nakkole something wasn't right.

His face was pale and he was perspiring, his eyes blinking rapidly.

"Dulcee, we need to stop," she said, wrapping her arm around Gavin's waist and ignoring his protest as he did so.

Dulcee shook his head. "I carry you both. Can't stop here. Maras come soon. Ogaro come soon."

Dulcee reached for Gavin, but Gavin pushed the big hands away. "You will not carry me. We will stop for a bit and continue on when my mind is clear."

"Gavin—" Nakkole said, but Gavin was already falling, the weight of him dragging her down.

In the next instant, he was flat on his back and she beside him. If not for his shallow breathing, she would have thought him dead.

"Maybe elf bolt made him sick?" Dulcee said, bending to scoop Gavin into his arms.

Elf bolt? "What elf bolt?"

"In shoulder. I find him with blood on shoulder, elf bolt hole. They tried shoot him again, but Dulcee stopped them."

Sweet Avalon. She'd thought he'd been weak from lack of food, sleep, and water. Thought perhaps the shock of his heritage had made him collapse. An elf bolt wound could be fatal to a mortal, and since Gavin was only half fae, all of her other worries were cast aside.

"How far until we reach Annwyn, Dulcee? Can we make it there before morning?"

"If we not sleep."

Gavin's wound needed tending by Abunda before the poison had a chance to seep farther into his blood. They would have to press on without stopping for rest in order to reach the full light of Annwyn and the river there.

If they did not, her entire journey would have been for naught.

For Gavin might very well die before he'd begun to fulfill his destiny.

Eighteen

Gavin remained unconscious throughout most of their remaining journey through the dwarf mines, Sanddine, which, to Nakkole, was both a blessing and a curse. While every moment he remained asleep meant less time to accept the future he was facing, it would allow them to quicken their travels to Annwyn, would allow Gavin to feel less pain, and would also allow Nakkole more time before answering his questions.

She stayed her pace in front of Dulcee and Gavin, preferring to be the one who encountered any trouble first, since she was far less burdened than Dulcee.

They had just begun the last incline of their trek through the caves, and her legs were throbbing in protest. As long as she didn't think too much about it, she could press on.

Ahead of her was a brilliant glow of sunlight, bright and welcoming, casting aside the cavern's shadows and calling her home. She quickened her pace, pausing only long enough to call back to Dulcee. "I'm going to go on ahead, Dulcee. The Annwyn River is just past the first copse of birch trees when you leave Sanddine. I will be there, calling for my mother to come heal Gavin. Hurry and find me there."

Without waiting for his reply, she all but ran toward the light. The sun embraced her like a warm cloak, and she nearly sank to her knees in relief. She was free of the darkness, of the silence, of the filth. The beauty of Annwyn surrounded her now, trees and flowers as far as her eyes could see. Even from the entrance to Sanddine, she could hear the Annwyn River's song, rolling and rippling with the sweetest sounds to her White Lady ears. She would have wept had she not been in such a hurry.

Her legs carried her of their own accord, toward the river and away from Dulcee's huffs and groans. The sooner she could get to the water, the sooner she could call for her mother. To her surprise, however, she had barely placed a toe in the water when Dulcee laid Gavin upon the grassy bank. His long strides had caught up to her quickly.

"Undress him," she said, her own gown already disappearing as the water sweetly kissed each inch of it. "He cannot be healed with so much clothing."

She slipped under the water and allowed it to run its fingers through her hair. When she next rose, she spread her arms in front of her and began the call to her mother.

Nothing happened. No ripples, no swirling leaves. Abunda would not refuse her call willingly. A lump formed in Nakkole's stomach, worry crept into her throat and burned her eyes. "Mother?"

Still nothing.

"Bring him to me," she said, finally turning to look at Dulcee. He had Gavin's naked body in his arms. "Put him in my arms and leave us for a bit, please, Dulcee. I need no distractions."

And truthfully, she wanted this moment to be shared in the privacy of only her and Gavin. Perhaps Dulcee's presence was what kept Abunda away. Her mother had a great sense of knowing when it was safe to reveal herself and when it was not. Perhaps she saw Dulcee as a threat, and why wouldn't she, when Nakkole had believed such before she had come to like him so well?

"Where me go?" Dulcee asked, stepping into the water.

He set Gavin carefully in Nakkole's arms, and with the water's aid, she held him easily, as though he were naught more than a large child. She cradled him against her chest, relishing the feel of his naked flesh against hers, recalling the memory of their lovemaking.

"Cross the river. Do you see that patch of clearing on the other side?" She nodded in the direction of the opposite bank. "It would be a great help if you would set up a place for our rest, maybe build a spot for fire. I will create flame when I come to you."

Looking rather pleased, Dulcee nodded. "I catch fish! I good fisher."

"Splendid. You catch fish. When Gavin and I come, I will create the fire and we'll eat the wonderful meal you give."

Dulcee wasted no more time. He walked across the river, his head remaining above the surface even in the deepest part. The moment he was gone, Nakkole stared down at Gavin's sleeping face, and she felt as though her very bones were melting. There was no anger, no disdain aimed at her just now, just blissful peace, and she truly wished she could say with confidence that one day, he would look at her thus while awake.

"Mother of water, mother of my flesh. Show yourself, our prince refresh. Elvish poison taints his blood, send to him a healing flood."

Still, her mother did not appear. Nakkole's hopes that it had been Dulcee's presence keeping Abunda away slowly died. "Please, Mother?" she whispered, leaving the formal calling behind in favor of a daughter's honest plea for help. "I've never needed you more. Please, come to me. Gavin could die!"

Slowly, a tiny whirlpool swayed before her. It grew bigger, swirling with foam, fallen leaves, and bits of debris. Gasping, Nakkole watched as all of the river she could see began to churn. Abunda had never used so much force to show herself. Unease trickled through Nakkole, and she inched her way toward the bank, afraid, for the first time in her life, of what might be in this water.

Her bottom hit the sandy shallows, and Gavin moaned in her arms. She could go no farther without dropping him. She could not get him safely from the water on her own. Casting a longing glance at Dulcee's big form across the river, she longed to shout to him for help, but knew that he would attempt it and the strong current would wash even him away.

Gavin's bare thighs rubbed hers as he lay cradled on her lap. He moaned and snuggled against her breast.

Swallowing her fear, she glared at the snakelike ripple making its way toward her. "Show yourself!" she demanded.

The ripple stopped, as though confused. From her distant spot in the river shallows, she could see the ripple's faint, white outline, and her breath caught. Relief, warm and worthy of tears, overwhelmed her.

"Your Majesty! Please! I did not know it was you. Your son, he needs you."

The white form moved, reshaping itself, and Nakkole could now see what she knew was Arrane's beard, floating on the surface. A moment later, a very real man stood before her, naked to the waist, his long white hair flowing around him, making him look more like Poseidon than the king of good fae.

"Bring him to me," Arrane's image said.

For a long moment, Nakkole could not move. During her experiences with Arrane, she had come to know he could materialize a part of himself, such as he had with his beard at Grey Loch when he'd held on to Nakkole. But she hadn't known he had the power to truly form his whole self like this. It was awe inspiring, especially when she knew his spirit still swam in the lakes of Arran, ill and pitifully frail.

"Bring me my son, Nakkole. Tell me what has caused this."

Arrane held out his arms, his gaze never leaving his son's face. She had seen Arrane angry and she had seen him pleased, but she had never seen him so devastated, so uncertain. It terrified her. For if King Arrane was frightened for his son, it could only mean that Gavin had been wounded far worse than she'd thought.

She wanted to remind him that this was not her fault, that she had been removed from guarding Gavin by Arrane's own command. But she wisely held her tongue.

"The ogre said it was an elf bolt, but I'm not positive

since I was not there. When I found him, the wound had already been inflicted," she said, walking slowly toward her king.

Gavin's wet hair caressed her shoulder. Handing him to his father left her feeling empty and oddly bereft.

Arrane lowered his torso beneath the stream, pressing Gavin's head to his shoulder. Nakkole watched the king's eyes well up, watched his deep intake of breath. Her heart stilled its beat as she watched the scene unfold before her. This was the first time Arrane had held his son in more than three decades.

"Leave us," Arrane whispered, finally prying his gaze away from Gavin's face. "You and I will speak of your disobedience when I'm through."

Disobedience? Did he not know that she and Beanie had been attacked on their way to the Isle of Arran?

She said nothing in her defense and turned back toward the grassy bank. As she stepped from the water and lowered herself to sit on the cool grass, her gown slowly crept back onto her body, offering her a bit of a shield from the biting breeze.

Arrane closed his eyes, tilted his head back, and released his tight hold on Gavin, holding him at arm's length. Slowly he revolved three times in the water, Gavin's naked body floating atop the surface. Arrane lowered his head and pressed his mouth to the gaping wound in Gavin's shoulder. The action brought Nakkole to her knees in panic. No. He was not—

Nakkole watched in horror as a tiny, black hole formed on Arrane's shoulder. It spread, turned the size of an apple, and looked as though it was days old. Her gaze drifted to Gavin and she watched his wound slowly disappear. His head turned, his eyes opened.

And for the first time since childhood, he stared into the face of the father who had just sacrificed a piece of his soul in exchange for Gavin's life.

Nineteen

❦

The Desolate Caves of the Otherworld

Gavin had escaped.

Elphina's private chamber was silent to all but the sound of her deep, heavy panting. She pressed her brow to the cold, clay wall, determined not to give in to the panic threatening to suffocate her.

When would it stop? These defeats cast against her by her own blood? When would it be *her* turn to be the victor over those who, by all rights, she should belong to?

Her desperation cooked a rage inside her. She would have killed the peches who'd failed to bring Gavin to her if she could afford to do so. But she couldn't risk more losses within her small army, no matter how pathetic they might be.

The worst possible scenario was taking place. Gavin was in the Otherworld, yet not in Elphina's clutches. Arrane's army could, and likely *would*, find him first, and no matter what Elphina boasted to her mother, she knew she didn't stand a chance of defeating her father if Gavin was at his side.

Not without the Master Trinity.

Choking on her anger, she seized Gavin's sword, which now hung on her wall, and hurled it across the room. The weight of the weapon brought her to her knees, and the loud clamor of sword against stony earth struck her deaf for a long, agonizing moment.

Two succubi hand servants rushed through the curtained doorway, the sight of their green flesh inducing Elphina to gag.

"Are you hurt, Majesty?" one of them asked as the other reached down to help her queine to her feet.

Once she was steady on her own two legs, Elphina jerked away from her servant's hold. "Leave me in peace," she muttered, too weary to screech at them as she wanted.

As the succubus who'd assisted her bowed out of the chamber, the other retrieved the sword and hung it on the wall once again. When she continued to stare overlong at the weapon, Elphina's temper began to boil to the surface once again.

"I said leave. Me. In. Peace."

The succubus glanced over her shoulder at Elphina. "Aye, Majesty. But the jewel is cracked. Just there." She pointed to the chipped amber in the center of the hilt. "Thought you should know."

It seemed nothing was to go Elphina's way. Even the Sanddine dwarves wouldn't want the damaged stone, which meant her brother's weapon had now lost its only bit of value.

Elphina moved to rip it from the wall and order its destruction when she saw something thin and yellow protruding from the cracked amber. Curious, she pulled at it until a tiny scroll slipped through the fracture and rolled itself into her palm. Tiny words stared up at her, sending a jolt of excitement through her veins.

"Fetch Lucette," she muttered, stretching the small scroll for a better view.

Krion save her. If this was what she thought it was, then Arrane's throne was as good as hers. Elphina smiled, rejuvenated by her realization.

"Just try to ignore me now, Father. Just try."

The Kingdom of Annwyn

Gavin wasn't quite certain how he knew the man holding him in his arms was his father, but the moment he opened his eyes and stared into the deep gray gaze, he simply knew.

Opening his mouth to say something, anything, to break the horrible silence, Gavin closed his eyes and tried to focus, but no words would come. The bright sunlight penetrated his eyelids, making words all the more difficult to find. When last he'd been awake, he'd been in the depths of those horrid caverns with Dulcee and Nakkole.

Nakkole.

Where was she? He tried to move his head, but the man—his father—had such a strong hold on him that he found it difficult to make even the slightest movement with his neck.

"Where am I?" he finally managed.

"Annwyn. You were badly wounded by an elf bolt. Do you remember?"

The man's deep voice sent vibrations through Gavin's naked body.

How the bloody hell had he lost his clothing? And why was he lying naked in this man's arms? Struggling, Gavin managed to work his way free and raked his feet along the sandy shores of the river, searching for footing.

"I see the questions in your eyes, my son. Speak them, for we have little time for answers."

Gavin licked his lips, his throat dry and in demand of water. Where to begin? He had so very many questions that needed answering, but they all seemed too important for mere words.

He would start with the most simple, though he was certain he already knew the answer. "Who are you?"

The man smiled, but did not laugh. Gavin studied him closely, realizing that he was truly only a watery image. His tall body was visible beneath the surface, but transparent as though a ghostly vessel. His torso, standing high above the water, however, looked very much real, and having just pulled himself from those large arms, Gavin knew they were as real as he.

"I am King Arrane, ruler of light fae from Normandy to Scotland and beyond. I am husband to Lady Geraldine of Grey Loch, and father to you, the McCain. But I can tell this news does not surprise you. You knew the presence of your father when you first felt yourself in my arms."

Gavin watched the king's long, white beard curl its tip and push away a few stray leaves that had ventured too close.

"My father," Gavin said, the haze clouding his mind slowly fading. "It was Laird Bruce McCain who raised me. Lady Geraldine knew only one husband, and he was the McCain, not a creature such as you. Perhaps you planted your seed in my mother, but such a simple act does not make one a father."

Arrane's gaze swung away, but not so quickly that Gavin missed seeing the sheen of moisture that welled in his gray eyes. "You are right. And it is sorry I have been for all these years that my duty as your father was sacrificed. But because you do not know my presence does not mean that I am not there, Gavin the Immortal. I know your life as well as you do."

A sob called Gavin's attention, and turning he spotted Nakkole perched on the riverbank, her arms wrapped around her knees as she watched him with his father. He turned back to Arrane, his hands balled in fists, anger eating away the childlike curiosity that had been his first response to finding his true father.

"I've yet to be told why I was brought here. All this time you have not cared to show yourself to me. You allowed me to be ignored by my fath—by Bruce McCain and a mother too ill to know I existed, my only companion that of another lost child called Alec whom I discover was your servant all these years. Now, you show yourself. I'll know the reason."

Arrane shook his head. "I came to you several times. You and I spent mornings together away from the keep you called home."

The memory of the meadow of larkspur and clover, of

trying to learn how to create life, flashed in Gavin's mind. The memory had been real.

Arrane's image offered a faint grin. "And in my absence, I felt your despair in that cursed home the McCain made for you, and sent Alec to you to serve as a companion."

Looking for a distraction, Gavin glanced at his wounded shoulder and found it healed without even the smallest of scars to show for it. Understanding washed over him as easily as the water. "So, you saved my life and now you wish for something in return? This is why you finally show yourself to me. Very well. Tell me why I was stolen by those horrid creatures in the caves, why I should believe your tales of a father's invisible protection."

"Gavin . . ." The voice belonged to Nakkole, and it came from just behind him. He had not heard her enter the water, but little about her surprised him anymore. "Do not be so cruel to him—"

"I did not ask for your interference, Nakkole. Leave us," Arrane commanded, his dark eyes narrowing their gaze over Gavin's shoulder.

"Mind how you speak to her," he heard himself saying.

Arrane's brow lifted and he half smiled.

"He saved you, Gavin. You were dying. Arrane gave you his own mortal half to save your life."

"Leave us!" Arrane shouted the command this time, his long, thick finger pointing at the riverbank. "This is no concern of yours."

"Is this true? You say the mortal half of me was dying, but what of this unnatural side? What would have become of me had you not come to my aid?" Gavin stared intently at Arrane, wishing he could peer straight through the man's steely face to the thoughts in his mind.

Was it him, or had Arrane's image waned? Did the torso now seem a bit transparent?

Gavin hugged himself, awaiting Arrane's answers. He now felt the chill of the water and a glance at his white, softening fingertips told him he'd lingered too long.

"You are a being of two worlds," Arrane started, lowering himself deeper into the water so that only his head protruded from the surface now. "Your mother's and my own. An elf bolt cannot kill the fae prince, but it would have killed the McCain heir."

"Your human self would have been no more," Nakkole offered, clearly unable to stop herself.

"And what will happen to you now?" Gavin asked Arrane, still as unsure about all of this as he had been when he'd met Dulcee hours ago. "Nakkole said you gave me your own in exchange for my life. Your own what? Human self? How can the king of good fae even possess a human self?"

"When you arrive at the Isle of Arran, I will have more thorough answers for you, my son. For now, I can only offer this, for my body will not survive if I do not return to it in Arran soon. Your mother is through and through mortal, but once the faery prince grew in her womb, a bit of his power and fae self seeped into her blood and allowed for a soul kiss."

Gavin shook his head. "A what?"

"A shared kiss between our kind once a child is created, is an exchange of souls, in a way. Your mother offered a bit of herself to me, and I gave a bit of myself to her. It is such that if we are ever parted, we still belong to one another, and while tradition required we spend our lives pining for our loves should separation occur, our shared souls allow us to live despite it. Your mother and I would both be long dead had we not exchanged that rite of love."

A long, heavy silence filled the air and Gavin knew they awaited his reaction. He had none, for he was still struggling to understand it all. Was that what kept his mother alive all this time? Her soul exchange with Arrane? Lord knew, most women did not live long in the weakened state that had consumed Geraldine in these past years. But still . . .

"Isn't it dangerous to give a fae king any sort of mortal spirit? Shouldn't it be easier to kill him?" he asked, his teeth beginning to chatter.

"I would live on, but would lose my bond to your mother."

"Stop loving her, you mean."

"Never!" Arrane seemed to shout the word. Then, in a softer voice, he drifted toward the riverbank. "Come, let us get you dry and dressed while I try and explain a bit better."

Grateful to be getting out of the water, Gavin followed the image of his father, which looked more and more like a mere watery reflection than the vivid man who had stood before him moments ago. He was fading away, and Gavin panicked, wondering if he'd ever see the man again, if he'd ever have all his questions answered.

This was his father.

His father!

So many emotions came with the acknowledgment of such a relationship. Pride at the awesome figure who had sired him, relief that he had a face to go with the memories, anger at the lies and the loneliness he'd been left with all this time.

Gavin climbed the sandy bank, looking for his clothes. He had just reached the grass when he realized he was already fully clothed. Not in the plaid he'd been wearing earlier, but in a pair of black breeches, white, shimmering tunic, and black leather boots that reached his knees. A heavy weight pulled at the upper left of the tunic, and he looked down to find the McCain brooch fastened there. He fingered it briefly, then reached up, feeling his hair, which was dry and tied at his nape with what felt to be a ribbon.

More magic. Would he ever grow used to it?

"You asked if I would stop loving your mother if my mortal side died," Arrane said from the water. Gavin turned to give him his attention, easing himself to sit on the bank, his legs still unsteady. "You must understand that loving your mother is something that will never end for me. Our exchange of souls was permanent and unbreakable. Destroying my mortal side, however, would make the pining for her in our separation fatal."

"Then you are not immortal?"

Arrane chuckled. "Nothing is immortal. I can be murdered as easily—well, not *as* easily I suppose—as any human. But death will not find me on its own."

"Unless," Nakkole added, sitting beside Gavin on the grass, "the death is in the form of pining for the love separated from him."

Arrane nodded. "Everybody has one other soul put here to complete them. Your mother was that for me."

"And you gave me your mortal self to save mine? So you could die, pining after a woman you haven't seen in years?" Gavin asked, his voice thick and heavy. "Why bother? Why not allow me to become fully fae?"

Arrane's mouth opened, but no sound came forth. His image faded away, leaving only slight ripples in its wake.

Bounding to his feet, Gavin nearly dove into the water to grab for the spot in which his father had last been standing, but Nakkole seized his arm and pulled him away from the shore.

"'Tis no use. The magic only lasts a short while. His body has called him home."

The wind around them crackled and roared, no longer a breeze but a fierce, biting entity. Gavin shivered, his teeth chattering uncontrollably. "I'm helpless here. I have not received all of the answers to my questions, and yet I am expected to . . . God in heaven, I still do not know why I was brought here!"

"Alec has saved your life on many occasion, you've said. Your father has just done the same for you. I ask if you will repay that debt as often as you have repaid it with Alec, or will your resentment of your father force you to turn your back?" Nakkole's voice was a whisper, yet stronger than a scream.

Gavin jerked his head toward her and watched her long fiery hair whip around her face in the wind, her gossamer gown blowing behind her, straining the front of the fabric against her body. She looked like an angered goddess, like Diana just before the hunt.

"How can I answer when I do not know what you are asking of me?"

"Your father's mortal self is inside you now, just as his fae self has always been. It was his only weapon against the heartsickness that will claim his life now that he has passed it to you because Geraldine is not with him. His love for your mother will kill him, and he will begin to die slowly."

Dying of love? Gavin caught himself before he laughed outright. "Then you are asking me to fetch my mother and bring her here?"

"Nay. There is no time for it. While he will weaken,

Arrane is too strong to die of the pining straight away, but he will be easy prey for those who intend to kill him."

"But it seems it would solve everything to simply bring my mother to Arrane. Then he would be a strong king again—"

"Nay," Nakkole interrupted. "The part of Geraldine that lived inside Arrane now lives inside of you. Geraldine would have to part with another bit of her soul in order renew the king to the strength he once possessed."

"If she loved him, why shouldn't she wish to?"

Nakkole nodded slightly. "She could, but the result would be far more life-altering than the first soul kiss. She would never be able to leave our world again—would be more fae than human."

Gavin didn't think that sounded like too much of a sacrifice to save the man Geraldine supposedly loved so deeply once. But rather than voice that opinion, he said instead, "Still, bringing Geraldine here would at least give her a chance to live again."

That there had been such an easy solution that might have given him the mother he'd always wanted fired a new anger in his belly. Damn her wants. What about *his* wants?

"If her body survived the journey, aye. But Arrane would never go against Geraldine's wishes and bring her here against her will. Until she wishes to return, he will not force her."

Gavin frowned. Not force her? Hell, he wouldn't give a damn about his wife's wishes if he could save her life by disobeying them. Nor did he care about his *mother's* wishes. The first thing he planned to do when he could escape this world was snatch his mother up and bring her here. She would live if he could manage it. He could finally have . . . a mother.

With a sigh of frustration, he wiped his hands over his face.

"He's the king of fae. Surely he has an army unlike any other. Why should he need me?"

"He has no one to lead them now, Gavin. Arrane's throne has been threatened, and he knew it would be you who saved his kingdom. It is why I was sent to you, to begin training your powers and to protect you from those who would see you dead before your father could send for you."

A soft humming distracted Gavin momentarily. He glanced across the river and saw Dulcee spearing a fish with a long, sharpened stick. He pulled the stick from the water and laughed gleefully at the fish flopping on its end.

"I am certain you are curious to know why your sister is trying to murder your father?" Nakkole asked, stepping in front of him, blocking his view of the jovial ogre.

"Nay," he lied. "But I *am* certain you will tell me."

"Elphina, your sister, is after your father's throne because she is his firstborn and believes she's entitled to it. Because she's half succubus, King Arrane cannot allow her into his kingdom. The only way to get what she wants is by force."

"A force more powerful than the king's?" he scoffed.

"If she succeeds at finding the Master Trinity, yes."

He studied her, far more curious than he would ever admit. "The what?"

She sighed, rubbing her hands over her face, obviously as tired as he was. "The Master Trinity. Long ago, there was a power conductor of magic called the Sphere of Life, and a dark king had harnessed its power to fuel his own evil ways. To destroy that power, your father used his own magic to shatter the sphere, separating each power contained within it so that one sphere became three Orbs of great power. The Master Trinity. The enchantment cast them into hiding, where no one, not even King Arrane, knew where they fell. We've found one, the Orb of Truth, but the other two are still out there somewhere. We can only pray we find them before Elphina can."

"And if she does?"

"Then she can raise the dark king from his grave—creating a foe just as powerful and far more angry than your father."

He stared at her, at her mouth, which had spoken lies since the day of their meeting, at her dress woven of magic. He reached out and stroked her bottom lip with his thumb. "You have caused me many problems, Nakkole. Until you appeared, my biggest quandary was trying to learn to be laird. Now, I must learn of things I do not believe in, must learn to be a prince, must forget all my mother taught me about the nonexistence of magic. Now I am to bend and do your favors, without asking aught in return? How grand of a man you must think me to be!"

"I do," Nakkole whispered, her cheek pressing against his palm, but her gaze drifted toward her bare feet. "I do think you the grandest of men, Gavin. That is truth. And I also believe you'll choose to fight your sister because of all she's taken from you."

He stared at her for a long moment. "You mean my mother? I should do this because Elphina's responsible for my mother's illness?"

Nakkole nodded. "And because she kept you from a father who would have raised you. She's responsible for Alec's injury, your injury. Even your man Rufous died because of Elphina's eagerness to get to you."

Gavin's head jerked, the bubble of anger in his belly exploding with a sudden rush of venom. The pain of Rufous's death reopening to bleed inside him all over again. "Rufous?"

"Oui," she said, softly. "He died as he slept because he was mistaken for you." She winced. So did Gavin. "The maras were after his . . . your . . . soul."

He closed his eyes, swallowing the bile that crept up his throat. Rufous was dead because of him. Killed by Gavin's sister.

Even if he had no desire to help his father secure his kingdom, he would kill Elphina for stealing Rufous's life.

She was as good as dead.

Nakkole watched Gavin's jaw clench, saw the pain that had come to him with thoughts of Rufous. Her heart hurt for him, but there was naught she could do to bring back his friend. She pressed her palms to his chest and stretched to the tips of her toes, pressing a soft kiss to his lips.

"There are many in our world who have lost loved ones, just as you lost Rufous, and all at the hands of your sister. 'Tis why we need you on our side." He glanced down at her, his eyes shining with anger so cutting, she had to look away.

Her fingers found their way to the chain around his neck, where they nervously played.

"I will fight for my father, will see justice done to my sister," he said.

Nakkole gripped the small pebble dangling from the chain.

"But I'm no prince, Nakkole. I'm a laird . . ."

Pain pierced her chest. Tangible, real pain no words could inflict. Her legs suddenly felt very numb and her fingers felt on fire.

". . . And I'll go back to being a laird when this is all over . . ."

His words faded into nothingness as Nakkole's knees buckled. Her thoughts turned white, foggy, muddled, as she sank to the ground, pulling Gavin with her as she clutched his necklace in her fist. In her mind, she was sitting alone on a grassy bank and in her arms . . . Sweet Avalon, she was holding a babe in her arms—a babe with Gavin's black hair and the mark of fae around its blue eyes.

She wasn't certain how it had happened, but deep in her heart, Nakkole knew without doubt she was being shown a glimpse of her future. As her mind cleared and the rush of blood faded from her ears, she could feel Gavin shaking her, could hear his voice calling out.

This was why Arrane had been desperate to get Nakkole to his isle, why he'd seemed just as concerned for her well-being as for Gavin's.

"Gavin," she whispered, her vision clearing enough to see his blurred face hovering in front of hers. "I . . . I think I'm carrying your child."

Twenty

～

Lady Geraldine McCain awoke slowly, her head and tongue heavy, her eyes blurred. She awoke in such a manner often, but this time, she felt a bit different. More aware, perhaps. Aware enough, anyway, to see that she was not in her bed, not in Grey Loch.

The walls around her glittered with purple specks. The floor beneath her bent and bobbed. Once before she had found herself in such a place—a day when Arrane had arranged for them to travel in a house faery's bubble to the golden shores of Annwyn. They'd feasted on a meal set upon the grassy banks, but it had been the journey that had fascinated Geraldine the most that day.

For a horrid moment, she suspected she was suffering delirium. She couldn't possibly be in such a contraption again. Or could she?

She blinked away a bit of the blur, her gaze settling on the small form of a short woman with purple curls bouncing down her back.

"Who are you?" Geraldine asked, surprised to find her voice worked.

So many times, she'd wished for her voice. Now here it was, as simple as though it had never been absent.

The purple-haired woman turned around and greeted Geraldine with a crooked grin. "You're awake." She curtsied, the knot of curls atop her head drooping to the left. "A pleasure to meet you, Your Majesty. My name is Nina."

Geraldine's head would not clear fully. Though she did feel stronger than she had in years, she could not bring herself to sit upright. "Nina. Where . . . why—"

"Don't tire yourself, Majesty. King Arrane will want you strong and fit when we finally reach 'im."

"Arrane?" At the mention of his name, Geraldine forced her eyes open so wide, they burned.

"Aye. Says you've asked to come home. That's where I'll be takin' you."

Dear God. Geraldine lay back against the cushiony wall of the bubble and struggled not to cry with relief. He'd heard her. He *had* been near Grey Loch. She'd known it in her bones but hadn't allowed herself to raise her hopes too high.

This was why she felt more alert now. She was closer to Arrane. Closer . . .

"My son?"

Nina's face fell. She turned her attention back to directing the bubble, but said, "He's been taken, but don't you worry. The king'll make sure he's brought home as safely as I'm bringing you."

The cool burn of tears trailed down Geraldine's cheeks. Gavin was taken. Ill prepared for what he faced, and it was all her fault. She'd taken him from those who could have explained his destiny, would have taught him how to fight these enemies he didn't know existed.

She rolled onto her side and came face-to-face with a young lad she'd didn't know. "Who—"

Nina sighed. "That be your wee guardian. He put up a struggle when I tried to claim ye. Had to take a candlestick to his head to make him calm. He's still out cold, but I think he should have his wits about him again by the time we arrive. I checked. He's still breathing."

Well, that was something, anyway. The interior of the

bubble was filled with chilled air. Geraldine wrapped her arms around herself to keep from shivering.

"Why did you bring him?"

"Seemed cruel not to. He would have wakened and found you gone. As he was supposed to protect you, he would have been blamed for your disappearance, I'm thinking."

Yet another innocent involved in this fight because of her.

The bubble shifted left. Geraldine mustered the strength to brace herself to keep from rolling into her young protector.

"How long?" she whispered, her throat aching for water.

"Och. I imagine we'll be there in a day or so. Would be sooner, but we've already missed the tween times of the mist gates. We'll have to wait until they open again tomorrow."

Geraldine nodded, opening her eyes again. A day or two. After spending what felt like an eternity away, she was finally going home. She was going to be reunited with Arrane, her son, and her kingdom.

Annwyn

Nakkole stared at Gavin's pale face, her heart in her throat and her stomach in a knot. She wanted to cry, not only because now that she carried Gavin's heir she possessed a fear for her own life that she hadn't experienced before—for her death in this battle would mean her child's death as well—but also for the simple joy of knowing Gavin's seed grew inside her.

"I understand now," she heard herself saying. Gavin remained silent, his jaw open, his eyes glazed. "Why Arrane wanted me to return to the Isle of Arran posthaste. He was worried about another heir's safety. Our child. He saw our child within me when I stepped into the lake and he held me."

"But . . . how . . . What just happened to you? How can you know so soon that you carry my child, Nakkole?" Gavin narrowed his gaze and clutched his hair in his fists. "I feel as though I am going mad."

Her heart ached for the weariness in Gavin's face, his defeated expression. "I'm not certain how I know it's true. I just do," she whispered, cupping his cheek in her hand. "Let me call for Dulcee to carry us across the river. We'll eat and fill our bellies while we try to understand this."

Gavin didn't reply as she shouted across the river for Dulcee to come fetch them. She watched Gavin from the corner of her eye, saw the shock that crept deeper into his mind now that what she'd revealed was finally sinking in. How could she begin to console him when she could not even console herself? Her mind drifted as Dulcee pounded his way across the water toward them. She was going to be a mother—*the* mother to the next heir of Arran.

❧

Dusk settled around the small fire, but it was Annwyn's dusk and therefore night traveled quickly on dusk's tails here. Dulcee had been proud to show Nakkole and Gavin his *trick* of fire, which had truly been naught but flint given to him by his brother, Ogaro. Apparently, Ogaro had let Dulcee believe the flint was magic, and Nakkole wasn't about to correct the sweet ogre.

While she would have preferred berries, the fish roasting over the flames smelled splendid, and her stomach ached from wanting.

Gavin remained silent, not uttering so much as a word of thanks when Dulcee handed him the first bit of fish and drink of water. He barely cast even the slightest glance at Nakkole, but his avoidance of her nearly came as a relief, for every few moments she caught her hand straying toward her belly, still awestruck by what she knew grew there, and she did not want Gavin to see how very pleased she was becoming over their child. She wanted his reaction to the news to be his own. Until then, she would struggle to show no more reaction of her own.

"You like fish?" Dulcee asked, holding out a stick tipped with trout toward her. "No know if White Ladies eat fish."

Smiling, she took the stick gratefully. "We eat most anything so well prepared, Dulcee. Thank you."

Beaming with pride, Dulcee sat on a fallen tree, causing

the ground to shake in response. She watched in shock as the ogre pushed his entire meal into his mouth, holding it by its tiny tail, then pulled it free again, his teeth raking the small bones clean of meat. Dangling the small skeleton over the ground, he waved his fist and threw the bones into the forest.

Nakkole shuddered and plucked free a small piece of the flaky meat and carefully placed it on her tongue.

"You sleep here. Dulcee sleep there." Dulcee pointed in the direction from which they'd come. "I make sure no baddies come from Elfame."

Before she could protest, Dulcee stood from his tree and crossed the river. Swallowing, Nakkole warily glanced at Gavin, wondering if he felt the heaviness of their seclusion as she did. Without Dulcee, she was ever so aware that no one else would bridge this horrible gap that had formed between her and Gavin. No one would fill the vow of silence they seemed to have sworn to one another.

From behind lowered lids, she watched Gavin pick at his food, his head hung low, his shoulders even lower. How was it that one so strong could look so utterly defeated?

Because of you. Because you came into his life and changed everything familiar, everything safe.

But it would have happened anyway. All of it. Elphina would have come for Gavin whether or not Nakkole and Timpani had ever arrived at Grey Loch.

But he wouldn't be feeling so betrayed had you not become so forbiddenly close to him.

That was one bit Nakkole could find no argument with. Gavin's situation was not her fault, but his despair had been helped a great deal by her mistakes.

"Show me your powers."

Gavin's request was so softly spoken, so unexpected, Nakkole nearly dropped her food in surprise. He hadn't moved, hadn't so much as glanced at her.

"You don't wish to talk about the babe?"

He didn't look at her. "I cannot yet. My mind is too full. I need distraction."

Distraction? She could think of nothing else *but* the babe. Swallowing the morsel on her tongue, she took a long swallow of water, then set her meal aside. "I told you once. I do not have your powers. Mine are only those of creation and concealment."

Finally, Gavin looked up from his meal and studied Nakkole. "And yet you were sent to train me? Why? With the danger you knew was coming, why wasn't a more deadly fae sent as my guardian, my instructor?"

At least he no longer refused to believe their stories. This was good, for now he could begin focusing on the challenges that lay ahead rather than what he believed to be real and imagined.

"Why I was chosen, I cannot say, and that is the truth of it. I know only that my interest in humans was thought to be a useful tool. But White Ladies, our queine and Mother, Abunda, mainly, have been Arrane's most loyal servants all these centuries. I do believe he trusts no others as he trusts us."

"Centuries. My God. How old *are* you, Nakkole?"

She smiled, hoping to ease his wariness. "Not much older than you, my lord. In your world, I would be considered far too old for marriage or bearing children, but in my own, I am merely a healthy young lady entering the second phase of her life."

The phase between girl child and woman. The part of her life when swimming naked in her streams wasn't a mere fun outing, but a sensual, decadent bath of the senses. But Gavin was not yet ready to understand the passage of time in her world, would cringe to know his father had been king for well over two hundred years, and if not for his growing weakness without Geraldine, would likely live many more centuries, as well.

As it was, however, Arrane had just given the last of his mortal life, the life Geraldine had gifted him with in their soul exchange, to Gavin in order to preserve the half of Gavin that was not born fae. Doing such had been a painful loss for Arrane, Nakkole knew, for it meant possibly losing the compassion he ruled his kingdom with, the compassion he'd gained only by taking a bit of humanity within himself during that fateful kiss with Geraldine.

"I don't understand," Gavin said. "What good is the

power of creation in a situation such as this? It seems Arrane would have thought it better to send someone with the power of destruction, or some such, as Dulcee said I possess."

"Again, I can only say that I believe trust was Arrane's bigger concern. He knew without doubt he could trust us to do our job, to guide you even though we could not actually show you your powers. There are no others he trusts more."

And look how badly I mucked that up, as well. It was unlikely Arrane would be calling on her services again in the near future—if ever.

"No matter how badly I have erred with you," she continued. "White Ladies are wonderful guardians. We guard our own streams and rivers every day, have often aided lost, worthy travelers. We are brave and strong, and while we are not the most powerful of fae, we know the meaning of loyalty."

Gavin chuckled and shook his head. "Aye. What loyalty you have is amazing. Truth to tell, you came into my home, claimed your loyalty to my mother and to myself, and all the while held secrets so devastating you knew my entire world would be shattered."

Nakkole stood, then sat on the boulder across from him, wishing to look him directly in the eye. "I claimed no real loyalty to you in the beginning, Gavin. My loyalty has always been to my mother and Arrane. Only when Arrane told me I was to return to his isle without you did I realize my loyalty had changed direction along the way."

His steely eyes turned black as they narrowed on her. "Because you carry my child. If your loyalty did in fact change, it was toward your child's father, not toward me as a man."

It was his first real acknowledgment of their child, and it sent a tremor up Nakkole's spine. She was having a babe with this man. This wonderful, strong warrior.

"I did not know of the child when I realized my loyalties had changed," she whispered, leaning toward him from her perch on the boulder. "I knew only of you and the feelings that stirred in me when you looked at me, touched me, kissed me."

She ran her thumb over his bottom lip, parting his mouth to reveal white teeth, then caressed his lips with her own.

Gavin started to pull back, but she grabbed his neck, hoping to show him the truth of her words through action, instead. She kissed him with every ounce of emotion welling in her now. Aggressively, she pushed her tongue into his mouth, teasing his until he complied and gave her the reaction she so needed.

Moaning against her mouth, Gavin dropped his food and seized Nakkole around her waist, dragging her from her boulder onto his lap.

"I hardly think Mother would approve."

The familiar voice brought a startled gasp from Nakkole. She leaped from Gavin's lap, pivoted, and found Alec and Timpani scowling at them from the trees.

"A pity," Gavin said, his breath still as irregular as Nakkole's. "It seems our rescuers have arrived."

Twenty-one

~

Gavin glared at Alec and Timpani, irritated that they'd cost him the intimacy he'd just been gaining with Nakkole.

"Thank Avalon, you're both alive and well!" Timpani said, the disapproval on her voice falling away as relief etched itself on her comely face.

"Where are the others?" Nakkole asked, greeting her sister with a tight embrace.

"What others?" Gavin could feel Alec watching him from Timpani's side, but Gavin refused to meet his gaze. He still wasn't sure how he felt about Alec's part in all of this, and until he'd settled it all in his mind, it was safest not to engage Alec at all. He wished he'd thought more on what he wished to say to the man.

Nakkole looked at him nervously. "I had to enchant a few of your men in order to gain their willingness to help us rescue you." She glanced back at Alec. "Did they remain at Grey Loch?"

"We must have passed you in Elfame or entered through a different faery ring, because we've already been to Arrane's isle." Alec finally turned his attention to Gavin.

"Robert, Markham, and Brock are all there with your father. They are safe."

"Oh," Nakkole said. "We were delayed a good deal by Gavin's wound, but now that he's sound again, we should have no more difficulty."

Gavin took a slow, purposeful step toward Alec, his fingers curling into a fist. "You gave *my* men orders to come to such a place—"

"Nay, Gavin." Nakkole grabbed his arm and pulled him toward her. "It was I who commanded your men. They had no choice but to obey me."

"Let us not fight." Timpani glanced down at him, obviously worried that violence was about to be done. "We'll give you two a moment to gather yourselves, then we'd best be on our way."

Alec turned to follow Timpani without another word.

His silent retreat bothered Gavin all the more. Where were his apologies? His pleas for forgiveness?

"Wait," Gavin called. "Alec . . ."

Alec spun around, his expression soft, but wary. "Aye?"

What was he to say? He could think of nothing. "Never mind."

Alec nodded. "Very well, then."

He turned to follow Timpani, leaving Gavin staring stupidly after them. Needing to say something, anything, he called out once more. "Wake the ogre while you wait. He sleeps by the entrance to the dwarf mine."

He listened as Timpani whispered to Alec while they departed. "He can't mean to bring the ogre with him to Arran. King Arrane will be furious."

Nakkole's soft sigh called Gavin's attention away from his confused thoughts of Alec. Now was not the time to focus on Alec's betrayal. Nakkole carried Gavin's child. He had to get her safely to Arrane. Everything else would have to wait.

❧

Nakkole walked quietly beside Gavin, watching as Timpani and Alec strode in front of them, their pesky arguments great indications of their attraction for one another. He worried over every little thing Timpani did, and she fought his protection each time.

It wouldn't be too long, Nakkole thought with a smile, when she would probably be attending their wedding. It hadn't escaped her notice, however, that Gavin had yet to speak to Alec, let alone watch him with Timpani as she had been doing. She'd seen him glance up occasionally, but his gaze never lingered for more than a brief moment, his stare always narrowed. A tension hung between the two men like a bowstring ready to snap in two.

"All right then. That's control and creation. I think I understand the use of both," Gavin said to Dulcee. "Destruction I used on the wall in Elfame, and I know I focused all of my anger on the stone, causing it to collapse."

Nakkole winced at the mention of his anger. Had his gruff feelings toward her softened even a bit since then? Would it truly matter if they hadn't?

He'd already stated firmly he had no intention of remaining in the Otherworld, and she certainly couldn't live in his world without losing a good deal of the magic that was in her blood and soul. And if Gavin did return to Grey Loch, their kingdom would be in dire straits searching for a new possibility for a future king. King Arrane could not possibly live much longer with Geraldine so far away. What was to become of their kingdom?

She stared at the trail ahead of them, forcing herself not to think such thoughts. It was up to King Arrane to decide what was to happen next.

"What of this communication Nakkole claims I have? What is it and how does it work?"

"It's not something you can use as you do the others, per se," she answered when Dulcee shrugged his overly large shoulders. "It's something that will happen when you need it most."

"But what sort of communication is it?"

Nakkole wasn't certain how to describe what it was he wanted to know. "It's not a power I've ever seen work. I don't think you can fully understand it unless you're doing it. I'm not even certain communication is the correct word, but it is the one that is used." She paused, stepping over a small mud puddle in her path. "Have you ever thought of a person and had that person appear a short while later? Or wondered if a person was all right, only to have them tell you they are, as though you asked them aloud how they fared?"

Gavin glanced at her, taking her arm to pull her around yet another puddle. As they walked farther out of the Annwyn wilderness toward the largest part of the river to the north, the ground beneath them grew soggy and difficult to tread upon.

"I once wanted to ask Alec where his parents were but was afraid to ask him. A moment later, he brought up the topic, himself. Is that what you mean?"

"In a roundabout way, that is right," Timpani said from in front of them. She slowed her steps, leaving Alec to guide them alone. "In a way, your power of communication is a way of prying into someone's mind. While you don't have the ability to read their thoughts, you can silently plea to them to speak them aloud. It's almost as if they'll hear your voice in their head and think it is their own."

Nakkole could see that of all that they'd told him of his abilities, this one intrigued and frightened Gavin the most. He said nothing more and walked on as though his legs carried him with no direction from his mind.

"Think of a question you'd like answered," Timpani said.

Gavin stared at Alec, uncertain how to proceed. He focused on the back of Alec's head. "Just think of a question?" he asked.

"Aye," Nakkole whispered.

He thought of asking for the truth of their friendship, but decided he wanted that matter spoken about with no magic between them. Best to let this experiment be about more simple matters. But what?

He'd seen the brief exchanges shared between Timpani and Alec and wondered what was happening there. Was there a love match between the two?

" 'Tis difficult having such feelings for a White Lady, is it not?" Alec said, finally turning to face Gavin. His eyes widened as though he had spoken without thought, and he cast a furtive glance at Timpani. "Was that your question?" he asked, glaring at Gavin.

That had indeed been his question. What a discomforting magic to wield. No one should have such power over others.

"It was a fleeting question in my own mind," he explained.

Luckily, neither Timpani nor Nakkole had seemed to understand the nature of his silent question at all. They were involved in their own topic of conversation.

"Yet you placed the inquiry in my head, regardless. 'Tis nearly as dangerous a power as destruction." Alec's glare of anger lessened only a bit, but his tone was still heavy with irritation.

Gavin's self-restraint was being sorely tested. What right did Alec have to be irked with *him*? That right belonged solely to Gavin at the moment.

"'Tis better if he uses the power for its other purpose, rather than that of answering questions. 'Tis what it's better suited for," Nakkole said, drawing herself into their conversation. "Though I admit, it is probably a lot more difficult."

Curious, Gavin momentarily forgot about his frustration and focused his attention on the flame-haired beauty at his side. "Other purpose?"

"I know Arrane uses his power of communication for *actual* communication, rather than a one-sided mysterious bit of questioning. He uses it often with our mother and queine, Abunda, when he wishes to know information she may have or wishes to tell her of his own, but cannot appear to her at that moment. I'm not sure, exactly, how it works, but it's almost as if he calls out to her with his mind until she answers."

"Then your mother, this *Abunda*, has the power of communication, too?" Gavin asked.

"Nay. The power is loaned to her during the times he needs it, I think. When he calls out to her, it's as though he's sharing the power when she answers. It is gone again once he's done with her."

Alec cleared his throat. "He uses it on me frequently."

Gavin's heart wouldn't allow him to ignore the opening Alec had just provided. "To convince you to befriend me?"

Everyone stopped walking at once, except Dulcee, who continued on as though nothing had occurred. In all his years of friendship with Alec, Gavin had come to read his emotions as well as his own. He could see the guilt and burden of truth written deeply in Alec's eyes now.

"Were you truly ever loyal to me, Alec? Or was it only my father who held such an honor?" Gavin asked, his voice thick and wavering. He didn't wait for an answer. He stalked off after Dulcee. The anger he had suppressed filled him from head to toe.

"Gavin, wait!" Nakkole called.

"This is not your fight, Nakkole," Alec said. "He will not forget our friendship.

"I have never betrayed you or acted disloyally," Alec said a moment later, catching up to Gavin. "And I never needed convincing to be your friend, Gavin. Never."

Gavin spun around and slammed his fist into Alec's jaw.

Timpani screamed. Nakkole gasped. Gavin swung again.

Alec caught Gavin's fist before it contacted his face, but Gavin brought his left hand up, pounding it into Alec's stomach, causing the man to double over. "God's blood, Gavin!"

But Gavin wasn't listening. He brought his fist down again, and again, and when he felt a hand grab his arm, struggling to keep him from pummeling Alec to death, he shoved it away.

From behind him, he heard a cry, then a thud. Wrapping one hand around Alec's throat, Gavin craned his neck to see where the sound had come from.

To his horror, he saw Nakkole sprawled out at the base of a tree, blood trickling down her forehead.

Twenty-two

~

𝕻akkole's still body lay bleeding and silent.

Gavin stared down at her and swallowed the shout of horror creeping up his throat. He hadn't meant to hurt her, but in his fury with Alec, he'd shoved her away, apparently slamming her into the tree behind them.

"Do you see now?" Timpani screamed at him, bending beside Nakkole to cradle her head in her arms. "You hold so much power within you that your temper can be a deadly thing!"

Alec choked, clutching his throat where Gavin had been throttling him a moment before. Nakkole moaned, bringing a hand to the cut on her brow. He wanted to touch her but dared not. All around him was proof of his uncultivated power and the destruction it could bring. He was flooded with memories of the battlefield and the carnage he'd always left in his wake.

This was all a mistake. A horrible mistake. These powers should not belong to him.

"I'm all right," Nakkole murmured, pushing herself up to sit. "I'm fine."

Truly, her head pounded something fierce, but the look of

devastation on Gavin's face forced her to feign a smile. While it did indeed hurt to have her body thrown like some limp thing against the tree, it humbled her to see the force of Gavin's powers come to life. He was the rightful heir in every way now. He would be the Kingdom of Arran's salvation.

That thought brought her hand to her belly. Carefully prodding her stomach, she checked for any tenderness that might have come from being thrown. Everything felt as it should. She exhaled a sigh of relief.

Had Abunda felt this protective when she'd carried Nakkole in her womb?

"Let us go," she said, taking Timpani's offered hand of assistance and rising to her feet. "The sea folk await our arrival at the river's source."

Woozy, she swayed on her feet. Then a sudden rush of movement caught her in its flurry, and she found herself being swept into the air by hands as large as her own head. "Dulcee! Put me down."

"We go faster if I carry. Come." Dulcee led the way, and from her perch on his arm, Nakkole watched Gavin linger in place for a long moment, then grab Alec by the arm.

Afraid another fit of temper was on the horizon, she motioned for Dulcee to stop. "Gavin, please. Leave him be."

Alec was staring at Gavin, but made no move to defend himself. When Gavin thrust out his hand, Alec didn't even flinch. Nakkole watched with tremendous relief as Alec slipped his hand into Gavin's and shook it firmly.

"You've saved my life a number of times—" Gavin started, but Alec interrupted.

"And you mine."

"Aye, and I yours. Whatever motivated you to be loyal to me, I will not question it . . . not while I am here, amidst strangers. I've trusted you thus far and pray I'm not wrong in trusting you now."

Alec clasped Gavin's shoulder. "'Tis glad I am you've opened your eyes." He grinned and rubbed his jaw. "You're a stubborn ass with a brutal fist, though."

"A truce then, until I know the truth of you." Gavin didn't appear quite as lighthearted as Alec. His face was still tense, his posture ready for battle. But he did resume following Dulcee.

Alec followed as well, falling into stride beside Timpani, who was staring up at him with a worried expression. "You've always known the truth of me, Gavin, and I believe you'll one day apologize to me for doubting my intentions."

Gavin grumbled, but said nothing else. The remainder of their walk was spent in quiet peace, the songs of the birds and rush of the waters the only sound as they grew closer to the river's source. Nakkole could smell the sweet scent of her familiar waters, could hear the light kiss of tide upon sand.

"We're here," she said, grateful when Dulcee set her on her own two feet. She fell into step beside Gavin. "We'll be crossing to the Isle from this spot."

Gavin stared around at their surroundings, and she tried to see the wealth of beauty through his eyes. Where the river poured into a spacious lake, ferns, trees, pink and white blossoms all edged the rim of the waters. A bird twittered, a butterfly soared; the only sounds belonged to nature and the heavy breathing of her companions. The thick fog clouding the depths of the lake, hiding the secrets that lingered there.

"Where's the Isle?" Gavin asked, squinting into the distance.

Nakkole smiled. She knew exactly where the Isle now floated. She could feel its nearness in her blood. Could sense the vibrations of the misty shield. But Gavin would feel no such thing. Not yet.

She raised her arms in the air and tilted her head back. "King Arrane, if it is your will, reveal yourself so we might find our way."

The waters rippled. Two large, white clouds parted and a ray of blinding sun shattered their divide. The large mist in the center of the lake lifted, and there it was. The alabaster palace perched on an isle drifting many feet above the lake. It lowered as they watched, a sign of trust and welcome, until the sandy shores lay just atop the water's surface.

"There," she said, her heart suddenly full. "That is our destination."

Gavin's eyes were wide, his mouth slightly open. She

knew from here, he would not be able to see the full beauty of his father's home, but watching such a massive structure appear from, quite literally, thin air, had to have stunned him.

Alec elbowed him in the ribs. "Time enough to stare later. We must cross."

It took a long moment for Gavin to shake himself from his stupor. Nakkole waited for his disbelief, his demands for explanations.

Instead, all he said was,"I see no boats. How are we to cross?"

She smiled, not fooled at all by his suddenly calm composure.

Alec sighed. "'Tis the part of this journey that took me the longest to get used to."

Gavin lightly touched Nakkole's cut forehead, his eyes questioning her. "What does he mean?"

She could have smiled, anticipating his reaction when she told him of their travel companions. "Sea folk. They'll carry us across on their backs."

"Wha—"

His question was cut off by a loud clicking sound coming from the water. Another followed from the other end of the waters, until finally, a black cloud of hair emerged from just beyond the shore. With human hands, the creature pushed the mess of hair from its face, revealing a stunning sculpture of beauty.

Raventail. The leader of this small pack of mermen stared at her with a wide grin on his face.

"Oy, Raventail! 'Tis prompt you are!" Timpani called out, waving frantically at their longtime friend.

"Aye, and undependable you remain. I was told of no ogre needing passage to Arran."

"Dulcee swim. Dulcee know how," the ogre said, grinning with pride.

"Gavin swim, too," she heard Gavin mutter beneath his breath.

Narrowing his eyes, Raventail turned to stare at Gavin. "He the prince?"

Nakkole nodded. "Can you not see the resemblance to

Arrane? How many did you bring? I do hope you knew to bring transport for Alec and Timpani."

Raventail let out a shrill whistle, which brought forth three more mermen, each similar in build.

"Here we all are, enough to carry the lot of you, though your reference to us as mere transportation wounds me deeply."

Smiling, feeling like the self she had lost from the moment she stepped out of her Norman home, Nakkole did the White Lady–ish thing and batted her eyes in mocked flirtation. "Ah, now, my good Raventail. You are much, much more, as you well know."

Raventail grinned and groomed his hair with his fingers. Just as quickly as it had come, the smile vanished when he once more stared at Dulcee. "Does His Majesty know he is to be entertaining a wicked ogre?"

"I'm not certain, and Dulcee is anything but wicked."

The merman grunted and motioned his men closer to the surface. "Very well then, let him swim. We need to leave now. Arrane was very clear that he wanted you here as quickly as possible."

"Are you sure you can manage, Dulcee?" she asked.

"Can walk most of way."

Nodding, Nakkole resumed her role of leadership and walked toward Raventail. Gavin grabbed her arm. "I'm not certain what we are to do."

She smiled and laid a comforting hand on his. "These great creatures are the horses of the seas," she whispered, careful not to let Raventail hear her compare him to a beast. "You'll ride them the way you ride a steed, only you'll be using their hair for grip, rather than reins. They'll do the steering. Don't dare try to guide them by pulling on their hair, or you'll likely find yourself struggling to swim to shore on your own."

"I think I'll swim with Dulcee."

Nakkole rolled her eyes. "You'll drown. The currents midway through this river are legendary. Not even the Prince of Light could hope to survive them. You'll have to trust the mermen. Unless you've managed to perfect your power to control something as strong as the currents, the mermen are the only way."

Gavin frowned, looking all the more uncertain. "Then I shall ride the one you call Raventail . . ."

Nakkole opened her mouth to protest, but Gavin held up a hand to silence her. "*I* will ride with him, Nakkole. I do not like the way he looks at you."

She fought a smile. "Very well, then. But you should know he has been trying to woo me for far longer than you."

Seeing the spark of jealousy flash in his black eyes, Nakkole's smile would no longer be restrained. She liked his possessiveness. She left him and joined Timpani and Alec, who had already chosen their rides. Nakkole approached a merman she had met only once before, Coralton, and politely waited for him to turn his back to her so she could mount.

Gavin approached Raventail, wondering what the odd creature would do if he challenged him to a fight. More than likely, he would drown Gavin. Still, he did not like the way Nakkole had flirted with him, even if he did have the tail of a fish hiding beneath these clear waters. From his spot on the shore, he waited while the others mounted the mermen, staring in awe at the slick, black tail that wriggled beneath the surface. Raventail indeed. It looked . . . slimy.

Gavin shuddered and made his way into the lake, noting that he could barely feel the water through his odd leggings.

"Have faith, young prince," Raventail told him, casting a quick glance at Gavin from over his shoulder. "I would not dare drown the rightful heir to Arran." He shared a smile with Nakkole and what looked to be a wink. "Even if you do challenge my efforts to woo the sweet Nakkole."

Without taking care to be gentle, Gavin growled and jumped onto Raventail's back. Raventail let out a soft *oomph*, then glared back at Gavin.

"Just because I vowed not to drown you does not mean I cannot have my own sort of fun with you," Raventail said, grinning.

A moment later, he ripped away from the shore, nearly bucking Gavin from his back. He dipped beneath the surface, rising only to allow Gavin to sputter out a mouthful of water.

Gavin gave a warning tug on the mane of black hair wrapped in his fist, and all he received in return was boisterous laughter from the fellow beneath him.

"Oh, the fun!" Raventail shouted, and for the first half of their journey did not stop dipping Gavin in and out of the water, and side to side. By the time the merman finally slowed his pace and calmed his path, Gavin's stomach was queasy and he was certain his face was green.

Raventail paused, turning in the water so they both had a view of the riders lagging behind. The three other mermen circled around the lumbering ogre, whose head was now pressed chin to water as they'd reached the middle of the river.

"You'll have to swim now, Dulcee. Are you sure you're able?" Nakkole called, the red-haired merman beneath her pulling to a stop beside Dulcee.

"Dulcee not scared of water." Dulcee frowned, and though it looked as though he was attempting a whisper, Gavin clearly heard the rest of his confession even from his distance. "Dulcee's stomach hurt. Arrane no like ogres. Dulcee afraid of Arrane."

"Nonsense!" Timpani said from above a blond merman. "You're a friend of his son and now a friend of the king because of it."

"Dulcee? Friend to Arrane?" The ogre's face beamed, his eyes widened. "We go now. Me like friend."

❧

𝔄rrane pulled legs that felt as heavy as solid oak over the side of his bed, knowing he needed more sleep, but needed awakening even more. As always, Balaster, Arrane's personal attendant, stood at the foot of the bed, ready to toss Arrane's cloak over his shoulders and fuss about his lordship's untidy appearance.

"Any word?" Arrane asked, peeling his tired bones from the mattress and holding out his arms so that Balaster could slip the cloak over him.

Balaster fastened the cloak at Arrane's throat with a brooch made of pearl and amber, Arrane's stones of choice.

Arrane stood, grabbed his mother-of-pearl cane with the amber crystal tip, balancing long enough for Balaster to pull Arrane's long silver hair from beneath the cloak and lay it over the soft silky fabric.

"No word. The merfolk say Raventail and his band of friends left here to retrieve your son early this morn. We assume they will arrive in time to sup with us."

"A feast, with the best sort of foods the Isle has to offer. I want my son's welcome to be memorable and enjoyable for him. Come morn, he will have time enough for the seriousness of the minions camping on our borders."

Balaster muttered under his breath, as he was wont to do, and Arrane turned to face him. "Again with the muttering, Balaster? I thought we'd tamed that wild tongue of yours?"

Balaster, an elf by birth, an outcast by his kind, stood tall and proud, jutting out his chin with defiance. "'Tis your army, Your Majesty. They think you are proving to be senile in your tender years. They believe a strong king would put the concern of his people over his need for festivities over the welcome of a son."

Arrane chuckled, not in the least offended. Most of the Isle's army were still young and eager for adventure. They did not yet understand the strategy that often lay in the most mundane of conversations and goodwill.

"Be certain to tell them that if they do not make Prince Gavin feel welcome, the safety of those we protect will no longer be an issue, for we will have lost this battle before it has truly begun."

Arrane stooped to allow Balaster to slip the crystal crown of Arran onto his head, then cast a scrutinizing glance into the looking-glass that covered a good portion of the eastern wall of his bedchamber. The crown was made up of three amber leaves entwined with a pearl deer, a pearl clam, and a pearl sun. The emblems of those he protected—the earth, nature, the sea, and the sky. The Kingdom of Arran's perfection embodied in a simple piece of head jewelry. The same crest marked Arrane's throne, his cloak, his staff, and his shield.

"If Gavin chooses not to lead our fight," Arrane continued, "we stand no chance."

"They are eager, Your Majesty, not foolish. They'll show your son the kindest of welcomes, even if they'd prefer to rally him directly to the barracks to begin talking strategy."

Through the looking-glass, Arrane smiled at Balaster and gave a slight nod. "See that it is so. Now, leave me be for a few moments while I ready myself to greet my son."

＞

In any place where there had once been shadow, there was now light. Even where the trees should have cast shade, only light shone, and it nearly blinded Gavin. From his spot atop Raventail, the merman, the river had calmed, and he could see only a blinding white glow along the shoreline. Odd, for darkness had fallen not long ago, and by all rights, it was still eve-tide, yet it looked like the brightest of morns.

"We are here?" he asked, his stomach knotted at what lay ahead.

His father. In the flesh, as real as the river around him.

"Aye. The king seems to have wanted to ensure our safety by bringing us daylight. You should have no problems reaching the palace safely," Raventail replied.

So, Arrane controlled the elements? Or was this time being manipulated, instead?

"As much as I'd like to have you on my back for the rest of eternity, I do have an army to see to on the northern side of Arran. Unless you'd like us to break our guard against those camping there, I suggest you take your leave of me now," Raventail said.

Gavin glanced over his shoulder to see Nakkole and Alec's mermen reach the shore and deposit them gently into the water. Timpani's merman did the same, leaving only Gavin atop Raventail.

"Right," he murmured, throwing his leg over the side of Raventail's back, then lowering himself into the water. "Thank you, I suppose, for that . . . interesting . . . journey."

"My pleasure." Raventail grinned and winked.

And then he disappeared beneath the water, and his black tail kicked atop the surface, spraying Gavin in the face. Cursing, Gavin stumbled toward the bank where the others waited for him, only bright silhouettes of their bodies visible in front of the blinding light.

The moment he dragged his left foot out of the water and into the staggering light of shore, the grass beneath that foot became visible, a flash of green so small in comparison to the white and yellow shadows around it. Thrown a bit off balance by what he was seeing, he stepped forward, moving out of the water, and the patch of green grew a bit.

Magic. It was as if a light shield or cloak had been cast around this isle, for when he looked back in the direction from which he'd come, he could no longer see the lake. Feeling a hand on his arm, Gavin glanced down to see Nakkole standing beside him, a smile on her beautiful face. Gavin shuddered, and without thinking, pulled her hand from his arm and gripped it in his own fist.

"What is this?" he whispered, the hairs on his nape prickling in his tension.

"Your father's way of making it more difficult for Elphina's army to attack. Most of them cannot approach the light, but it will only last a short time. 'Tis one reason your presence is needed here so badly." Nakkole's vivid eyes dampened. She stared up at Gavin beseechingly. "Your father's ability to cast magic is not at all what it used to be. He is weak, Gavin. And without you, he stands no chance of defending his home and his body against those who would see him dead."

Why should he be overwhelmed by such sadness for a man who had abandoned him long ago? Gavin didn't understand why her words affected him as strongly as they did, but he squeezed her hand tighter and stepped toward the others.

"Then this is the magic of creation?" he asked. Would his own abilities allow him to cast such beauty?

"*Oui.* Come. Let me show you your birthright."

Her words froze Gavin's feet in place, even though Nakkole pulled at him to follow her. *His birthright?* Surely they didn't believe he had come here to claim his title as prince? They must know he would assist them in their plight and then return home, mustn't they?

"Nakkole . . ." he started.

"I know, Gavin. No one expects any decisions from you yet. Come. Just follow me to the palace. We'll worry about your responsibilities to two lands later."

Slightly comforted by her ability to read his tension, Gavin gave in and followed Nakkole farther into the light.

He allowed her to lead him, still fascinated at the color that seemed to expunge the blinding light with each step they took. He could now see several trees to his left and right, but the light surely must be making them look so odd, for the branches and trunk were shimmering with gold, the leaves with silver.

Fruits of all shapes dangled from the highest branches, their color so deep and rich, they looked as though they'd been dipped in jewels. Apples as glittery as rubies, pears in all shades of amber. Dew crusted the blades of grass at Gavin's feet, making them shine so brightly he half expected to hear the crunch of emeralds beneath his boots. Gavin's heartbeat accelerated. He felt as though he were stuck in a vivid dream.

A courtyard of sorts became apparent, but rather than a stone wall, the circle barrier looked to be made of pearls. Flowers of all types were beautifully planted around the inside of the wall, and as they stepped into the courtyard, he could smell a familiar scent on the wind. His mind instantly took him back to Grey Loch and his Scottish heritage.

"Do I smell heather?" he asked.

She guided him over a marble path, through the garden. "Your father planted it for your mother before she left . . . to make her feel a bit more at home."

Gavin tried to picture his odd, old mother in a place such as this. To him it was like sliding his leg into the sleeve of his tunic—it just didn't fit.

Ahead of them, the light swept away as if by fog, revealing marble steps, pearl columns, and a castle several times larger than Grey Loch's keep. The entire structure looked to be made of crystal, or glass, but if Gavin shifted just so, the light moved, and the structure looked more like alabaster and pearl. Turrets bordered all sides, the arrow slits carved into shapes of all kinds, rather than the simple rectangle of

Grey Loch's design. Gavin could hardly breathe. This magnificent fortress made his warrior's heart pound ferociously.

"Welcome," Nakkole said, waving her hand out in front of her, gesturing to the grandeur all around. "Welcome to your birthright, Prince Gavin. Welcome to the Palace of Arran."

Twenty-three

~

All around them the light trickled away, revealing another sort of blinding whiteness that was so very welcome to Nakkole's weary eyes. The Palace of Arran. She darted a quick glance at Gavin, who still stood openmouthed at the sight before them. She'd watched him drink it all in, this grandeur of pearl, marble, and alabaster, while Timpani and Alec ventured forth to announce themselves at the massive white oak door.

Gently, she slipped her hand into Gavin's and urged him toward the steps leading to the palace entrance. "I assure you, there's much more beauty to be seen inside," she whispered.

She'd only visited Arrane's palace once, many years ago, but she could still recall the grand interior as easily as if she'd stood there yesterday. She wanted Gavin to see it, too. Thus far, most of what he'd been shown of her world had been dark and menacing. She wanted him to know of the goodness, the beauty that she loved so dearly.

"You mean to say this is what I inherit if I choose to believe I am the heir?" Gavin asked, his eyes blank as though dumbstruck.

Nakkole's free hand sought her belly. She lay it there for a long moment, then said, "Aye. And your child after you."

His gaze traveling to her belly, Gavin's body gave a tiny shudder. He scowled. "Is it possible, I wonder, for a man's mind to explode with an abundance of information? I'm asked to absorb this odd heritage of mine, this magic running through my veins, your and Alec's deception all this time. This . . . *palace* that I'm sure is on no map, and the knowledge I have sired an heir."

He pulled at his hair and squeezed his eyes shut. "If I had a decent amount of time to think on only one of these matters, perhaps my head would not ache so badly. I've not even had time to ask you how you feel about being the mother of my child. My *illegitimate*, magical child."

Nakkole's heart fluttered. That he should even consider that a worry brought such tender feelings toward him that her knees truly went weak. "When you've had proper time to consider your own feelings, we can discuss mine. For now, let us greet your father."

She gestured toward the now-open door where a tall man clad in white and silver stood glaring down at Alec and Timpani. Alec was putting up a fuss over some matter, and Nakkole could hear Timpani's demand to see Arrane.

"I will not let you pass unless you surrender your weapons. No one comes into the Palace of Arran armed except the king's men," the man said. As he shook his head, his white-blond hair fell over his face, covering a piercing green eye.

"You know me well, Balaster," Alec said through gritted teeth. "Let us pass."

Balaster craned his neck to peer over Alec's shoulder. "You've brought an ogre? Alec, surely you know better. You've never been allowed to enter with your weapons, now you expect that courtesy as well as that of bringing in such a beast to sit before His Majesty?"

"This is not an ordinary visit, Balaster, as you well know," Timpani chimed in.

"Let them pass," a low, overpowering voice said from behind the partially opened door. "Now is not the time to make our friends surrender the weapons they will be in need of so soon."

Balaster swung around to face the voice, pushing the door open wide enough to reveal a white-robed figure looming behind him. Balaster swept low into a bow, then held his arm toward the group of them awaiting entrance.

"They've brought an ogre," Balaster said, his voice eerily calm.

"You dare make your prince await entrance here?" Arrane asked, his gaze settling on Gavin.

Balaster's face whitened. He cast his stare to the white, marble floor. " 'Twas only because I was wary of the ogre.''

Beside Nakkole, Dulcee sighed and stepped away from the stairs. "Dulcee go. Know Dulcee shouldn't come."

Lightly shoving Balaster from his path, Arrane stepped over the threshold, revealing himself completely in the afternoon light. Nakkole nearly gasped aloud, but caught herself in time. Her king looked so very old, so very ill, as though the time he'd been evading all these years had finally found him and settled itself like a cloak over Arrane's skin.

"Dulcee, is it?" Arrane asked, leaning heavily on the staff he carried in his right hand. "I know you are responsible for saving my son. You are welcome here for as long as you wish. This is your home, if you choose it to be so."

Dulcee gasped, his gray-green eyes alight with glee. "Dulcee live in Arran? Arrane like Dulcee?"

Nakkole reached out and patted his arm. "*Oui*. Arrane likes Dulcee. You are welcome here, just as I told you you would be."

The ogre reached up and scratched the sporadically placed red hairs atop his head. He leaned down so that his hot, sticky breath fell on Nakkole's cheek and whispered, "Dulcee not fit through door."

Arrane's laughter was as strong as his hearing. He lifted his staff and the white oak door behind him widened and stretched. "I'm quite certain I can manage to find ways to make you comfortable, Dulcee." Arrane's smile lessened. He turned his head to stare at his son, and Nakkole thought she saw moisture dampen his eyes. "My son."

Nodding his head, Gavin made no other move to greet his

father in turn. A lump forming in her throat, she took Dulcee's arm and took the remaining steps quickly. "The four of us shall leave you to greet your son properly," she said, sending a commanding glance to Timpani.

With one last gaze at Gavin from over her shoulder, Nakkole silently pleaded with him to be kind to the old king, to forgive him for things not his doing. Then she led the others through the enormous door and into the palace.

Gavin watched as Nakkole disappeared inside, his stomach knotted with anticipation and awkwardness. His first meeting with his father had not truly occurred, for Arrane had not been more than an apparition when he healed Gavin. Now, however, the imposing, though wan figure stood before Gavin, his features so very familiar it was chilling.

Swallowing the tension in his throat, Gavin did the only thing he could think to do. He swooped into a bow and lowered his head. No matter his feelings of resentment over having grown up in such blind ignorance, this man before him had sacrificed his health, his loving bond with Geraldine, to ensure Gavin's life. He was owed nothing less than Gavin's respect.

"Your Majesty," Gavin said, his stare steadily fixed on Arrane's bare, white feet. "I thank you for your efforts to save my life."

A hand, cool and firm settled upon Gavin's head. "Rise, my son. My tired bones will not allow me to bow to you, but it is you who deserves such appreciation."

Though he did not rise, Gavin did lift his head to stare up into his father's face. The sunlight above cast an eerily angelic glow about Arrane's silhouette, the sheer brightness of it making Gavin's eyes water. "I have done nothing."

Arrane's hand slipped to cup Gavin's chin. It was as though he could feel all the years of Arrane's life in the man's frail fingers.

"My son, you have come to the aid of a kingdom you know naught about, a father you did not know of until days ago. Surely that is something in itself. A lesser man would have returned home, would have understood he had no true obligation to save something he thought abandoned him years ago."

Gavin's voice was lost to the constriction of his throat.

Arrane's smile was wide and bright. His black-gray eyes flickered in the sunlight. He swept his hand toward the entranceway. "Let us feast and enjoy the night. Later, we can speak of the army camped at our borders. If you have the desire to help our plight, we do not have much time to decide what needs to be done."

So many questions begged to be asked, but somehow Gavin managed to keep his grip on them, recognizing the weariness and pleading in the old man's eyes. His father's eyes. Gavin's questions could wait until he'd better phrased them in his mind. For now, he would go along silently and allow only his mind to scream those incoherent inquiries.

He stopped thinking altogether, however, when the first glimpse of the palace interior was revealed to him. The first thing that caught his attention was that he could see his reflection in no less than a dozen surfaces—from the immaculate marble floors to the crystal ceiling. His face stared back at him through the golden stairs, through the jeweled tapestries than hung upon the walls. He couldn't stop his jaw from falling open in appreciation any more than he could control the gasp that followed.

"'Tis beautiful," he whispered.

Arrane reached for Gavin's arm. Gavin instinctively pulled away, not yet ready for such contact with his father. In an attempt to hide his discomfort, he cleared his throat and turned toward the tapestry hanging beside him. Amber and pearls were woven into a thin, shiny fabric so artfully as to create a stunning replica of Arrane's profile. The only other stones Gavin could see in the work of art were a glistening dark gray stone that made up the portrait's visible eye, and a trickle of what looked like shimmering diamond dust that trailed from the corner of the eye to the bridge of the nose.

It looks as though he's weeping. Casting a quick, uneasy glance at Arrane, Gavin's stomach tightened at the sight of the damp streaks marring the visible skin above his beard. Had he been crying?

Nonsense. Utter nonsense.

Arrane cleared his throat. "We can begin our welcoming

feast as soon as you are ready. I assumed you might like a bath, perhaps a nice rest before eating. If I was mistaken, I'll send for your companions, and we can dine now."

Gavin's gaze fell to Arrane's hands, both of which now gripped his staff tightly in front of him, wringing the wood in his gnarled fists.

He's uneasy, Gavin thought. *He's feeling as awkward about this reunion as I.*

The knowledge of this eased the tension in Gavin, and he had a moment of pity for the old man, shoving the bits of resentment that still lingered in him to the back of his mind. "A bath would be heaven, as would a brief respite on a real bed."

His hands stilling on the wooden staff, Arrane smiled and nodded. He turned and headed toward the golden staircase, glancing back once to gesture for Gavin to follow.

Adjusting the bow on his shoulder, Gavin took one last glance at the amazing tapestry, only to find the trail of diamond dust gone and a wan smile splayed across the profile's face.

Brouillard Noir—The Black Fog

Queine Elphina sat on the makeshift throne, created from three muddy logs and a cushion brought from her underground palace, placed in the center of the bog known as the Black Fog. Normally, the sulfuric stench would have been intolerable to Elphina's delicate sense of smell, but just now, she was too focused on the reason they were here to pay the smells much notice. She turned Gavin's sword in her hands, studying the amber stone in hopes of discovering more secrets within. When Lucette suddenly appeared at her side, Elphina nearly pierced her hand.

She looked at her mother. "You bring me news?"

"Certainly, but not the sort you hope for." Lucette eased onto the muddy earth, the bog all around them gurgling and bubbling with thick, black ooze. "Geraldine is in our world. She's traveling in a house elf's bubble."

Elphina's insides turned cold. "Where is she now?"

Lucette shrugged. "If she made it through the Sanddine Caves, then she's likely already in Annwyn."

Which meant she was far too close to Arrane for comfort. She was likely already rejuvenating by the nearness of her soul match, and thus, so was Arrane.

Elphina stood and cupped her hands around her mouth, letting out a yell shrill enough to stop the dozens of creatures around them. They froze in their search, wide-eyed and trembling, to look at their queine.

"You have until nightfall to find the damned orb!" she screamed. "What are you staring at? Search, you pathetic imbeciles."

Her chest heaving for breath, she fell back onto her cushion, nearly desperate enough to plop into the muck and search herself. That it would likely come to that before the day was through made her hand tremble with anger as she reached into her gown for the tiny scroll that had been caged in Gavin's sword.

"Read it again," Lucette muttered.

Only because she was about to do so anyway did Elphina obey. She unrolled the scroll and squinted to read the small print. "Truth of the ancient oak. Knowledge of the deepest lake. Creation of the darkest earth."

That was it—those three sentences had filled her with such hope earlier, and now she wasn't even certain she'd been accurate in their meaning. But she'd made Lucette tell her where the Orb of Truth had been found by Arrane's people. It had been buried in the roots of the oldest oak in the Annwyn forest. Ancient oak. They had to be right. The message had to be the locations of all three orbs. Which meant the Orb of Creation must be here, in Brouillard Noir, for nowhere on earth was the dirt and soil darker than in the Black Fog.

"We'll keep looking, Elphina," Lucette said.

Elphina glanced at her, disturbed by what she saw in the succubus's eyes. She was looking at Elphina in a way she'd never done before—the way a mother looks encouragingly at her child.

Quickly glancing away, Elphina nodded. "We must do so

before Arrane and Geraldine are reunited. I'm not certain I can beat him if he's strong again."

"If we find the orb, you can. With the Orb of Creation, you can raise an endless army against him, daughter. You can win this. You can kill your father and your brother and, once you find the last orb, together we can raise King Krion. Darkness will rule again . . . and *you* will be its queine."

Twenty-four

~~

The Palace of Arran

Nakkole wiped her hands on the front of her gown and readied herself to knock on Gavin's chamber door. He'd been given the uppermost chamber in the highest tower of Arran, a room meant to allow a bird's eye view of the goings-on around the Isle, normally used by the king's most-trusted man. That it was given to Gavin said much of Arrane's intentions for his son, but Nakkole was certain the young prince would not realize the gesture for what it was—the highest proof of faith and appreciation.

This would be the first she'd seen of Gavin since Arrane had shown him to this chamber. Gavin had rested, bathed, and had been given more than enough time to ponder his fate alone. But now . . . now a reception waited to begin below.

Pixies, White Ladies, house fae, and so very many more species of fae had journeyed from near and far to attend this greeting of their prince, and his tardiness in meeting them would do much to shake their faith in the outcome of the looming war. Such creatures were limited in their powers, but were swift and mighty for what they were. Arrane needed their allegiance, and their hopes of defeating the dark magics, and because of his gradual weakening over these years without Geraldine, Nakkole knew they could well choose to leave his aid and flee for their lives rather than fight for them.

"Gavin?" she called, rapping lightly on his door.

For a long moment, she heard nothing, then the sound of heavy, shoeless feet crossed toward the door. The massive barrier opened and revealed her prince, his white tunic clinging to his chest with remnants of his bath, his black hair slicked behind his ears, laying softly on his shoulders.

"I'm not certain I'll ever grow comfortable with my clothing dressing me the moment I emerge from water. Is it natural?"

She gazed at the shimmering white tunic he wore so beautifully. "*Oui*. Your father's greatest powers come from the water fae. This is what happens to those born of water. My hair, too, dries almost immediately."

He reached up and smoothed his wet hair, his eyes flashing with some emotion that darkened them into smoldering coals. "The night you were wounded—you really *were* at the loch, weren't you?"

Nakkole found herself staring with longing at his full mouth. She swallowed again and felt herself nod.

Gavin's gaze fell to her belly. He reached his hand out and placed his palm against her navel. "And our child? Will he have powers like mine? Or, should you bear a girl, will she be a White Lady?"

Smiling, Nakkole folded both of her hands over his on her belly. "He, or she, will be more of you than me. Only Abunda, my mother and queine, can give birth to White Ladies, until, that is, she has chosen a new White Lady queine."

"Then you and Timpani are sisters?"

Nakkole chuckled. "We are. I have twenty-six sisters in all."

Gavin's jaw dropped. "You mean to say she's birthed twenty-six daughters from her own body?"

"*Oui.*"

"And who is the father of all these children?"

Nakkole shrugged. "That is knowledge only the White Lady queine possesses, though we are all pretty certain the mermen are responsible. 'Tis why I never took Raventail's flirtations seriously. I've always possessed a fear that he might be a brother, or perhaps even the father of one of my sisters."

"How old is this mother of yours?"

Grinning, Nakkole imagined his reaction to meeting the beautiful, youthful Abunda this evening. "She has been alive for ninety-six summers."

"Ninety-six—"

"Ah, good. You're up and about," the interruption came from Balaster. "His Majesty requests the presence of both of you below. We've many hungry folk about."

Balaster swept his hand toward the golden staircase. "This way then."

Nakkole palmed Gavin's elbow and guided him alongside her, following Balaster down the winding stairs. "Come," she said. "I am anxious for you to meet my mother."

A glimmer of a grin surfaced on his too-serious face. "I admit to be a bit anxious of the meeting, as well."

The climb downstairs took a good amount of time, for there were six floors in the palace, but because she made the journey at Gavin's side, so close their hands continually rubbed one another, Nakkole did not mind the long walk. They reached the bottom in silence, and when Gavin's foot descended the final step, he stopped and turned her to face him.

"A moment please, Balaster?" he said without gracing even the quickest of glances toward the elf.

"Of course, my lord. I will tell the king you'll be along presently."

Nakkole watched Balaster pass through the large white doors leading to the great hall, her stomach twisting into knots at the intensity of Gavin's stare. She willed herself to meet his gaze, the power of it beckoning her. "Did you want something of me?" she asked, her voice shaking.

His throat rose and fell in a deep swallow. His gaze turned sharp and intense. Gathering both of her hands between his own, he cleared his throat and took a deep breath, his chest rising with the intake.

"It seems my life is changed forever, and once I enter those doors, I know there will be no more hope that this has all been a dream." He licked his lips and pulled her into his arms. His hands rubbed her back and she pressed herself against his chest, drinking in the strong masculine scent of him. Her arm moved beneath his, cupping his back, kneading his muscles, offering whatever comfort she could give.

"What is it you want from me?" she whispered. Whatever he asked, she would give it willingly. At this moment, there was naught she wouldn't do for him.

"This. No matter what will happen to us in the future, I need your strength now."

He all but choked on those words, and a lump formed in Nakkole's throat. She was willing to stake her life on the fact that he'd never required strength from anyone before. That he asked for hers to borrow now gave her hope that they might find their way through these difficulties.

But to what end? What exactly did she believe might happen between them? That she carried his child did not change the fact that he was royalty and she was not. He was of one world and she of another. Why should she believe he would leave behind his people in order to lead those he barely knew?

Close to tears, and unwilling to spill them, Nakkole stretched to her toes and pressed her lips to Gavin's. "Have my strength," she whispered against his mouth.

He took what she offered, gently prying her mouth open with the tip of his tongue. She fed off his hunger and hoped he fed off hers. When finally he broke their kiss, he left his forehead pressed against hers.

"Stay by my side?" he asked, releasing his hold on her waist to pull her arms from around him. He clasped her hands, squeezing so tightly her fingers throbbed.

His breath warmed her nose, sweet and heavy. Nakkole sighed and rocked her head against his, nodding. "I'll not leave you for the entire evening."

He breathed heavily, moved his head, and kissed her firmly on the brow.

Turning, keeping only one of her hands in his, he faced the closed, great hall door. Such pride filled her then, she nearly wept from it. Her prince, her kingdom's savior.

Uncertain, yet unwavering. There was naught else she could ask of the father of her child.

As though it had been waiting for their approach, the door swung inward, framing them in the jamb. The chaotic chatter rumbling throughout the massive great hall came to an abrupt stop. The room was crowded with bodies; short, fat, slim, tall, winged, two-legged, four-legged. And all of them were turning to gawk openly at Gavin now. He squeezed her hand. He was perspiring, his hand clammy.

"They are loyal to you," she whispered, her gaze moving over Timpani, Alec, Robert, Brock, Markham, Arrane, and finally, Abunda.

Her mother smiled, her beautiful red lips parting to reveal perfect white teeth. Her black hair glimmered beneath the candlelit, crystal ceiling, her circlet crown catching all the colors of the colorfully garbed crowd.

"Daughter," she whispered, approaching Nakkole and Gavin with outstretched arms. "'Tis relieved I am to have you returned safely . . . with my grandchild, as well."

Heat filled Nakkole's cheeks. How many others knew? She opened her mouth to properly greet her mother, but already Abunda's attention had moved to Gavin, her gaze appreciative as she looked him over from head to foot.

"A handsome, comely prince we have." Abunda curtsied, though she never lowered her gaze from Gavin's face. "I trust you did not take advantage of my daughter?"

The heat in Nakkole's cheeks crept to her neck. "Nay, Mother. And this is not the time for such talk."

Abunda smiled and nodded, taking a step back toward Arrane.

"*That* is your mother?" Gavin whispered rather loudly. "She looks as young as you."

It wasn't often that she resented her mother's beauty, but just now, it made Nakkole painfully aware of her own paler attributes. "Beautiful, isn't she?"

"Comely, aye." Gavin stared down at her and offered a smile. "But she lacks the fiery locks I've come to desire in my women."

A smile formed in her soul and spread through her belly before settling upon her lips.

Gavin had no time to say aught else, for Arrane clapped his hands loudly, calling the room's attention onto himself.

"Goodly people of fae," the king said, raising his arms above his head, then moving them to gesture toward Gavin. "Join me tonight in welcoming home my son, your prince, the future king of Arran."

A loud cheer rang out and Gavin's hand gripped Nakkole's tightly. Suddenly, they were overwhelmed by the group of fae stepping forward to surround them. Nakkole knew they expected her to step aside, to allow for more room for Gavin's admirers. But she had given her word not to leave his side, and unless he left hers willingly, no force would move her from her spot.

She was pushed and jostled about as each loyal being knelt to pay homage to Gavin. The affair lasted a long while, until finally Brock, Robert, and Markham were the only ones who had not kneeled. Gavin placed a solemn hand on Alec's shoulder as the man rose to his feet in front of him. His gaze seemed to finally settle on Grey Loch's men, his mouth twisting into a grin.

Without releasing her hand, he stepped toward his men and greeted them with a nod. "What do the three of you make of this madness?" he asked them.

Robert smirked. "I'm not certain what I make of it, but I do hope I awaken from this odd dream soon."

Gavin looked again at Nakkole. "They are no longer enchanted?"

She shook her head. "Nay. My glamour would have worn off long ago. If not, Timpani would have dispelled them so they would have their wits about them in Elfame."

"We will be able to return home, won't we?" Markham asked, his fingers pressed against the hilt of his sword, his eyes darting about the room with curiosity.

"Most certainly," she agreed, deciding not to mention that they would not remember any of this once they had gone. "King Arrane shall send you back as soon as he deems it possible."

"Well, then," Brock said, his barrel chest heaving with what she could only assume was relief. "Beautiful place, this is."

"I'll not be leaving until those who are after our laird have been caught," Robert said. "You have my blade for as long as you need it."

Gavin opened his mouth to respond, but a high-pitched, tinkling sort of music began to play just behind them. Nakkole turned to see two pixies blowing on beautifully carved reeds, their wings fluttering, keeping them steady in the air. The tune was eerily pretty, and Nakkole found herself stepping closer to Gavin, urging his arm around her waist.

"Dance with me," she whispered, her body already swaying to the music. "Like the night we met. Dance with me."

Again, Gavin looked as though he wished to speak, but instead he obliged her, pulling her into his arms. All around them, couples began the ancient dance of the fae, and Nakkole decided it better not to mention to Gavin that his body knew these steps, though he had never been taught them. Their feet moved quickly as they spun around and around. The magic of the dance allowed for no collisions with the other pairs, so she let her stare remain fastened to Gavin's. His eyes smoldered. He licked his lips.

Then, he licked hers.

Nakkole shuddered and gave herself over to their kiss. Their tongues danced together in perfect rhythm with their feet. Perfection. Pure perfection. Before she could brace herself, Gavin snatched himself away from their kiss. It took Nakkole a long moment to realize what had caused his withdrawal. All around them, the crowd had circled, clapping mercilessly, roaring their cheers.

Her gaze darted to Arrane's, then Abunda's, and she waited for their disapproval.

None came.

Relieved, Nakkole managed to find a chuckle from somewhere deep inside. She looked up at Gavin, a wan smile on her face, hoping to soothe his unease, even if only a bit.

Arrane thrust his staff high above his head. A loud clang sounded, and the many tables scattered around the edges of the great hall were suddenly covered with platters of food.

"Let us feast!" commanded Arrane, then he raised his goblet in salute to Gavin.

~

Geraldine stretched her legs inside Nina's bubble. Every bit of her body felt renewed, though a tad sore from being cramped inside the small sphere for so long. They'd only stopped a few times to eat and to stretch, but with each breath closer to Arrane, Geraldine's body came a bit more alive. She longed to leap from the bubble and dash to the Isle, if only to prove to herself she could.

Beside her, her young protector, Luke, was quietly picking at his nails. At least the color had come back to his face. When he'd first awakened that morning to find himself trapped in the bubble, he'd panicked. He'd grown no more calm when Geraldine and Nina had explained to him the reasons he was no longer at Grey Loch. Now, it seemed he was content to dwell in silence, perhaps still thinking of all they'd told him.

She could understand what he must be feeling. She still remembered well what it had felt like to awaken in the Otherworld after stumbling into a faery ring whilst chasing after what she'd thought had been a butterfly. The pest had turned out to be a pixie, which was why Geraldine had been able to enter the mist gate, and from that point on, nothing had been what she'd expected. If Arrane hadn't discovered her near the Annwyn River that day, Geraldine suspected she would never have found her way out.

But now she was back of her own free will, and anxious to seek the man who'd been her savior. Eager to see their son. To hold him, touch him, love him as she'd longed to do throughout her illness.

"Gavin," she whispered, pressing her cheek to the bubble wall.

"We are at the shore, Majesty," Nina said. "We need only to ask the king to reveal his Isle, and you'll be home."

"And Gavin will be there?" Luke asked, his voice filled with hope.

Geraldine smiled, her heart full of joy. "He will be. And I'm certain the king will see fit to send you back to Scotland if you so choose."

She stood and patted her hair, her plaid, her face. "Do I look as young as I feel, Nina?"

Nina smiled and dipped the bubble toward the ground. "You look as lovely as a queine ought to."

The bubble burst, revealing the earth beneath them. Geraldine wasted no time. She closed her eyes, her heart soaring. *My love, I am here. Reveal to me our home.*

And then came the light of alabaster walls and crystal turrets bouncing off the pink hues of sunset.

"I am home."

❧

akkole felt the tension drain from Gavin's taut grip on her hand, and she gently guided him to the largest table at the head of the room. "Come," she said. "You will share my platter."

Without a word, he followed her and took the seat she showed him. He collapsed onto it, looking ready to flee at any moment. She couldn't blame him in the least. All this attention given to one who had lived with so little of it throughout his life had to be overwhelming.

"What is this?" he whispered, staring at the long, rolled green leaf stuffed with mushrooms and pheasant.

"Kelp-crusties." She smiled at his horror-stricken expression. "They're really quite good."

To prove to him that the kelp-crusties were indeed edible, she lifted one from the trencher and bit into it. Juice ran down her arm, but the taste of this food she had loved since childhood made its mess forgivable.

As she lifted the kelp-crustie toward Gavin's mouth, he leaned away like a child being forced to eat an adult's food, his face contorted into a grimace. "I think I'd rather not."

"Please?"

Again, he opened his mouth to refuse, and she took advantage, shoving the remainder of the crustie into his mouth. He threw up his arms and choked, his gray eyes glistening with water. Then, as she knew he would, he began to chew, a pleasant expression consuming his grimace.

"Not bad," he said, his mouth full of food. "Bit chewy, though."

"Here." She picked up the goblet of cream sitting before him and handed it to him, her own mouth watering for a sip. "Drink this."

He took it and drained the goblet. Then, to her immense satisfaction, he picked up another kelp-crustie and stuffed it into his mouth.

Smiling, Nakkole sipped from her own cream goblet, savoring the sweet taste as it dampened her throat.

Gavin cleared his throat. "If you keep that expression of pleasure on your face, I will not make it through the rest of this feast without claiming you."

Startled, she nearly dropped the gold goblet on the ground. She caught herself, the cream lapping over the goblet's rim, splashing her dress only to dry immediately. Gavin chuckled and placed his hand upon her thigh. He settled it there, making no motion to do anything inappropriate, though he very well could have and no one would have been the wiser. She was slightly disappointed that he didn't try to reinforce his threat by sneaking his hand up her gown.

"You're doing it again," Gavin said, leaning close to whisper in her ear.

Nakkole jumped and reached for a crustie, unwilling to meet his gaze less he read her thoughts. "Doing what?"

"Looking . . . enthralled. Like your mind is on far more pleasurable things."

She turned and dared herself to look him in the eye. "You make me think of such things. 'Tis your fault. Be a good lad and leave me be."

"Lad?" His eyes widened with amusement. "So, you're speaking like a Scotswoman now?"

But she was never able to answer. Gavin's stare had left her and was focused over her shoulder. She could see by his intense stare, his slack jaw, that he would not hear her now. Curious as to what held his attention so tightly, she turned in her chair to look in the direction of the great hall door.

There, standing in the doorway, was his mother. Queine Geraldine of Arran.

Twenty-five

~

$\mathcal{L}$ady Geraldine, the mother Gavin had never truly known, stood in the doorway of the palace's great hall. Her dark, graying hair lay matted against her face and down her arms, but it was the wide smile on her face that beckoned his attention.

He hadn't seen his mother smile in—well, never.

Gavin dropped the kelp-crustie he'd been eating and fought to breathe. The crustie landed with a soft thud on the trencher he shared with Nakkole, but there was no other sound in the room.

No one spoke a word, even as a small lady in drab brown dress and one of Gavin's youngest men, Luke, stepped up to stand beside Geraldine.

Geraldine glanced nervously about, her gaze lingering on no one too long.

Then, her gaze met Gavin's, and for a long moment, she held him mesmerized. Her eyes dampened, and she released a soft "Oh."

Her sob echoed throughout the still-hushed room, until finally Arrane cleared his throat and stepped forward. He raised a shaking hand into the air, and immediately, Geraldine's sobs ceased.

"You're alive and well," she whispered, stepping toward Gavin.

Gavin wanted to stand, wanted to shout his many questions at the woman who had never had any answers to offer. But his legs would not allow him to move. He could only sit and watch while his mother greeted his father, the sight overwhelming him and making his throat burn.

At the table beside him, Nakkole squeezed his hand. "Gavin, look."

As if he could do aught else. The sight of the years being washed from Geraldine's face was awe inspiring. The tiny lines vanished beneath a youthful glow. The streaks of gray throughout her hair darkened to fresh blackness. It seemed as though time and trials left her body in a simple washing, leaving a vibrant young woman standing before them who looked no older than Gavin himself.

He gasped, turning to Nakkole for answers. "What—"

"The soul exchange," she said, giving his hand another squeeze. "Your father's presence has healed your mother's body, given her the youth she possessed when they joined their souls."

Quickly, Gavin glanced toward Arrane, expecting to see the same dramatic change wash over him. It did not. Time still marred the ancient-looking face. Silver hair still hung halfway down Arrane's back. Weathered, fragile-looking hands still clung to the wooden staff.

As though sensing Gavin's bewilderment, Nakkole leaned closer and said, "He will not return to his former self. The piece of Geraldine that kept him alive and young for so long is within *you* now. He surrendered it to keep your mortal self alive, remember?"

"Your queine," Arrane's voice called out in a trembling baritone. "Your queine stands before you all, and yet I do not see you bestowing the respect she rightly deserves."

Gavin turned to look at his parents and watched his mother shake her head at Arrane's words. "Arrane, nay. I am no longer their queine."

No one seemed to hear her quiet plea, however, for in a

graceful wave around the room, each standing body knelt to pay homage to Geraldine McCain.

Gavin turned to question Nakkole and found she, too, had lowered herself from her chair to kneel before Geraldine. Alec, Timpani, Luke, Robert, Markham, and even Brock, each bowed to Gavin's mother as though they did not question why they should. Only Arrane and Gavin remained upright.

Lord, but his mother was beautiful. He had not seen enough of her during his lifetime, but he could appreciate her youthful glow, her flawless features.

Slowly, Arrane turned his head to stare at Gavin. "My son. Please come with us into my private chambers. I wish to speak to you and your mother alone." A forced smile curled on Arrane's lips, and he turned his attention to the others in the room. "Please, everyone. Enjoy the festivities. We shall return shortly."

With no time wasted, the music started to play once again, and Gavin found himself being prodded forward by Nakkole. "Go," she whispered. "I'll be here when you return."

"You said you would not leave my side."

"And I shan't. But you shall leave mine. It is not my place to intrude on your family's reunion."

She carried his child in her womb. Did that not make her family?

Gavin chose not to say so out loud, however, and complied with his father's wishes. He followed Arrane and Geraldine out of the great hall and through another set of doors across the corridor. Unlike the great hall, this chamber was not so brightly lit, nor did it possess the grandness of decor. Instead, it looked very much like Gavin's own drab solar at Grey Loch. A writing table, a few benches, some tapestries. But that was all.

When the door closed behind them, Geraldine glanced briefly at Arrane. "Thank you for honoring my request to come home. I wasn't certain you would."

Arrane looked ready to respond, but Geraldine's attention had already settled upon Gavin. "Are you all right, Gavin? I must know what happened to you, why you disappeared."

God, he'd nearly forgotten how low her voice was, so different from Nakkole's airy, soft sound. Hearing his mother speak his name now, after all these years of silence, hitched his breath in his throat.

"You are well?" he managed, wanting to reach out and make certain she wasn't an apparition like Arrane had been in the loch.

She wrung her hands in her skirts. "More and more well each moment I stand here."

Gavin nodded, his head throbbing to an unsteady beat. "I'm . . . not quite certain what I'm meant to say."

"Say nothing," Arrane said. "'Tis your mother and I who have the explaining to do."

But his relief and hope over seeing his mother alive and youthful wasn't enough to bite down the temper boiling inside him. "Aye, you do. You . . . you could have returned here anytime? Could have become well and young and alert . . . could have been a mother to me, but chose not to?"

She reached out a hand to him, but Gavin ignored it.

"I wanted only to keep you safe," Geraldine whispered. "I thought that if I distanced us from your father, your sister would not find you so easily."

He threw up his hands. "What good is safe if it means being miserable? And now . . . now I find myself learning things I should have known long ago. Could you not have at least prepared me for what has come to me now? My heritage? My abilities?"

"Gavin, please." Geraldine stepped cautiously toward him. "Let me just look at you. Just for one moment. I've waited so long . . . I can hardly believe the man you've grown into."

"Answer me, Mother," he said, though he didn't move away when she cupped his cheek.

Geraldine whimpered and slipped her hand around his neck, pulling him to her. For the first time in his memory, he was being embraced by his mother, and God save him, he could not pull away. He wrapped his arms around her frail bones and buried his face in her neck, fighting the urge to weep like the child he'd been when he'd lost her.

"Why did you not love me enough to live?" he whispered, resting his brow on her shoulder.

He could feel her sobs beneath his face and hands. She pressed her cool, tear-slickened lips to his cheek and pulled away from him, wiping away her tears as she did so. "I loved you enough to die."

Gavin's chest tightened. He'd waited a lifetime to hear those words from his mother. "I always kept you close to me," he said, reaching beneath his tunic to pull free the charm he'd given her so long ago. "I took this from you when you became too ill to care whether you had it or not." He pulled it off his neck and slipped it over hers. "You should have it now, if you want it."

Her face lit up. She cradled the tiny stone in her palm, her sobs beginning anew. "The stone you found in the loch. I remember." She pressed it to her lips and stared at him, a smile growing wide on her face. "Thank you."

Gavin grunted his reply, suddenly far more uncomfortable than he had been a moment ago. "I want to know it all," he said, finally. "Everything that led me here today."

"I had hoped," Arrane said, nodding, "that, given the troubles nearly on our doorstep, tonight would be a pleasant one. But, it seems we must put our merriment aside in order to discover some badly needed truths."

Arrane turned his back to them and rubbed his hand along the crystaleque wall at the back of the chamber. "A moment please, and you shall have your answers."

The back of Arrane's head tilted, and Gavin thought he heard a bit of muttering. Then, the two sconces on either side of Arrane's hands parted like shutters, opening the wall to a large, black, rectangular hole. He reached inside, then turned back to Gavin, holding out a pearl as large as an infant's head.

"Here." Arrane held the pearl sphere out to Gavin. "Take it. Let your mother gather herself, and seek your answers here."

His gaze searching for his mother's reaction, Gavin found only a serene expression. With a resigned sigh, he took the large orb from Arrane's hands and cupped it in his own. It weighed nearly nothing, which baffled Gavin, for it looked solid and heavy. He glanced up, waiting for Arrane to explain.

"That is the Orb of Truth you hold in your hands."

"The Master Trinity," Gavin muttered.

"You know of it?"

He nodded, his gaze remaining transfixed on the Orb. "Nakkole told me a bit about it."

"Ask your questions. It will show you what you seek. The Orb's memory does not wane as ours does, nor does it exaggerate or mold truths."

"And it's just going to *show* me the answers?"

"Just ask it," Geraldine said. "I shall have more of my wits about me when I've become accustomed to staring at my son as a fully grown man."

He knew exactly how she felt. Lord, but her sudden, youthful appearance still shocked him. It was as though he stared into the eyes of a sister, or perhaps a young cousin. But his *mother*? He studied her for a long moment, studied Arrane's treatment of her as they stood side by side without touching, without so much as looking at one another. *Soul exchange.* They looked as connected as two strangers. Even if what Nakkole had said was true, and Arrane had lost his soul connection to Geraldine, wasn't Geraldine's connection to him still strong? Surely it must be, or else she wouldn't have changed so drastically. Where, then, was the emotional reunion, the pained expressions of a love so long withheld? Was Arrane angry that she'd left him? Gavin wondered how fierce a danger had faced his mother to make her sacrifice her true love to escape it. What had happened to Geraldine to make her flee from the place she so obviously loved?

The Orb in his hands shook violently. Gavin stared at it, gripping it tighter to keep it from crashing to the floor. From the center of the sphere, a white glow appeared, and what resembled a fog filled the center. Confused, he looked to Arrane for answers. The king wore a wan smile, nodding his head.

"You must have questioned it, for it answers you now whether you believe or not."

Fear coiled around Gavin's chest. He stared with narrowed eyes into the center of the sphere, and watched as a vision of his mother, the way she looked now, filled the fog. She walked hand in hand with a young man in white robes. The man's long, black hair reached his backside, but was tied back at the sides with a gold ribbon. It took a moment for Gavin to see the man's face clearly, but once the eyes came into view he nearly dropped the Orb again.

Arrane. A youthful, comely Arrane who smiled at Geraldine as though no other existed in the world. She, in turn, stared up at him with adoration in her eyes and reached up to touch the young Arrane's cheek.

"Your wish has been granted," the image of his mother whispered. "I carry your child."

Gavin's throat formed a knot the size of his fist at the announcement, and he found his gaze drawn to the image's flat belly. Was he inside her now, when this memory had taken place? For he knew now that was what he watched. A memory. Whose, he wasn't yet sure, but he felt the truth of it in his soul. His mother reached for Arrane's hand and placed it on her stomach. Arrane's eyes were filled with unshed tears and Gavin could have sworn he felt the physical presence of their love for one another, for him, reach from within the pearl walls of the sphere to touch his soul.

Then, the image of his parents was swept clean of the Orb. Geraldine was suddenly alone in the memory, walking along a beautiful trail in an emerald-green forest. She stooped to pluck a wild rose from a thorny bush, and when she stood again, he could see her belly was full and straining against her flowing, amber-colored gown.

Gavin rubbed his finger along the image. This was the mother he had wanted to know so badly, the one who had never really existed for him. But, here, in this orb, she was real, and she glowed with happiness, happiness he knew—could feel—came from knowing true love for her husband and more important, for her child.

The Orb trembled again and a faint scream echoed from its core. Gavin brought it closer to his face, trying to peer through the chaos that seemed to have taken over this private memory.

A green-tinted creature with long, stringy gray hair

clawed at Geraldine's image. Another pushed her from the front, slamming her body into the trunk of a tree.

"Please, Lucette!" Geraldine shouted. "I am with child!"

A loud, cackling laugh shattered Gavin's frayed nerves. He fell onto the bench behind him, never taking his gaze from the images playing out in front of his eyes.

And now the creature had his mother by her hair, her long claws raking threateningly across her slender throat.

"I have already given Arrane his heir," it screeched. The creature's hungry eyes swept over the length of Geraldine, and she reached a thin, gnarled finger out to caress Geraldine's belly. "This *thing* inside you has no rights here!"

She lunged for Geraldine, but before she could sink her claws into her neck, a fist knocked her away. A figure stepped into view . . . Arrane. "Run, Geraldine. Return to the Isle."

"Run?" The creature pushed herself to her feet and sneered at Arrane, green ooze dripping from her lip. "There is an army of us, Arrane. That child is as good as dead—as is your precious queine."

Geraldine whimpered and stepped away. Then, she turned and fled, leaving the creature and Arrane staring after her.

Gavin waited, but no other image came to him from the orb. Uncertain what was expected of him now, he gently handed the priceless sphere back to Arrane, then turned to face his mother.

"You returned to Scotland after that attack?" he whispered, shaken by the sight of his mother's tears streaking glistening paths down her cheeks.

Geraldine nodded and took a tentative step toward him. She looked to Arrane, who still remained silent. Finally, the king closed his eyes and drew in a deep breath. "She sacrificed her happiness and our love because she thought she'd be saving the life of our child. I'm not so certain I could have been as strong."

Geraldine sobbed but did not look away. "But I did not trust you to protect Gavin."

"How do you place the life of your child in the hands of

another? I cannot fault you for your actions, Geraldine. I abandoned my anger toward you long ago."

Gavin cleared his throat, uncomfortable with the emotion smothering him. "So, you left the fae world," he said. "You returned to your father, and when he died, you turned to Bruce McCain. Mother, you were already married. How could you have said your vows to McCain, as well?"

She shook her head. "It is a sin I will surely pay for when my time comes, but I do not regret it."

Gavin buried his face in his hands, confused. Wearily, he looked at his father. "She didn't trust you to keep me safe, but you didn't trust her, either. You sent Alec to keep watch over me."

Arrane nodded, looking old and tired. "I needed eyes and ears to venture places I could not go."

Leaning back in his chair, Arrane held out his hand. "Create wine," he said.

A moment later, a fine crystal goblet appeared in Arrane's hand. He leaned across the table and handed it to Gavin. Gavin took it, remembering how it had felt to create the life in the dead butterfly so many days ago. Ask and ye shall receive, he thought, a faint smile curving his lips.

"I sent Alec to you only because I knew you were a young boy who would be curious of the world. If ever you were in danger, that was when Alec was bound to guard you."

"He was only two years older than I. What a mighty force of protection he would be."

"You are alive, are you not? Alec was an unfortunate boy who had no one in this world to call family or friend. He stumbled into a faery ring during the times of 'tween and saw much of what a boy his age should know nothing about. I recognized in him the strength of a man your age now."

The pounding in Gavin's head worsened by the second. "I need to think on all of this, to clear my mind," he said. He did not wait for his parents' approval. He couldn't leave the confining room fast enough. But as he reached the doorway, he turned back to his mother. "I am truly happy to see you looking so fit, Mother. It pleases me that you've come. I hope you both will give me time to understand what it means to have two parents, when my whole life, I've had none."

Without waiting for a reply, he closed the door and strode through the main corridor. Sighing, he passed the great hall and listened to the music wafting out from the door cracks. He was in no mood for festivities, and though he longed to simply keep on in search of solitude, he needed to see Nakkole. With a swing of his arm, he pushed open the hall door and stood there for a long moment watching the festivities.

In the far corner, Nakkole sat where he had left her. As though sensing his presence, she jerked her head up. Her gaze focused on his, a smile artfully decorating her face. It fell as quickly as it had appeared, and a frown took its place. In an instant, she was out of her chair and making her way toward him. She did not pause to ask him questions. Instead, she simply put her arms around his waist and pulled him to her, offering in her embrace both her strength and her understanding.

Twenty-six

~

The silence in Arrane's private chamber thudded heavily in Geraldine's frazzled mind. She could feel Arrane's intense gaze boring into the top of her head as he held her in his arms, consoling her when he should be screaming at her in anger.

What did one say to the man she abandoned so many years ago? The man she'd not trusted to protect their child. Searching for her courage, she found it wanting, but still forced herself to look into his eyes.

Heavens, but she was too old for this. Throughout her journey to this place, she had felt her strength slowly begin its return with each breath as she grew closer to Arrane. When she saw him in the great hall, she had felt the power of time slip away from her, had felt her renewed body as it healed from her reunion with her soul mate. Still, she felt so old . . .

She took in the sight of Arrane's aged face, his silver hair. She had been so relieved to find Gavin unharmed, to finally lay her weary eyes upon a son her illness had stolen from her, that she hadn't allowed herself to truly see Arrane for what he had become.

With trembling fingers, she reached up and traced the deep grooves around his eyes, following the wrinkle to his brow and above. "I have returned. The part of your soul you gave to me is renewed, and I felt the years slip away. Why—"

"I gave your soul away, Geraldine. I will not be healed by your nearness as you were by mine."

Gave it away? But that wasn't possible. "To whom? Why?"

"Gavin did not come through his journey unscathed. He was pierced by an elf bolt. He would have lost his mortal half had I not transferred to him the bit you gave to me."

"Gavin carries my soul?"

Arrane smiled and cupped her cheek. "Hasn't he always?"

Geraldine relished the strength in his hand, but would not let herself be swayed. "Aye, he has. But had he lost his mortal half, he would have been full fae. Surely, that would have benefitted your kingdom?"

"Geraldine, until I met you, I did not rule Arran with the fairness it deserved. I did not hold the necessary compassion within myself, nor did I understand the grandness of life in its fullness. Should Gavin lose his mortal half, he would not be as good a king as he could be. He would lose the part of himself that is truly good, for even light fae, by nature, have a sinister side."

"As do mortal men," she interrupted.

"*Oui*, but Gavin's mortal half is good and pure. It will keep his thirst for power and greed at a distance, and it is all that is keeping him from being as unconscionable as Elphina and her mother. Geraldine, had I not been given a piece of your goodness, I cannot guarantee I would not have welcomed my daughter into my kingdom in order to share the ruling of all the fae everywhere."

Her heart swelling, Geraldine reached to her toes and placed a feathery soft kiss on Arrane's lips. "We share a child, Arrane. My God, how he looks like you. But did you see? He has my mouth, I think. He is no longer in my womb, but together we created a whole being. Surely we can take part in another soul exchange."

He smiled, but it did not reach his eyes. "If I did not love you as much as I do, I would rejoice in your offer to share yourself with me once again."

"Then why do you not?"

Arrane released her shoulders and sighed a heavy sigh. "You love your Scotland far too much. Another soul exchange, and you would be forever forced to remain here."

Her heart light with relief, she laughed. "Is that all? Arrane, had I not feared for Gavin's safety I would never have left! You are my home and always have been. I care not where that home may be."

"Nay, that is not all, though I do admit it cheers my heart to know you wish to remain with me. You would be forever changed as well. We cannot partake in the exchange and have it be one-sided. I have already given you a bit of myself, and it lives in you still. For you to give me back a piece of yourself would mean receiving even more of me. You would be as Gavin is, half fae."

Geraldine swallowed. As much as she'd always admired Arrane's gifts and thought his kind lovely, she had never wanted the magic herself. The very thought frightened her to her core.

But not, however, as much as the thought of living once again without this man that she loved. For him, she would do anything.

"Arrane?"

"*Oui?*"

"I give myself to you." She smiled and wiped a tear from his cheek. "Kiss me."

She waited for the warmth of his mouth to capture hers, but instead, he rained a damp trail over her neck and down her throat. It didn't matter that time lingered on his face and hands—he still possessed the ability to make her heart race. But the tangible desire she'd felt within him a moment ago vanished. She lifted her head to find him staring at her chest with such scrutiny, she squirmed. "What is it?"

"This . . . this is the charm Gavin found as a child?" Arrane's long, thin fingers plucked the chain dangling from around Geraldine's neck, sliding it through his hand until the small amber stone that hung from it lay flat against his palm.

"Aye, why? Arrane? What's wrong?"

He met her gaze, a soft smile curling up the edges of his mouth. "May I?"

She nodded, allowing him to slip the chain from her neck. She attempted patience while she waited for him to speak, but after several minutes was about to break the silence with the demand he return her necklace. She wasn't given the chance.

"You and our son have brought it home, Geraldine. This is no ordinary jewel." Then, to Geraldine's utter astonishment, Arrane threw back his head and released laughter so loud, she was forced to cover her ears.

When he finally calmed, he cupped her chin and tilted her face toward him. "It's the Orb of Knowledge."

Geraldine's gasp was cut off by Arrane's kiss—a kiss so powerful, she knew he'd be a different man when it finally broke.

❦

Nakkole felt as though she floated—like a leaf abandoning its mothering tree to explore the world on its own. Only she wasn't alone. She was in Gavin's arms, being carried up the golden staircase to the destination of his choosing. She clung to his neck, kissing every bit of bare skin along his throat that her lips could find. He moaned, and she could feel him taking the steps two at a time, as hungry, she hoped, as she to find solitude in a chamber above.

"I need your sword, Gavin," a deep, intrusive voice said from the bottom of the stairs.

The moment broken, Nakkole stepped down, turning with Gavin to stare at the man who'd interrupted them. Arrane stood at the foot of the stairs beside Geraldine, and the very sight of her king made Nakkole's knees weaken.

Beside her, she felt Gavin stiffen. Nakkole, too, found it hard to comprehend what she saw. Arrane stood before them nearly as young in appearance as Gavin, his long, silver hair, now as black as night, his skin taut and flawless. Gone was the stooped posture born of time, for Arrane now stood tall and strong, and clearly ready to take on whatever posed the threat at this moment.

"Arrane?" Gavin's voice was all but a whisper.

Arrane glanced down at himself, as though expected to find his white robes gone. "Am I so unrecognizable?"

"Aye, Your Majesty, you are," Nakkole said, rushing down the stairs. She threw herself to her knees, desperately choking back her sobs. *This* was the king she remembered from her childhood. The king who would leave no doubt as to the victor of this battle against Elphina.

"Rise, Nakkole." Arrane helped Nakkole to her feet and briefly embraced her before turning his attention back to Gavin. "Your sword, son. Where is it?"

Since Gavin didn't look capable of speech, Nakkole answered in his stead. "It was taken from him, Majesty. In Elfame."

Arrane's newly bronzed face paled. "Taken? By whom?"

Gavin visibly shook himself from his stupor and slowly made his way down the steps. "The peches that dragged me into this world, I assume. I had it with me when they took me. It was gone when I awakened."

Arrane muttered something beneath his breath.

"What is so important about his sword?" Geraldine asked, looping her arm through Arrane's.

Arrane let a moment of silence hang in the air before answering. "The enchantment I cast that split the Trinity was so powerful, even I didn't know where the stones fell. I had a son and a wife who could very well be taken and used to weaken me enough to gain such knowledge from me. I couldn't risk knowing the location of the orbs. But, because I knew the day might come when we would need to find them in order to prevent someone else from doing so, I cast the knowledge of each location onto a tiny scroll. A scroll that is, even now, buried in the hilt of your sword."

Gavin's gaze swung to his mother. "Bruce McCain said you'd made him swear to give me that sword."

"I didn't know. I knew only that your father wanted you to have it." Geraldine bit her lip and stepped in front of Arrane, forcing him to look down at her. "Why didn't you tell me what was in it?"

"Because if anyone else discovered what was in that

sword, Gavin could be used to torture the information out of you the same as I."

Anger slowly made Nakkole forget the respect her king deserved. This secret should have been revealed long before now. "You knew Elphina was searching for the Trinity. What better time to bring that sword here and fetch the rest of the Orbs before she could find them?"

"Why not simply steal the sword and leave Gavin be?" Geraldine demanded, obviously as angered by Arrane's secrets as Nakkole.

Arrane smiled weakly. "Because I thought I'd be long dead before the need to find those Orbs would come. Even if you'd brought the scroll to me, I would not be able to read the locations."

"I don't understand any of this." Gavin eased himself onto the bottom step, sitting and looking as though he felt queasy.

"I enchanted the scroll so that only my bloodline could read what was written upon it. Foolish, I see that now, but I never expected Geraldine to return and restore my youth. I could have enchanted it so that only I could read what was on it, but I thought for certain I wouldn't last that long. I could only pray that you could be persuaded to return here with that sword, and that you might read it."

Nakkole understood well enough. Arrane had thought this war of Elphina's would come to pass when it was too late for him to stand against her. He'd been counting on his son to fight this battle. And now, the sword was gone, leaving two of the Trinity out there somewhere.

She gasped. "Elphina. If Gavin can read the scroll—"

Arrane nodded, tiny patches of pink returning to his cheeks. "Then so can Elphina. I never thought in a million years that she'd get her hands on that sword. And even if she had, why would she look for something within it that only I knew existed?"

"Avalon save us if she does! The Orb of Knowledge and the Orb of Creation are still out there. Should she find them, her cause will be greatly benefited," Nakkole said, fighting to keep disrespect for her king out of her voice.

"Gavin found the . . . Orb of Knowledge years ago."

Geraldine pulled a long chain from her breasts and dangled a small amber stone in front of them. "He gifted it to me when he was a child, only I was unaware that it was more than a jewel until Arrane told me a few moments ago."

Nakkole recognized the stone as the one Gavin had been wearing. He'd had the Orb all along? All this time?

She gasped, her hand flying to cover her mouth. "The babe. I was holding this Orb when I saw . . . when I *knew* I carried your child."

Gavin's brow furrowed. "I wondered how you knew, but I didn't dare ask for fear of learning of yet another bit of magic to confuse me."

"I'm going to have a grandchild?" Geraldine asked, placing a hand over her heart.

As Nakkole nodded, tears filled the older woman's eyes. "I believe so." She looked at Arrane. "You knew of the babe when you ordered me to come to you, didn't you?"

Arrane's smile was faint, his worry for the Orbs still quite evident. "I did."

"A sweet babe! Amidst all this ugly hate and war. 'Tis a blessing!" Geraldine threw her arms around Nakkole, nearly knocking her off her feet.

Unsure what to do, Nakkole held her lightly.

"Later, Geraldine," Arrane said. "We will celebrate our new heir. But just now, the Orbs require our full attention."

Grateful to no longer be the center of attention, Nakkole backed away and all but plastered herself to Gavin's side.

Gavin wrinkled his brow and rubbed his chest as though he felt the weight of the stone still dangling there. "So this is the Orb of Knowledge?"

Geraldine nodded, an enormous grin on her face.

"Well, that explains why I've found myself knowing things I shouldn't since my arrival in this world," Gavin muttered, a scowl on his face.

Arrane smiled. "Indeed."

"Why is it not locked away with the other?" Nakkole asked.

"I considered it," Arrane said. "But I believe placing both Orbs in the same place would be foolhardy at best. Better to

split them up." He turned to Geraldine and held out his hand.
"May I?"

Geraldine nodded and slipped the chain from around her
neck. She handed it to Arrane, her gaze watching it lovingly
as though she was reluctant to let it go.

Arrane palmed the Orb, closed his fingers around it
tightly. "I used the power of Creation to fashion a replica of
this Orb. I placed it in my solar with the Orb of Truth.
Should anyone know to look there, at least I will have prevented the theft of both." He opened his fist and dangled the
chain in front of Gavin. "I think it best if *you* place this one
in safety. No one else needs to know where you've hidden it,
and I trust you to keep it safe."

Gavin didn't reach for the Orb. "I appreciate your trust,
but I'm not certain I want to be the Orb's keeper. That is a
powerful weapon, best left to one who knows the hows and
whys of this world. Best left to someone who intends to stay
and guard it."

Nakkole's chest tightened at the mention of his leaving.
The jovial, passionate mood she'd reveled in moments ago
now lay shattered all around them. Gavin would leave. He
was not hers. It was growing more and more obvious he had
no intention of even considering staying in the Otherworld.

It was all she could do not to cry like a silly human. The
mortals' notion of love . . . my, but it seemed to be catching!

Geraldine grabbed for Gavin's hand, then plucked the
chain from Arrane's fingers. She pressed the Orb into
Gavin's palm. "'Tis as it should be. What you do with it is
your choice, but this Orb belongs to you. Perhaps Nakkole
can help you find a place for it, and when you're ready to return to Grey Loch, you can carry it with you and hide it
there."

Nakkole bit into her bottom lip so hard, she nearly cried
out with pain. It was all she could do to hold her tongue
against chastising Arrane and Geraldine for giving in to
Gavin's desire to return to Scotland so easily. Arrane's youth
had returned, which meant the kingdom no longer needed
Gavin to replace the king so soon. But what of a mother's
need for her son? A father's? What of a woman's need for

the man she was just coming to know and love? A child's need for its father? What of *those* things?

She felt the pull of Gavin's stare and looked up to find him watching her. "Will you help me find a place for it?"

Unable to speak for fear of giving in to her tears, she nodded.

Arrane clapped his hands together. "Well then, that settles it. Take care of the matter as soon as possible and we'll only have one other Orb to worry about."

"The Orb of Creation," Geraldine said.

Gavin slipped the chain around his neck and stuffed the Orb of Knowledge beneath his tunic. "What sort of mischief could Elphina possibly achieve with only one Orb?"

Arrane smiled wanly, looking tired despite his newly youthful appearance. "She can create an army that could bring us to our knees."

Twenty-seven

~~~

Gavin could not sleep, and after all that had occurred that day, it was no wonder he felt the urge to pace his chamber—or better yet, run circles around the Isle. He felt as though a stampede of horses charged through his blood, and he had nowhere to release his pent-up energy. Everyone else in the palace had long since found slumber.

The chamber he'd been given was truly spectacular, but there was little here to hold his attention. Even the large, stone bath set into the floor like some Roman structure did not beckon him. A bath would help him sleep, aye, but the water the servants had brought up to him earlier had already grown cold, and would only waken him further.

He truly considered the idea of running around the Isle, but had a feeling he would pay dearly for it should anyone discover he was out unguarded. The last thing he wanted or needed was for more concern over his welfare.

So instead, he paced. And paced. Until only a few hours before cock's crow, a light tap on his door offered the distraction from his thoughts that he so needed. He opened the door to find Nakkole there, wrapped in a blanket, a look of determination on her face.

"What are you—"

She all but lunged at him, wrapping her arms around his neck and smothering her face against his shoulder. "I had the worst nightmare, so vivid, in fact, I had to inspect my chamber for any signs of maras." She squeezed him more tightly. "I dreamed you were dead, that Elphina was queine of this palace, and the light shone no more."

Gavin patted her back, breathed in her wonderfully familiar scent. "As you can see, I'm alive and well . . . if not extremely tired."

She pulled back, her eyes wide. "I didn't mean to wake you. I just had to make certain you were all right."

He laughed and hugged her back to him. "I haven't even laid down yet."

She stared up at him, her lips plump from fresh slumber. He ran his thumb along them and she kissed it lightly. He lowered his head and she met him halfway, stretching to the tips of her toes to reach him. Gavin welcomed her warmly, hungry for whatever solace she offered.

Something odd drove the force of her kiss, and he was certain it was not simply lust, but emotion as well. His groin tightened and strained against the odd black leggings he wore.

"You didn't come here for this," he whispered, moving to bury his face in the crook of her soft neck.

"Nay, but I will stay for it if you'll allow it." Nakkole's hand moved to cup the back of his head, her fingers clinching a fistful of his hair.

Gavin groaned, his entire body suddenly ablaze. He scooped her into her arms and carried her to the bed. Sitting on the edge of the soft mattress, he settled her on his lap and once again devoured her mouth.

Trailing a finger over her breast, he continued on until his hand rested against her flat belly. He gave momentary consideration to the child there, *his child*, before moving to cup the tender mound between her legs. She gasped and opened her thighs wider for him. The blanket she'd had wrapped around herself fell into a heap on the floor, exposing her private curls to his starving gaze and touch. He stared at her, reveling in the sight of her now-bare breasts.

She stood from his lap, pulling him up with her. Her hand found the laces of his breeches and tugged them loose. She knelt to remove them, the sight of her head at his waist a painfully beautiful scene. He dared not breathe or touch her for fear of losing all composure. Every movement, every bit of clothing she discarded from his body, scorched him like flame. When she'd finished her task, he seized her by the waist and bit at her throat playfully, wishing he could devour her inch by inch.

When Nakkole's palms pressed against his bare chest, her fingers fondling his nipples, he could take no more.

He moved to place her onto the bed, but she stepped away. "Nay. Not there." She stretched to kiss him, placating him with a gentle stroke to his neck. "Let me show you?" she muttered against his mouth.

Confused, Gavin did as she asked, nearly whimpering when her flesh left his, her kiss gone. Nakkole walked to the corner of the room and stuck her foot into the stone bath filled with water that must be far too cold to be comfortable by now. She didn't even flinch. Instead, she bent, offering him a highly arousing view of her backside, and placed her hands into the tub. A moment later, a faint steam rose into the air, and she stepped into the bath. She turned to him and held out her hand, her eyes promising only heaven, and Gavin walked to her without question.

Taking his hand, Nakkole guided him into the water and pushed on his shoulders until he sat on the rim. The water was hot—a trick of magic, no doubt—but he hadn't the care to ask her about it. She kneeled in the water, and her lips brushed against his inner thigh. Blood pounded in Gavin's ears at the feel of her tongue so close to the part of him that throbbed for her. Unable to stand, he lowered himself beside her, watching as she stretched out on her back, the bath so large, even a man the size of Gavin would find comfort stretching out in it.

"My soul is of water, Gavin. I want to show you the beauty of it."

As she stared at him, her eyes glittered and her hair seemed to lighten to the soft embers of fiery gold. He allowed her to pull him on top of her, her wet body slick be-

neath his, and he fell easily over her, his legs gliding between hers. He could have wept for the sensation of their
bodies swaying together in the light ripple of water. To alle-
viate the need driving him mad, he crushed his mouth to hers
and plunged his tongue inside, drinking in the taste of her,
the feel of her. Nakkole moaned into his mouth and raked
her nails down his ribs and waist. She cupped his backside,
pinching and scratching, even as her hips moved against
him.

His hardness nicely cuddled in the folds of her silky heat,
her movements nearly sent Gavin into premature ecstasy. "I
cannot wait."

It was an apology of sorts, but Nakkole didn't seem to
mind. She wrapped her legs around his waist and lightly nib-
bled on his jaw. "Nor can I. Find me, Gavin."

He did, and the feel of her tightly wound around him was
powerful enough to allow him to forget all that had happened to him these last few days.

His thrusts came easily and effortlessly as the water
pulled him to then fro, deep then shallow. Together, they
found their release and fell weak inside the steaming pool.

Gavin collapsed against Nakkole, his energy spent from
the ferocity of their lovemaking. His full weight crushed
against her tiny body, but, when he tried to ease himself off
her, she held him steady.

"Please," she whispered. "A moment longer."

And so he waited, inhaling the sweet, springtime fra-
grance of her nakedness, his hands tangled in her long, wet
hair. After a few short moments, he could feel her chest rising more deeply as air became more difficult for her to
grasp. He withdrew from her body, moved to her side and
drank in the sight of her glowing body.

"There!"

Nakkole's cry startled Gavin enough to sit up quickly,
sloshing the water from the tub. "What?"

She was pointing at the crystal mirror hanging above the
tub. She raised up and pressed her finger to the small amber
stone in the bottom left corner. An identical stone marked
the other three corners, as well.

"This is where you should hide the Orb of Knowledge.

Look." She rose to her knees, giving him a delightful view of her backside. "See if the Orb will fit where this stone is."

His heart slowing to normal pace, Gavin lifted the chain on his neck so that the Orb was beside the small amber. It looked pretty damned close in size.

"Will it work?" Nakkole asked.

Gavin smiled, "I believe so. I'll see if I can loosen one of the stones in the morning. Damned, but they look nearly identical."

His gaze raked over her glazed eyes, her pert nose and her full, swollen lips and he no longer cared about the stones. He stared at her breasts and their pink crests, then slowly allowed his gaze to move to the belly that cradled his child.

His child.

He knew naught of being a father, of being a parent at all. He'd never possessed either, in all truths. How would he possibly know how to love this child the way he'd never been loved, himself?

"I know nothing of fae children." In fact, he knew nothing of children of any kind. "How long before our child is born?"

He knew the question would be foolish if put to a normal woman, for they had only joined once before this and the answer should be simple enough. But for all he knew of the fae kind—which was little to nothing—Nakkole could have this fae child in as little as a day or as long as a year.

"'Tis no different than the ladies of Scotland or elsewhere. Just before spring, I suppose."

Eight moons would come and go until then. Plenty of time for him to prepare himself for fatherhood, and yet three years could pass and he would still feel ill equipped. "I should hate you, Nakkole. And yet, I cannot. Why? What is it about you that makes me forget your lies and deceit in favor of wanting to hold you and keep you safe?"

He hadn't meant to speak his words aloud, but there it was all the same. Nakkole turned so they floated nose to nose. Her breath warmed his face, and her fingers trailing slowly over his jaw warmed his heart. God save him, he was feeling much too much for this lass.

"Should I apologize, then, for your not hating me? I cannot, for I am so very glad to think we might someday be friends again."

Friends? Is that where she saw them headed? And what of their child? Surely she knew he would not allow his child to be born without the security of wedlock. Her words bit cruelly in his heart, but he held back the bitter reply perched on his tongue.

Nakkole watched Gavin's eyes flicker and darken. "Did I say something wrong?"

Her body still burned for his touch, but the coldness now residing in his eyes kept her from reaching out to him. He left the tub, left her side, and she watched him walk to the hearth and tamper with the small fire burning within. His clothes slowly began to dress him, as was the way in this world with any born with powers of water. She immediately missed the intimacy of seeing him as bare as he'd been a moment ago.

When he didn't respond to her question, her heart skipped a painful beat. The truce they'd found was a fragile thing and she loathed the thought of destroying it. But what had she done? She'd only said she'd hoped they might be friends again. Was that what bothered him?

Surely not. Surely he knew as well as she did that any prospect of a future together was impossible. No matter that she loved him more each moment she spent with him. That such loving was slowly leading to a passion she hadn't thought she'd ever be granted. He was her prince and, he had already stated that he was going to be leaving to return to Scotland when this ordeal was over. She had no right to pretend more would become of their relationship.

"Gavin," she whispered, pushing herself out of the soothing water. She allowed her body to dress itself as she waited for Gavin to respond. He didn't. "Why is it that each time we make love, I seem to make you angry?"

He looked at her, tired pockets lining his eyes that hadn't been there moments ago. "I'm not angry," he said. "Just thinking."

"Will you talk to me?"

He studied her in silence for a long moment, then finally tugged at his hair, his face twisted in frustration. "This is a fine mess we find ourselves in, is it not?" He collapsed onto the bed, reached for Nakkole, and dragged her onto his lap. "I've been fighting the answer to our dilemma because of my duty to Grey Loch, but the truth of the matter is, my choice had been made from the moment I made love to you in Scotland."

A smile spread throughout Nakkole's body and she thought she might drift away from the lightness now filling her soul. He was going to stay! He realized his duty to this kingdom and his child was his destiny, not what lay in Scotland. She flung her arms around his neck and showered his face with kisses.

"You'll be happy here," she said, resting her cheek against his. "I promise, you won't miss Scotland after a while."

"Not miss— Nakkole, I cannot stay here. Is that what you thought . . . ? Nay, my duty to my people still stands."

He cupped her chin, forced her to look at him even while she felt her heart crumble with each word he spoke. It was all she could do not to burst into a horrid display of tears and run screaming for her mother to heal her hurts.

"But, you said—your duty to Grey Loch?"

"Aye. My duty to marry a lass from a strong, wealthy clan. That simply cannot happen now. You and I will marry—here on the Isle if you'd like your family to witness the ceremony. And once my sister has been dealt with, we'll return to Scotland."

Marry? Another piece of her heart chipped away. "Return to Scotland?" Nakkole's throat ached terribly as she constricted the tears climbing up it. "I cannot return to Scotland, Gavin."

His hold on her slackened, but his body beneath her grew rigid. "Of course you can. You're carrying my child, Nakkole. You can't possibly believe I'll allow you to remain here and have my child grow up without a father as I did."

Nakkole pushed to her feet, her body shivering now. "My blood is tied to the waters here, Gavin. Should I leave this place and my waters for too long, my magic will slowly die."

He stared at her accusingly, his eyes narrowed, his jaw

muscle clenched. "And you care more for your magic than for the well-being of our child?"

"It's not so simple as that. I'm full fae, Gavin. I belong *here*, not tied to two worlds as you may be. If my magic dies . . . *my soul* dies."

This seemed to calm him, seemed to soothe a bit of the anger in his eyes. He sat beside her once again, but took care not to brush against her.

She reached out to him, but he waved away her touch.

"I don't wish to see you hurt," he said. "But, do you believe your king, my father, will allow a bastard child to rule all of this?"

"Bastards are a human worry. They are not seen here as unworthy. It's far more common for a fae to be born a bastard than to be born in wedlock in our world. Your child, our child, will rule here without prejudice from anyone."

Gavin took a deep breath and bowed his head into his hands. For once in his life, the fight had been beaten out of him. What was he to say? He wanted Nakkole for his wife, wanted to drag her back to Scotland and create the family he'd longed for as a child. But he couldn't very well force the issue if it meant Nakkole's life would be put at risk. If her life and soul were indeed tied to the waters here, he couldn't ask her to relocate.

"I have to return to Grey Loch, Nakkole. I've left much there undone."

And the truth of it was, he still needed to prove to himself that he was worthy of being their laird, that he could lead them into being a strong clan, that he could be useful, damnit. Here, he was nothing more than the son of a powerful king. Had Arrane remained frail and near death, Gavin might have truly considered staying, for it would have meant this kingdom needed him. But with Arrane's newfound health, Gavin was no more needed here after this battle than was Luke or Robert.

"My child," he said, his voice raw, "will not grow up without his father. But I do not wish him to grow up without his mother, either." He looked to Nakkole, found her eyes glassy, her face pale. "So how do we solve this matter?"

The light of her faint smile didn't reach as far as her eyes.

She rose to her feet and stood with her back to him. "There are four seasons in a year. I'm certain we can think of some fair matter to share the raising of our child."

She walked slowly to the door, opened it, then paused. When she looked at him from over her shoulders, her lifeless, tired expression brought Gavin to his feet.

She smiled faintly and shrugged. "It seems you'll be free to marry a Scottish lass, after all."

"Nakkole . . ." he started. But, she'd stepped into the hall and closed the door before he could discover what he'd meant to say.

Twenty-eight

~

After a morning spent working to hide the Orb of Knowledge within the mirror in his chamber, Gavin went in search of Nakkole after spending the remaining hours of night reliving the gut-wrenchingly defeated expression she'd worn when she'd left his chamber. He could have strangled himself for ruining their time together, for so obviously hurting her.

He meant to make up for it by inviting her on a walk to explore the Isle. But as he searched the palace, he found no sign of her. Instead, he found Arrane sitting alone in his solar, studiously examining the Orb of Truth as he sat behind the small table in the corner.

He glanced up, his taut expressioning softening when he saw Gavin. "Good day, son."

Gavin nodded, then gestured to the Orb. "Is it showing you anything?"

Arrane scowled and set the Orb upon the table. He folded his hands in front of him and heaved a sigh. "It showed me something this morning, but I keep checking again in hopes of better news. None has come."

"Can you not ask the Orb of Knowledge?"

"It would be no use, either. Unlike the Orb of Truth, it merely supplies facts, not secrets. Should I ask about the Orbs, my head would simply be filled with knowledge regarding them."

"What did the Orb of Truth show you?" Without awaiting an invitation, Gavin stepped into the chamber and took the seat across from Arrane. He stared at the Orb, but saw only the clouded marble structure. No image cleared its center as it had when he'd peered within it last eve.

Arrane pinched the bridge of his nose. "Elphina has found the Orb of Creation. As I feared, your sword led her straight to it."

His sword. The vacant spot where it normally hung on his waist still itched to be filled. "Then it is a blessing the other Orbs are in our possession."

"True, but the Orb of Creation is powerful in its own right. Elphina will no longer have to wait for her maras to gather the souls of the dead. She'll be able to create her army herself. Oakmen from oak, redcaps from toadstools. Succubi, incubi, and banshees from the bones of the dead. She'll even be able to better prepare them with weaponry and armor from items as simple as stone."

Amazing. Had he possessed such a tool in Scotland, the McCains might have been the most powerful clan in the lands. "What does this mean for our fight?"

Arrane looked at him from over his hand, his brow raised. "It means learning your powers has never been more important. There is no time to waste, Gavin. I'd like you to spend the afternoon with me. Let me guide your magic until it is under your control."

Gavin sat in silence for a moment, unable and unwilling to fully commit himself without a good deal of thought. He considered what having fully developed powers might mean for the remainder of his life. How would he manage to keep them hidden from those at Grey Loch who might find them frightening? The church, the people, the allies he'd hoped to gain. They would suspect witchcraft or possession, most likely. How was he to cope with that?

"I'm deadly with a sword, Arrane," he said, finally. "And

far more comfortable with my blade than I could ever be with magic. Let me fight this battle my way."

Arrane's thin mouth pursed and he rose to his feet. "I want to show you something." He turned and pulled a sword from its sheath on his hip, a sword he hadn't been wearing the night before. Then, he handed the weapon to Gavin and thrust out his other arm. "Cut me."

"I'm sorry?" Gavin placed the weapon on the table, certain he'd heard wrong.

"I want you to cut me. I want to show you why magic is vital in our war with Elphina."

"Nay." Gavin backed away from the table, growing slightly annoyed. "Cut yourself, then."

Arrane nodded. "Very well."

And to Gavin's horror, he lifted the sword, stretched out his other arm, and ran the blade's edge down his palm. Blood dripped from the open cut, but before Arrane could place the sword back in its sheath, the skin closed around the wound, sealing shut, and the blood ran no more.

"Magic?" he asked, feeling foolish for voicing the simple question aloud. Of course it was magic. What else could perform such a trick?

"*Oui*, magic. That sword was crafted by a human weaponsmith. It possesses no enchantments. Therefore, it is no threat to our kind." He smiled at Gavin. "I wouldn't be surprised to learn that you've been wounded in battle and had no knowledge of it many times. The fae half of you likely mended itself before you could even feel the first sting."

Gavin had never allowed another's sword close enough to find out. "And if I took that sword into this battle?"

"It would be useless." He bent, and when he rose again, he held in his hand a dagger. "Now this, on the other hand, is a fae weapon. Enchanted to cause mortal injury to those of fae blood. They are hard to come by, but I have been collecting such for years."

Gavin took the dagger from Arrane. Its blade was golden and shiny. It looked more like an accessory than a deadly weapon. As Gavin was turning it over in his hand, Arrane snatched it and ran it down his palm where the other sword had cut him. This time, the blood dropped onto the table long enough to create a nasty puddle of red.

"You didn't need to illustrate your point so vividly," Gavin said. "Put it away."

Arrane laughed and ran his fingers over his wounded palm. The cut vanished, sealed once again. "Had I not the power to heal myself, that cut would have needed tending. You see now why your magic will be necessary in this fight?"

He did, and the notion didn't sit well with him at all.

"We can begin your lessons straight away—"

Gavin shook his head. "I need to find Nakkole. After noon meal, I'll return here and we can begin."

Arrane shoved his dagger beneath the sleeve of his long, white robe, and contemplated Gavin. "The White Lady . . . you like her a great deal."

"I suppose," Gavin said, uncomfortable with the fatherly tone of Arrane's voice.

Nodding, Arrane leaned back in his chair, his eyes narrowing slightly. "And I'm also presuming you mean to try to take her back to Grey Loch should you leave here. You should know, she'll never be able to live permanently in your world."

Relieved that Arrane knew Gavin would resume his lairdship come the end of this fight, Gavin nodded. "She's already explained to me why she cannot return with me." He frowned then. "We're likely to divide the raising of our child throughout the year. My son or daughter will not grow up without his parents."

Guilt bore into the gray of Arrane's eyes. "I am truly sorry I could not have saved you from that situation, Gavin. I cannot say so enough."

Clearing his throat, Gavin strode for the door, and with great effort, cast his father a last glance.

"Then I ask that you watch over my own child when I am not here to do so. Be my eyes when he is in your world and be as good a grandfather as you couldn't be a father."

He closed the door and left his father alone to ponder his words.

❧

He found Nakkole sitting in a circle with her fellow White Lady sisters. Each of them was beautiful, but his gaze was riveted on the sight of Nakkole. She was laughing, her head thrown back, her hair flowing about her face in the breeze. She truly was the loveliest woman he'd ever seen.

He was tempted to leave her be, let her reunite with her sisters without intrusion. But his time in this place would hopefully be short, and he needed to make certain she held no anger at him when it was time for him to leave.

"Nakkole." His deep voice sounded strange and gruff among the feminine giggles that it seemed to have summoned.

The group of women watched him, each whispering something to the sister beside her. A few continued their giggles, and others smiled in quite the flirtatious manner. Gavin squirmed beneath his skin. If he'd been born with the ability to blush—which he was certain he had not been—he would have done so now.

Nakkole rose to her feet and tilted her head toward him. "Good day, Your Majesty."

She was still upset. Not that he could blame her. He wasn't exactly in a jolly good mood himself. He summoned his most calm expression, a pleasant smile, and far more cheeriness than he truly felt.

"Aye. I thought perhaps you might accompany me on a walk." Several White Ladies tittered. Gavin ignored them. "I would like very much for you to show me the Isle."

She approached, blessedly stepping away from the prying ears of her sisters. "I don't know this isle much better than you. I only came here once as a child. And, besides that, you should not be wandering around unguarded."

He grinned, a genuine grin this time. "Are you not a guardian faery?" When she frowned, he lifted his head to gesture to the turrets above. "Look . . . we are watched. I promise not to stray from their sight. Does that satisfy you?"

She shrugged, still not looking him in the eye. "I suppose, though as I said, I'm not certain what I could possibly show you. Mayhap my mother, or your father, should be the one to escort you about."

Reaching out to her, he brushed a stray hair from her cheek. "But they are not such lovely company as you."

Her flinching beneath his touch soured his mood all the more, but he struggled not to change the pleasant expression he hoped he wore.

"You may throw stones at me while we stroll if it pleases you."

At that she smiled, though she looked away as she did so. When she turned her gaze back to him, she nodded. "A short stroll, then."

Satisfied, he allowed her to guide him around the pathway that circled the palace. At the southern end, they came upon a garden blooming with every color ever created. Nearly a hundred feet of hedgerows constructed a sizable labyrinth, bordering the land between river and forest. In the fields just west of the labyrinth, fawns and does grazed freely, unbothered by the strangers approaching them. Gavin and Nakkole watched them in silence for a long while, until, eventually, Gavin sat on the thick grass and pulled Nakkole down beside him.

Unsure of what to say to her, he chose the topic that had been bothering him this morning. "Arrane wishes to begin my lessons with magic."

"Good," Nakkole said, leaning back on her hands, her attention still fully centered on the pasture filled with deer. "You should learn them as quickly as possible."

"Will you help me? I mean to say, I don't wish to look completely ignorant when I go to him this afternoon. Perhaps a quick lesson here?"

She shrugged. "What do you wish to know?"

She smelled so sweet, his stomach rumbled. "Tell me about my ability to control.

You said I've been using this all along."

"*Oui*. Gavin the Immortal." She faced him, her gaze studying his hair rather than his eyes. "'Twas more than your impressive skill with a blade that kept you alive all these years, I think."

Hearing her say such did not surprise him. He'd always felt as though something larger than himself had been at his side on every battlefield he'd ever fought on.

"Show me."

"I cannot. The power of control is not within me. You share the powers of your father. My powers as a White Lady are limited to cloaking and creating. That is all.

"All power works in a similar manner. It's in here," she said, pointing to her head. "And here." She pointed to her heart. "If you can focus both onto what it is you wish to do, and you have the power within you, you can manage anything."

She felt around the grass beside her, found a stone and held it up. "When you were on the battlefield, and an opponent's sword was about to cut you through, how did you stop it from piercing you? How did you maneuver him and his blade away from you?"

Gavin closed his eyes and recalled the last battle he'd fought. Alec had been at his side, and Gavin had not been the one about to be run through. A man larger than Gavin had charged at Alec, his sword raised. But Alec had been engaged with another foe. Gavin had been surrounded on all sides, unable to get to his friend in time. Panic had been all consuming. He had focused on the man's sword until he could almost feel it in his hand. He had prayed, silently ordering the man's sword to the ground, and the man had dropped it, holding his hand as though it had been burned.

"I concentrated," he said. "At that moment, nothing else was as important as having that man lose his sword."

Nakkole nodded. "You willed it, and it was so."

The bit of news disturbed him. It was more than unsettling to know he had such a power within him and had been using it unknowingly all this time.

"Here," Nakkole said, opening her palm, revealing the tiny stone. "Concentrate and command this stone to roll away from us."

She set the stone upon the grass. Narrowing his eyes, Gavin stared at it, willing it to move. As it stayed as still as, well, a stone, he felt extremely foolish.

"You have to want that stone to move with your whole being," Nakkole offered.

Then perhaps he'd have more success if he tried to make Nakkole smile in his direction.

He sighed and focused on the stone, his eyes open so wide, they began to water. The pebble twitched, and as though caught in a burst of wind, it tumbled and spun, rolling a good five feet away. He blinked, the concentration broken, and the stone stopped and fell onto its side. Gavin muttered beneath his breath and refocused. This time, the stone came tumbling back toward them, resting just beside Nakkole's knee.

Like a child wishing to impress his father, he looked forward to showing Arrane this trick he had learned.

"I'm here," Gavin said a couple hours later, sticking his head into Arrane's quarters.

Geraldine was perched on Arrane's lap and, at Gavin's appearance, leaped up, a faint pink staining her cheeks. She hurried past Gavin, pressing a gentle hand to his shoulder as she left him alone with Arrane.

Gavin watched her go, still astounded that the bedridden, elderly woman he'd watch fall more ill each year could now be so young and vibrant.

"Come in." Arrane motioned for Gavin to close the door, then stood and beckoned Gavin to the back of the chamber. Much like when Arrane had opened the secret vault where the Orb of Truth resided, he chanted a few words and the shelves along the back wall slid forward then to the side, revealing yet another chamber behind them. "I want you to see this before we begin."

Someone knocked and Arrane turned his back to the newly revealed chamber. "Ah, good, they're here." He opened the door and Brock, Robert, Markham, and Luke entered, each wide-eyed and curiously looking about.

"Fancy." Luke exhaled, a broad smile on his face.

"Why are they here?" Gavin asked, greeting each of his men before turning his query to his father.

"Because they need to learn this bit, just as you do." Arrane disappeared into the chamber he'd opened, returning a few moments later with one arm toting five quivers, the other gripping four swords.

"Halt," Gavin commanded, holding his hand up to prevent his father from approaching his men. "This is not their fight, Arrane. They, like me, have no notion of the fight awaiting them. It was my choice to aid you, not theirs. I will not have them unwillingly fight for what is not, nor ever will be, theirs."

Arrane studied him, but finally nodded and set the weapons down. "Very well." He turned to Gavin's men, looking them over. "This is not your fight. Should you choose to return to Scotland now, we will not think lesser of you for it."

No one moved for a long moment. Then, to Gavin's surprise, it was the youngest of the bunch, Luke, who broke the silence. He stepped forward and swept low in an awkward bow. "You are not my king," he said to Arrane. Then, he bowed toward Gavin. "But you are my laird, Gavin. You have my sword, for whatever that is worth."

Gavin smiled and clasped Luke's arm. "It is worth a lot, my friend."

"The laird's fight is my fight, as well," said Robert, jabbing his elbow into Markham's ribs.

Markham coughed and nodded. "Aye. Mine, too."

With a heavy sigh, Brock shook his head. "Well then. Can't be the only coward to flee, now can I? You've my loyalty for whatever purpose it serves you, Laird Gavin."

Before Gavin could express his appreciation, Arrane clapped his hands together, his face beaming with pleasure. "Wonderful. Now, here . . ."

He handed a quiver to each man, and gave all but Gavin a blade. He disappeared again, this time appearing with five bows. These he set on the table, then perched himself beside them before turning to grin at his audience. "Now, as I told your men earlier, Gavin, I wish them to become familiar with the weaponry of fae. It shouldn't take long to become familiar with the differences in these weapons as opposed to the ones you normally wield."

"What sort o' differences?" Brock asked, eyeing the sword in his hand with suspicion.

"Well, that sword should feel no different than your current one, so it will take no getting used to," Arrane answered. "But it glows because it's enchanted . . ."

Gavin listened as his father explained to his men the same reason for the enchantments that he'd given Gavin this morning. Why did he need to be here for this? He was wasting valuable time that could be better spent on his magic or, even better, with Nakkole.

He watched the men swing the swords about, watched them play in mock battle.

"It's no different at all." Robert clutched the hilt of his human-made sword at his hip. "Am I to replace this one?"

Arrane nodded. "It would be best if you did. You're welcome to keep the blade I've given each of you. Consider it a gift for your services to my son. And, when you return home, if you prefer to keep your old blades instead, keep in mind the ones I've given you are made from pure gold. They'll fetch you a nice sum."

Arrane's eyes twinkled with humor as he watched the humans. Gavin, too, couldn't help but smile, given how well he knew Robert and Markham. The pair were likely already struggling to figure out how many favors from a wench such a weapon might bring them.

Luke, however, had turned his curiosity to the quiver and bows he held. The lad was decent with a sword, but was one of Gavin's favored marksmen. "And these? What sort of enchantment do these hold? Or is it the same sort?"

"The bows look a tad small to me," Brock grumbled.

And it was true enough. Each of the five bows on the table looked small enough to better fit a woman than a strapping Scotsman.

Standing, Arrane moved to Luke's side. "Pluck an arrow from that quiver, Luke."

Luke looked at Gavin for approval. Gavin gave it in the form of a curt nod. Reaching for an arrow, Luke licked his lips, obviously anxious to see the magic his favored weapon might possess. He plucked one from the bunch and gasped with delight when another immediately took its place. Gavin couldn't help but smile. It was no wonder only three arrows filled the quiver. There was no need for more as they replenished themselves with each use.

"Clever," he said, testing out his own arrows. He looked to his father and gestured to his bow. "But, this isn't likely going to fit comfortably over my shoulder."

"Won't it?" Arrane chuckled. "Why don't you try it out then?"

Frowning, Gavin slid the bow over his shoulder as he would normally. To his amazement, the wood and string stretched to accommodate his size. Robert and Bruce roared with laughter. Luke stood still, muttering, his eyes wide. Markham eagerly grabbed his own bow to give it a go.

"Go now, the lot of you." Arrane strode to the door and held it open. "Practice with your new weapons until you know them as well as you know your own." He looked to Gavin. "Stay, please. We're not quite finished."

Gavin nodded and watched his men leave, pleased that they'd found such delight in this world that had to have confused them all. When the door was closed once again, he played with his quiver of arrows, plucking them from their spots, watching them reappear again, while he waited for Arrane to continue their discussion.

He glanced up to find Arrane gone, but could hear him moving about the secret chamber. When he came back, he held yet another sword in his hands, this one a remarkable beauty.

"Its blade was made of silver on this side," he said, showing Gavin the long, shining blade. He flipped it over in his palms to reveal a darker shade of metal on the other side. "And this side of gold."

He handed it to Gavin. On the hilt, the same markings that made up several pieces of furniture in the palace had been carved. A deer, a clam, three leaves, and a sun, each entwined with the other, jeweled with pearls and amber stones. He'd never quite seen anything like it.

"My father gave it to me when I was first strong enough to lift it. It should have been yours years ago. It would please me if you took it now."

Gavin looked up to find his father watching him with

glassy eyes. Unsure of what to say, Gavin nodded. "My thanks. It's . . . beautiful."

"It's priceless." Arrane ran his finger over the hilt, tracing the outline of the engraved emblem. "The deer represents the lives we guard, a clam for the ocean, leaves for the forest. The sun . . . well, we are all the guardians of light here. Together as they are, they make up our world and all that we protect and are charged to keep order of."

The sword suddenly felt far more heavy than it had a moment ago. "You know I wish to return to Grey Loch. Such a gift should be given to whomever will become king when you no longer are."

Arrane grinned. "As I've been saving this sword only for *my son*, it is yours. No obligation is attached."

Gavin's throat felt swollen and tender. "My son shall carry it one day as well."

Arrane laughed, but it seemed to Gavin that the glossy sheen in his eyes had only deepened. "There is no shame in gifting it to a daughter, either."

Gavin smiled. "Nay, there isn't."

"Now, enough of this." Arrane cleared his throat and fell into the chair behind the table. "Let's discuss your powers, shall we?"

Twenty-nine

~

Gavin winced and stared at Arrane. "My magic. I don't believe I will ever grow used to hearing of such."

Arrane nodded as though he understood. But how could he possibly? He'd used his magic since he was born. Gavin was a fully grown man expected to accept and control his powers after a lifetime of never knowing about them.

"You will, as easily as you now understand the magic of those arrows," Arrane said. "An open mind is your best weapon just now, Gavin."

"There is still so much I don't understand, so much you've yet to show me. How can you expect me to learn all I need to know when war is on our doorstep? It would be as foolhardy as me sending a man into the throng of battle when he'd just been handed his first sword."

"Just because you have not been aware of it does not mean you have not been using your magic, as I'm quite sure you've come to realize." Arrane leaned back in his chair.

"Quite possibly," Gavin agreed. "But fighting an unknown enemy is far more difficult than fighting one you've faced before."

The truth of it was, he hadn't cared to know about the

enemy until now. But as he sat here with his father wearing a sword that carried his family's history, he very much wanted to know what had brought them all here.

"Tell me why we fight this war. Tell me of my sister."

Arrane's eyes widened and something unnameable flickered within them. "You will listen with an open mind, an open heart?"

"I doubt little could surprise me any longer."

"Then I shall tell you what I can." Arrane took a deep breath. "You see, the world must keep a careful balance between light and dark, sun and moon, good and evil. When one holds much more power than the other, everything is affected." He rubbed his brow. "This is no simple matter to explain."

"When there's too much rain, the earth floods," Gavin said. "When there is no rain at all, there is drought. I understand balance well enough."

Arrane's lips curled into a smile. "Very well. Then you might appreciate what could happen if the dark magics of the world far outweighed the light. And that is exactly what happened thirty years ago."

"Dark magic reigned?"

Arrane shook his head. "It tried to. You have, or *had* an uncle. My brother, called King Krion—"

Gavin frowned. "Another king?"

"Aye, another king. For if there is a majesty of light . . ."

"There must also be one of dark. So where is this king now?"

"Entombed in the walls of the Desolate Caves where your sister makes her home. He is being held prisoner by my magic. When Akrion, Krion as he is known, became too greedy, his actions forced me into war in order to ensure the balance in the world. Krion had sent a succubus by the name of Lucette to enchant and seduce me in hopes of breeding a dark child whom I would be forced to accept into this kingdom."

"My sister, Elphina," Gavin muttered. "You didn't accept her into this kingdom."

Arrane shook his head, a sadness in his eyes that made Gavin sorry he'd asked. "I could not, which is why she fights me for it now. The three stones we told you of . . . one of which you gave your mother . . . as you know, they became the Master Trinity. Together they were once the Sphere of Life, and if ever rejoined, will be the key to freeing Krion from his prison."

"So, that is why Elphina wants the Orbs? I thought she only wanted the power they alone would bring her. She must have been searching for them long before now. Why the sudden need to fight her? Why the sudden fear?"

Arrane looked away, his eyes closed, his mouth taut. "Because *you* were found. Your aid could provide Elphina a victory against me. But with you at my side, she wouldn't stand a chance."

The muscle in Gavin's jaw ticked. Anger and disappointment moved him from the chair to pace the chamber. "So I'm naught more than a pawn. You would never have come looking for me if I didn't have the power to destroy your daughter or your brother?"

"That's not true." Arrane rose, walked to Gavin. He thrust out his hand, placing it on Gavin's shoulder, keeping him from walking his paces, forcing him to listen. "I would never have let you go at all if you hadn't been in danger. I cared more for your life than the security of my throne. Dark fae don't hold much power in the human world—at least, not the same sort they wield here. You would never have been safe in any place of magic. It was your mother's desire to hide you in the human world and I respected her wishes until Elphina discovered your location through the Orb of Truth before we snatched it from her minions."

Gavin turned his stare to the window, trying desperately not to ruin the truce he'd found with his father, the peace of accepting all he was being told. He saw Dulcee walk by, wielding a stick as large as a tree trunk, playing as though he was engaged in a fight. Gavin couldn't help but smile at the sight, but the realization that everyone in this world was affected by this war calmed him even more than the humorous sight of the ridiculous ogre. There was no time now for the indulgence of self-pity.

He exhaled his frustration and sought a calmer voice. "It seems I was doomed no matter where I lived."

"Not doomed. Blessed. You hold the key to it all, Gavin."

❧

Gavin sat with his father for the remainder of the afternoon and well into evening. They took supper in his quarters as Gavin showed Arrane the use of control he'd learned with Nakkole that afternoon. Arrane had seemed pleased, and they'd pressed on to discover Gavin's ability to destroy and to create, until eventually, he'd managed to start and put out the fire in the chamber's hearth without the use of flint.

Now, as the palace began to settle for the night, Gavin's head felt full to bursting. He pushed himself away from the table. "I will practice more of the creation and destruction in the morning. If I learn aught else, I'm likely to forget everything."

Arrane, too, looked weary, but he shook his head and gestured for Gavin to sit again. "Our time is short, Gavin. We've made great progress today, but until you've mastered these powers, you won't be as strong as you could be. We haven't even tried your skill with communication."

"Nay, and I'd like to see how it works, but not tonight." Tonight, he wanted to seek out Nakkole and see if she'd welcome him as warmly into her body as she had the last. Needed to see if she'd warmed to him at all since he'd left her this afternoon.

With a sigh of defeat, Arrane led Gavin to the door. "Very well. First thing tomorrow."

Gavin nodded. "First thing."

"Good eve to you then." Arrane smiled, pressed a hand to Gavin's back, then started down the corridor.

At the foot of the stairs, they found Nakkole and Geraldine engaged in conversation. Arrane placed a kiss on Geraldine's cheek in greeting. Gavin nearly did the same to Nakkole, wanted to very badly, but wasn't sure the gesture would be welcomed and therefore refrained. He regretted it the moment she turned and smiled at him.

"How did the training go?" she asked. Her long, wild curls were bound at her neck with a ribbon, and she expelled a hearty yawn.

"My son is a fast learner," Arrane answered when Gavin did not.

Nakkole's body grew hot beneath Gavin's intense stare. He was examining her, inspecting each inch of her face. She could feel it. She liked it. She wanted the same feeling for the rest of her body.

After spending the morning irritated and saddened by their discussion the night before, she'd had time to calm herself. Their outing in the fields had helped, as well, and she'd forced herself to remember that everything in Gavin's life was changing. If she truly cared for him, she could afford to be patient with him.

And she *did* care for him. She loved him. Each time she saw him, her heart leaped and her skin tingled. And while she knew her love for him was never going to lead to a life spent by his side, she would eventually grow content with knowing she'd enjoyed him while he was here. When the time came, she would love him enough to let him go.

As Arrane and Geraldine ascended the stairs together, Nakkole allowed herself to reach out and cup Gavin's cheek. "Come to bed with me?" she whispered, emboldened by the way his eyes darkened at her touch.

He leaned down and ki·sed her softly. "You're no longer angry with me?"

"Perhaps," she teased. "But there are many ways you can make it up to me."

Gavin growled deep in his throat, his tongue sliding between her lips and delving into her mouth. She sighed with contentment, wrapped her arms around his neck, and allowed him to all but drag her up the stairs.

But they barely reached the top floor when their interlude was shattered by a high squeal from overhead. She glanced up, and felt Gavin grip her arm. Above them, a purple pixie fluttered, clutching her throat, her little eyes wide with terror.

"What is it?" Arrane bellowed.

The pixie covered her eyes with her teeny hands. "Attack! They have attacked. Cutter and Wingleaf are dead, gone forever!"

Arrane and Geraldine appeared, flustered but alert, at the

end of the corridor. As Geraldine covered her heart with her hand, Arrane hurried to them and seized the pixie in his fist, demanding she gain control.

"Cutter and Wingleaf?"

The pixie nodded, once again burying her face in her hands. "The south border of Arran, Your Majesty. An army marches onto Arran soil as we speak. Cutter spotted them, and he and Wingleaf tried to come and warn you, but the army shot them down with faery bows afore they could get to safety. I saw only because I was having a bit of rest on a window ledge above stairs."

Arrane's gaze flickered to Gavin, and he released the pixie from his grasp. "It seems we have no time to prepare you further, my son. Are you still willing to aid us?"

Not a soul breathed in the corridor. It seemed it had filled with curious eyes and ears, each awaiting their prince's answer.

Finally, after a tense silence, Gavin gave one curt nod. "I still am not confident in my powers, but I certainly know how to lead an army and am not afraid of a challenging fight." He glanced at the pixie, and Nakkole listened as everyone around her seemed to release their collective breaths. "What are their numbers?"

The pixie glanced around, her puffy eyes wide. "I—I do not know. One hundred? I saw only a few banshees, several oakmen and succubi, and many maras."

"Find my men and bring them to me," Gavin commanded the pixie.

Slowly, people began to fill the hall, spilling out from their chambers. Ever the king, Arrane cleared his throat and once again called everyone's attention to him. "Arm yourselves, all who intend to fight with us. A hundred does not complete their army, so for certain this is only the first of many battles their wicked queine plans for our war."

He led them into his private quarters, and Nakkole watched as he opened a passage to a hidden room.

"My armory," he said. "Choose your weapons."

The crowd flowed into the chamber, one by one leaving again, armed and ready to fight. Nakkole found herself standing alone in the corridor with only a worried, frightened Geraldine for company.

"There are nearly fifty of us here," Nakkole said, patting Geraldine's arm reassuringly. "And hundreds more on our borders. This is not a battle we will lose."

Her eyes welling with tears, Geraldine nodded. "I ken. But, Nakkole. I just found him again. I canna bare the thought of losing him again so soon."

Nakkole didn't know whether Geraldine meant Arrane or Gavin, but chose not to ask. "And you will not. Come, Geraldine. Let us fetch our own bows and make certain we bring them back to us alive and well."

❧

G avin slung the faery bow over one shoulder, fastened the satchel of arrows around the other, then unsheathed his sword, blood pounding in his ears. This was what he knew— the fight, the preparation of battle. Every sense and nerve within him came alive in anticipation.

Addressing the room of fae, Arrane said, "Take care with your lives this night. They are worth more to me than ridding my lands of each of our foe. You have my thanks, and the promise of a feast like no other once we have our victory."

A cheer sounded across Arrane's audience. Then, with the oddest, shrillest battle cry Gavin had ever heard, Arrane's army rushed from the room to begin their fight.

"You five, come with me," Gavin said, grabbing Alec before he and the others could leave.

Alec, Robert, Brock, Markham, and Luke followed Gavin from the chamber, not even pausing as Arrane begged them to be safe. They passed Nakkole and Geraldine in the corridor. Both women had bows slung over their shoulders and small, golden helms upon their heads.

"What is this?" Gavin bellowed. "You do not think to fight."

Geraldine glared at him and shoved him from her path. "Bloody hell I do. This is my husband's home, and I will not sit by while those monsters try to destroy it."

Gavin let Geraldine pass, though he wanted to reach out

and throttle her. She was Arrane's problem, however, for Gavin had his own fiery-haired she-devil to contend with. The stubborn look upon her face warned that she would be as difficult to command as Geraldine.

"You do not know me at all if you believe I would sit here and wait while this battle sheds blood at my feet. I'll have you safe!"

"And I'll have you safe!" he said, seizing her by the arm and forcing her to follow him into the great hall. "You carry my child, Nakkole, the heir to this kingdom. Do not be foolish!"

Nakkole's face fell and he knew she understood his reasoning. She would not be reckless and endanger their child's life.

"You must be cautious," she said. She leaned into him, burying her face in his neck. "Promise me, you'll take more care out there than you ever have before. Promise you'll remain Gavin the Immortal."

He nodded against her hair, rubbing her back gently. "You promise to stay here?"

The great hall door creaked open and Luke stuck his head in. "I'll stay with her, my laird. I've a bow and arrows and there are plenty of windows from which to take part in this fight from here. I'll make certain no harm comes to her . . . You are far better served with my bow, rather than my sword."

Wise lad, Gavin thought. Luke had not yet mastered his swordsmanship, but he was a damned fine marksman.

"If she tries to flee, tie her down," Gavin said.

"There's no need. I will remain here if only to protect our child." Nakkole wiggled from his hold, placed a soft kiss upon his cheek, then stepped back.

Unsatisfied with her pathetic farewell, he pulled her to him and set a forceful, bruising kiss upon her lips before she could utter a word. Then, he stepped away and left Luke to guard her.

Arrane stood at the end of the corridor instructing Balaster and seven other elven soldiers to stand guard in his private quarters. They were to watch the vault that now held the Orb of Truth.

"I'll protect it with my life, Your Majesty," Balaster said, taking his position among the other elves.

Gavin shoved the large, marble statue of Arrane in front of the door, barring Nakkole from any attempts to escape. He believed she would do what was best for their child, but he was taking no chances.

❧

The first thing that caught Gavin's attention was his ability to recognize all of the creatures fighting against Arrane's followers. The flow of fae running over the hill in their direction was made up of the oddest army Gavin had ever encountered.

And likely the most dangerous.

Succubi wailed and clawed their way through pixies and dwarves. A banshee hissed and easily slit the throat of a small brownie with its sharp nails, then turned her attention to Gavin's men.

He roared and set loose an arrow that pierced the banshee's heart. It shrieked and disappeared into nothingness.

"Gavin, behind you!" Alec called out.

Gavin spun, pulling his sword from its sheath. Three oakmen slung their small axes directly at Gavin. He ducked, falling on his backside, and rolled out of the way as another oakman brought his axe down toward Gavin's head.

Blood oozed from the oakman's mouth. It dropped to the ground beside Gavin, Brock's sword piercing it from back to chest. With a grunt, Brock freed his weapon and pulled an arrow from its satchel. He spun around to face another group of oakmen heading toward them from the gold-and-white-treed forest. Their small brown faces looked nearly human, save for the yellow, glowing eyes and beaklike noses. Their small bodies were stout and strong, and they were well armored against an arrow attack.

Behind Gavin, Alec and Robert fought diligently against a pack of banshees.

"These . . . are . . . the wicked . . . creatures who attacked . . . us at Grey . . . Loch," Alec said, swinging his sword each time a banshee got too close.

Alec's fear of the banshees was evident in his eyes, but still, he fought them without backing away.

As though sensing Gavin's presence, one of the banshees turned and flew at him. It bared its blood-tinged fangs and aimed at his throat. Swallowing his trepidation, Gavin waited until it had nearly sunk its fangs into his flesh. Then, he unsheathed his sword, forcing the banshee to impale itself upon the cold, sharp steel.

It wailed and disintegrated into a pile of debris.

Across the way, he caught a glimpse of what he'd first thought was another banshee because of the flowing black garment swirling about it. But it was no banshee. It was Gavin's mother. She was running toward the palace, casting fevered glances over her shoulder. A moment later, a small, hairy mara leaped from the forest trees, descending upon Geraldine even as she tried to run faster.

A look at Alec caused Gavin's hesitation. His friend was surrounded in a very uneven fight, but he'd handled worse. Swearing, Gavin tore off in Geraldine's direction, praying Alec's skills with his sword would aid him well.

Glaring at the mara as he ran, Gavin concentrated, trying desperately to recall how he'd destroyed the wall in Elfame. A burning hatred and anger drove his legs faster. Without taking his gaze from the mara in pursuit of Geraldine, he pulled an arrow from his satchel and placed it in the bow. But he never got the chance to fire the quiver. In the next moment, he felt his power release itself and the mara's body split into a dozen pieces and landed all over the field.

Dropping to his knees, Gavin silently pleaded for the world to stop spinning. He could sense he was no longer alone. As his strength slowly began to return, he managed to glance up long enough to see a banshee diving straight at him.

With a curse, Gavin fell onto his back. He watched as an arrow flew into the banshee's chest. Thinking for a moment that his own arrow had flown free of his bow, he reached into his satchel to rearm himself, only to find the bow still armed.

The arrow had not come from him.

Rolling his head to the side with what little strength he

could muster, he saw Geraldine standing above him, her bow still aimed where the banshee had fallen.

"I sacrificed everything to protect you years ago," she said, offering him a hand. "I will not allow it to have been for naught."

Thirty

～

The cries of the banshees were deafening. Keeping her head low, Nakkole knelt beneath the window in the great hall. She poked her head up to survey the field outside, aimed her bow, and let loose an arrow that vanquished one of the horrid creatures drifting toward the open window.

"Luke! The other window! They're trying to get in." She grabbed another arrow and shot through the heart of yet another banshee.

A quick glance at Luke proved he was partaking in a battle of his own, his bow releasing a succession of arrows that resulted in eerie wails and screeches outside.

"I have not seen Gavin or Arrane," she called, ducking back below the sill in order to steady her heart before taking aim once more. "I've not seen Abunda, either."

Panting, Luke sank to the floor, resting his head below his own windowsill, his cheeks red, his chest heaving. "If I know Laird Gavin, he'll be trying to fend off any more of these beasts before they can cross onto the Isle."

Then those who had already crossed would have an easier time of it.

She wanted to be out there with them, watching over

Gavin, her mother, her sisters. But she knew her place was here, protecting the babe in her womb, the heir to this kingdom. What was she to do?

"I must know they are all right, Luke. You must go and make certain they are safe."

Luke glared at her, rose to his knees, and aimed his bow out the window again. Nakkole chanced a glance out of her own. The field on this eastern side of the palace was now clear.

"I won't be going anywhere," Luke said. "I made my vow to protect you and that's what I mean to do."

"You can see for yourself, there is no one—"

"Nay, lass! Now, hold your tongue and busy your eyes—"

The sound of a loud *whip* sang through the air, and Nakkole watched with horror as a small battle-axe flew through Luke's window. He wheezed, his eyes widening. The axe met its target with a thud, knocking Luke backward. As he landed, Nakkole scooted long the floor toward him, her heart in her throat, staring at the axe now imbedded in his chest.

Oh, Avalon. This could not be happening.

"Luke? Luke, you must listen to me." He stared at her, his eyes not quite focusing on her face. "Hang on . . . do you understand me? I'm going to find help. Hold on until my mother can heal you!"

Nakkole tried to move, but found her skirt was held tight in Luke's fist. "You . . . must . . . stay."

Pulling herself free, Nakkole fought her panic and peered out of the window through which Luke had been hit. He was right, and she knew it.

Somewhere out there was the owner of the axe that had fallen Luke. Before her fear could persuade her to stay put, she stuck her head out the window. To her great relief, she thought she caught a glimpse of Abunda dashing around the corner. Nakkole stuck her head out farther and called for help. An eerie silence greeted her, but there was no sign of the oakman who had thrown his axe at Luke, nor of Abunda. Where were the sounds of fighting? The screams of pain and battle cries?

But before she could complete a second scream for help, a hard blow to her head left her world in utter blackness.

~

 rrane found Geraldine and Gavin huddled under the shelter of trees. Arrane hurried to them as a trio of banshees swooped from the trees to their left, urging Arrane to run even faster.

Quickly, on legs with newly given youth, he hurried toward the two most significant people in his life. He raised his staff, stepping in front of Gavin, pushing his son and Geraldine behind him. As he prepared to let lose his own power of destruction, a shrill whistle sounded. The banshees paused in their descent, and the oakmen paused in their approach. All of them turned toward the sound. Without a backward glance, all of the dark creatures fled for the trees, leaving in their wake only a chilling silence.

Why had they retreated so abruptly? There had been no obvious victor in this battle.

"They're fleeing," Geraldine said, gripping his arm in her shaking fist. "Why?"

Arrane cursed. "A distraction. Quickly. Into the palace. The Orbs!"

Panic seized Arrane's chest as he led his wife and son into the palace. He stopped to look at nothing, his mind and legs set on reaching his private solar as quickly as possible.

"The Orb of Knowledge," he called out to Gavin. "You hid it well?"

"Aye."

"Go, make certain it's safe. Be quick about it and return here." Already, Arrane could see doom spilled along the corridor. Three elven soldiers lay soaked in blood, their bodies empty of life. As Gavin leaped over them and darted upstairs, Geraldine and Arrane stumbled into his chambers, a cry of outrage on Arrane's lips awaiting release.

Four more soldiers, dead and bloodied. Balaster's blank expression staring at him from the corner of the room, though, blessedly, he still breathed and appeared unharmed.

The open, secret safe in which Arrane had placed the Orb. Just as Arrane had feared, the safe was empty.

"What happened?" he asked, his voice shaking. He snapped his head toward Balaster. "How did this happen?"

Balaster's expression did not change, though he fell to his knees and scurried to Arrane's feet. He bowed his body before his king, lifted his head to stare up at him with eyes now brimming with tears.

" 'Twas my doing, Majesty. Succubi. They attacked. Four were . . . dead before I could even raise my sword."

Arrane's hands itched to snatch the elf up by his hair and strangle him. "Yet you seem unharmed."

Balaster's lip trembled. "Be-bewitched, Majesty. One moment I was filled with anger. The next I would have died if they'd asked it of me."

Arrane's understanding and sympathies were buried beneath pure fury. "She has the Orb, then."

Balaster nodded. "Aye, Majesty, but that's not the worst of it. It was the witch, Lucette, who charmed me. I-I told her . . ."

Arrane grabbed him by the shoulder and dragged him to his feet. "Told her what!"

"I told her the other Orb in the safe was a replica."

"Arrane, let him go," Geraldine said from somewhere behind him. "Do not forget you, too, fell for Lucette's magic long ago." She was suddenly at Arrane's side, her hand upon Balaster's shoulder—a far more gentle touch than the one given by Arrane. "You didn't know where Gavin hid the other Orb, so she can't have gotten it."

Balaster nodded. " 'Tis true, that, my lady, but I told her Gavin knew where it was hidden." He dropped his gaze and fell, once again, to his knees. "She told the other succubi they were to take Lady Nakkole as means to barter for the last Orb."

❧

Once Gavin had made certain the Orb of Knowledge was still hidden safely in his chamber, he all but ran back downstairs. He didn't stop at his father's solar as he knew he should. Instead, he rushed toward the Great Hall, eager to see how Luke and Nakkole fared. As he was pushing the large statue of Arrane out of the door's path, however, Arrane joined him, a look of desperation on his face. His father stared at the statue with narrowed eyes, and in the next instant, it shattered into a million pieces, leaving the doorway unbarred. Gavin didn't have time to question the use of Arrane's power, however, for the king pushed open the door and rushed inside.

The moment Gavin stepped through the great hall doors, the sight of Luke lying all alone in the large room gave Gavin his first real taste of fear. Nakkole was gone.

Luke sat against the wall, his bloody hand clutching his chest. The moment he saw Gavin, his eyes seemed to sparkle with life that had not been there a moment ago. "They . . . took . . ."

Gavin hurried forward, his heart heavy on his tongue, in his legs, in his throat. "Who, Luke? Where is she?"

He fought to find compassion for Luke's injury. It would not come. The only thing that mattered was Nakkole and the child she carried within her.

"She . . . window." Luke slumped forward. "Took her . . . from . . . window."

"Lucette took her," Arrane said, his voice eerily calm. He walked past Gavin, then knelt beside Luke, laying the lad's injured body on the floor. "She means to trade Nakkole for the final Orb."

Gavin watched, struggling to remain calm, knowing it would do no good to flee Arran to search for Nakkole until he knew where she may have been taken. Arrane pressed his hands against Luke's wound, blood seeping through his fingers.

"Where have they taken Nakkole?" he asked, his teeth gnashing.

Arrane tore open Luke's tunic and dug his fingers into the gaping hole in the lad's chest. Gavin flinched, but did not look away. "You'll not give your sister what she wants by going after her," Arrane said.

How could he sound so calm while stating something so devastating?

"The hell I won't. Tell me how to find her."

Arrane spared him only a short glance, his attention focused on Luke. In that short, fleeting glance, however, Gavin caught a glimpse of panic, of fear.

"You cannot go to the Desolate Caves, Gavin," Arrane said. "Elphina has two of the Orbs now. We cannot allow her to claim the third."

"Do not tell me where I can or cannot go." Gavin spotted Abunda in the doorway and turned his questioning to her. "Where are these caves?"

Abunda opened her mouth to speak, but a quick glance from Arrane silenced her.

Outraged, Gavin bellowed. "Tell me, or all of your efforts to get me here will have been for naught. I will not fight for those who will not fight for her!"

"I will take you," Alec said. Gavin looked up to find his friend standing beside him, offering his hand to assist Gavin to his feet. Gavin took it, staring Alec in the eye. "These creatures will be ready for an attack of the fae kind, but they will be unprepared for the sort you and I employ in times of war."

"We cannot have both heirs in jeopardy!" Arrane raged.

Gavin opened his mouth to release his anger toward his father, but the sight of Geraldine stepping into the room silenced him.

"Would you not go after me, Arrane?" she asked.

A tear rolled down Geraldine's cheek. She turned to Gavin. "Son, I am done trying to desperately to protect you at all costs—especially when that cost is your happiness. It frightens me beyond anything that you intend to venture into such a darkness that Elphina's kingdom is known to be, but I understand that quality of life is sometimes worth such risks. She makes you happy. Save her." Geraldine bowed her head. "Save *yourself* as I never could."

Without giving another thought to his parents, and with his mind consumed by Nakkole and their child, Gavin rushed upstairs to pry the Orb of Knowledge from its hiding place. If handing over the Master Trinity to Elphina guaranteed their safety, he would relinquish it willingly.

Brouillard Noir—The Black Fog

Nakkole clamped her teeth down on a hairy, bony hand. She felt a crunch, then heard a howl. The hand gripping her face let go, and the horrid mara that had been attached to her back fell to the ground. Nakkole spun, kicking the creature in its belly, searching for her breath in the thick, heavy haze shrouding this dark place.

She took a moment to look around, relieved to find herself seemingly alone, save for the whimpering creature at her feet. The succubus who had attacked her on the Isle of Arran was nowhere to be seen.

Nakkole had glanced only the briefest of glimpses of the rotten creature, but it had been long enough for her to realize her attacker had not been Elphina. The succubus's skin had been green, not blue, and there had been no mistaking the creature's old age. Lucette, perhaps.

Something brushed her ankle, and Nakkole jerked. Around her, dark, slimy trees reached their branches toward her, their legs rooted in black, bubbling mud. She glanced down to find her dress soiled in the nasty substance, the flesh of her legs covered in the ooze. Immediately the need to retch overwhelmed her, doubling her over. She heaved up nothing, but between the stench of the bog and the throbbing in her wounded head, she heaved thrice more before her body strengthened enough to let her stand upright again.

"You've awakened."

The light, tinny voice startled Nakkole, nearly causing her to tumble backward in the muck wrapped around her ankles. She turned to find four succubi staring at her, and in their center sat Elphina, crowned with a wreath made of dead twigs. "For once my mother has done something ri—"

"For what purpose have you brought me here?"

The queine's eyes narrowed, her thin lips rounded into a smile. "You have not guessed?"

Nakkole shuddered. All she knew of Elphina were the descriptions passed on from others. She'd not been prepared for the regal grace, nor the beauty staring back at her now. True, parts of the queine were malformed, but still, the loveliness of her face so closely resembled Arrane and Gavin that Nakkole was having difficulty remembering the true nature of the woman before her.

"What could I have guessed in the few moments I've been awake?" Nakkole said, stepping backward as the five-some slowly approached her.

"She bit me, Your Majesty. I did not have time to let you know she'd awakened," said the creature at Nakkole's feet.

She found his prone body with her feet, stepping hard and purposefully on his small hand. He squealed and sank his teeth into her ankles. Nakkole bit back a gasp and brought her foot back, catching the horrid beast in the chin.

"Tie her to the Cyprus," Elphina said.

Nakkole stumbled in her hurry to flee. The four guards around the queine approached her quickly now, leaping across the water as though they were enormous frogs. In their hands, two of them carried lengths of rope. If they caught her now, her chance for escape would diminish all the more.

Focusing on the muck preventing her stealth, she narrowed her eyes and quickened her steps. "Create earth," she whispered.

Nothing happened. Cursing, she closed her eyes and tried again, this time speaking a bit louder. "Create earth, create earth, create earth . . ."

She felt a tug on her arm the same moment the ooze between her toes vanished. She opened her eyes, finding the guards pulling on her from both sides. Beneath her feet, the bog had turned to solid dirt. Nakkole's feet took hold of the firm ground. She delivered a kick to the succubus on her right, knocking it backward. The two remaining guards increased their speed, but Nakkole turned and fled across the magical path.

"Catch her! Bring her to the caves!" she heard Elphina call out. "Gavin will go there to find her."

Nakkole ducked beneath a large branch, leaped over a fallen one. She could feel their presence so close behind her. And with no knowledge of how to escape this kingdom, she was as good as theirs.

Hot tears scorched her cheeks. Elphina meant Nakkole to

be the bait that would ensnare Gavin. She swung around a
tree that blocked her path and turned right where the dirt
trail divided. She would not be the trap that led to Gavin's
death.

❧

Gavin ripped a sleeve from his tunic and tied it around his
nose and mouth to help keep the stench of the bog from
distracting him. He watched the sleeve grow back to cover his
arm, tore it off again, and handed this one to Alec. Alec followed Gavin's lead, tying the garment over the lower portion
of his face, and once again, a new sleeve mended itself to
cover Gavin's bare arm.

"How can you be certain she was brought here?" Gavin
asked Alec, his voice muffled beneath the fabric.

"Just beyond those Cyprus trees lies the Desolate Caves.
Elphina would want to take Nakkole somewhere where we'd
know to look for her."

Gavin squinted, trying desperately to peer through the
darkness around them. Not even the stars dared to penetrate
the blackened skies here to offer light. He recalled being in
the caves of Elfame, wanting desperately to see, when the
peches had attacked him. He had created the ability to see
then, and he focused hard now to do the same.

A moment later, he could better see the outlines of large
trees and the boiling muck beneath his boots. Alec would not
have such an advantage, but if Gavin was careful, he should
be able to guide his friend through the trail ahead.

"Do you know the way?" he asked, quietly sliding his
sword from its sheath.

Alec armed himself as well and shook his head. "No one
else ever dares enter the Black Fog for fear of being lost to
it forever."

Gavin muttered a curse, fighting the helplessness creeping throughout him. "This way," he muttered. "I see a trail
ahead."

They walked in silence for a few moments, finally coming to a thick path made of fresh dirt. When he no longer felt
Alec at his side, Gavin turned to find him kneeling on the

dirt, his hand cupping a fistful of the earth, slowly letting it slip through his fingers.

"What is it?"

Alec glanced up, holding the dirt out to Gavin. "She's been here."

"How—"

"There are no pathways here. Certainly none of dry dirt. All land here is muddied and foul, but this is as fresh as that of Grey Loch's forest."

"How can that be?" Gavin knelt beside Alec, setting his sword across his knees in order to scoop a handful of dirt into his fist.

"I'm not certain, but if I had to wager a guess, I suspect the power of creation used by someone in need of a quick escape caused this."

"Nakkole." Gavin rose, scanning the trail for any sign of footsteps. Alec rose as well and they walked side by side in silence, both searching the ground for any sign of Nakkole. With their limited vision in the darkness, however, Gavin held little hope for finding anything useful.

He'd just about given up when he spotted the small imprint of a human foot along the trail. "There. She has been this way."

Fear confounded Gavin's breathing and uncertainty pressed his mind. He'd never truly known fear such as this, for when approaching a fight, his own life had little mattered to him. Now, however, it was not his own life that lay in peril. Failing could mean Nakkole's death, his child's death.

He adjusted his grip on his sword, noting with frustration that his palms were damp with sweat. Something large and solid appeared just ahead. Gavin reached out, pressing his hand to the cold, hard stone.

"The caves," he muttered.

Alec stepped beside him, running his fingers along the outer cave wall as he made his way along the path. "But where is the entrance?"

Squinting, Gavin searched the wall for an opening. He considered using his power of destruction to create his own opening, but doing so would sound a rather loud alarm for his sister.

He swore and kicked the wall. "What good are these damned powers if I can't use them when they are most needed?"

"And why can't you?" Alec turned, and Gavin could see hope light up his darkened eyes. "You could destroy the wall—"

"And everyone in the kingdom would hear it."

Alec scowled, then said, "Creation?"

It was worth a try. Gavin concentrated on a mossy stone etched into the wall near his head. "Create a doorway. Create. Create."

Nothing happened. The stone remained solid and Gavin's frustration built. "It's no use. It took forever for me to simply learn to create a small fire and I nearly killed myself in the process."

And as there was nothing here to control, that power was useless to him as well.

But there was one other power he possessed . . . one that might be the key to finding Nakkole before any harm could come to her. When Alec tried to speak, Gavin held up a hand to silence him and closed his eyes, leaning his head against the cave behind him. He could probe others' minds and they were likely to respond to his inquiry, but that would be of no use to him here. Not with Nakkole so far away that he could not hear her answers.

But she had also told him that he would be able to communicate through his mind, no matter the distance, with any other being who held the power, and there was only one other person he knew who would be able to speak to him in such a manner.

Arrane. Arrane, if you can hear me, answer me now.

Silence. Gavin squeezed his eyes more tightly shut, as though by doing so, he could open up his ears. He wasn't quite certain what he expected to hear, but when a quiet voice that did not belong to him filled his mind, he instantly knew it belonged to Arrane.

I am here, son. Are you safe?

Relief pumped blood to Gavin's heart, causing his chest to pound with new hope. *Aye, but I can't find the entrance to the cave.*

To the east, amidst the Black Fog.

'Tis where I am. Arrane, I need to hear from Nakkole. I need her to tell me where she is . . . how to find her.

Another silence, and Gavin could all but feel Arrane thinking.

I will see if I can locate any water holes within the caves. If I can find her, I will tell you the path to take.

If you can find her, you can save her before it is too late.

I cannot. My body will be here, in Arran. There is little I will be able to do in spirit form. I will do what I can, Gavin, but I'm afraid her life is still in your hands.

Gavin didn't bother to reply. He could feel Arrane's absence in his mind. He opened his eyes to find Alec staring at him with a worried expression.

"Communication?" he asked Gavin.

Gavin nodded. "I still don't understand all these rules of magic. Arrane appeared to me in the river. He healed me, held me, and yet he cannot free Nakkole in that form."

Alec offered a sympathetic smile. "He can appear through water to oversee his kingdom, and it takes very little magic to do so. But to manifest even bits of himself through such portals is all-consuming. He would be defenseless should he do so now. If there was another attack on the Isle . . ."

"He would not be able to defend his people," Gavin finished. Arrane would not want harm to come to Nakkole, but he would not sacrifice his kingdom for her. Not even for the grandchild that grew in her belly.

Gavin?

The feminine voice in his head made him jerk, knocking his skull against the stone at his back. His heart raced.

Nakkole?

You must go back! This is a trap meant for you. They do not want me, Gavin. They want you. Run, now, while you can.

How was it possible that he could hear her?

Arrane loaned me a bit of his power, just as he does with Abunda. I think he believes I'll be more successful in persuading you to turn back than he was. This power won't last long, so heed me. Turn back afore it's too late.

Like hell he would.

Where are you? Tell me how to find you.

Run. Now! Elphina has two Orbs. You must run. She won't let you leave her kingdom alive.

Gavin kept his eyes closed and choked back his panic in fear of losing Nakkole's voice.

Then tell me how to find you quickly. It's not me she wants, it's the Orb of Knowledge.

You must return to the Isle at once, son. This was not Nakkole any longer, but Arrane, and suddenly, Gavin's head felt ready to explode. There were far too many voices running amok in him, and yet, he was terrified to let them go.

Gritting his teeth, Gavin slammed his palm against a nearby tree. *If you are truly concerned for my safety, Nakkole, then tell me where the hell you are so I can be quick about finding you. The longer you take to tell me, the more danger we are all in!*

No more voices cried out within his mind. He dared to open his eyes and found Alec scowling.

"What is it—"

Nakkole can no longer hear you so don't bother listening for her, came Arrane's voice. *She is in Elphina's throne room. Follow the path you are on until the trail bends right. You'll find the cave opening there. The burning sconces will lead you to Nakkole. Elphina has made the way easy for you.*

Gavin had already opened his eyes and pointed the direction to Alec before Arrane could finish his instructions.

I'm gathering an army to follow. But, should I not get to you in time . . . be safe.

Determination moving him swiftly along the path, Gavin swallowed and clutched the Orb hanging from his neck. *There is a reason they call me Gavin the Immortal. I intend to live up to that name.*

Thirty-one

～

After what seemed an eternity, Gavin and Alec found the entrance to the Desolate Caves exactly where Arrane had said it would be. They spent several more moments walking silently through the tight twists and turns provided by the muddy earth walls. Gavin didn't like it down here one bit. Being in these caves was too much like being in Elfame, the caves he'd first awakened in, confused and, for the first time in his life, slightly afraid of the unknown.

They followed the path lit by sconces just as Arrane had instructed for a while longer, then Gavin stopped and held up his hand, motioning for Alec to still his movements.

"Someone is ahead. I hear voices."

Gavin quieted his thoughts and focused his ears. Several voices echoed from a path that descended even farther below the earth, quiet yet urgent in their discussion. Careful not to walk loudly, he and Alec stayed their course, pressing their bodies against the walls in an effort to remain hidden. The path once again separated left and right, this time encircling a room bright with light.

Sapphires shimmered from the ceiling, the walls, and decorated a throne perched atop a stone dais. The jewels gave the room a blue hue, haloing the dozens of creatures sitting upon the floor. But it was the slender, hauntingly beautiful woman in the throne that held Gavin's attention. He couldn't mistake her sharp nose and deep-set eyes, for he'd looked upon them each time he'd glimpsed his own reflection.

His sister. Elphina.

A painful tug pulled inside his chest. He'd always wanted a sibling, someone he could look out for, who would care whether Gavin lived or died. It was why he'd treasured Alec so much—the man was the closest thing to a brother Gavin had ever known.

But now he'd found another who shared his blood . . . and he was going to have to kill her. Nakkole and his child's safety demanded it.

Gavin bit back his bitter resentment and took in the sight of his opposition. There were at least fifty creatures in this room alone, and though he and Alec had encountered no one else in the caverns, he was certain a great many more were positioned in the tunnels, likely awaiting the queine's command to fight.

"How long before Arrane's army arrives?" he asked Alec.

"I'm sure they'll find this place more quickly than we did, but it could take a while. The quickest way to travel would be in that house fae's bubble, but any army that could fit in there would be too small in number to do us much good."

Gavin had feared as much. He continued scanning the chamber, searching for any sign of Nakkole.

A bright white glow pulled his attention to the right wall. Three stone pedestals stood there, two of which were topped by Orbs. A white one the size of Gavin's fist—the one that had caught his attention—and the larger Orb of Truth.

Just one last stone that would reputedly raise his uncle, the Dark King Krion.

Gavin fingered the stone at his neck, suddenly uncomfortable with the weight of it. This was going to prove far more difficult than he'd imagined. Perhaps if they waited just a little longer, Arrane's army would come and the odds would not be so—

The crowd of seated creatures shifted, clearing a path near that cursed wall. Elphina stood, and for one breath-stealing moment, Gavin could have sworn she'd looked right at him.

In the next instant, however, she was speaking to her army. Gavin didn't hear a word she said, his gaze fixed on a cage now revealed in the path the creatures had created.

Nakkole. Gavin could hear naught else for the blood pounding in his ears. The mother of his child was caged like a wild animal. He could see her small fists gripping the bars holding her prisoner, as well as the shimmer of her gossamer gown.

There was no time to wait for Arrane's men. He and Alec would have to work quickly to free Nakkole.

Gavin held up a hand at Alec, then pointed to the tunnel that circled to the right.

"Follow that path and see if it leads behind Elphina. If we can find another way in, we won't have to fight our way through this horde before reaching Elphina and Nakkole," he whispered.

If Alec discovered a way into the rear of the room, Gavin would stop at nothing to distract Elphina and her horde to give Alec time to escape with Nakkole. Even if it meant his death.

As Alec turned to go, Gavin grabbed his arm. "Should you spot the chance to free Nakkole, do not wait for me. Take her to Arrane immediately."

"I'll not leave you," Alec said. "You do not even know your way back."

"Then pray I can be quick in finding you on your path. Now go!"

When Alec disappeared around the corner, Gavin sheathed his sword and pulled his bow from his back. Desperately trying to steady his breath, he pulled two arrows from his quiver and armed the bow. A shadow moved into the open pathway at the rear of the chamber, and a moment later, he saw Alec's dark head appear, deliver a quick nod in Gavin's direction, and Gavin expelled breath he hadn't been aware of holding. Alec was near enough to Nakkole that he could get to her if given the chance.

The time to fight had come.

He concentrated on the locked cage, focusing all of his mind on his power to control.

The lock fell to the ground, calling the attention of everyone in the chamber, and Gavin made his move.

Nakkole, if you can still hear me—run with Alec . . . Now!

He pulled back, straining against the bow's limit, and let loose both arrows. Two of the creatures closest to him howled and clutched their chests. After that, chaos broke out, and as he'd hoped, the creatures ran in his direction, leaving Alec a clear chance at freeing Nakkole.

Gavin hurried and fired another arrow at one of the screaming beasts, then pulled his sword free. He barely had time to raise his weapon when the first of the monsters bit into his leg. Soon, he was covered from head to foot in the wee beasties. He collapsed to his knees, struggling to peel one of them from his back, another from his chest.

Gavin the Immortal. He focused, willing the creatures from his body. A few of them fell, leaving him just enough time to raise his sword. The moment another creature flew at him, he impaled it on the end of his weapon.

But it was the sound of Nakkole's bone-chilling scream that had him back on his feet and fighting for his life in earnest.

Thirty-two

~

𝕬 lec was dead.

Nakkole's scream echoed so loudly in her own ears, her brain felt shattered into disoriented pieces in her head. Time slowed as she stared down at Alec's prone body, and she gaped at the horrific sight of the spear-shaped stick protruding from his belly.

One moment, she'd thought she'd heard Gavin in her head again, telling her to flee, then Alec had been pulling her free of her cage, and the next he'd been attacked by an enraged succubus.

A painful tug at her head brought time back to normal passing. Nakkole looked up to find the succubus snatching her hair, and she struggled not to be dragged from the throne room. She dropped to her knees, hoping her weight would be too burdensome for the foul creature, and her gaze found the glint of steel near Alec's hand.

His sword.

She reached out, inching her fingers along the ground, fighting back tears as the succubus pulled harder on her hair. All around them, frenzied chaos and screaming carried on so loudly, Nakkole could no longer tell which of the sounds belonged to her.

The possibility that Gavin could be at the center of this fight urged her arm farther still, until the cool feel of steel slid between her fingers. She wrapped her fingers around the hilt of Alec's sword and pushed herself to her feet, jerking her head back violently. Her head slammed into the succubus's body, knocking the creature off balance.

Seizing the moment, Nakkole spun around, the weight of the sword keeping her slightly bent. But as the succubus lunged at her once again, Nakkole summoned the strength to raise the weapon. The succubus pierced its own belly upon the tip of the sword and let loose a shrill cry before dropping dead to the ground.

Nakkole barely had time to pull the blade from its belly before she found herself surrounded by half a dozen more of Elphina's army.

Standing over Alec's body, she guarded him, her gaze darting from one creature to the next until it finally settled upon the most beautiful, yet terrifying, sight she'd ever seen. Gavin. One, two, three creatures fell quickly to his skill with his sword. The weapon she could barely lift with both hands, he wielded as easily as the wind maneuvered the leaves.

But even such deftness in battle would not hold against such an enormous army. She knew Elphina had hundreds of other guards ready to pour out of the tunnels at her command. Gavin and Alec had lost this battle before they'd ever stepped into it.

Run, she begged him silently. *Go to Arran.*

There was no response to indicate he might have heard her thoughts. Only the sound of her thudding heart in her own ears.

The circle of maras and succubi inched closer around Nakkole, and she forced herself to look away from Gavin. She lifted the sword in front of her. Spinning to face each of her opponents in turn, panic crept throughout her. She was surrounded on all sides.

"Step back!" she screamed. But, knowing they had her cornered, the creatures only grinned at her.

With the stealth of a wildcat, Gavin was suddenly next to

her. She reached out a hand to touch him, needing to make certain he was real. When she laid her hand upon his shoulder, he winced and she pulled away. He was wounded.

Nakkole shook her head, dislodging all thoughts from her mind save those which mattered now—keeping them alive. She turned her back to Gavin's, guarding them from those behind them, while Gavin faced those in front. Alec's sword was far too heavy, but if she could just grab his bow . . .

As if reading her mind, Alec groaned, calling her attention to him.

He was alive.

Relief nearly brought her to tears as she glanced down and saw his bow at his side. She snatched it, dropping the sword to the ground beside him. He pushed himself up on his arms and even in the darkness she could see his pained expression.

"Lie down," she whispered, bending slightly to scoop up his quiver of arrows. She saw the spear protruding from Alec's belly and winced for him. "Sweet Avalon, just lie down."

"How many are back there?" Gavin whispered over his shoulder.

She counted quietly. "Four."

"Five on my side. Can you fire that quickly?"

"I can fell two before they retaliate," she confessed.

"When I count to three."

Nakkole nodded, knowing he could not see her do so. Her voice was lost somewhere beneath the fear in her belly and the bile in her throat.

"One . . ."

She stared into the eye of the mara she intended to kill first.

"Two . . ."

It smiled and reached out a long, thin hand toward her, flashing its claws.

"Three!"

Nakkole fired the arrow between the mara's eyes. It howled, but the second shot was fired before the first victim hit the ground. By the time she aimed a third, another mara was upon her, leaping through the air, baring her teeth.

Nakkole flinched, bracing herself for the pain to come. It never did. The creature screamed. When Nakkole opened her eyes, she found Alec's arm raised, his sword plunged into the creature's belly.

She opened her mouth to offer thanks, but a succubus moved to strike. She aimed her bow, and let loose another arrow, catching it in its nonexistent heart.

With no other creatures on her side of the fight, she whirled around to aid Gavin. He needed none. Only one other creature remained, and as Gavin raised his bow to bring it down, the creature dashed from the chamber, fleeing for its life.

"Coward!" Gavin screamed. His face was blood red, his chest heaving, and his hand still holding his steady aim on the bow.

Nakkole reached out and eased Gavin's arm down, forcing him to look at her. "There are hundreds more, Gavin. Elphina . . . where is she? We must get Alec to safety before she can return with more than we can fight."

He stared at her, his eyes blazing with fury. He blinked, shouldered his bow, then grabbed Nakkole by the shoulders and pulled her roughly to him. He held on to her as though afraid she would disappear. She choked back a sob, breathing in the scent of him, sweaty, dirty, and so very strong.

Alec's groan forced them to pull apart. They stepped away from one another and glanced down at Alec. He was sitting now, the spear in his hand.

"God in heaven, that hurt!" Alec wheezed.

"You didn't just . . . you can't just . . . Gavin!" Nakkole sputtered. "He pulled the spear out of his own belly! He'll bleed to death."

"It had to be removed so that I could carry him." Gavin stared down at Alec, admiration in his eyes. "You have my gratitude, friend. But, if you die now, you'll force me to kill you."

Alec managed a brief chuckle and collapsed onto his back. "Where's the . . . ogre when you need him? I'm not . . . likely to make it . . . back to the palace alive . . . if I have to rely on your scrawny . . . arse to carry me."

Gavin smiled, but Nakkole would have sworn she'd seen

his eyes dampen for the briefest of moments. "Breathe deeply, my friend. I'm going to have to toss you onto my shoulder."

Nakkole watched with her heart in her throat as Gavin stooped and struggled to pull Alec over his shoulder. He managed, wobbling where he stood, then grunted for Nakkole to lead them out of the caves.

The sound of hundreds of running feet, however, kept her frozen in place.

"She's going to have every tunnel filled with her army," Nakkole said.

Gavin swore, his gaze darting about frantically. He set Alec back on his feet and tucked his arm under his shoulder to help hold him up. "We're going to have to fight our way through. Can you walk if you hold the walls for support?"

Alec nodded, one hand clutching his wounded belly. Blood oozed between his fingers. His jaw muscle twitched, and he pointed to the tunnel on the far side of the chamber. "Go . . . the way . . . we came. Only way I know . . . to get . . . out."

With Nakkole and Gavin on either side of Alec, each burdened with a bit of his weight, they started slowly for the exit.

When they reached the center of the chamber, however, Nakkole shifted Alec's weight toward Gavin and hurried to the three pedestals by the wall. She stared blankly at the empty vessels, her heart dropping to her toes. "They're gone."

"We'll come back for the Orbs, Nakkole. I still have the third." Gavin grabbed her by the arm and led her out of the throne room. "Right now, I want you safe."

Nakkole could say nothing. The Orbs had been so close—within their grasp. Now they were gone, perhaps never to be found again.

"Ready your bow," Gavin said, his fist clutching tightly the hilt of his sword. His taut expression screamed his alertness.

Nakkole wished Arrane's gift of communication had lasted a bit longer, for the need to know Gavin's thoughts just now would do wonders for her confidence.

As it was, she was certain they were all walking to their deaths.

As they approached the first curve inside the tunnel, Gavin held up his hand in silent instruction for Alec and Nakkole to stay back. He raised his sword, and in the next instant, disappeared from sight.

Nakkole held her breath, torn between following Gavin and staying behind to make certain Alec remained safe. When she heard Gavin's loud curse, her devotion to him won out, sending her dashing round the corner after him. What she found sent her to her knees with tears.

Never so pleased to bow to anyone in her life, she tilted her head back and smiled up at King Arrane.

"You said you were sending an army," Gavin was saying. "I did not expect you to come, yourself. Who is defending the Isle?"

Arrane bent and held out his hand to Nakkole. She took it and swayed to her feet, dizzy with relief and gratitude for his arrival.

"I was wrong to tell you not to come here," Arrane said, releasing Nakkole in order to place his hand upon Gavin's shoulder. "Had it been Geraldine in danger, I would have left everything behind to save her. You were right to do the same for Nakkole."

A cough from the path they'd left behind brought the reality of their precarious situation back to Nakkole. "Alec, Your Majesty. He needs you."

Knowing Arrane would follow, she hurried back to their wounded friend, who now sat slumped against the wall, drenched in sweat and blood.

"Ah, what a mess I find you in," Arrane said, squatting beside Nakkole. He pried Alec's hand from his wound and placed his own over the gaping hole. "Close your eyes."

Alec obeyed. Arrane, too, shut his eyes and as he worked his magic. Nakkole watched as, one by one, familiar faces stepped into the tight pathway behind him.

Gavin. Abunda. Dulcee.

Timpani. Beanie. Robert, Brock, Luke, and Markham.

Behind them, dozens of elves, dwarves, and White Ladies

stepped into view. And with all of them came a new hope for escape.

Hot tears burned Nakkole's cheeks. She ran to Abunda and threw her arms around her neck. Abunda buried her face in Nakkole's hair and rubbed her back in such a soothing manner, the effects were immediate. Nakkole's body relaxed and her heart slowed.

When Abunda finally released her, Nakkole found herself speaking aloud the very thoughts that had been consuming her since the succubus, Lucette, had stolen her from the Isle. "I thought I was going to die, Mother. That my child was going to die."

And before Nakkole's weeping could start anew, Abunda pressed a firm, but loving kiss upon her brow. "I would never allow such, Nakkole. But the battle is not over yet. We've a war ahead of us before we can be free of this place."

Abunda left Nakkole's side and approached Arrane, who was helping a healed, though still pale and trembling Alec to his feet. Timpani pushed past their mother and wrapped her arms around Alec's waist—whether to support him or embrace him, it was hard to tell.

"Instruct the Bean-Tighe to take my daughters to Arran. The wounded one can travel with them," Abunda said.

Arrane shook his head, his face grim. "I cannot. Nakkole must stay." He looked to Gavin. "I wish you to return to the Isle with Timpani and Alec."

Gavin ignored him. "Nakkole goes as Abunda suggested."

Arrane looked from Gavin to Nakkole. "Your work is not done here, Nakkole. I cannot win this war without you. I wasn't quite certain what I needed to win this war with my daughter, but now I am certain. As your king, I am asking that you stay."

The need in Arrane's stare caused a wave of foreboding to wash over Nakkole. "What could *I* possibly do for this war, Majesty?"

"She's done enough already," Abunda interrupted.

Arrane didn't even spare Abunda a glance. He was solely focused on Nakkole. Her trust in her king grew, and she knew without doubt that he would not ask something of her without reason. "Tell me what to do."

He tore his gaze from her long enough to nod at Beanie. "Take Timpani and Alec to Arran. Nakkole and Gavin will be staying."

Beside her, Gavin's entire body stiffened in protest. Nakkole gripped his arm. "I'll not leave," she said. "Save your fight for our enemies. Not your king. I trust the safety of our child to him, but even more, I trust our child's safety to *you*."

The muscle in his jaw ticked a rapid tattoo before he glowered at Arrane. "Very well, but there better be a damn good reason for putting Nakkole and my child at risk."

Arrane nodded. "You must know I'd give my life before allowing harm to come to my grandchi—"

A loud clatter of pebbles resounded from the tunnels around them, cutting off Arrane's words and putting everyone on guard. Arrane pointed at Beanie. "Go now."

In the next moment, Beanie, Timpani, and Alec disappeared inside the golden bubble. They watched it drift from the tunnel above their heads, then Arrane gripped Nakkole's shoulders and once again bore his intensity into her.

"You know the defense of the succubi?" he demanded, obviously not willing to waste much time in talk when the battle was so near.

Nakkole nodded. "They cannot be killed by any male."

"What?" Gavin asked. "That is what you need Nakkole for? Abunda is here, and she's not delicate with child!"

"Any succubus could be killed by any female. This is true. But Elphina has the added protection of being my daughter, which means she can only be killed by a female carrying my blood. The child within Nakkole is young, but it is my blood. Do you understand?"

Nakkole's knees gave slightly, as though the weight of the world truly pushed her toward the earth. "I must be the one to kill Elphina?"

All around them, gasps of surprise and protest sounded. Both Abunda and Gavin stepped on either side of Arrane, looking at him as though he'd grown a spare head.

It was Abunda who spoke. "You wish to pit my Nakkole

against Elphina? Arrane, I have never questioned you, but
Nakkole is no warrior. What you ask of her is impossible.
Elphina will kill her without straining a muscle."

Nakkole didn't balk at her mother's lack of confidence in
her abilities, for the same doubt was assailing Nakkole. But
the weary, drained glaze in Arrane's eyes held her attention.

"I haven't time to explain much more," Arrane said,
glancing over his shoulders at the tunnels behind them. "I
ask only that you try. I will be with you, Nakkole. I will not
leave your side. Should you be wounded, I will be there."

Nakkole knew how difficult this request must be for
Arrane. For all of Elphina's wickedness, she was still his
daughter, and ordering her death had been something he'd
not been able to bring himself to do until now. If he thought
there was no other way to win this war than to slay his own
child, Nakkole knew their position was even more grave
than she'd feared.

"What should I use?" she asked, twisting her shaking
hands into a knot. "To kill her, I mean. Somehow, it doesn't
seem as simple as firing an arrow into her heart."

"When the time comes, you will know what to do." He
grabbed her hand and pulled her into an embrace. The gesture caught Nakkole by surprise, and all she could do was
allow him to cling to her before Gavin pulled them apart.

"They come." He pointed toward the tunnels where shadows grew larger and more ominous. "There is no more
time."

Arrane nodded and held up his hands, calling forth the
group of elves lingering behind them all. "Nakkole is to be
guarded with your lives. Surround her on all sides until I
order you to part. Abunda, your White Ladies should be able
to ward off the peches and maras with your bows. Ginks," he
said, addressing the king of the Sanddine dwarves, "the oakmen are all yours. Lead the dwarves against them, axe
against axe."

He looked to Gavin. "There should be no banshees here.
They won't travel beneath the earth, but I will need your
men to fight through the succubi and ogres. Keep a watch for
the succubi's glamour. Don't allow them to enchant you."

"What about Dulcee?" came a booming voice. Nakkole

glanced up to see Dulcee's worried face peering down at them from Gavin's side. "Dulcee kill ogres. Dulcee big like ogres."

Nakkole smiled through her fear and lightly touched Dulcee's arm. "You would kill your own kind, Dulcee?"

He grinned, hot air wooshing from between his missing teeth. "To save Nakkole, Dulcee would kill Ogaro himself."

Stretching to her tiptoes, Nakkole planted a kiss on the highest part of the ogre that she could reach—his belly. "I am proud to call you friend, Dulcee."

He sniffed and nodded, then turned to glower at the elves. "Watch her well. She dies . . . you die." He looked to Arrane. "Dulcee lead the way."

Arrane nodded, and all around Nakkole, elves formed a protective barrier. Then, they were moving, slowly shuffling her along the dirt path. Ahead, the sound of screams and bodies being hurled against the walls had already begun.

❧

Gavin wiped the sweat from his brow, the rush of battle urging him on, despite his constant need to check on Nakkole. Thus far, there had been no real challenging foe, but the farther they traveled, the more the enemy seemed to increase.

With each new creature that fell beneath his blade, the image of Nakkole facing off with Elphina chilled him to the bone, making his need to kill all the stronger. If he could just get them out of this tunnel, perhaps that confrontation could be avoided.

He stopped at the fork that divided left from right and searched the walls for the familiar sconces he'd followed when he and Alec had arrived. Both paths were dark, but his gut told him to turn left. Just as he was opening his mouth to tell Dulcee which way to go, Arrane's calm and even voice broke through the crowd.

"Right, Dulcee."

Gavin stopped, waiting for Arrane's troop to catch up. When they reached him, Arrane ordered everyone to halt.

"The path out is to the left," Gavin said.

Arrane nodded. "It is. But we cannot leave until our battle is won. We press right, where Elphina is waiting . . . hiding."

"But if we can escape these caves, there is no need for—"

"There will always be the need, Gavin. And should we wait, then perhaps Nakkole will have birthed your child and my blood will no longer grant her the ability to end this once and for all. We do this now."

Gavin's anger tightened the fist holding his sword. "Then you are purposefully endangering Nakkole and our child!"

"If we do not end this now, then it will be *you* endangering your child. Do you think that, should we let your sister live, she'll not come after your child again and again until she finally receives what she wants? She waited over thirty years, Gavin, but she came for you . . . didn't she?"

No matter what happened, his child was in danger. For a brief moment, he thought of the worries Grey Loch had provided him and missed them dearly. The tiny troubles of the clan would be so welcome just now.

More weary than he could ever remember being, Gavin slowly tilted his head back to nod to Dulcee. "We go right."

Thirty-three

~

Elphina ran her sharp nails against the polished sapphire walls of her private chamber. So close. Everything she'd wanted her entire life had been within her grasp, only a breath away from seeing life. The Master Trinity. Hers. The Dark King Krion. So close to rising once again to the power he was meant to wield.

Gavin McCain, her brother. Her enemy. He'd ruined everything. She'd had him right where she'd wanted him—surrounded by numerous minions who would see him dead. And yet he still lived. How was it possible?

Even Arrane would have had difficulty fighting off so great a number on his own. Gavin should have been dead. Her trap should have worked!

But she still had two Orbs. If she could hide them . . . get her hands on the third one, there was still the possibility King Krion could be raised from his earth-and-stone coffin.

She stopped in front of the door, listening, barely breathing. The echo of metal against stone, against flesh rang throughout the tunnels outside her chamber. She searched the cavern, desperately seeking a place to store the Orbs.

With the sound of a familiar voice, her frantic search

froze. Arrane. In her kingdom. She knew she should find another place to hide, should run now and secure the safety of the two Orbs she still possessed. But she didn't move. She was lulled into immobility by the sound of Arrane's voice, an ache building in her chest and climbing up her throat as she heard him bark orders at someone.

How many had he brought? How many had he thought necessary to murder his only daughter?

Something warm and wet trickled down her cheek. As she moved to brush it away, she caught a glimpse of herself in the looking glass across the chamber, her gnarled fingers brushing across her face.

Monster. Gruesome and deformed.

Screaming her outrage, she lashed out, shattering the glass, then dropped to her knees, leaning her head against the door. Life had been unkind to her, but she had adjusted well. She ruled this Desolate Kingdom as well as her father ruled Arran. He had no right to try to take this from her as well! No right at all.

His son he barely knew, yet defended so eagerly. While his daughter he'd never set eyes upon, and loathed with every bit of his soul. It was a folly he would die for—as soon as she could regroup and form a new plan.

❧

Gavin gasped for air, turned, and plunged his sword into the belly of an approaching succubus. The horrid creature squealed and pulled away from the weapon, but did not vanish into thin air as the banshees had done during the battle on Arran. Instead, she looked only slightly weaker, but seemed to have no intention of complying with his wish that she die.

"The bloody bitches aren't dying," Luke said, gritting his teeth and raising his sword in front of him. Like Gavin, the young lad had fought half a dozen succubi to no avail.

"You won't be able to kill them. Just keep them at bay so we might get past," Arrane called out from over Gavin's shoulder.

The tight formation surrounding Nakkole grew tighter as

the tunnels became more and more narrow. For that, Gavin was grateful. Nothing of any size would be able to squeeze through their group to get to her.

"Why can't we kill them?" Brock asked.

An arrow whipped past Gavin's head and straight into the heart of the succubus he'd been fighting. The creature vanished into a pile of black ash.

"What the—" Confused, Brock glanced over his shoulder in the direction from which the arrow had originated. "How did you—"

"Succubi can only be killed by females. It's a protective power so their sexual targets cannot harm them when they mate," Abunda answered instead, reaching across her body to unsheathe a small but fierce-looking dirk. "You men can help keep their numbers back, but best if you focus your energy on the ogres Arrane sensed up ahead. There are enough of my White Ladies here to deal with the succubi."

The tunnel twisted sharply to the left, and from Gavin's point of view at the head of the group, it looked to be a dead end. A large, round boulder blocked the exit, and the door to their right was shut. Gavin pushed on the door, then gave it a swift kick, but it didn't budge. His toe throbbed like hell, but as he lifted the hilt of his sword to attempt to bust through that way, Arrane's voice stopped him.

"Won't do you any good, son. That's your sister's private chambers. She'll have used magic to bar it from your attempts to enter. Sealed tight, I imagine, though if you lot can manage to give me a few moments, I'm certain I can find a way to break through."

Arrane didn't wait for agreement. He threw his head back, his mouth moving rapidly to words none could hear. Gavin turned slowly in his spot, glancing about anxiously for any sign of more creatures lying in wait for attack.

Nothing moved save for the nervous jerks from his companions. Then, so slowly he thought he'd imagined it, the boulder at the end of the tunnel moved. A small gap formed around the circular stone. It was as though the boulder were shrinking, not rolling away.

He pointed his sword in that direction, calling Brock and Luke's attention there.

"What is that?" Luke asked, his face draining of what little color remained. "That's no bloody stone."

"Nay . . . it's an ogre." Gavin's entire body tensed, ready to spring into action as he watched the boulder stand on two legs and realized what he'd thought to be stone had really been the curved back of a creature twice as big as Dulcee.

The lit tunnel darkened. Gavin looked up to the ceiling and stared in frozen fascination as an enormous, distorted shadow shifted overhead. One glance behind him revealed its source. Two more ogres blocked the path from which they'd traveled. They were trapped. The only way out of this small enclosure was through three creatures that took up more space than the entire army Arrane had brought here.

"Holy blessed Mother," he whispered. His heart hammered in his chest. Never in his life had he been afraid of a fight, but as he stared into the deep yellow eyes of the ogre closest to him, smelled breath that stunk of rotting human flesh, and watched a hand roughly the size of an infant human child reaching out toward him, Gavin's confidence exploded into an utter sense of helplessness.

As the ogre's hand grew nearer, Gavin ducked and stepped back through the crowd until he reached his father's side. "We must run. Leave Elphina, Arrane. Let me worry over her another day and take Nakkole and my child to safety now."

But Arrane didn't seem to be able to hear Gavin's plea. His gaze was focused on the locked door, his mouth still moving in silent speech.

Gavin looked to Abunda. "I'm taking Nakkole from here."

Abunda smiled the smile of a woman facing her own demise. "It's too late for that, my prince. There is no where to go but through those ogre's bellies."

A loud clatter pulled Gavin from his own fear long enough to allow him to maneuver back to the front of the group. Robert lay on the floor in a crumpled heap.

"What happened?" he asked. The group around him pushed closer together, forming a tight circle around Nakkole and Arrane.

"Fainted." Brock nudged Robert with his boot, then hurriedly pointed his sword at the approaching ogres again. "Never live that down, he won't."

There was nothing to do but fight and pray that, should he be killed, Arrane would prove powerful enough to pull Nakkole out of this mess safely.

Taking a deep breath, he lifted his sword and let out a roar that sent pebbles rolling down the walls. He plunged forward, thrusting his sword toward the nearest ogre. The tip of the weapon found its mark just below the ogre's throat. It staggered backward, but did not fall. In the next instant, he, Brock, Markham, and Luke were flying toward the wounded ogre, knocking it off balance until it landed with a thud on the hard ground.

Two, three, four swords jabbed at the enormous belly, until slowly, the heaving movement of breaths stopped completely.

"Two left," Markham muttered, raising to his feet.

Unfortunately, the two remaining ogres looked even more hungry for blood now that one of their kind had been killed. Chaos erupted around them. Arrows popped free of their bows as the White Ladies joined in the fight. Small axes zoomed overhead, lodging themselves into walls, ogre feet, ogre arms, as the dwarves, too, took up arms.

But soon, the dwarves were distracted by at least three dozen small, bearded men who suddenly appeared around the corner. They dashed through the ogres' legs, around their bodies, rushing at Arrane's small army.

"Oakmen!" Ginks, the dwarf king, shouted. "Melee ye of Sanddine. Our time to fight is upon us!"

Gavin and his men kicked out at the little creatures as they inched toward the next ogre. "If the four of us fight one ogre at a time, we might have a chance."

A loud crack distracted them from their target, however. The door to Elphina's private chamber had opened, and Arrane and Nakkole were gone.

✦

akkole's legs trembled. Even her bare toes shivered at the reality of standing inside Queine Elphina's private chambers. The same blue jewels that had made up the throne room were here, as well, casting an ominous aura about the place. But it was the heavy presence of sadness that kept Nakkole from following Arrane farther into the chamber.

Not *her* sadness. The sort of melancholy that lingers in a place where loneliness is all that is known.

She reached out and grabbed the back of Arrane's sleeve. "I cannot be here."

She was crying, she realized, and brushed her fingertips across her eyelids. A tear dripped from her eye, and Arrane brushed his thumb along her cheek. The sadness lifted from her, swallowed up by the light of goodness that accompanied Arrane wherever he went.

"What a sweet gesture," said a quiet voice.

Arrane spun around and put himself between Nakkole and Elphina, who had appeared from the shadows in the corner of the room.

Elphina tilted her head, peering past them at the doorway. "This is all I am to receive? My father and his pitiful White Lady servant? I thought I demanded more respect."

"The time has come for this war between us to end, Elphina. I cannot allow you to threaten my family any longer."

Elphina rushed forward, half laughing, half screaming, until she was nose to nose with Arrane. "I am your family, Father! Me!" She pulled back slightly, staring at him through the eyes of a madwoman. "What purpose do you have in seeking me out? You cannot kill me. Cannot harm me. I am half succubus, and you are incapable of causing me harm."

Arrane remained silent. Elphina circled him, her gaze briefly falling on Nakkole. "She is to be your weapon, you think? You brought a female with you to try to rid yourself of me once and for all." She smiled. "Surely you have not forgotten that I am your child, Father. The mixture of good and evil within me protects me from your White Lady as well. I am the only female tied to you by blood. None can kill me."

Nakkole stepped back, pressing her shoulders against the

wall for support. Arrane was trying to communicate with her, but she was so frightened, she couldn't focus on his words. She closed her eyes, trying to focus.

You have my power to destroy, Nakkole. I loan it to you now. Reach within yourself and use it now!

Nakkole swallowed.

Now, Nakkole. Hurry, for I cannot protect us from her here.

Elphina walked back to Arrane and studied him.

Can you not shield us, Majesty? Protect us while I fight her?

I had to break her shield on this door in order to enter. No other shield enchantment will work here for days. Concentrate. She is summoning power. I feel it.

Nakkole bit back tears, focused on Elphina, and pushed all of her hatred and disgust from her eyes, through the air, and into Elphina's chest. Elphina flew backward, slamming into the wall so hard, a lit sconce split in two and crashed to the floor.

Elphina screeched. Nakkole reached behind her and pulled an arrow from the quiver. Arrane stepped aside, his presence calming her enough to steady her hand.

As Elphina righted herself and bared her teeth, Nakkole released the arrow and waited for it to meet its mark.

❧

Gavin forgot about the ogre he and his men fought. Desperate to reach Elphina's chamber and protect Nakkole, he left them all, pushing and shoving his way through the mob of skirmishes. He tripped . . . or so he thought. In the next instant, he was dangling by his ankle near the ceiling of the tunnel, his face directly in front of the largest set of eyes he'd ever seen before.

"Ogaro!" a familiar voice shouted.

The grip on his ankle loosened, and Gavin fell face-first into the dirt. He fought for breath, rolled over, and stared up in awe as Dulcee plowed into the ogre three times his size. The ogre could crush Dulcee's head with one hand. They collided, tumbling to the ground.

Dizzy, Gavin stumbled to his feet, raised his sword, and drove it through the large ogre's foot. It howled and kicked out, catching Gavin in the nose. The crack of bone breaking brought a swallow of vomit to his throat. He choked, coughed, then swallowed back his revulsion long enough to find his anger again.

As the ogre reached down and plucked the sword from his toes, Dulcee attacked. He shoved the ogre's head in the crook of his arm and twisted violently until a crack far worse than Gavin's nose had made echoed around them.

Dulcee dropped the ogre to the ground, a large, round tear plopping onto his bloodied chest. "I kill Ogaro."

His chest heaving, Gavin limped over to Dulcee and knelt at his feet. "You saved my life, Dulcee. You've earned my loyalty forever."

Dulcee nodded, cast another saddened glance at his dead brother, and sighed. "Ogaro bad."

And with that, Dulcee took up Gavin's place in the battle between human and ogre, aiding Brock and Markham and Luke as they fought to bring the last of them down.

Gavin rose to his feet and rushed through the crowd, this time arriving at Elphina's chamber without delay. An arm thrust out, preventing him from stepping deeper into the chamber.

"This must be settled between *them*." It was Arrane, and his gaze was ever watchful upon Nakkole and Elphina.

Elphina was fighting to stand, a wound to her chest spreading a circle of blood through her velvet cloak. An arrow protruded from the wound. Elphina glanced down at it, seized the end, and yanked, screaming out as she pulled the arrow free.

Gavin flinched, certain that the removal had caused more damage than the original injury.

Elphina froze in place at the sight of Gavin. "Brother," she wheezed, clutching her chest, her head lulling slightly. "My family, all in one place."

"Your mother is not here, Elphina. She is the reason we cannot be your family." Arrane's voice was eerily calm and emotionless.

"Because she is succubi?" Elphina pushed away from the

wall and approached them. Gavin stood in front of Nakkole, wanting desperately to push her out of the chamber and take his chances fighting his sister alone.

"*Oui*," Arrane said. "Because she is succubi. Because she made you succubi."

"She made me. Succubi or not, I would not exist without her." Elphina smiled a smile that sent a shiver over Gavin's flesh. "Perhaps that is what you wish. That I never existed at all."

Arrane shook his head, but said nothing. Something akin to remorse flashed in his eyes, but rather than speak, he looked toward Nakkole intently, as though speaking to her with his eyes.

Gavin turned slightly, watched Nakkole swallow and take a hesitant step around him. As Elphina continued to speak words Gavin no longer had interest in hearing, Nakkole narrowed her eyes upon the succubus.

It took all of Gavin's willpower not to reach out, to try to protect her. That Nakkole alone could defeat Elphina was cold comfort.

The air in these caverns was beginning to make Gavin's head spin. Elphina's cackle swam like a distant echo in his ears. It took every bit of strength within him to look in her direction.

She was studying Nakkole, smiling and coughing. A tiny spray of blood spit between her fingers and stained Nakkole's gossamer gown. Nakkole didn't notice.

"Back, bitch!" Elphina screeched, raising her arm. Nakkole was lifted from the ground and sent soaring into the far wall. Her quiver of arrows clattered to the ground along with her bow. Gavin made to move toward her, but Arrane reached her first, lifting Nakkole to her feet.

"You think this child can destroy me?" Elphina asked. "You care for her. You aid her and let me bleed from her arrow. You care for her, and yet you allow her to challenge me? She cannot kill me any more than you can, Father. She is not filled with the blood of Arran."

Nakkole inhaled tiny breaths, testing her ribs for any breaks. Barely aware that Arrane was gripping her arm, she watched Elphina in a blue fog. From the corner of her eye,

she saw Gavin in the doorway, but Arrane's power grew
steadily inside her, allowing her to keep her focus on the task
at hand.

Her confidence, while growing with Arrane's power, was
not so strong that she deluded herself into believing she
could win this battle against Elphina. Her blood tie to Arrane
was in the form of a tiny, unborn child—hardly large enough
to wage war against a powerful, dark queine.

Nakkole was outmatched and wise enough to realize
such.

Calling the attention of everyone, Arrane let out a startled
noise that sounded like half choke, half yell. His eyes
widened, and he rushed past Nakkole.

"You're not meant to be here!" he roared. Nakkole froze
at the site of Geraldine in the doorway. Where had she come
from? She was supposed to be on the Isle of Arran.

Elphina took advantage of their distraction. She bent, and
when she stood once more, she was holding in her hand a
sword Nakkole recognized as Gavin's. She raised it.
Nakkole screamed. Arrane swung around and knocked his
forearm against Elphina's hand, just as she was lowering the
blade toward his heart. The weapon clamored to the ground.

In the next instant, Geraldine was pulling on Nakkole's
arm, all but shoving her to the center of the chamber. "I have
Arrane in me, his soul, his life's breath. You carry his blood
in you through his grandchild. Focus, lass. Destroy."

Elphina paled. Her mouth fell open. "Grandchild?" She
looked to Arrane. "You knew of this?"

Nakkole could feel power seeping into her arm from
Geraldine's grip, knew the woman would somehow let
Nakkole know the moment to strike, and prayed to Avalon
that it would work.

"It never should have come to this, Elphina," Arrane said.
"You were meant to live a quiet life with your mother. It was
you who began this war, but it will not be you who ends it."

Elphina stumbled, reached once again for the sword, and
was rushing toward Arrane before any of them could antici-
pate her intentions.

Arrane, obviously startled, stepped back. The tip of the
sword pressed against his pure, white robe. A small, red

stain spread slowly near his navel. A silent command from Geraldine sent a surge of energy through Nakkole, and with the power of destruction, they sent Elphina to her knees. It was as though the bones in her legs had crumbled to dust, destroyed, useless. She collapsed onto her back. Arrane staggered and fell to his knees beside her.

Elphina raised an arm toward Arrane, but it too crumbled and fell limp at her side. In silence, Arrane ran his hands beneath Elphina's cloak. He turned, in his hands, the Orb of Truth and the Orb of Creation. He placed them on the floor beside him and bent his head, turning away from the onlookers behind him.

It was over. Elphina was dead, and no one dared say a word as Arrane wept silently over his daughter's body.

Thirty-four

~

Late that evening, everyone seemed put back together. Alec would live, and, in fact, was beginning to act as though he'd never been wounded at all. Arrane had saved his life, as well as healed Gavin and himself. Once they'd returned to the palace, Arrane had taken a long, private moment in his quarters. Gavin had thought he'd needed time alone, but when Arrane had rejoined the crowd, he assured them all that the Master Trinity was safe once again, and even jested that, this time, he'd found better hiding spots for each—this time, no one would find them. Since there was no way to destroy the Trinity, it was the best they could hope for.

Despite Arrane's efforts to be jovial, however, everyone seemed to be in silent agreement that celebration over their victory should wait until their king's grief over the death of his daughter wasn't as fresh. Gavin now leaned wearily on his bench, his food cold, the new quiet in the hall heavy and awkward. He glanced to Nakkole, who dozed charmingly with her head upon his shoulder. God above, but she was beautiful. He wanted to hold on to her and keep her safely by his side now that he'd come so close to losing her forever.

Odd, but the fight that should have drained him seemed to have energized him instead. He could no longer remember any good argument for leaving the Otherworld to return to Grey Loch. His people would be fine as long as they were given a good laird to take care of them. His reasons for returning had been to prove to himself that he could be that laird, that he could be vital to people who needed him.

But the truth of the matter was, the people who needed him were *here*. Nay, he would not be king, but he would be a father to a child who would require his guidance. He could be a husband to Nakkole if she let him. To them, he could be as important as he needed to be, just as they were essential to him.

He bit back a grin as Nakkole's eyes fluttered open and she slid her arm into the crook of his own. "You look pensive," she whispered.

Gavin smiled, sleepiness weighing on his mind and body. "My men be leaving first thing in the morning, once our farewells have been made."

Nakkole's smile fell and she opened her mouth to reply. But before she could speak, Arrane's voice captured the attention of the Hall.

"Enough of this!" Arrane stood, bracing his hands on the table, his gaze roaming slowly across each body in the hall. "I appreciate the somberness you've all taken part in on my behalf, but we fought a good battle today, prevented the worst from occurring. We should celebrate. Dance and make merry. The living is what matters this night."

A round of grumbling circled the room, and after several long seconds of this, a few beings stood and lifted their goblets into the air. "Tonight, we make merry!"

The rest of the crowd seemed to catch the delirium. Laughter erupted. Pixies began their song. Couples walked arm and arm to the clear center of the chamber and began to dance.

"Shall we make merry, Nakkole?" Gavin asked, pressing his lips to her ear. He kissed the tender lobe, waited for her to sigh. She did not.

She pulled away, looking tired. But there was something more to her expression, something withdrawn and empty that hadn't been there moments ago. "I think I've only just realized that I'm going to lose you."

While the others in the hall danced merrily, hailing their king's newfound health and youth, he seized Nakkole by the arm and guided her into Arrane's private chamber.

The moment the door closed behind them, he kissed her.

When he finally pulled away, Nakkole was breathless, her expression dazed. "What was that for?"

He smiled, nuzzling her ear with his nose before he stepped back to look at her. "Marry me."

"Pardon?" She blinked, her brow furrowed.

"I said, marry me. Surely there's someone here who can lead us in our vows."

Nakkole stepped away and turned her back to Gavin. The thought of marrying him made her stomach flop, made her almost giddy. But she was no child to be comforted by a ceremony that, in the long run, would mean nothing. "Marry you before you leave? Why would you wish to be tied to a wife you'd never see?"

"Have you plans to go somewhere then?"

She pivoted. "I told you. I cannot return to Grey Loch—"

"Ah, and since I will not be there, either, there is no dilemma. I have no home here, so wherever yours might be, I'm certain I can make comfortable enough for myself."

Nakkole's knees weakened. The room took on a haze that hadn't been there a moment ago, and she found herself searching for a chair. She collapsed into one in the far corner and studied Gavin through her blurred vision. There was no mockery on his face, no signs of jest. He was wearing a smile, but it was born of genuineness.

"A home?" she whispered. "You wish to see my home?"

"Aye, and, if it's suitable, perhaps make mine there as well. Otherwise, I'm certain Arrane will be more than happy to have us stay here."

"Gavin." Nakkole lowered her head toward her knees, fighting for breath. She didn't dare get her hopes up, but, Avalon save her, it sounded as though Gavin meant to stay in the Otherworld! "What exactly is it that you're trying to say? Please. State it as though I were a four-year-old lass, for apparently I'm too dense to play along with your games."

He stepped toward her, his eyes dark, his smile wide. He kneeled, clasped her hands in his, and placed a kiss to her knuckles. "I wish you to be my princess, Nakkole. I don't need to prove myself to Grey Loch's people. I needed to prove myself to . . . myself. The people who need me are in this chamber. You . . . our child. The people I love."

"The people you . . ." All the breath in Nakkole's body evaporated into nothingness. She gasped, felt Gavin reach for her arms and haul her to her feet. She was still fighting for breath when he pulled her against him.

"The people I love. Nakkole," he kissed her lightly, "I'm a fool not to have realized it before your life was in danger, but the truth of it is, whether you carried my child or not, I would have fallen in love with you. 'Tis odd that I feel the need to thank my sister, of all people, for forcing me to realize that those I need the most are here, in a world I never knew existed. I'm asking you to marry me, if it's not too late."

"What better night to perform the ceremony than this one?" Nakkole and Gavin turned to find Arrane and Geraldine standing in the doorway. Arrane had spoke and he wore a smile nearly as broad as the one plastered on Geraldine's face. "I am fully capable of seeing the two of you wed."

"Does this mean you're staying?" Geraldine asked.

Nakkole's jaw dropped. "He said he loves me," she whispered, and immediately felt ridiculous for muttering those words aloud.

"Of course he does, silly girl." Geraldine swept into the chamber and threw her arms around Gavin before pulling away and stepping to Nakkole's side. "You should have seen the way he took charge the moment he found out you were in danger. I knew then that my son wouldn't be happy away from you."

"Nakkole." It was Gavin's voice she heard now, clear and nearby. She looked up to find him backing her into the corner of the chamber, a pleasing glint in his eyes. "I'm not sure I even realized it was love till I knew you'd been taken by the succubus. But it's been a while since I've known that the thought of leaving you here and returning to Grey Loch was not bringing me the joy it should have."

"But your people—"

"Robert can lead them as well as I ever could," he said. "I have a father now. A mother. Both are worth far more than leadership over any clan. But even more than that, I have our child, and I have you. If you don't wish to marry me, if you reject me now I will know it's not because I ran back to Scotland in order to prove something to myself. I'm staying here, whether you wed me or not, but truth be told, I want you for my wife more than I've wanted anything in a very long time. I love you, Nakkole. If you believe naught else, believe that."

Her hands trembling, her heart daring to believe what her mind could not, Nakkole turned her head, slowly looking toward Arrane. "Wed us, Your Majesty, so I can make him mine."

"A splendid choice," Arrane said. "I've known this would happen all along."

"Oh, you did, did you," asked Geraldine.

Arrane smiled. "During one session with the Orb of Truth, I asked if Gavin would ever come to accept his place here, knowing I wasn't likely to receive an answer. You see, the Orb is for finding the truth of what has been, not what will be, so I knew I was asking for the impossible."

"And?" Gavin asked, grabbing Nakkole by her waist and dragging her to his side.

"It showed me something that I would never have expected to see. It showed me what would bring Gavin home. What it was that would make him give up everything familiar to remain here, with our kind."

Nakkole's heart leapt. "What was it?"

Arrane smiled and tucked two of his fingers beneath her chin.

"It showed me you."

"It showed you *me*?" Nakkole squeezed Gavin's hand. "What could I possibly have to do with bringing Gavin home?"

"You are his destiny, Nakkole—nay, let me finish. The

Orb does not lie, and that it offered me a glance into the future is proof of the importance of your role in my son's life."

"But you said it could not show the future."

"And I was certain it couldn't. It appears that I, like any other man, can actually be wrong from time to time." He smiled down at Geraldine, who in turn beamed up at him, then returned his gaze to Gavin and Nakkole. "So, is there to be a wedding? There are guests aplenty in the Great Hall as we speak. Might as well turn this into a wedding feast."

Nakkole looked to Gavin, waited to see if he would back down now that the reality of his words was staring him in the face. Rather than take back all he'd said, however, he nodded at his father.

"Tell them the ceremony will take place in a few moments . . . *if*," he looked questioningly at Nakkole, "the bride says yes."

"Yes," she heard herself whisper. "I will marry you, Gavin McCain."

Gavin's smile was so wide, all Nakkole could see was a flash of white teeth before he pressed his lips to hers. He dipped his tongue between Nakkole's warm lips. For a long moment, she felt only the wondrous, slick feel of her mouth pressed to his, but then, a strange thing happened.

Something hotter than air, thicker than water, swum down her throat and filled her body to capacity. Her heart seemed to enlarge, her vision cleared, and she could hear more vividly than ever before. It was as though Gavin was inside her, completely inside her, and it made her hunger for him, yearn for him.

Nakkole clutched Gavin's shoulders and felt her own hot tears running down her face. They trailed along her cheek and dipped across her lips, their salty, wet taste mingling in the intense kiss. As clearly as she could feel Gavin's lips on hers, his tongue in her mouth, his hands on her waist, she could feel his soul enter her body and mingle with her own. She sobbed as she felt a bit of herself leave, never to return, as it entered the body of her soul mate.

There was only one reason this would happen between her and Gavin now.

Her eyes burning, she stepped away, breaking the kiss

and the spell-like bind between them. She placed a gentle hand on her belly and whispered, "My soul is yours, your soul is mine. Gavin . . ."

He stared at her with clouded eyes, swollen lips. "A soul-exchange?"

She nodded, her head fogged by numerous, confusing thoughts. "A soul-exchange."

Gavin laughed. His laughter was so boisterous, so catching, that soon Arrane and Geraldine had joined in. "That settles it then," he said.

Still baffled by what had just occurred, Nakkole asked, "Settles what?"

"You're stuck with me." Gavin grinned and lifted Nakkole into the air. "Forever."

"We shall definitely hold the ceremony this night," Geraldine said, laughter still ringing in her voice.

"I don't believe there is time to waste," Arrane said. "They look eager to have their wedding night."

Nakkole felt the heat creep into her cheeks and she buried her face in Gavin's chest. She felt his laugh. "Come now, lass. I thought White Ladies didn't suffer embarrassment."

"Embarrassment? Is that what this horrid emotion is called?" she asked, glancing up at him.

"Indeed, it is the reason you blush now." He did not seem perplexed that she didn't know the name of such an emotion. "I promise to show you many different reasons for blushing later, when we are alone," he said, leaning down to whisper in her ear.

He cheeks inflamed, Nakkole decided that blushing could not be *all* bad, after all.

"Then in turn, I shall show you many different ways of being loved."

Gavin blinked down at her, and she could have throttled herself when his eyes turned moist. Damn her insensitivity. The man had lived without knowing even one kind of love his whole life.

His mouth brushed hers and he rested his brow against her own. "I'm certain you can make up for a lifetime of my ignorance of such a thing."

Nakkole wrapped her arms around his neck and kissed

him with every bit of love in her heart. If it took her the rest of her days, she would make up for all the love he had lost throughout his life. When she pulled away, the teary stares of Arrane and Geraldine told her that they, too, would see to Gavin's education.

"Welcome home," she whispered.

Gavin bent and scooped her up in his arms. He stared into her eyes and she wrapped her arms tightly around him. "Home," he replied, "has never looked more beautiful."

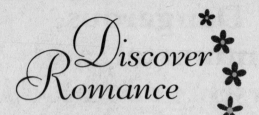